THE STILL SMALL VOICES

ALSO BY S. A. SEDLAK

Bury Her Gently

THE STILL SMALL VOICES

By

S. A. Sedlak

All characters, names, places, and incidents in this book are fictitious, and any resemblance to actual persons, living or dead, events, or locales is purely coincidental.

First published by AuthorHouse 07/27/04

ISBN: 1-4184-6463-5 (e-book)
ISBN: 1-4184-2602-4 (Paperback)
ISBN: 1-4184-2603-2 (Hardcover)

This book is printed on acid free paper.

AuthorHouse
1663 Liberty Drive, Suite 200
Bloomington, IN. 47403
1-(888)-280-7715 (Toll Free)
www.authorhouse.com

Life is the continuous adjustment
of internal relations to external relations.

Herbert Spencer:
Principles of Biology

For my mother

who understood

Part One

Edward

1

On a warm, tranquil, sunny Thursday morning in June, Edward T. Aldworth, of the small town of Mapleville, Massachusetts, and Jonah L. Willis, of Chicago, graduated from Harvard Law School. It was the day that Edward's parents had planned for their son since the moment he had been born. For Jonah, it was merely a dream come true. Both of his parents had died in an automobile accident when he was four years old, and his only living relative now was an arthritic, partially deaf grandmother who lived in an old dilapidated house alongside the Elevated Tracks—or the L, as it was mostly called in those days. Jonah had been sponsored by Doctor Frank Hassur, of Oak Park, Illinois, who had no children of his own, and who had for many years treated the frail black woman and had watched her grandson grow up to be a brilliant young scholar.

Except for the holidays and vacations, the two boys were inseparable friends during their stay at Harvard: they were roommates and both had graduated with high honors. They also liked the same things—books, music, popcorn and jelly beans, skinny girls who smiled a lot, and long, quiet talks about politics.

This day in June, then, was the start of their first real separation.

After the Commencement:

"Jonah, I want you to meet my parents now. They're outside in the hall, waiting."

"I've been thinking about that, Ed. Maybe you ought to go home first and tell them about our plans. Then I could meet them."

"What d'you mean *could* meet them? They're right out there now. They won't care if you're black, if that's what you're thinking. They don't worry about things like that."

"I know, Ed, but I'd still feel a lot better if they knew everything beforehand."

A short silence.

"You haven't changed your mind about going to New York, have you? Because if you have, I'm not going either."

"I haven't changed my mind. I'd never change my mind about that."

Another short silence.

"Okay. I'll go home first, but you've got to promise you'll come to the house as we planned. It's important to me."

"Sure, Ed, I'll promise."

"You wouldn't go back on an old buddy now, would you?"

"Naw...I'd never do that. You know that, Ed."

"Cross your heart then."

"I done crossed it."

"And stop talking like an *ignorant nigger.*"

"I ain't no ignorant nigger no more, Ed. No, sir!"

They laughed now and slapped each other on the back. Edward said he would telephone just as soon as he broke the news to his parents. Then they parted.

Jonah's promise to come to the house was sufficient for Edward: he had never lied to him before, and there was no reason to think he would begin now, especially when they had such great plans going for the both of them. That letter from the big New York law firm, Pratt, McPherson &, Rettig, was indeed a rare opportunity, and they both knew it. How expensive the paper had looked, how impressive the writing! The letter had stated quite simply (but most encouragingly, too) that the firm was going through a quick changeover, and that it now needed two young dedicated law school graduates to fill a sudden and enormous void left by an elderly, retiring senior partner. So, in two weeks' time (that was how long Edward thought he needed to straighten things out at home), he and Jonah would be going to New York City, to start their law careers together.

Edward was happy on his graduation day. He felt sure that everything would turn out just fine for him and Jonah.

Waiting until his friend was completely out of sight, Edward walked briskly out into the hallway and gave his parents his best smile. He kissed his mother on the cheek and shook his father's hand, then stepped back from them for a moment, to look at them standing there together—much the same way as a photographer who is ready to snap a picture, except that Edward was seeing his parents through the lens of his conscience mind, through all the years of his young life.

He knew he would never forget how they looked at this precise moment.

They were tall, slender people, dark-haired and dark-eyed, well-dressed for the occasion: his mother wore a pale green dress with a long-sleeved matching jacket, white shoes and purse and gloves, and a single strand of pearls which Edward had given her at Christmas; his father, a dark gray, pinstriped suit with a white shirt heavily starched at the collar (which would promptly start to irritate his Adam's apple at three that afternoon) and a deep maroon silk tie pierced by an 18 karat gold stickpin, which had belonged to Edward's grandfather, John. From under the left lapel of his father's suit, Edward could see the stalwart bulge of the big horn-rimmed glasses: though his father refused to wear them at social functions, he felt undressed without them. They were as much a part of his attire as were his socks and shoes.

Edward could see that his parents had taken great pains in dressing for that day. Everything had to be just right, and he was proud of them.

Edward was the Aldworths' eldest child and only son. His sister Suzanne, who was going to be nineteen that summer, looked just like him: she had the same thin, delicate face—the short, upturned nose, the bright dark eyes, the dark wavy hair. In fact, the two looked so identically alike, that Roger and Adele Aldworth often remarked to their friends that they thought they had a pair of twins on their hands. But there the resemblance between brother and sister ended rather sharply: where Edward was quiet, oftentimes shy, his sister was lively and thoroughly outgoing; where he was quick to please, she resented even the slightest interference in what she considered to be her own private affairs. Since the life of an eighteen-year-old girl—especially that of a pretty, outgoing one—is usually brimming over with exciting events, these "affairs" often as not extended beyond the boundaries that had been set for them and consequently, her parents' interference in them at times seemed overbearing to her. She would show a terrible temper whenever she couldn't get her way. But despite the girl's strong will, Roger and Adele had made plans for their daughter as well. Upon her graduation from Mapleville High School, she had been whisked off to her mother's school, a small Catholic college in Paxton, where it was hoped the good sisters there would be able to curb some of her vivacious tendencies. There she was to remain until she fulfilled the required years of education, or promised herself in marriage to some suitable, upstanding young man. Though the Aldworths were old-fashioned parents, they were practical ones as well: they did not consider a proper marriage for their daughter any less worthy than a good formal education.

Unlike his sister, Edward had always tried to please his parents. In fact, it was like a second nature for him. He had gone to Harvard because they had wanted him to, but he had never regretted it. He had been happy there. The teachers had treated him well, and he had made many new friends. And of course he had met Jonah.

Looking away from his parents now, Edward remembered his first day at Harvard: he had gone back to the dormitory for something he had forgotten (he couldn't even remember what it was any more), and there was this very lanky, cropped-haired young black standing over his bed, holding on for dear life to a battered suitcase full of crumpled old clothing. Dark eyes flashing, broad shy smile. Had the black hand reached out first, or had he?—he couldn't remember that any more either; but they had instantly become good friends, on a day when both had badly needed a friend.

Jonah's just like me, Edward thought now. He won't go to New York alone either. He'll stay in Chicago, and take care of his sick grandmother, and never go another place again in his whole life. So Edward knew that he had to go to New York. But he didn't want to hurt his parents. He wanted them to be happy these two weeks.

His mother suddenly touched his arm. "Edward, wasn't there someone you wanted us to meet?"

"He's left already, Mother. I'm afraid we've missed him."

"Oh." She looked confused for an instant. "Is there anything else you must do here?"

"No, I'm all through now. I've said goodbye to everyone."

"Well..." his father said then, turning slowly around to look at the diminishing crowd, "I suppose we ought to be getting on home, too. What d'you say, son?"

"Sure, Dad." Edward smiled at him. "It'll be great to be home again."

"And for good this time, eh? No more rushing you back to school..." The elder man, who was several inches taller and graying profusely at the temples, placed an affectionate arm about his son, saying, "I know I don't have to tell you what this day means to your mother and me. We're proud of you, son."

"I know, Dad."

They all walked slowly now, to the door—then outside and down the steps, over to the car: it was an old 1959 Chrysler, dark metallic blue, polished and gleaming in the bright sunlight. Edward had to smile at the sight of it: So the old clunker was still hobbling along. He had never been quite sure whether it would make all those long trips back and forth to school, but it had, and now here it was again, today, waiting to take him home. It was probably as glad as he was that it was all over. Well, in two more weeks he wouldn't be needing it any more. He'd be riding the New York Subway!

His father suddenly stopped in his tracks and looked back. "I put your things in the trunk, Edward." Edward smiled and nodded his thanks: his father had always put his things in the trunk. Edward watched him take out the keys and open the back seat door for his mother: she gathered up her skirts and got in.

"You look thinner, Edward," she said through the open door. "Have you been getting enough sleep?"

"Of course he has," Roger Aldworth told her quickly, giving his son a wink. "The boy's never looked better."

"I feel fine, Mother," Edward said, smiling at her. He closed the door for her and waited until his father walked around to the other side of the car and got in behind the wheel, then slid onto the front seat beside him. Then he watched him turn on the motor: it made a low, groaning noise—caught, sputtered out, caught again and sputtered out again. When it was finally running fairly smoothly, he asked: "How's the Chrysler doing these days, Dad?"

"Just fine," his father answered calmly. "Just needs a little tune-up. Marty was supposed to check it over before we left, but he got too busy."

Marty *too* busy? Since when did Marty get too busy to check over the Chrysler? He had always managed to do it before. Edward wondered if the two hadn't had some words again.

"What about Ben? Doesn't he do tune-ups any more?"

"He's not at the garage any more. He quit to work for his cousin. Kenneth's there now."

"*Kenny Habich*? He's working for Marty now?"

His father nodded solemnly. "Got the job the day after he graduated from high school. Disappointed Otto too. He had his heart set on the boy going to college."

Edward leaned back in the front seat now, and watched his father slowly turn the wheel—creep into the long line of traffic: a loud angry horn sounded directly behind them, but he only half-heard it. He was thinking of Mr. Habich, the butcher, now. Why should he be disappointed about Kenny working for Marty? Kenny was the "grease monkey" of Mapleville, and as far back as Edward could remember, he had always been crazy about cars. While all the other boys were home doing their homework, Kenny could be seen in the dreary light of his father's garage, tinkering with some jacked-up jalopy. Well—now the only difference was, it was Marty's garage.

10

Edward waited until the Chrysler found its place in the traffic, then said: "Kenny'll make a terrific mechanic, Dad. It's what he's always wanted to be."

"I don't doubt that," his father returned, his voice solemn now, "but it's still not the same as going to college."

Edward didn't say anything more. He knew that once his father took on that tone of voice, there was no use trying to convince him. Besides, he didn't feel like trying to convince anybody that day. He was too happy.

They turned down Memorial Drive, and Edward looked out of the side window and watched all the old familiar buildings going by: *Leverett, Gore, Standish, Eliot.* In the bright sunlight they appeared like wrinkled-faced old men bidding him goodbye. He gave them all a silent fond farewell, wondering if he'd ever see them again. Everybody said they'd come back some day, but would they?

"Feeling a little homesick already?" his father asked, smiling now.

"Sort of," Edward answered, looking away from the window.

"Nothing to be ashamed of. I nearly bawled like a baby when I graduated. And so did your mother."

"Did you ever go back to see your school?"

"Oh, sure. Once. But it wasn't the same any more. All the teachers I had known were gone, or dead. There's only one graduation day, Edward."

They came to a corner and stopped abruptly: Edward saw a shiny new white Lincoln Continental swerve majestically around them. The

11

driver looked back and shook his fist angrily. Then the Chrysler started up slowly again.

"Well, Edward..." his father said, placing both hands loosely on the wheel, "what do you want to do now? Take it easy for a while?"

"I don't think so, Dad. I'd sort of like to get started in something right away."

Roger Aldworth laughed and glanced up at the rear-view mirror: "Did you hear that, Mother? Looks like we've got ourselves an ambitious son."

"It's not that I'm ambitious, Dad," Edward started to say. He felt his heart pounding suddenly. How easy it would be to tell them right now, this moment—about the job in New York, and Jonah; but easy for whom? He could at least wait until they were home. Nothing was going to run away. "It's just that," he went on, "most of the guys at school have got something going for them already. I don't want to be left behind."

"Well, I wouldn't worry about that too much," his father said, patting him lightly on the knee. "Things have a way of working out themselves. Besides, your mother and I would like to see you enjoy yourself for a while. You've earned it."

"Oh, I intend to take two weeks off at least," Edward said quickly.

"*Two weeks?*" Roger Aldworth laughed again. "That'll hardly get your mother started on spoiling you."

Mrs. Aldworth moved to the edge of her seat now: "There's a lot of people waiting to see you at home, Edward."

"Who, Mother?" Edward turned around to look at her.

"Oh…Tom Rowley's back from school, and Georgie Mathews. And Cynthia Forst…"

Tom Rowley, Edward thought, the boy who lived down the block. The most popular boy at Mapleville High, and the one voted most likely to succeed. So Old Fish Eyes was home already. All during grammar school days, Tom had his little concession going: every day he would have something hidden away in his pockets, to show the boys at recesstime. That is, if they had their pennies. Crickets, grasshoppers, lightning bugs, horseflies, even once a wiggly little garter snake. Edward remembered how he had always given his pennies eagerly to see these "rare" attractions. He had been Tom's regular customer, and once had been allowed to view a swarm of vicious bumble bees in a dirty pickle bottle, for nothing. But somehow Fate had taken a hand in it, and the lid of the bottle had come off, and one of the bees had stung him on the arm. Tom had laughed like crazy. "That's on the house too, Ed," he had said. Tom was always laughing at somebody's misfortune.

Now, Georgie Mathews was different: he was the nice pudgy little kid that nobody ever bothered with, until he got to drive his father's car to school. Georgie had barely been sixteen then, and the whole town had talked about it: how foolish it was to trust a boy that age behind the wheel. Weren't they always getting into some kind of trouble? But the truth was, as everybody found out later, that the Mathewses hadn't any choice in the matter. Mr. Mathews' eyesight was failing badly. He had several unsuccessful operations, and now needed Georgie to drive him to and from work each day. Mrs.

Mathews herself was too frightened to even touch the wheel. And since Mapleville High was in the same direction as the grocery store where Mr. Mathews was working, it seemed senseless to make the boy come all the way home again with the car, so Georgie was allowed to take it to school. It wasn't much of a car, just a rattly old Ford, but all the kids had made a big thing out of it, and Georgie became a celebrity overnight.

Now—who was this Cynthia Forst? The name sounded familiar and yet...

Edward turned to his mother again: "Who is Cynthia Forst?"

"Oh, you must have forgotten all about her," she replied. "She was the little girl you used to walk to Sunday School, remember? Her parents moved to Worcester when she was eight. Well, they're back in town again. Mr. Forst has opened a new drugstore on Ames Street, and Cynthia's working at the bank. She's Mr. Rydin's secretary."

Oh, *that* Cynthia Forst, Edward thought glumly. The neurotic little girl with the awful black circles under her eyes. How he had hated to walk her to Sunday School each week. She was forever crying, kicking up a fuss, and he had almost had to yank her arms out to get her there. Then, when they arrived, all the boys in the class would be waiting outside for them, on the front steps, with their playful little jeers. "How's your little girlfriend today, Eddie?" "What's she crying about now?" "Did you try to stick it in her on the way?" Then somebody would always make a big guffaw, and they'd start shouting and scuffling on the stairs, until Big Breasts Mary Lou Patterson, the teacher's assistant and pet, would poke her blond tousled head out the door, to shake a finger. "You better stop that right now," she'd warn, "or Miss Brown's gonna send notes home to your parents!" But nobody ever stopped, and Miss Brown never got around to sending the notes. Somebody once said she was only too glad to have a class to teach. Well...the girl had caused him embarrassment, but he had never been able to tell his parents about it, because the Forsts were close friends of the family. Anyway, he doubted whether they would have done anything. The girl was always quiet and well-mannered in front of grown-ups.

Well, at least he didn't have to worry about that any more. He didn't have to see Cynthia Forst again, if he didn't want to.

His father was talking to his mother again: "Edward doesn't know who Mr. Rydin is. He wasn't at the bank yet, still in Chicago, when Edward worked there last summer." Roger Aldworth turned to his son: "Mr. Rydin's the new bank president."

"Oh," Edward said thoughtfully. "What happened to old Mr. Conover?"

"He retired shortly after Christmas. His asthma finally got the best of him."

Poor Mr. Conover. Well, he was getting pretty close to eighty, a ripe old age for retirement. Edward remembered the small, bent figure that had hissed and coughed down the bank corridors: Mr. Conover seldom spoke to anyone, and when he did it was usually nothing more than a blurt. Sometimes you couldn't help wondering how an old man like that could run a bank, but people said he'd been doing it for forty some years, and a right good job of it too. The Mapleville Bank wouldn't be the same without him.

They came to a traffic light. Edward waited until the green light flashed on and the Chrysler passed through the intersection, then said: "How's Suzie, anyway?"

"Oh, she's fine," his mother answered. "She couldn't come with us today. She was committed to a party—Priscilla's."

Priscilla Eckert. Edward clicked that one off in a hurry: tall, strong-boned, brown-haired Priscilla: Suzanne's best friend and tennis partner. He wondered if she was still biting her nails down to the quick. "What kind of party?" he asked.

"Oh, you know," his father put in dryly. "One of those pajama things. Except now they call them *weekers* instead of overnighters."

"They do not," Mrs. Aldworth retorted gently. "The party's only going to last three days. Suzanne should be home tomorrow."

"Well, let's hope so," her husband said. "That's long enough to sit around in pajamas. All they do is talk about boys, and they do that anyway."

Edward had to laugh now. It was funny how his sister always managed to cut through the serious tone of the family. He could see her now, sitting cross-legged on Priscilla's bed, laughing and talking up a storm. Suzanne was always having a good time.

He realized suddenly how much he had missed his sister: she hadn't come home for the spring vacation as she had promised she would, and he wondered why. He'd have to ask her about it when he saw her—that, and why she hadn't answered any of his letters either.

16

He slumped down in the front seat and looked out of the window again: they were moving so slowly now, he could almost count the bricks of the buildings going by. Well, he had two whole weeks— enough time for everything. There was no need to rush anything or anybody.

2

At eleven o'clock the following morning, in one of the upstairs bedrooms (the blue room) of the simple white frame house on Hobson Road, Edward woke from a deep, pleasant sleep to find his sister standing by the bed. She was holding a large cumbersome breakfast tray, grinning from ear to ear.

"Well, good morning!" she said in her usual quick, bouncy voice. "The Honorable Attorney has finally arisen and the day is now in session!"

Edward smiled at her sleepily, then yawned and pulled himself up slowly from the covers: leaning back against the tall headboard of the bed, he tried now to focus his eyes on her more clearly. She looked cute as a button this morning, he thought, even prettier than the last time he had seen her. Short, fluffy dark hair—white shorts, white sneakers, red-and-white checkered blouse. There was a reddish dot on each of her cheeks, too. Positively healthy, he thought, just the way a girl her age ought to look. "When did you get home, Suzie?"

"Oh, about a half hour ago," she replied. "Priscilla and I had a game of tennis, then she drove me. She wanted to come up to say hello, but I told her you sleep in the nude at home. That scared her off. I guess she's still got that silly old crush on you."

"You shouldn't be telling your friend a lie like that," Edward said, not knowing whether to laugh or scold her. But Suzanne was always saying things like that, and you would have had to scold her all the time. Besides, he didn't want to scold her this morning. He was too happy to see her.

He watched her set the tray down on the bed. "What's all this for? I could have gone downstairs."

"No, you couldn't. Mom said you were to have breakfast in bed the first morning. She had to go to the beauty shop, so I got stuck fixing it. We're having company for dinner tonight."

"Who, do you know?" Edward lifted one of the covers of the dishes, carefully.

"No, and I don't care to," his sister said. She plopped down heavily on the bed, by his feet, and watched him a minute. "Incidentally—you don't have to poke around like that. It's all perfectly edible: orange juice, two boiled eggs, toast and coffee. I had a cooking class at Mapleville High, remember?"

"Ah ha. That's the one you almost failed in." He gave her a teasing smile.

"Almost but not quite," she retorted. "I happened to pass on *breakfasts*." She wrinkled her nose at him.

"Well, then I won't have to worry about this one, will I?" Edward said, laughing. He picked up the glass of orange juice and drank it down quickly, then began shelling the eggs, making a small, neat, white mountain alongside the dish. He saw that his sister was watching him more intently now: a tiny furrow had formed between her dark brows. She's probably worried she won't please me, he thought. She knew how he liked his morning eggs prepared (boiled three minutes exactly) and had probably used her mother's minute-timer so as not to make a mistake; and he, in turn, knew how much she hated to have to work in the kitchen. Her mother had what to do to get her to wipe the dinner dishes occasionally. Yet, this morning she had made him this breakfast.

He hurried along. When the eggs were all shelled and salted and peppered in the dish, he heard her give a small sigh of relief.

"So what's new, Suzie?" he asked her, pausing a moment from eating.

"What do you mean?"

"You know what I mean. What have you been up to, since the last time I saw you?"

"Oh," she said, "I thought Mom and Dad told you."

"Told me what?" He buttered the toast without looking at her.

"I've decided to quit college. I'm not going back in the fall, or ever."

"And what did they say to that?"

"Oh, they didn't like it much. Especially Mom. You know how she feels about that old school of hers. According to her, there's just two things a girl my age ought to be doing—going to college, or getting married."

"And you don't want to do either one right now," he said, finally looking at her.

"No."

"So—did you convince her?"

"You can't convince her, or Dad, you know that. But we're talking again. That's why I couldn't go to your graduation yesterday. It would have only started it up again."

Edward nodded understandingly. "So how was the pajama party, then? Did you have a good time?"

"There wasn't any party. Priscilla and I just made it up, so I wouldn't have to go with Mom and Dad."

"Oh," he said, trying not to look surprised. He picked up the coffee cup, took a few sips, then looked back at her over the brim, wondering how many times she had done that—made up excuses. Was she in the habit now of lying to her parents every time she wanted to get out of doing something? Had she lied, too, about why she hadn't come home for the spring vacation? Since his parents had made no mention of it in their letters, he had assumed her excuse had been acceptable; but now he wondered if it really was. He knew he ought to ask her about it now, it was the perfect time for it, but the more he thought about doing it, the less fair it seemed. Wasn't he going away himself now? Besides, she was almost all grown up, and he had no right to pry. Yet he knew if he did ask her, if he had to know, she would tell him the truth. She always did.

Setting the cup back on the saucer, he said: "Didn't you like college at all?"

"Oh, sure, I liked it fine. But I don't want to go to school any more. I'm not smart like you, Eddie. I'm not going to be some great lawyer or anything."

"And who says I am?"

"Mom and Dad think you are. They never gave me much hope. They just sent me to college because Mom went. Anyway, you were the one who always like school."

"Nobody *always* likes school," Edward said, trying to correct her gently. "There were plenty of times when things got rough and I felt like quitting too."

"But you didn't," she told him quickly. "That's the difference between you and me. You wanted to graduate, and I don't."

"Then, what do you want to do?" He couldn't think of anything else to say now.

"Oh, I haven't really thought about it yet," she said. She leaned back on her elbows and gazed up at. the ceiling, meditatively. "I guess I just want to have a lot of fun for a while, and not think of anything too seriously."

Edward had to laugh now: Wasn't that his old Suzie talking? There was no need to worry, after all. "And after that—or haven't you thought that far ahead?" He was teasing her again.

"Oh—then I'll probably just get married like Mom wants," she said, straightening and looking back at him.

"That sounds like a last resort."

"It probably is. I'll be twenty-one or-two by then."

"A drastic old age!" He smiled. "What about boys? Are you still dating Steve Delingham?"

"Oh, sure," she said, casting her eyes down now, "we're going steady. Mom's happy about that at least. That's the only thing she's ever approved about me—my dating Steve."

"It can't be as bad as all that," Edward said, smiling quietly now—trying to be a little more serious because she was. But it was true—or at least part of it was: his mother had always been pleased about Steve. But what mother wouldn't be? Steve was the tall, good-looking, red-haired boy who had been crazy about Suzanne since she was fourteen. He was also the only son of the Delinghams, who owned the big paper mill just outside of town, where Edward's father worked as head-bookkeeper. Every girl in Mapleville envied Suzanne for dating Steve, and every mother of every daughter probably envied her mother too. That was just how things were between mothers and daughters.

"I think you're wrong about Mother though," Edward added. "She approves of a lot of things about you. And so does Dad."

"No, they don't," she returned quickly. "You don't know, Eddie. You've always done what they wanted you to do. You went to Harvard."

"That's true," he admitted, picking up the cup again, "but then I didn't always want to, either. At first I thought I wanted to go with the other guys, to their schools. It seemed so lonely going off by oneself. Then, one day, I got to thinking that maybe there was a guy somewhere who wanted to go to Harvard, and couldn't, and I realized how lucky I was."

"Well," she said, thinking over what he had said, "maybe it's not so bad when you agree with them some of the time. I never do."

"Who knows—you might still change your mind about school before fall comes." He hoped she would, but he couldn't say that. She'd think he was taking sides.

"But I won't. I know I won't." She smiled then— "But let's not talk about me any more, Eddie. What about yourself? You haven't said a word about what you're going to do, now that you've graduated."

"Well…" he said, feeling suddenly excited just to be able to talk about it, "I guess things are pretty well settled for me already. I've got a job with a law firm in New York. I start in two weeks."

"*Really?*" she said. Her dark eyes became two enormous, perfectly round Os, and Edward had to laugh again. "You're not kidding, Eddie?"

"No, I'm not kidding." He told her the name of the firm.

"It sounds real important."

"It is. The Placement Director at school said it's one of the biggest law firms in New York City. There were two openings, and I was lucky to get one of them."

"Oh, that's wonderful, Eddie," his sister said, clasping her hands together. "Did you tell Mom and Dad about it?"

"No, but I will—soon. I was going to tell them yesterday, on the way home, but then I thought I'd wait a few days. I didn't want to spoil things for them right away."

"Well," she said, looking a little disappointed now. "I wouldn't wait too long, if I were you. You're going to spoil things anyway." She studied his face. "You're not afraid to tell them, are you?"

"Of course not. Why should I be afraid?"

"Oh, you know—how they're always telling us what to do. Now that they know I'm all through with school, they're going to work that much harder on you."

"Don't worry, Sis, I'm going to New York. I've got to go. There's somebody depending on me—rather, we're depending on each other."

Her face brightened. "Somebody I know?"

"You haven't met him yet, but I wrote about him several times. My roommate—Jonah Willis. He's got the other job with the firm."

"Oh, the black guy with the brain," she said quickly. "I remember him. Mom and Dad talked about him once."

"What did they say?"

"Oh, just that you told them he was super-smart and all."

"Well, he is. He's about the smartest guy I've ever known, but he doesn't know it himself. He's awfully shy about a lot of things."

"You mean—about being black?" She looked sympathetic now.

"That, and other things too. For instance, you know how most of the guys at school have got middle names? Well, he doesn't have one, so he made his up. He calls himself Jonah L."

"After the famous prizefighter, *John L. Sullivan?*"

"No. After the train tracks that run alongside his grandmother's house. He said they were the closest thing to him in his whole life, next to her."

"He sounds as if he's got a good sense of humor," his sister concluded.

"No, he was very serious about it."

"You like him a lot, don't you, Eddie?" she asked, smiling again.

"He was my best friend at school."

"Tell me..." She leaned back again, slowly—"What's it like, having a black for a best friend?"

"Well, I guess it's just like any other best friend," he told her. "You trust one another, try to help one another whenever you can."

"Was he the one who helped you through all those rough times you mentioned?"

He nodded. How perceptive she was now! She had certainly grown up since the last time he had seen her. "Whenever I had trouble studying for an important exam, he'd just skim through his own work and help me. I owe him a lot, Sis."

"And now you want to try to help him back," she said, "by going to New York with him. Right?"

"Well...I don't know if I'll be helping him that much," Edward said. "He'll probably end up helping me again." He laughed. "Anyway, we'll be together. It's a big break for both of us."

"He sounds real nice, Eddie," his sister said. "I hope I get to meet him someday."

"You will. He's coming to the house just as soon as I tell Mother and Dad about the job."

"Oh," she said with a frown, "that ought to be another big surprise for them. You've never had a close friend before. They won't be able to get used to it. They won't know how much this job means to you."

"Oh, everything'll be all right, Sis," Edward told her confidently. "You'll see. Once they meet Jonah, they won't mind my going away so much."

"I hope so, for your sake," she said. "Anyway, it'll be the first time *you'll* be asking them for something. That ought to be interesting." She glanced down at the tray now, and saw that he was through eating, then stood up and looked at her wristwatch. "Oh, God," she said, "it's nearly twelve o'clock. You've got to get dressed. Mom wants us to do some shopping, and I promised Steve we'd meet him at B's for lunch."

"For *lunch*?" Edward laughed and fell back slowly against the pillows.

"Well…" she said, putting her hands on her hips and eyeing him haughtily, "you'll just have to pretend on a Coke or something. Steve won't know the difference anyway. Besides, *every*body doesn't sleep to eleven o'clock, you know. *I* happen to be starved." She picked up the tray and started to leave, then stopped—stooped over to kiss him on the forehead.

"What was that all about?" Edward asked, both pleased and embarrassed at the same time.

27

"That's for being my big brother and a couple of other things you don't know about." She went to the door. "Now, please hurry. We don't have *all* day."

Edward waited until she closed the door behind her, then jumped out of the bed and went over to the windows. Outside, the late-morning sunlight looked warm and golden like tinsel on a Christmas tree. It really did feel great to be home again, he told himself, even if everything wasn't exactly the way he had planned. But didn't his father even say, things had a way of working out?

Whistling, he hurried into the bathroom.

About twenty minutes later, Edward came down the stairs into the living room, still whistling. He was showered and shaved, dressed in a new pair of light blue trousers and a crisp white shirt. His dark wavy hair had been vigorously brushed and combed, lightly pomaded, so that no wisp of curl would disturb its smooth, caplike appearance. His face looked radiant with happiness and anticipation.

This was to be Edward's first day at home. Yesterday could hardly be counted, for he and his parents had arrived quite late in the evening; after a quick snack in the kitchen, every one had gone directly to bed, feeling weary from the long strain of graduation day. Now, this morning, completely rested from his late-hour sleep, Edward was feeling like most young people feel on their first day after graduation—that the world was indeed a nice place in which to live.

Although he was sure that everything would turn out just fine for him and Jonah, he knew that everything would not simply fall into place without some effort on his part. He knew his parents too well for that. Much better at times than did his sister. Suzanne could only judge them by the prejudices of her will—her needs and desires to be free from their "crushing" guidance; but Edward had no such prejudices, and he had never minded their guidance. In fact, he felt grateful for it. So he was able to see them in a much clearer light than his sister could. To him, they were just small-town people, who, like their parents and grandparents before them, had been contented to live out their lives in one place: Mapleville. All their ambitions, their sacrifices, had settled there with them, too. So it was no wonder that they would expect their children to want to do the same thing.

Edward knew what a terrible blow it would be, when they found out he was going to New York.

He realized that going to work in New York was not the same thing as going off to college; before, it had just been a matter of time when his parents would have him home again. Now, this job had a certain finality to it. Even though he would be spending the holidays and vacations with them, as before, he would be making a home for himself somewhere else. All his expenses would be entirely his own. For some parents, this is the most difficult time in life—the cutting of the parental cord. They have built their whole existence around helping their children, then suddenly the nest is empty. The little birds have flown away. Life becomes empty, too. Though Edward had tried to pay for as much of his college education as he could, by

29

working at the Mapleville Bank each summer, his parents still had to bear the brunt of it. But they had never once complained. They had been all too happy to make the necessary sacrifices so that he could go to Harvard.

Edward, being a devoted and conscientious son, understood most of this; but not being a parent himself, he could not understand all of it. So he imagined the rest. In his heart of hearts, he felt that once his parents understood why he was going away—once they realized he wasn't doing it to hurt them, they would be as happy about it as he was. Everything would be all right then.

Already the night before, he had worked out a plan on how to break the news to them—a sort of mental synopsis of how things might go: the different scenes that would take place between them and him. First of all, he would drop little hints to each one, separately. He would begin with his mother, for she was the easiest of the two (though his sister would never have agreed with that), and preferably in the warmth of her kitchen, where she was most contented. She always liked to have someone around her while she worked. He would tell her that some of his friends were thinking of going to New York, to look for jobs, because the opportunities there were much better, and she would probably agree. She always liked to go to New York herself. Then—after that, he would speak to his father: after dinner would be the best time for him. He would be sitting in his big brown leather chair, feeling comfortable and contented after a good meal, with the evening paper sprawled out in front of him. His father usually enjoyed a good robust conversation after dinner. With him, though, he would have to be more specific—he would say he had spoken to some one at the Placement Office at school, about a job in New York, and that he was giving it a lot of thought. His father would no doubt make some comment afterward, and Edward would just listen. Then, later, his parents would discuss it together, compare notes, and approach him. It was then that he would tell them everything about the job, and Jonah.

Yes, that was how Edward had planned it. But now, standing at the foot of the stairway, gazing out over the large rose-colored living room, with its flowery chintz slipcovers and wide bay window that looked out upon the front lawns and the tall shadowy elm trees of Hobson Road, and the almost harsh, pin-point neatness that always prevailed there just hours before company arrived, he realized that he had left one thing out: other people. During the next two weeks, all sorts of people would be infiltrating his life—people who would come to the house to congratulate him and wish him well, people to whom he had given no place in his plan. Like tonight. Company for dinner. Well, he just had to get used to it. He had to realize that there were other people involved too, that they had their own plans, and that it wasn't just him and his plan. At this point, Edward made an important agreement with himself—possibly the most important agreement he would ever make in his whole life: he promised himself he would be flexible. Even though Time was of the essence (he still felt the two weeks were adequate), he would never allow himself to get impatient. He would give his parents enough time to get used to the idea of his going away. One thing was for certain now, though—

he couldn't keep putting off telling them. His sister was right about that. The longer he waited the harder it would be, and the harder for them to accept.

Thinking of all this and remembering that Time was of the essence for his sister too, Edward hurried through the living room into the dining room, then to the kitchen, looking for her; but she was no where to be seen. Nor had she been anywhere upstairs either. In the old days, just about this time, she would have pounced upon him from behind some door, giggling her head off; but that was over too. She was too old for games like that. Looking about the kitchen again, Edward noticed that the back door was slightly ajar: a narrow stream of sunlight poured through, crossing over the polished yellow tiles of the floor. So that's where she was—outside. Smiling, he pulled the door open and stepped out onto the porch.

She was sitting behind the wheel of the old Chrysler, which was parked in the driveway under a huge sprawling maple tree, dressed as before in the white shorts and red-and-white checkered blouse, except now she had a tiny flimsy white scarf tied about her head. The moment she saw him come out, she frowned: "God, I thought you'd never be ready. It's almost twelve-thirty! Steve won't think we're coming any more."

She watched her brother close the door, hurry down the steps over to the car. "Do you want to drive?"

"No, you do it." He got in.

She waited a moment longer, until he was comfortably settled on the seat beside her, then turned on the motor and drove out to the street; then, before turning the wheel—before making the final sweep onto Hobson Road, she took another look at him: How nice he looked this morning in his new blue trousers and white shirt. She had always prided herself on having the handsomest brother in town, and the best-natured one too. None of the other girls' brothers would have let them drive them around like this, on their first day at home. It would have deflated their egos. But her brother wasn't like that. He was so agreeable, so easy to get along with, and that was precisely his trouble. If, for only once, he would get angry at something or someone—even her—things might be different.

Now he was smiling at her again, that trusting, pitiful smile, and all the things she had been thinking about just moments before he had come out—of his being such a slowpoke at times, and of Steve waiting impatiently at B's, worrying that his father would be angry if he was just a few minutes late from lunch—all these things which had irritated her so much then, now quietly slipped away and, thankfully, she looked at the placid, smiling face beside her. Because her brother was so agreeable, because he was so easy to get along with, she loved him dearly. And to think that she had almost missed seeing him again. To think that she had almost not come home this time either.

In the past week (actually from the very first moment she had arrived at home from school), it had crossed her mind many times, that since she had no intention of going back to college in the fall, she probably should have stayed away from home the entire summer.

33

That way she would have avoided all the bickering that had taken place between her parents and her. She had friends at school who would have gladly put her up, and it would have been fun. And it certainly would have served her parents right, to worry about her a little. Then, when she did come home, they would not be so eager to press the issue about school, for fear she might just go off somewhere again. But, no, she had come home because she had wanted to see her brother. She had promised him that she would be home for spring vacation and had broken that promise, and she knew how disappointed he must have been. She had done something else besides—hadn't answered his letters. Well, she hadn't answered them because there was really nothing she could have written that would not have hurt him even more. Nothing truthful. And she didn't want to lie to him. Well…at least she was home now, when he needed her. At least she could say that she was obeying her parents about one thing: if they had known about her brother going away, they would have wanted the family to be together these two weeks.

Although it was against her better judgment to obey her parents all the time, she knew she ought to try to obey them once in a while. After all, they *were* her parents, and she did love them—in her own way. Even if she could, she would not have traded them for any other parents, but she certainly would have liked to trade some of their old-fashioned ideas for more modern ones. Well, if she was stubborn, it was only because they were stubborn too. Now, her brother was different from all of them: he didn't have a stubborn bone in his whole body.

She hoped that for once her parents would be fair. She knew how much this job meant to her brother (she had seen how excited he got, just from talking about it), and they ought to let him have it. After all, they had their way with him long enough. He had always done everything they wanted without complaining, and now it was their turn to do something for him. They ought not try to hold him back.

She hoped they wouldn't—actually she believed they wouldn't (how could they be so heartless?), but still she was worried. She knew how determined they could be, and how pliable her brother was in their hands. She was afraid that in the end they would break him down. They would not do it intentionally, of course, but they would hurt him just the same. They would think of a million excuses (she was getting pretty good at that now herself) to keep him home, to make him feel guilty about leaving, until he would have to stay. And the pity of it all was, if they did succeed, they'd think they were doing the best thing for him.

Well, she thought, it didn't matter so much about herself—if they made her go back to college, for she'd probably end up doing all the things they wanted her to do anyway. She knew that some day she would marry Steve because he was the only boy she had ever liked enough to marry. She would marry Steve and have babies, and live the rest of her life in Mapleville, just like her mother. She would bury herself in the little town, become as rich and miserable as poor Mrs. Delingham (she could even imagine herself wearing those horrible drabby dresses of hers), until one day no one would remember any more what the real Suzanne had been like. And Steve—he would

35

bury himself in the paper mill, become more and more like his father each day. Well...she wasn't going to complain about that. By then, she'd have lived a little. But her brother deserved something better. He had worked too hard at Harvard, to be buried anywhere. He deserved his chance in New York.

It was funny, she told herself now, that since she had done the one inexcusable thing in the Family Rule Book (there were actually two, but the other she considered more personal), had decided to quit college without any regard for her parents' feelings, she had for the first time in her life begun thinking of other people besides herself. Always it had only been Suzanne—Suzanne's happiness, Suzanne's pleasures. It must mean that she was a woman now. Well, she certainly felt like a woman, and because she felt like one, she was sure she was doing the right thing about quitting college. Oh, maybe she'd regret it a little someday, but by then there would be other more important things to think about. Now, it was just a waste of time and money. What had she actually gotten from that one year at college? About the only thing she could say she had learned, hadn't come from a teacher or a textbook, but rather a relationship she had with a boy. No, a man. He alone had taught her something about life, about loving people and being loved; and though it had lasted—this relationship—for only a short time (for as long as the spring vacation itself), the knowledge she had derived from it would be hers for the rest of her life. It had been more than an infatuation, more than what she had ever felt for any other boy—perhaps even more than what she felt for Steve, whom she had known all her life. True, there were some guilty feelings attached to it (these she blamed on the prudent way she had been brought up), but, on the whole, she could say she was a much better person because of it.   Of course, it wasn't something she could boast about to her friends (certainly not to prudy Priscilla), and it certainly wasn't something she could write about to her brother. He had always put her on a pedestal. So she hadn't answered any of his letters. She had just let him think she was too busy. She had let him blame it on the excitement of a first year at college.

Now, of course, he knew that was not so. He had asked her how she had felt about college, and she had told him. And she was sure he had wanted to ask her about the spring vacation too, but something had stopped him. Probably his good nature again. Well...she was grateful for that much. How could she have possibly told him the truth, with that gentle, trusting smile staring at her like that? Or worse yet, lied to him? No, it was better this way. She would make it up to him some day. And as for the boy (why did she persist in calling him that, when he was nearly five years older than she was?), she would probably never see him again, anyway. Neither one had wanted to make more of it than it was. It had merely been a time for reaching out to someone, for needing someone, and she had needed someone for a long time to bring her to her senses.

Now they were turning off Hobson Road—turning away from the rows of neat white frame houses and their lawns of greenery, and the tall old elms, toward the business section of town: Main Street. To the left was the old Mapleville Bank with the new building going up alongside of it (she wondered what her brother would say about that. All the construction workers were away at lunch.), and across from it, the park, with its small steepled church, where she and Steve would be married one day. Then came the stores—Emeline's Lingerie and Apparel Shop, the barber, the butcher and baker and grocer, the drugstore, the General Clothing Store, and the florist and hardware stores, and over there on the corner, B's Snack Shop, the only thriving place in town. Without B's she would have gone crazy.

Steve's new red sports car was parked out in front. How she hated it already! With his flaming red hair, it made him look like a fireball coming down the street. Well, at least he had waited for her. Sometimes she got so mad at Mr. Delingham, she could *scream*!

"There's Steve's graduation present from his parents," she said, pointing out the car to her brother.

"That's quite a present," her brother said, turning his head to admire it. "Speaking of cars—how did Dad get to work this morning without the Chrysler?"

"Mr. Delingham drove him. They had to go over some books or something."

"I thought Mr. Delingham didn't get down early any more."

"He didn't used to, but he started up again. Since Steve's been working there."

"Oh, Steve's working at the mill already?" Her brother smiled. "How does he like it?"

"I guess he likes it all right," she answered almost curtly, "but it wouldn't do any good if he didn't. He can't do anything about it anyway," and with that turned the corner sharply and parked between the florist's rusty green van and the hardwareman's dirty Buick— which made the old Chrysler look pretty good.

3

B's Snack Shop was crowded, which was usually how things were at half-past twelve on a working day in the small town of Mapleville. All the employees of the Delingham Paper Mill who were on the first lunch shift and who hadn't brought their lunches to work that day, had made a mad rush there. But Steve had managed to get a table.

The moment he saw Edward and Suzanne enter, he stood up and grinned, thrusting out his hand: "How've you been, Ed?"

"Just fine," Edward answered, smiling back and feeling the strong grasp of the tall, freckled, red-haired young man in the tan plaid sport jacket and orange bow-tie. Steve hadn't changed at all, Edward told himself; he still didn't look like a Delingham. He remembered the young boy who had come to the house for his first date with Suzanne—tall then, too, dressed in an old worsted woolen jacket, with a stocking cap pulled down low on his forehead and ice skates slung any which way over his shoulder. All you saw were the freckles and the big grin. Nobody would have said Steve looked like a Delingham then, either. "How's yourself these days?" Edward asked him.

"Oh, I can't complain," Steve said, bringing forth another wide grin. They all sat down at the table then: Steve helped Suzanne with her chair, but she didn't seem to notice. Then he looked back at

Edward and said, "I'm working for my dad now, you know. At the mill."

"Yes, I heard," Edward said. "That's a nice-looking graduation present you've got outside."

"Oh, the car..." Steve said, "it's okay, I guess." But he looked pleased with the compliment. "I've always wanted a sports model. My dad was after me to get something more conservative, for the business end, you know—but then I thought, heck, you don't graduate from college every day."

"That's true," Edward said, smiling again. "How're things going at the mill?"

"About the same. You know how the mill is."

And that was true too: Edward knew how the mill was. Seldom a day would go by, that his father wouldn't be talking about it—the new accounts and the old, the rising costs of materials, prices, wages. He had heard it all, in all the variations there were, and there was no need to ask Steve about it.

"Well..." Steve said brightly, looking at the both of them now, "what's everybody going to have?"

"Eddie just wants a Coke," Suzanne answered, "and I'll have a hamburger and a chocolate malt."

"Me too," he said. His flat little blue eyes rested on her admiringly now, as he watched her pull off the white scarf and shake her dark curls free. Then: "What kept you so long? I thought you weren't coming any more."

"Eddie overslept, and I had to fix his breakfast. House orders."
There was a tinge of resentment in her voice now.

"Oh, that's okay," Steve said good-naturedly, looking back at
Edward. "I don't mind waiting, just as long as I get back by two.
That's my dad's lunch hour. He likes to have me around to keep an
eye on things while he's gone."

"What Steve *really* means, Eddie," Suzanne said with a long face,
"is that Mr. Delingham likes to have him around so that he can keep
an eye on *him!*"

"Well…it's not exactly a snap working for your own father, you
know," Steve told her, looking slightly hurt but not angry. "I don't
just sit around all day, with my feet propped up."

Suzanne ignored her boyfriend's remark and went on talking to
her brother: "Mr. Delingham makes Steve work overtime every day.
Even on the days he knows we go to the movies."

"That's just until I get to know the business better," Steve
explained to Edward. "Suzanne doesn't realize how much there is to
learn. It's not like going to school any more. You don't have the
time to fool around."

Edward nodded in agreement. "That's something we're all going
to have to find out. But at least you can say you've got a sure thing
going. It's not like the guy who doesn't know what he's falling into."

"I know," Steve said, the good-naturedness coming back to his
face again. "I don t mind the extra hours. The way I've got it figured
out, in a couple of years I'll be practically running the whole business.
My dad's already talking about semi-retirement. Then Suzanne and I

can get married." He gave her an affectionate grin. "My dad even promised me a house for a wedding present."

"You two ought to be feeling very happy about the future," Edward said, smiling at the both of them, and noticing that his sister wasn't looking happy at all.

"Oh, I am." Steve leaned forward and rested his elbows on the table, grinning again: "What about yourself, Ed? How do you like being through with school now?"

"I like it, but I can't seem to get used to it. I keep thinking I've got a class to run to." Edward laughed.

"I know what you mean. I felt the same way when I first got home. But you'll get used to it, and then you'll be glad it's all over. The studying and everything."

"Well...I don't think I'll ever be through studying though. Not with law—"

"No, I guess not," Steve said quickly, turning a little pink with error. "Not with law. I keep forgetting that being a lawyer is a lot different from running an old paper mill." He laughed shortly. "Do you have any idea what you'll be doing now?"

"Sure he has," Suzanne put in, smiling at her brother. "Eddie's going to New York City—aren't you, Eddie?"

"Oh, yeah?" Steve said, looking surprised. "Taking a little vacation, Ed?"

"No, silly!" she said. "He's got a job there—with the *biggest* law firm in the country!"

"Well...maybe one of the biggest anyway," Edward said, laughing softly at the excitement he saw in his sister's face. He was beginning to get excited again himself.

"Oh, yeah?" Steve said again. He really looked surprised now: his soft pinkish mouth hung open loosely as he stared at Edward with curiosity. "I thought it was all set for you at the bank."

"Oh, I suppose it was—" Edward said, quietly now, "but then this other job came along. It offered a much better opportunity."

"Well, I guess you've got to follow the opportunities," Steve said, leaning back slowly in his chair. He was still watching Edward curiously. "I guess after you go to a school like Harvard, Mapleville just seems like small potatoes."

"I wouldn't say that," Edward told him. "I wouldn't leave here for just any kind of job."

"Me neither." Steve laughed suddenly. "My father would probably come after me with a shotgun!"

Edward laughed too, but he knew what Steve meant: no matter how great an opportunity was offered him, he could never leave Mapleville. His whole future lay at the Delingham Paper Mill. He would run the mill all of his life, just as his father had, until one day, perhaps, a son of his would graduate from college and enable him to go into semi-retirement.

Edward thought of all the boys who had envied Steve through the years—envied him the expensive clothes he wore, the fine big house he lived in, and now, of course, the new red sports car parked in front of B's. No other boy in Mapleville would ever get a present like that for graduation. But Steve, like everybody else, had to pay for the things he got. Even though he would be running the mill some day, he would never be able to call his life his very own, for behind every plan of his would always be his father's.

Edward felt sorry for Steve now. He thought how lucky he was, to be going to New York with Jonah.

The waitress came over to the table now: she stood with her pad and pencil, smiling at everyone. Steve gave her the order and watched her write it down—then, when she had left, said: "When do you have to leave?"

"In two weeks," Edward answered.

"That doesn't give you much time at home, does it?"

"No, but I was afraid to ask for more. They need someone right away."

"They always do," Steve said, authoritively now. "They always tell you that, so that they can get you in a hurry. It's the old employer's trick. They don't want to waste any more time than they have to, in case you don't work out."

Edward nodded.

"But I don't see that you have anything to worry about," Steve went on. "If you don't like it, you can always go back to the bank."

"He'll like it!" Suzanne interjected, throwing a swift warning glance at her boyfriend. "Won't you, Eddie?"

"Oh, sure he will," Steve said hurriedly, looking at her—then back at Edward: "Sure you will, Ed."

"Well…I'm going to give it a good try anyway," Edward said, smiling at the both of them.

"That's about all you can do," Steve said. "Who knows—it might even be easier than that school of yours. I heard Harvard can be pretty rough."

"I wouldn't say it's rough exactly," Edward said. "You've just got to buckle down, that's all. Or you find a lot of guys passing you by."

"That's true of anything nowadays," Steve commented, wrinkling his freckled forehead thoughtfully. "Too many eager beavers around. Everybody wanting to get rich." He laughed at his own joke. "Take my father's business, for instance—just ordinary salesmen, mind you, and they'll stand in line to break you if they can. You've got to be on your toes every minute."

Edward nodded again. Then out of politeness: "How was your school? Rough?"

"Oh, sure." Steve leaned on the table again: "And my dad wouldn't stand for anything but top grades. I really sweated out those four years."

"Don't believe a word he says," Suzanne told her brother, sarcastically. "Steve's never had a top grade in his whole life!"

"Oh…I don't know about that," Steve said, turning in his chair to look at her. "I thought I did pretty good in college, considering what I was up against. Otherwise my dad wouldn't have bought me the car."

"He would too! He promised you one for graduation."

"Not if I didn't graduate, though—"

"No, not if you didn't graduate. *Anybody* knows that. But you didn't *have* to get top grades!"

Steve shrugged his shoulders hopelessly now, and looked at Edward: "Your sister never likes to give a guy any credit."

Edward didn't say anything; he just sat there quietly, watching the both of them. He had never seen his sister act this way before—lash out at Steve: they had always gotten along well. Now it seemed as though she were trying to cut him down every chance she could. He wondered if it hadn't anything to do with her wanting to quit school— if she wasn't a bit jealous of him now. Maybe she had taken her parents' objections more seriously than she cared to have known. Well, if that was the case, all she had to do was change her mind again. She had done that many times before.

He heard her say now: "Eddie had a black guy for a roommate at Harvard."

"Is that right?" Steve said, looking at Edward sympathetically and forgetting his own plight. "Well, at least I didn't have that problem. Some of my friends had to put up with the black guys though."

"Eddie didn't have to *put up* with anybody!" Suzanne snapped. "They happen to be *very* good friends. In fact, they're going to New York together, to work for the same law firm!"

"Oh, yeah?" Steve said, staring at Edward again. "Don't you think that might hold you back some?"

"Oh, Steve!" Suzanne looked thoroughly disgusted with him now. "Sometimes you say the *dumbest* things!"

"Now what did I do that was so wrong?" he asked her, his face flushing to a deep pink—the maze of freckles almost obliterated. "Things like that still happen in this country, you know."

"Maybe they do, but they won't happen to Eddie and his friend! Eddie's friend is a *brain!* Eddie said he's the smartest guy he's ever known!"

"Well...that ought to make a difference then," Steve said, glancing at Edward somewhat sheepishly. "Some blacks are pretty smart, I guess." But he still didn't look convinced. It wasn't that he had anything against blacks, but rather that he had just assumed what he had heard all his life to be true: People always judged you by the company you kept. And right now, blacks weren't the best kind of company. They were putting pressures on big business, everyone knew that, and if you wanted to be on their side, then you had to expect some of the opposition.

"Oh, you make me sick!" Suzanne told him sharply. "You *guess*! That's all you ever do is guess, Steve Delingham! Just because your father has a few blacks working for him at the mill, you think you know all about them!"

"No, I don't," Steve thrusted out defensively. His patience was beginning to wear a little thin. There was just so much a person could take. "I was just pointing out a well-known fact—that some companies aren't as eager to hire blacks as they claim to be. They just do it because they have to."

"That's true," Edward intervened, trying to smooth things out. "I've even heard that some companies won't hire friends. You have

48

to go in separately for a job. So we're lucky that way too."

"Well…" Suzanne said, frowning emphatically, "they ought to make a law against it then."

And the conversation ended there. Edward was glad—he didn't want them to quarrel over Jonah and him. After all, it wasn't their fight. Suzanne had no right to say those things to Steve, for he had never really known a black in his whole life, so how could she expect him to feel any different? Besides, all this had happened before, he could have told his sister that. Friends at school had said the very same things Steve had, meaning no more harm than he. They had merely tried to be helpful. He was used to it now, expected it. And so did Jonah.

He looked away from them now and saw the waitress coming with the order: she was smiling pleasantly again. Edward was glad to see her, for she seemed the sort of person who could put one instantly at ease. And that was what they all needed now.

The girl's name was Rita Triplett: Edward had never seen her before this day, for she and her parents had just recently moved into town. She was seventeen, small and slender, with long shiny blond hair and glittering green eyes. She wore her black waitress-uniform more snugly than the other girls did theirs, to show off her nicely rounded little figure. Edward hadn't notice this though, for he was too occupied with the girl's friendly smile, but Suzanne, like most competitive girls her age, saw everything about her. Most of all, she saw that the girl was smiling a great deal at Steve—flirting with him openly. But at that moment she was so angry with him she didn't care.

Steve, on the other hand, didn't notice the girl at all. He was not in the habit of looking at other girls when he was with Suzanne. He had eyes only for her.

The waitress, however, had eyes for all three at the table: she knew something about each one of them. She was a very observant, nervy girl, and each time she placed something on the table, she would peer into the face of whom it belonged, thus being able to conjure a mental picture of that person long after she had seen him. First of all, she peered into Suzanne's face—saw her fine dark eyes, the short upturned nose, the dark curly hair. She also saw that Suzanne was attractively dressed (most of the small towns she had lived in had horrid little shops to contend with). Although she had not yet been formally introduced to Suzanne Aldworth, she felt she already knew her, by the bits of information she had gathered about her. She knew that she was the prettiest girl in Mapleville, that she was good at sports, and that she was now going steady with the town's rich boy, Steve Delingham. She also knew that the quiet, handsome young man at her left was her brother Edward (how could any one make a mistake about that, they looked so much alike), who had just graduated from Harvard Law School. Everyone in town was talking about it. The other young man at the table, of course, was none other than Steve Delingham himself—of the rich Delinghams who owned the big paper mill, where her father was working presently. On several occasions, she and her mother had met the elder Mr. Delingham, and he had frightened her terribly, so tyrannical-looking was he, with his long, straggly brows and thickset jowls, that she was glad now to see that his son wasn't anything like him. Steve looked cheerful, easy-going. She liked his bright red hair and blaze of freckles, and the haphazard way he had of dressing (most of the other boys in town were stuffy dressers, like their fathers—products of nearby colleges; but Steve reminded her of the New York State boys, whom she always greatly admired), and, of course, that cute little red sports car he was driving around in. Most of all, she liked Steve Delingham because he was hard to get. Everyone she had spoken to had told her of his deep devotion for Susanne Aldworth. "He won't even look at another girl," they had said, "much less give one a tumble." Well, she meant to get much more than a tumble out of Steve. When she was through with him, he'd be making somersaults over *her!*

Now, as she placed his food on the table (she had left it for last, so as to give him enough time to notice her), she leaned forward, lining up her small, rounded breasts with the level of his eyes, and smiled demurely, fluttering her long lashes ever so gently, just as the Mississippi "belles" had taught her to do, to catch a beau. But again Steve didn't notice her and, disappointed, she set the check down on the table and walked away.

But the instant the girl moved away, Steve picked up his hamburger and began eating—staring out into the distance: by chance he happened to catch sight of her walking down the aisle. For a moment he gazed at the quick, rhythmical sway of her little behind, then turned to Edward, saying: "Are you going to the dance tomorrow night?"

51

"What dance?" Edward smiled, holding the straw of his Coke in the air. "I didn't even know there was going to be one."

"I forgot to mention it," his sister said with some indifference. "It's just the Church Social. They moved it up from Christmas this year, as a sort of reunion for all the college kids coming home. You'd better figure on going though. Mom and Dad are."

"Oh, I don't mind," Edward said. "I haven't anything else to do."

Suzanne shifted her attention now to her boyfriend: it was the first time she was looking at him since their quarrel. "Eddie's expecting his friend to come in. He's going to stay at our house, until they're ready to leave for New York."

"Oh, yeah?" Steve said quickly, evenly—trying not to appear surprised again, even though he was. He didn't want to get back on the subject of blacks, for he had put his foot in that enough already. Even though Suzanne was talking to him again, he knew she was still angry. Well...if the Aldworths wanted to mingle with blacks, that was their problem, not his, and he didn't want to have to quarrel with Suzanne about it. He only hoped she wouldn't be angry any more by the time the dance came around tomorrow night. He had been looking forward to it, having a good time, and everybody was going to be there. If she insisted on making a scene there, she'd just make things worse for him. Already his father was upset about her wanting to quit college.

He knew, of course, that some of the employees in the restaurant had overheard their conversation, and how quickly gossip traveled at the mill: it would be just a matter of time when his father would hear of it too. "If that girl's going to be a Delingham someday," his father had told him that very morning, "she'd better start settling down. I won't have that attitude of hers in this family." And his father had meant it. Well, it was partly his fault, too. He had been too easy with Suzanne. He should have put his foot down a long time ago. But he hadn't wanted to risk losing her, for there were too many guys waiting around to pick up where he'd leave off. And she was the only girl in the world for him. He couldn't even imagine being in love with somebody else. But he knew he had to think of his father's side of it too: the family's position. Now that he was working at the mill, now that he was preparing for the day when he would have to run it all by himself, he couldn't let her go on talking to him like this. Especially in public. She should have known that herself. Well—he would just have to talk to her about it one of these days. He was hoping, though, that by the time they got married, she'd have settled down by herself.

Resolving not to worry about any of this now, though, to be his old, cheerful self again, Steve took another bite from his hamburger and grinned, saying, "Did you hear about Cynthia Forst, Ed? She's back in town."

"Yes, I heard," Edward said, forcing a smile now—hoping that Steve wouldn't dwell on that too long. Like him, he had certain subjects he wished to avoid, and Cynthia Forst was one of them. But she kept cropping up everywhere.

"You'll probably see her at the dance tomorrow night," Steve went on, enthusiastically. "I heard she gets around a lot."

"That's all he talks about now," Suzanne said sulkily. "You'd think Cynthia was *Ann-Margaret* herself!"

"No, more like *Lauren Bacall*," Steve corrected her, hunching his shoulders excitedly. "With those slanting eyes and slinky figure."

"*Lauren Bacall?*" She laughed stiltedly. "You don't even remember what she looked like, when she was Cynthia's age."

"I most certainly do!" Steve retorted. "I had to see every one of her movies. She was my mother's favorite movie star." He looked at Edward. "Wait till you see Cynthia, Ed—you won't recognize her. She's quite the siren now. There's some old guy who comes all the way from Philadelphia, to see her. Drives a big black Cadillac."

"Where did you hear that?" demanded Suzanne loudly.

"From the guys." Steve was grinning now like a mischievous boy.

"Well, I heard a few things myself," she said. "Straight from Cynthia too! She says all the boys in this town are *squares:*"

"I believe that," Steve said, chuckling, "from what she's used to running around with. I heard that Washington crowd of hers was pretty fast." He lunged toward Edward now: "Did you hear about her smoking cigars?"

"No," Edward answered, still trying to appear interested. But there was nothing that Steve could tell him about Cynthia that would have interested him. But he couldn't say that. He could see that Steve was enjoying himself now.

"Regular men's cigars," Steve went on to explain. "The big fat ones. Tom Rowley saw her light one up at the Albino's the other night. And that's not all..." He half-stood now and whispered in Edward's ear: "What do you think about that? Carries them around in her purse, just in case."

Edward nodded and smiled again; but Steve hadn't told him anything new. He had already heard about girls carrying contraceptives in their purses, and probably so did Steve. It was just that now it was a girl from Mapleville—some one everybody knew, and that made it shocking.

"She must have picked that up in Washington," Steve added. "She was supposed to be keeping company with some young politician there, until his wife found out." Steve laughed.

"That's not true," Suzanne burst out fiercely. "Cynthia told me all about it! There wasn't any wife—he just wanted to get married, and she didn't. So they broke it off. Cynthia's just *too* sophisticated for this town. That's why everybody's making up stories about her!"

"Then, what about that old guy?" Steve persisted. "He's no story."

"It just so happens he's an old friend of hers—an agent from her modeling days. He just comes down for a visit."

"I bet!" Steve laughed out loud now. "That must be some visit, eh. Ed?"

Edward nodded again—then, seeing a chance to change the subject, said, "You mentioned Tom Rowley a moment ago. What's he doing now?"

"Oh, Tom..." Steve's voice instantly lost its spontaneity. "He's working at the chemical plant, as a salesman. You know Tom—he wouldn't be happy unless he thought be was selling somebody down the river."

"Yes, I know Tom all right. That's one guy I don't care if I ever see again."

"Oh, yeah?" Steve looked surprised again. "I always thought you two were pretty good friends."

"No, we were never friends," Edward said. "I just hung around him, to listen to his gift of gab. Georgie Mathews was the guy I liked."

"Yeah. Good old Georgie..." Steve looked reminiscent now: "I always felt sorry for him, the way he had to drive Tom around all the time. Georgie had to do a lot of chores to make up for all the gasoline they used."

"Are they still as thick?"

"Oh, sure. Tom'd never let Georgie go. He knows he's got a good thing there."

Edward waited a minute now. "What's he doing? Georgie, I mean—"

"Oh, he's working at the chemical plant too. With Tom. Tom got him in the day after he was hired."

"In *Sales?*" It was Edward's turn to look surprised: he couldn't imagine Georgie selling anything, much less himself.

"No. General Office. I guess Georgie's leaning toward Management. It'd be a big joke on Tom, if he ended up running the whole place, including him."

"Tom would deserve it." Edward smiled at that. "How's Mr. Mathews doing these days?"

"Oh, he's blind as a bat now. Can't work any more. Georgie was just lucky to finish college when he did."

"Well, now that you two have had your old home week," Suzanne interrupted again, pushing her chair abruptly away from the table, "Eddie and I've got to go. We've still got Mom's shopping to do."

"I've got to run myself," Steve said, glancing down at his watch. "I'll just about make it." He watched her get up from the table. "Will I see you tonight?"

"I don't know yet." Her voice still held a trace of anger. "We're having company for dinner, and you know how Mom gets about that. You'd better phone first."

"Okay." He gave her another affectionate grin.

Edward stood up now, and reached for the check; but his sister stopped him. "Don't bother about that," she said, "it's Steve's treat."

"That's right," Steve said quickly. "My treat, Ed."

"Well—I'll just have to get you the next time," Edward told him.

"Sure," Steve said.

Edward followed his sister to the door—waited until she was outside, then turned to look back at Steve: the tall, red-haired young man was standing at the table now, hovered over, digging into his trouser pockets. He looked worried. Edward watched him take out a handful of change and lay it carefully on the table. He walked back slowly.

57

"I guess I must have forgotten my wallet at home," Steve said, looking up embarrassingly.

"It happens to the best of us." Edward reached into his pocket and pulled out a neatly folded five-dollar bill and set it down on the table, next to the check. "Will that help cover it?"

"Oh, sure," Steve said quickly, looking relieved. He pushed over his change. "That's more than enough." Then his face clouded again. "I'd appreciate it, if you didn't mention this to Suzanne. She thinks I'm rolling in money, now that I'm working at the mill. Actually, my dad doesn't give me—"

"You don't have to explain to me," Edward said. "We've all been in the same boat."

Steve nodded. "Well, thanks anyway. I'll pay you back as soon as I can."

"Don't worry about it. The next treat will be yours."

Steve nodded and forced a grin now. He watched Edward start to walk away—then: "Ed…I think I ought to tell you something. About your dad and mine—"

"Sure. Go ahead."

"Well…" Steve hesitated a moment. "You probably heard they were going over the books this morning—" Edward nodded. "Well, my dad happened to run across a mistake your father made in one of the ledgers, and he sort of blew his top. You know how fussy he is about those books." Steve gave a weak laugh now. "Well, anyway…one thing led to another, and your father got angry too, started bringing up the past, how my dad once promised him a raise and never gave it to him, and my dad said that if he knew anything about bookkeeping at all, he'd have known why he hadn't gotten it. That really made your father sore, and he took the books and banged them down on my father's desk, and went home."

"Well...they'll get over it," Edward said slowly. "They've had misunderstandings before."

"I know," Steve said, "but I don't want Suzanne to blame me for it. Here lately, we can't talk about anything without her flaring up. A guy can't help what his father does, can he?"

"No. And don't worry about it. My dad won't say anything to her. He wouldn't do anything that would spoil it for you two."

"I know. Your father's a nice guy."

"Well, I better get out there," Edward said, looking toward the door, "before Suzanne thinks something's going on here."

"Yeah," Steve said quickly. "And thanks again, Ed."

Edward hurried outside and found his sister sitting impatiently behind the wheel again. "What were you two talking about in there?" she questioned, as he got in.

"Oh—Steve just wanted to make sure I was going to the dance tomorrow night." Edward closed the door.

"Did he apologize?"

"For what?"

"You know—what he said about blacks."

"Oh, that." Edward looked out of the window. "He didn't mean anything by it, Sis. Steve's all right."

59

"That's your trouble, Eddie," his sister said almost sternly. "You never think people mean the things they say, but they do. Otherwise, why would they say them?"

"Oh…just to have something to talk about, I guess." He looked back at her and smiled.

"Men! Sometimes they're *so* disgusting!"

Edward laughed. "So what's next on the agenda, Sis?"

"The butcher and the baker." She picked up one of the small pieces of paper that lay between them on the seat and handed it to him. "Here—you take the butcher. You were always better at that."

And then they were driving down Main Street again.

4

Some things never change, Edward thought, and Mr. Habich's butcher shop was one of them: it still had the same drabby brown wooden front that it had when he was a small boy doing errands for his mother, the same pictures on the walls, of contented cows grazing in peaceful, emerald-green pastures. Even the tinkle of the tiny brass bell above the door sounded the same.

Edward smiled and stepped inside.

"Well...if it isn't Edward Aldworth," the butcher said, smiling back from behind the shiny white porcelain meat display case. He was holding a long, sharply pointed knife, preparing to carve a portion from a huge leg of beef. Mr. Habich was a short, stoutish man, with a narrow dense ring of curly black hair running about the back of his head: he always wore a heavy, floppy muslin apron, and his round fat face was every bit as red as the meat he sold. That was why the boys in town nicknamed him Blood Face.

"How's business these days, Mr. Habich?" Edward asked.

"You ask me a question like that," the butcher said, "with prices going up every day?" But he laughed. "Business is just business." He turned to the small, attractive middle-aged woman who was standing in front of the counter, dressed in a bright floral housedress, and said. "This is one of our smartest boys, Mrs. Triplett. Your husband must know his father—Roger Aldworth. He's the head-bookkeeper at the mill."

"Oh, I'm sure he does," the woman responded melodiously, resting her sparkling green eyes on Edward's face. "The name does sound familiar." She smiled. "We're the new people on Tyler Street. We live in that darling little white house with the picket fence—"

"Oh, Mrs. Bedler's house," Edward said, smiling at her politely.

"Yes, that's the one. The poor dear took sick suddenly, and had to go live with her sister and niece, in Norfolk. We're only renting, of course. We never stay long enough in one place to buy anything. My husband, William, is a machine set-up man. He's putting in a new line at the Delingham Paper Mill."

"Oh, I see."

The woman went on: "I was just telling Mr. Habich when you walked in, what a delightful little town this is. I'll certainly hate to leave it someday. We mostly stay in industrial areas, you know—dreary places."

"It must be interesting though," Edward told her, "traveling around the country like that." He was trying to be polite again.

"Yes, but it does get tiresome at times. Sometimes we wish we could settle down, like other folks. But I suppose we never will." She laughed melodiously now, "I always say, we're like a pack of gypsies—my husband, daughter Rita, and me."

Mr. Habich spoke now. "Edward's been doing some traveling too—he just graduated from Harvard Law School this week."

"How nice for you!" the woman said, her eyes beaming at Edward again. "I have a nephew who wanted to go there, but there was something about curriculum. He had to end up at Columbia University instead."

"That's another good school," Edward said.

"Yes, but it doesn't have the tradition Harvard has. When you think of all those great people who have gone there—you must be very proud to be part of it."

"Well…" Edward said, smiling again, "sometimes it makes you wonder if you can measure up."

"Oh, I'm sure a nice young man like yourself won't have any trouble," the woman said. "You'll be a great success."

Mr. Habich spoke to her again: "I always hoped my Kenneth would turn out like Edward here. Edward did right by his parents— he went to college and made them proud."

Edward didn't know what to say for a moment. "My father said Kenny's working at Marty's garage now. How's he doing?"

"Too good for his own good, if you ask me," the butcher replied bitterly. He looked back at the woman. "A man works hard all of his life, just so he can give his children something better than he had, and what does my Kenneth do? He takes a job as a mechanic! He wants to dirty his hands just like his father!"

"He'll make a good mechanic though, Mr. Habich," Edward said. "Some day he'll have his own shop, and then you'll be proud."

"I don't think so," the butcher said, shaking his head firmly. "It still won't be as good as going to college."

Edward didn't say anything more: he remembered how his father had said the very same thing. Most fathers thought alike: because they had worked hard for their families, their children, they thought they knew what was best for them. But sometimes the children knew better. Like Kenny. He had taken that job with Marty because it was the only thing he wanted to do, and even though it might turn out to be a mistake in the end, the choice was his. He couldn't blame it on anyone but himself. Mr. Habich had that much to be thankful for.

The woman was talking again. "Well…I always say we can raise our children, but we can't run them. We can't expect them all to be doctors and lawyers—somebody's got to do the other things. My, what a terrible state this country would be in without its mechanics! It would ruin the economy!" And she went on to tell briefly how a nice young mechanic had help fix their car on the way down there, so that they could keep their appointment with Mr. Delingham. But Mr. Habich was only half-listening. He didn't care about the woman's story or the country's economy—all he cared about was his son. And Kenny ought to be going to college like everybody else.

The butcher placed the woman's package on the counter. She turned and smiled at Edward: "Well, it was nice meeting you, young man. And good luck!"

Edward thanked her, then watched her go outside and climb into her brand-new Ford station wagon. When the woman drove off, Mr. Habich said: "Mr. Triplett's supposed to be one of the best machine men in the country. Cost Mr. Delingham a pretty penny, to bring him down here."

"What does he want new machines for?"

"To cut down expenses." Mr. Habich smiled almost maliciously now. "You know how he is. He wouldn't spend a dime, unless he thought he'd get a dollar back." He laughed.

Edward laughed along with him, then remembered how embarrassed Steve was in the restaurant, when he found out he didn't have enough money to pay for the bill. Everyone knew how careful Mr. Delingham was when it came down to spending money. It was almost a standard joke about town. Oh, sure, Steve had his nice clothes and new car, but he had to tote the mark for them—and even Mrs. Delingham herself had to wait for the semi-annual sales at Emeline's on "better" dresses, before she could splurge a little on herself. And of course there was always the story about how underpaid the mill workers were, how Mr. Delingham expected them to work twice as hard for the money they got. No, nobody could ever say Mr. Delingham was foolish when it came to money.

"Well, Edward..." the butcher was saying, "what can I do for you today? I see you've got your mother's list again. Just like old times, eh?" Edward smiled and gave him the piece of paper. "Hmm... big order for the weekend. Lamb and veal chops... Must be having company for dinner." Mr. Habich knew everything about everyone's eating habits.

Edward nodded. "I guess it's sort of a surprise for me."

Mr. Habich smiled, then went about his business. Edward watched the precision and swiftness of his hands: it always amazed him, how quickly the butcher could have the meat cut and weighed

65

and wrapped to perfection. The woman was right: no job was too big or too small, or less important than other jobs—rather it was a conglomeration of jobs, of people doing what they were best at, that made the world go around.

"I suppose you're getting ready to go back to the bank now," the butcher said, wrapping up the order.

"Well…" Edward hesitated, "I haven't really thought about it too much yet."

"No?" The butcher looked almost as surprised as Steve had. "Don't you like working at the bank any more?"

"Oh, sure," Edward said quickly. "I like it fine. But—well, I thought I'd just think things over for a while."

"Well, take your time. You've got your whole life ahead of you. I just wish my Kenneth would have stopped to think things over. Maybe he would have changed his mind about college."

Edward nodded; but he knew Kenny had thought things over. That was why he was working for Marty now. But he couldn't say that to Mr. Habich.

"Well, Edward," Mr. Habich said, setting the package down on the counter and reaching for his little black book—marking in the transaction, "it's nice to see you home again. Give your mother my best, as usual."

"I will, Mr. Habich. And thanks." Edward took the package and went out.

This time his sister was waiting with the car door open. "You were so long again," she said. "What happened in *there?*"

"Oh, Mr. Habich and I were just discussing jobs," Edward told her, getting in and setting his package alongside hers on the front seat. "He seemed pretty certain that I was going back to the bank, just like Steve was. That's the second person already."

"Everybody's going to think that," his sister said. "You've just got to get used to it."

"I know." He smiled. "Well—where to now? Home?"

"No. Dad wants me to show you something first."

"Another surprise?" He laughed.

They drove along silently then. Edward stuck his arm out of the window and looked about, then noticed the construction workers standing in a huddle in front of the bank. "What's going on over there? Looks like somebody's putting up a pretty big building next to the bank."

"That's what I've got to show you," she said, pulling over to the curb and shutting off the motor. "That's going to be the new bank."

"The new bank?" Edward looked at his sister thoughtfully. "What's going to happen to the old one?"

"Mr. Rydin, the new bank president, is going to tear it down. He said it's too old to do anything with. He's going to put up one of those big fancy banks, like they have in Chicago."

"He sounds awfully ambitious for being here such a short time. What does Dad think about it?"

"Oh, he's all for it. You know, anything for good ol' Mapleville. Mr. Rydin told him the new bank is going to be one of the finest in the state, that it's going to bring up the economy."

"I always thought Dad liked things the way they were. Mr. Conover would never have done it."

"That's precisely what Mr. Rydin said. He told Dad that Mr. Conover was too old to run the bank, that he was running it down into the ground. Holding back progress."

"He seems to be telling Dad a lot of things. They must be good friends."

"I guess they are. They're always talking on the telephone." She looked at him suddenly. "You don't think Dad's in cahoots with Mr. Rydin, over something for you, do you?"

"I hope not. It'd only make it that much harder for me to tell Dad about the New York job."

"Well, you're just going to have to do it," his sister said firmly. "It's not your fault, if he's making plans behind your back."

"Well..." Edward said, slowly now, "we're probably just jumping to conclusions. Dad wants me to take it easy for a while. That doesn't sound as though he's got something on his mind."

"Oh, yes it does. That's how they work it: they tell you to take it easy, then make all kinds of plans for you. They do it to me all the time." Edward had to laugh now. But his sister remained skeptical. "You wouldn't let Dad talk you into anything, would you, Eddie?" she asked worriedly.

"Of course not. I told you before, Sis—I've got to go to New York. Nothing's going to change that."

"Good! That's all I wanted to know." She started up the motor again. "Now, we better get these things home, before Mom goes into one of her convulsions."

Edward leaned back in the seat and watched her drive for a while. Then: "By the way—did Dad say anything to you about the Chrysler?"

"No. Why?"

"Oh—it's probably nothing. He just had a little trouble starting it yesterday, at school. It sounds all right now, though. Dad said Marty was too busy to check it over this trip."

"Well, I don't blame Marty a bit!" she said, turning off Main Street and onto Hobson Road. "He's probably tired of fixing it all the time. It'd serve Dad right, if it just stopped for good one of these days. Then he'd *have* to get a new car."

5

By the time Edward had carried all the packages into the house, his sister had gone off somewhere. "Where's Suzie?" he asked his mother, who was standing by the kitchen table arranging a platter of freshly baked chocolate chip cookies. She was dressed in a simple navy blue skirt and a white blouse, and her dark hair was piled high into thick rigid shiny curls at the top of her head. She looked different from yesterday—taller, much older. Edward didn't like the new hairdo.

"She had to go upstairs. Urgent phone call. Priscilla wants her to play another game of tennis before dinner." His mother made a quick little frown. "Sometimes I think they won't be satisfied until they run themselves ragged," she added. "After all, they only play each other."

"But you love it, Mother. You know you do."

"Oh, I suppose I do," she admitted. "I used to like to play tennis myself, when I was a girl. But I knew my limit. Those girls don't." She looked up at him now, with a smile. "Did you enjoy yourself today?"

Edward nodded. "We went to B's for lunch—Steve was there. He seems to be doing all right at the mill." He reached for a cookie and munched quietly. "Suzie said we're having company for dinner tonight."

"Yes, but don't expect me to tell you who it is. It's your father's surprise. He's in the living room. He's been waiting to talk to you."

"Oh, Dad's home already?" Edward asked—as though he hadn't heard what had happened at the mill between his father and Mr. Delingham. It was just quarter of three now. His father never came home before six.

"Mr. Delingham let him go home early today," his mother explained, "because you graduated. Wasn't that nice?"

Edward nodded again. "Well, I better see what Dad wants." He took another cookie and walked out through the yellow-tiled archway.

His father was sitting before the windows, at his desk—head bowed over a large, open book, glasses resting on the tip of his nose; the long, svelte fingers of his right hand were arched loosely over his brow, in quiet, thoughtful repose. Edward thought he looked especially tired that day—worn out. So his father had gone back to working on the books again... That meant the quarrel with Mr. Delingham was over. Well, he hadn't figured it to last too long anyway. There was no use worrying about other people's problems, especially when you knew how they were going to turn out.

He walked softly across the room, to the sofa, and sat down and waited. Presently his father lifted his head and said: "Mind giving me a few minutes, Edward?"

"No, go ahead, Dad. Finish what you're doing."

"Thanks, son. I've just got one more notation to make—" Edward sat quietly now, watching the long, svelte fingers run quickly down a wide column of figures—stop, reach out for a pad of paper and a pencil. Then his father jotted something down, tore off the sheet, slipped it into the book and shut it. "There! That's got it," he said, pulling off the glasses and laying them on the desk.

"I didn't know you were busy," Edward told him. "I could have waited until later."

"Nonsense," his father said. "I was just waiting for you to come home." He turned now in his swivel chair and reclined, resting his hands on the polished mahogany arms. "Well, how does it feel to be part of the household again?" he asked, smiling.

"Just great, Dad." Once again Edward related the events of the day.

"I'm glad to hear that your sister devoted some of her time to you anyway," his father said. "That's more than your mother and I have been able to get from her, since she's been home."

Edward smiled—then remembered something: "Oh—and thanks for the use of the car, Dad."

"Don't thank me! That's the least I can do for a son who's just graduated from *Harvard*." His father laughed. "So—did your sister show you where the new bank's going to be?"

"Yes, sir."

"What do you think of it?"

"It seems like a good idea," Edward answered, trying not to show his true feelings. Already he felt a slight resentment toward the new bank—and this Mr. Rydin, whoever he was.

"Makes your old town look pretty good now, eh?" Roger Aldworth said, laughing again. "I suppose you've been wondering what's going on around here, too?"

"Suzie said we're having company for dinner. Looks like somebody important."

"It is. Somebody *very* important, Edward—" His father leaned forward in the chair now: "Mr. Rydin, the new bank president. He's coming over to talk to you."

"Mr. Rydin?" Edward could feel his heart suddenly pounding. "What about, Dad?"

"He wants to tell you all about the new bank. It seems he's heard a lot of good things about you and wants to meet you. He's very much interested." His father paused to make a point. "He's a very busy man, Edward, and to come here like this, means something. Sounds as though he's got something on his mind worth listening to."

"Gee, Dad..." Edward waited a moment—then slowly: "I appreciate him coming here and everything, but I wish he wouldn't go through all the trouble."

"What do you mean, son?"

"Well...I'm not too sure about the bank any more. I mean—it was all right while I was going to school, but now I've been thinking along different lines."

"What kind of lines?" His father's eyes were fixed on him intently now.

"Well, to be perfectly frank, Dad—I've got an offer from a law firm in New York. Through the Placement Office at school. I've been giving it a lot of thought."

"You have?" His father sat very still in the chair. "You haven't committed yourself though, have you?"

"Well…no, not exactly." Edward watched the disappointment mounting his father's face and looked away for a second. "There's nothing definite yet. I can think it over for a while. But it seems to be everything I'm looking for."

"Oh, well, then…" his father said, resting back in the swivel chair again. "As long as you haven't committed yourself, you're still open to offers. It wouldn't hurt to listen to what Mr. Rydin has to say, to be on the safe side."

"Oh, I'll listen to what he has to say," Edward said quickly. "I just don't want to make any promises."

"Nobody's asking you to, son," his father said, sitting upright. "I'm sure Mr. Rydin hasn't forgotten what it's like to be fresh out of college, full of indecisions. Everyone goes through that. The important thing is that you make the right decision in the end."

Edward nodded.

"Of course," his father went on, "it would be worth your while to remember what a big man Mr. Rydin is. A big man with big ideas! He's going to do big things for our town, and anybody who gets on the bandwagon with him now, can expect to go right to the top."

Edward nodded again. *Bandwagon?* Since when did his father care anything about bandwagons? He had always plodded along his own way.

"All I ask is that you think over carefully what he has to say," his father said. "Give it the same kind of consideration that you're giving that other job."

"Sure, Dad. I'll think it over carefully."

"Good." His father smiled. "Another thing—maybe you better not mention that other job to your mother, until you're absolutely sure of it. There's no use upsetting her for nothing."

"Sure, Dad. I wouldn't want to upset her."

"I'm glad, son." Roger Aldworth reached over for his glasses now and slipped them back on, then opened the book to the exact page where he had stopped—where the sheet of paper with the notation was dangling out. "Well, I might as well get some more work done before dinner," he said.

"Sure, Dad." Edward didn't try to say anything more. He knew that this was not the right time to try to say anything more. His father had that book to work on—and besides, all he wanted was for him to listen to what the banker had to say. He could at least do that much.

He got up from the sofa and started for the stairs.

"Going up to your room now, Edward?" his father asked a minute later, smiling at him over his shoulder.

"I thought I'd take a little nap before dinner. I guess I'm still tired from all that excitement of yesterday."

"Good idea, son. I want you fresh and alert for Mr. Rydin tonight. And don't forget to wear your new suit—we're making *good* impressions, you know!"

6

Dinner was always served punctually at six-thirty at the Aldworth house, regardless of whether there were going to be guests or not; but this evening, everything had already been carefully laid out by five. The white linen tablecloth, the china, the silverware, the crystal candlestick holders and the goblets. Even the heavy curtains had been drawn closed, though there was still considerable daylight left, and the tiny lamps lit in the far corners of the living room where nobody ever sat at all, besides all the table lamps and various other lamps normally used each day on the first floor of the house. The small square ceramic dishes lay waiting on the cocktail table, with their delectable assortments of nuts and candies, and alongside Roger Aldworth's big brown leather chair, on its very own table, was the box of cigars which had been bought especially for that day—Mr. Rydin's visit. It had already been decided that the banker would occupy the leather chair that evening.

The whole anticipation of that night (the vital importance of it, that is) seemed to permeate throughout the house—sweep up the long carpeted stairway to the second floor as well as the bedrooms. In Edward's room (while he showered), his new dark blue suit lay across the bed with an immaculate white shirt and handkerchief, a light blue tie, and a pair of highly polished oxfords with "ironed" socks tucked inside. In Suzanne's room, the orchid ruffled bedspread had been smoothed out and the little cherub dresser-lamps kept lit for her arrival (which was presumed to be shortly). And in Roger and Adele's bedroom, all the tops of the cologne bottles had been put back and the room and closet set to order, after a hectic period of dressing. There, too, the lamps burned brightly. Like the floor below, every lamp in every room had been turned on, lest Mr. Rydin would find himself upstairs looking for the bathroom. The entire house looked like a brightly lit stage awaiting its most notable actor.

After his shower, Edward dressed quickly—slipped into his trousers and shirt and suit jacket, thinking that he ought to at least be downstairs at a decent interval before the guest arrived, since this evening was solely being given for his benefit, whether he liked it or not. So, at five minutes before six, he ran the brush through his hair for the last time, gave a final tug to the light blue tie, and scrutinized himself for five whole seconds in the mirror, telling himself that it just had to do. After all, it wasn't the President of the United States that was coming tonight but just some big banker from Chicago, who thought it was a good idea to put up a big city bank in a small country town.

At six sharp Edward left his room and started downstairs; halfway down he nearly collided with his sister, who was galloping around the corner like a runaway pony. "Oooops!..." she said breathlessly, instantly stepping out of his way. "*Pardon.* I'm late, and Dad's on a rampage again!"

Edward laughed. "Did you win your tennis game?"

"Ah ha. That's the fourth time in a row. You should have seen Priscilla's face!" She grinned, then looped a dark, damp curl off her forehead, turning serious. "I heard the news about Mr. Rydin coming tonight. What are you going to do?"

"Oh, it's all right," Edward told her. He didn't want her to worry. It was enough he had to worry about it. "I told Dad I'd just listen to what he has to say, that's all."

"Does he know about the job you've got in New York?"

"No. I didn't tell him. I just said I had an offer from New York. I thought I'd better wait with the rest of it, until all this is over. There's enough excitement around here already." He laughed, realizing he was beginning to make up excuses too.

"Well, you'd better be careful," she said. "They're going through an *awful* lot of trouble for you downstairs." She drew back suddenly. "Oh, there's Dad's head! Got to run!" and she scampered up the rest of the stairs.

Edward watched her go for a moment, then continued downstairs.

His father was in the dining room, hovering over the table, making a wry face and trying to determine where to set a last-minute dish of chilled celery stalks. The instant he saw Edward, he smiled and made a quick decision—placed the dish in the nearest available spot. "Well, Edward—how do you feel now? After your nap?"

"Just fine, Dad," Edward answered, smiling back. He thought he'd better not mention he hadn't taken the nap after all. It might only complicate things. Further.

"Good!" his father said. "We want everybody at his very best tonight." The elder man made another wry face and looked toward the stairs. "Do you know what your sister did today? Came home late! And after her mother told her explicitly not to! I'm going to have to have a good strong talk with that girl. She's got to start realizing she's got certain obligations to this family too!" He shook his head. "I just hope she's got enough sense now to dress properly. Can't understand why girls don't like to wear dresses any more. Your mother always did..." He gazed down at the table again. "Well—how does everything look to you, son?"

"Just great, Dad."

"Your mother really knows how to give a dinner party, doesn't she?" Roger Aldworth chortled now. "Mr. Rydin's looking forward to this evening. He said he can't remember when he's had his last home-cooked meal."

Edward didn't say anything; he just smiled and shoved his hands into his pockets. He didn't want to discuss Mr. Rydin now: there'd be enough of that later.

In a little while Mrs. Aldworth came into the room.

"Hello!" her husband called out to her cheerfully. "Your son said the table looks great."

"I'm glad." She beamed at Edward. She was wearing the pale green dress again—of yesterday, of his graduation—and the pearls, except now she had left the tiny jacket off and had tied a frilly white apron about her waist instead. Edward watched her go over to his father's side: with the new lofty hairdo, she looked taller than he did.

I don t like it at all, he thought. She's not herself. Everything about this evening is so artificial.

"I just hope that daughter of ours hurries now," Roger Aldworth told her, glancing at his watch impatiently. "It'd be just like her, to walk in when Mr. Rydin does."

"I'd better go upstairs and help things along," his wife said, taking her cue. She went to the stairs.

"And tell her I said she should wear a dress. I'm sick-and-tired of seeing her in those pants all the time!" Roger Aldworth looked back at his son: "Well, I suppose we might as well sit down and be comfortable, while we wait, eh?"

Edward nodded.

Together they walked into the living room; both sat down on the sofa. Then Edward noticed the box of cigars on the table next to his father's chair. Now his father was even afraid to sit in his own chair, lest it wouldn't be good enough for the big banker later on.

"Feeling a little nervous, son?" his father asked, after a moment or two.

"Sort of, Dad."

"Me, too." His father stood up suddenly. "What do you say we have a little father-and-son drink before Mr. Rydin gets here?"

"Sure, Dad." Now that really was something! Edward had never had a drink with his father before—not on his high school graduation day, nor on any of his birthdays, even his twenty-first. His father had always maintained that drinking was solely for social purposes, and then only sparingly: nobody ever got more sociable by drinking too much. Oh, there was the usual small glass of wine at the dinner table for holidays, if guests were present, but that was all: then the bottle had to be stashed away again. Edward remembered how his mother had to always dust it off before serving. Now—because this big city banker was coming to dinner, his father was trying to act differently.

Edward watched his father retrace his steps back to the dining room—open the serving cart. He took out the bottle of wine, filled two glasses, then put it back and returned to the sofa. "We're not exactly what you'd call a drinking family," his father said, mustering up a smile, "but I think the occasion calls for one, don't you?"

Edward nodded, then reached out for his glass. He gulped down half of the wine and watched his father sip his. Then about five minutes later the front doorbell rang. He made a move to answer it, but his father stopped him. "No, I'd better do it," his father said, setting his glass down on the cocktail table. He got up quickly and started for the door, then stopped—pointed to the ceiling: a low rumble sounded from above. "I had a feeling your sister wouldn't make it."

Edward finished drinking his wine, then set the glass down next to his father's; he stood up and watched the door open. The man who had been waiting there was big in many ways: tall, broad-shouldered, portly. He wore a light tan coat, a dark blue suit, a white shirt, and a silvery gray tie. His hair was brittle-gray and his face smooth and shiny, set in a hard, blunt fashion. But he had a hearty smile, which he instantly gave to Edward's father.

"Well, good evening, Roger!" he said jovially, stepping inside the room. He eyed Edward momentarily, then tossed off the coat and handed it to his host. Edward noted now that the man's suit was impeccably tailored, of the very latest style: the wider lapels. Well, he had bought his own dark blue suit just before Christmas. When you were going to college, you couldn't just be thinking about the size of your lapels! "I thought I'd have to be a little late," the man said. "There was a meeting this afternoon but I left my secretary to finish up for me."

"Oh, well…" Roger Aldworth said congenially. "We would have gladly waited." He hung up the man's coat in the nearby closet, then turned to his son. "This is my son, Edward," he said proudly. "Edward, Mr. Rydin…"

"Hello," the man said, putting out his hand. Edward moved forward to shake it, then waited—watched him maneuver hesitantly toward the sofa.

"Oh, no, Charles!" Roger Aldworth said quickly. "The chair over there—"

"Thank you!" the man said, drawing up now in front of the big brown leather. Edward sat down, thinking—he'll manage to fill it. "This *is* comfortable, Roger," the man said, laughing heartily.

Roger Aldworth looked pleased. "Have a cigar before dinner. In the box there—" He pointed to the table.

"I just might do that," the banker said, turning in the chair. He opened the box, took out a cigar and put it up to his nose. "I didn't know you smoked the same brand."

"Well...I don't indulge too often," Roger Aldworth told him, "but when I do I like the best."

Edward felt like cringing now—What a whopper that was! His father had never smoked a thing in his whole life, much less a cigar. What was there about this man, that made him feel he had to lie?

The banker turned to Edward now: "What about yourself, young man? Care to indulge?"

"No, thanks," Edward answered politely. "I'm afraid I haven't learned how to smoke yet."

"Good for you!" The man laughed heartily again. "Actually I hadn't got started myself, until I went into the banking business. Had it forced upon me, so to speak—but I give the man credit who can follow his own head!" He struck up his lighter now, sending up a thick, billowy dark cloud up to the ceiling. Just then Suzanne came down the stairs, with her mother. She was wearing a pale peach-colored dress, with a full skirt and a little white Peter Pan collar. With her dark hair and eyes, and glowing complexion, she looked girlishly lovely—but not happy. Edward thought the dress must have been a last-minute decision on her mother's part.

"Oh...here's my daughter Suzanne now," Roger Aldworth said, turning around to take hold of her arm. "Suzanne, I want you to meet Mr. Rydin—the new bank president."

"How do you do," she said rather stiffly, giving the man a carefully measured smile. Edward could see she didn't particularly like the looks of him either.

"Charming!" the banker said, half-rising and clenching the cigar delicately between his teeth. "Perfectly charming! I have a daughter too, you know—back in Chicago. She's staying there with her mother."

Roger Aldworth merely nodded to that: he didn't know too much about the man's private life, and didn't care to. A man's private life ought to remain private. All he cared about was that the banker was here tonight—meeting his son. "And of course you've already met my wife," he said, turning to her. He paused. "Well...now that we're all here, I suppose we can eat." She nodded, then went to the cocktail table for the two glasses.

Mr. Rydin immediately got up now and began squashing out his cigar.

"Take it with you, Charles," Roger Aldworth told him, trying to be accommodating.

"Oh, I never do that," the banker replied. "Spoils the taste of the food. When I eat I do nothing but eat.'" And he laughed heartily once again, rubbing his strong, rounded belly.

Then they all went into the dining room.

The dinner went smoothly enough, but Edward was glad when it was over: he had the misfortune of having to sit across the table from Mr. Rydin, who had scrutinized him the whole time. Mr. Rydin had the kind of eyes that could look straight at you without flickering an eyelash—dull, gray eyes which without the benefit of his hearty laughter were neither friendly nor unmercenery, but rather curious and ever-thinking. I wonder how interested he'd be, if I hadn't graduated from Harvard, Edward thought. He was glad when his father finally made the motion to leave the table.

Mr. Rydin rose slowly now—rubbing his belly again. "Splendid meal, Roger! Enjoyed every bit of it."

"I'm glad," Roger Aldworth said, looking pleased once more. He started to lead the banker back to the living room. "We'll let the women finish up," he said, and then turning to Edward: "Come along, son. This concerns you as well."

Reluctantly Edward followed them, but the last place he wanted to be now was back in that living room, listening to Mr. Rydin brag about his new bank. But it was too late to do anything about it.

He went and sat down on the sofa again, beside his father, while the banker followed the familiar path back to the brown leather chair. Then Edward watched him reach for the cigar box again. "Do you mind, Roger? Can't stand the taste of a dead cigar."

"Oh, no, go right ahead," Roger Aldworth said quickly—perhaps too quickly now, letting the man know he intended to please him at any cost. Edward thought: The big banker was not only overly ambitious, but extravagant as well. What was wrong with the other cigar? Couldn't he stand the taste of his own spit?

"Well, I suppose it's time to get down to brass tacks," Mr. Rydin said, leaning back with the fresh cigar and sounding suddenly abrupt. He looked across the room at Edward: "No doubt your father has informed you on why I'm here—"

"Yes, sir." Edward thought now: He certainly knows how to get to the point when he wants to. "My father said you wanted to talk to me about the new bank."

"That's right, Edward." There was now a certain formality about the man's voice—a businesslike quality, and Edward told himself he might as well be sitting in his office, getting an interview. Why had his father bothered at all? "Have you given the bank any thought at all, since you've been home?" the man asked.

"Well...frankly no, sir," Edward answered. He was trying to be polite and honest at the same time. "I've had an offer from a law firm in New York—which I've been thinking about a lot."

"Yes, I know. Your father told me." So...his father had already told him. That meant they were better friends than he had thought— "I'm sorry I wasn't able to get to you first, but that's the way things are sometimes, even in the banking business." The banker laughed shortly. "Do you mind telling me the name of the firm?"

"No, sir." Edward told him.

"Pratt, McPherson & Rettig...Yes, I've heard of it, and a very substantial firm it is, I must say. I don't blame you for letting it turn your head. I know what an offer like that can do to a young man just coming out of college. I've traveled that route myself, and let me tell you, it's not easy. The big city's not always what it's made out to be. Sometimes it just lets you become a number—one of the great many."

Edward didn't say anything. He just listened to what the man had to say.

"Mr. Rydin's originally from Wisconsin," his father put in. "Up around Madison—isn't that right, Charles?"

"River Falls, to be exact." The banker smiled slowly now. "So you see, Edward, I'm just a small town boy like you. 'Course, I've been one of the lucky ones. But I've seen my share, too, of disenchanted youths who had to turn tail and go home empty-handed. That's the sad part, Edward—never having the chance to succeed. It doesn't matter where you start from, or how you do it, as long as you end up where you want to be."

"But none of this applies to me," Edward felt like saying. "I've already got the kind of job I want. You're the real opportunist, and I'm not—you like pushing people around, things. I don't like you, I don't want to be like you, and that's why I don't ever want to work for you. I don't want the things you've got to offer." But again he said nothing.

"Now, Edward," the banker went on, leaning toward him, "I'm prepared to offer you something that's equally as good as that other firm offered you, if not better—a chance to do something for your own town. To be on top of things when the changes come!"

"Changes?" Edward looked confused.

"That's right," Mr. Rydin said. "No doubt you've had a chance to compare your town with the other towns you've seen during your travels—what do you think of it now?"

"Well...I've never really thought about it before," Edward said slowly, "but I guess it's just the same old town it's always been."

"Precisely!" The banker looked pleased with himself now. "It probably hasn't changed since the day you were born, or before that either. It just keeps on going along in the same old, backward way. Now, the new bank's going to change all that. It's going to revitalize the town, give it a facelift! Don't you think that's exciting?"

"Oh, sure..." Edward said. "A new bank might be nice—"

"*Nice?*" The banker laughed out loud. "No, Edward—I'm afraid that not even a bank can afford to invest money in something that's merely nice. Rather, it's the turning point—the changeover from old to new! *Progress*. That's what we're talking about here!"

Edward looked a little startled for a moment; then nodded. "Oh, I suppose it'll improve the town," he said, making an effort to get along with the man.

"It'll do more than that," the banker contended. He looked as if he were losing some of his patience. "It's going to change the whole town, its entire concept. Mapleville will be born again! That's the miracle of modernization, Edward."

"Well...some of the older buildings could stand a fixing," Edward admitted, "but outside of that, I don't think the town looks too bad."

"Of course you don't!" The banker seemed to be quietly raging within himself now— "You're like the rest of the people here. You can only see what you want to see. But I'm a stranger—someone from the business world—and I can see something entirely different. Do you know what I see, Edward? I see a town that's slowly coming to a standstill, that's slowly dying because of its backward ways and lack of initiative. *Decay*, Edward. That's what you've got to worry about!" The man paused—then went on less intently: "Of course you've got the paper mill here—but how long can you depend on that? Ten years? Twenty, thirty at the most? Suppose it were to close tomorrow, would the people here be able to go on supporting themselves? I doubt it. Without the mill, you haven't much left. Meanwhile, all the other towns are forging ahead, thinking of the future—building, tearing down, modernizing! Expanding! Do you want to see your little town squashed out in the end, Edward?"

Squashed out? That's a pretty strong statement you're making there, Edward thought. Mr. Delingham would never close the mill, and neither would Steve. They know what it means to the town. It'll be here long after you're gone. You're just saying these things to scare me, like you did my father—

"Now, I'm bringing the best people down here," Mr. Rydin continued, "the best architects and tradesmen, the best interior decorators. When I'm finished, the new Mapleville Bank will be one of the finest in the state. People will come from all around just to see it, and bring their business, too. The town will have a prosperity it's never known before."

And that's it, Edward thought glumly. *Money!* You don't really care about the town. All you care about is building that new bank of yours, so you can make more money. Well—I don't care about your bank either. Sorry!

"Well, Edward," the banker said, taking a short puff on the cigar and holding it away from himself, "what do you think now? Interested a little?"

Edward waited a moment. "Well…it sounds good, sir."

"Mr. Delingham thinks it's the hest thing that could happen here," his father told him, enthusiastically.

"Of course," the banker added, smiling broadly now, "we've got a definite spot in mind for you now, Edward. You will no longer be working as a teller. We're going to move you straight to the top!"

Edward nodded slowly—but didn't say anything.

"Mr. Rydin's not pressing you," his father said. "You don't have to give him your answer tonight."

"That's right," the banker said. "Think it over. Take as long as you like. Take the whole summer off if you want. 'Course, we'd have to know that you'd be ready to work when the new bank is completed."

Edward nodded slowly again—looked at his father, then at the man: "Well…I appreciate all this, but I'm not sure I'm the right person for the job."

"No?" The banker looked a trifle serious again. "Something bothering you?"

"Well—no, nothing's bothering me," Edward told him. "It's just that I don't think I feel the same way you do about the new bank."

"You don't?" The banker smiled quickly. "Then, how do you feel?"

"Well…" Edward hesitated. "I just don't think it's going to fit in, sir. I mean, it sounds too much like a city bank to me. People here are mostly farmers and mill workers—they're used to the old bank, the way things are. They're not going to like too many changes."

"But you *heard* what Mr. Rydin said," Roger Aldworth said quickly, nervously, moving to the edge of the sofa. "He's not only concerned about the people here. He wants to improve the whole town, bring in more business, people from other towns."

"I know that, Dad," Edward said, picking up momentum now that he had started, "but those towns have their own banks. Sure, people will come here once or twice, just to see how things are, but they'll get tired of it. Then they'll revert to their own banks."

"I'm afraid you've missed the point entirely, Edward," the banker said, sounding formal again. "We're dealing in *services*. Big city services. You may not be aware of it yet, but there's a lot of people around here who are looking for that precise thing. I'm not talking about the farmers or mill workers, but people like yourself, and your father—bookkeepers, lawyers, doctors. Businessmen who would like to dabble in high-grade stocks and bonds—investments—if they could only find somebody who could direct them properly. Now, with the new facilities, we'll be able to do just that. And we'll be giving them a brand-new modern bank to come to, besides. What could be better than that?"

Edward waited a moment again. "Well, I might be wrong..."

"If you're not, then I most certainly am," the banker said, laughing brusquely, "and I haven't been wrong yet. I've seen that same doubtful expression you have on your face a dozen times over, and each time I've proven it wrong. I've seen towns that were literally buried in neglect—calling out for help when it was almost too late to give it, then lo and behold! a new bank goes up, and they're thriving like mad. It's like a red feather on a cap, Edward. You've got to see it! Take notice!"

"But this isn't exactly a blight area, you know," Edward wanted to say. "This is just a small country town—people here don't care about the kind of progress you're talking about. If they did, they would have done something about it themselves. Nobody's been waiting around for you." But again he was silent. His father was eyeing him nervously once more.

"I think Mr. Rydin has heard enough about your opinions, Edward," his father said. "After all, he knows a lot more about the banking business than you do."

"Oh, don't stop him!" the banker said. "I'm always interested in hearing what young people think about the things I do. If I thought your son didn't have any opinions of his own, I wouldn't be sitting here now."

Roger Aldworth nodded his head appreciatively; but he didn't quite believe the man. He looked at his son: "Why don't you pour Mr. Rydin—all of us a drink now, Edward? Hmmmm?"

Edward did as he was told—he got up and went to the serving cart, took out the bottle of wine and three glasses. Just as he was about to open the bottle, he heard his father saying in the background: "Not that bottle, Edward—the *brandy*. Mr. Rydin never drinks wine after dinner."

Edward stared at the wall for a few seconds, then bent over and searched for the other bottle; when he found it, he took it out and set the wine back in its proper place. So now his father was even up on what *other* people drank. What happened to all those good old-fashioned principles? He filled the glasses and took them to the living room.

"Why—thank you, Edward," Mr. Rydin said, taking hold of one of them and smiling up at him. "I might as well warn you now—I intend to prove you wrong!" And he laughed heartily once again.

"Well…you know how the young people are today," Roger Aldworth remarked, making another stab at an apology. "They like to think they know best."

"And they should!" the banker insisted. "After all, the future belongs to them. We old-timers can just hold on to it for as long as we can." He looked at Edward in particular now: "We've got to learn to pull together. We cannot put ourselves on one side, and our children on the other."

Roger Aldworth nodded again—then gave a sudden loud, ludicrous laugh: "I guess you're right."

Edward stared at his father now, as he waited for him to take his glass; then turned away sharply and sat down. If he had any sense of humor now, he told himself, he would have thought it funny. But it wasn't funny. Was his father that desperate about this job the banker was offering, that he was willing to bend backwards for it? Make a fool out of himself? Well, if he was, whose fault was it? If he had told his father everything in the beginning, all of this could have been avoided. You couldn't go ahead and make a mistake, then expect to blame somebody else for it.

What I am talking about here, Edward concluded thoughtfully, is closing the barn after the horse has gone. I've got to think of some way to get that horse back in there—

He took a few swallows of his brandy and leaned back against the cushions of the sofa: his father was sipping again. Well, it wasn't that his father was so pious when it came down to drinking, but rather the way he had been brought up, just as it was the way he himself had been brought up (otherwise, why was he sitting here, listening to a man talk about a job he didn't even want?). Basically, you were the way your parents had made you, or had tried to make you, and if you didn't like that, if you wanted to change yourself, then you had to be prepared to fight them as well as yourself. His father had never wanted to fight anything or anybody, and that was how he had known the quarrel with Mr. Delingham wouldn't last too long. Even though his father was constantly complaining about the injustices at the mill, he was thankful to work there. He would have thought it more of an injustice not to be able to. My father's the perfect whipping boy, Edward thought, and now he wants me to be one too.

He swallowed some more of the brandy—

He remembered his Grandmother Martha well: a strong, silent woman she was—huge breasts and hands, forever moving, doing chores. From Martha Aldworth had come the dominant trait of the family: Limitation. Stern religion, the saving of one's soul through pure thoughts and actions. Edward wondered what she would have thought today, if she could see her only son having his *third* intoxicating drink in the very same day (Edward thought of the dinner wine his father had had to sip, too). She would have probably held up her hands in shame. Now, his grandfather John might not have minded at all. Edward always felt his grandfather liked to take a little nip occasionally—that is, whenever he was able to get out of range of Martha's watchful eye!

Now, on the other side of the family—the Malcomes, his mother's people—there existed a totally different kind of orderliness: they were quiet, soft-spoken people. Slightly gullible, perhaps, but forever plodding the well-trodden path. From them had come the old-fashioned constancy—the gentle but determined "plugging away" at things, which his sister Suzanne resented so much about her mother. But wasn't she herself like that at times? Maybe if she could realize this, she wouldn't be so quick to criticize her mother.

Well, it *was* funny after all, he thought, that he should be thinking of all this now—of all these people long gone. In a way, though, they were all here tonight, with their thoughts and convictions. He wondered whose side they were on—his father's and Mr. Rydin's, or his? He didn't think they would have wanted the new bank either.

He finished the brandy, felt a sudden surge of deep warmth inside of him. He was getting a little dizzy now. Well, maybe it was better to drink than to think. The more you thought about things, the more complicated they got.

He was about to get up from the sofa when he heard the telephone ringing in the tiny alcove off the dining room: a second later, Suzanne came rushing out of the kitchen, swinging an exhausted dishcloth. She looked somewhat strained herself, and bored. It's probably

Steve, Edward thought, calling to see if she can go out. Well, she'll be glad now. At least one thing was working out. He didn't want that botched up too.

Holding the empty glass now, he sat there for a while longer, listening to the two strains of conversation crossing over him—the one more subtle, coming from the alcove, and the other, hard and driving, like the steady beat of heavy rain: Mr. Rydin was explaining a financial matter to his father now, and his father kept bobbing his head up and down. All he needs is the apple, Edward thought. Thank God they had left him out of that at least! He got up and went back to the serving cart.

He poured himself another brandy and stared at the wall again: What exactly was he afraid of? All he had to do was tell his father and the banker that he had a job already. What was so difficult about that? But he couldn't even answer that himself.

He put the bottle down and stared at it now. Then he saw his sister coming toward him.

"Steve?" he asked, smiling quickly.

She nodded. "He wants to go for a ride. I just hope Dad doesn't make a big stink out of it."

"He won't. He's on good behavior tonight." Edward picked up the glass and held it out to her: "Want some? We're drinking brandy now—"

"No, thank you!" she said, pulling back from him and gazing off toward the living room. "I heard what Mr. Rydin said about the new bank. Dad's really going to be mad now, when you tell him you're going to New York."

"He'll get over it," Edward said quickly. "He's just charged up now."

"I don't know…" She looked back at him, with some misgivings: "I wish I had your faith in this family. Well—" She let her arms sag at her sides. "I might as well get it over with. Steve's waiting by the phone. I told him I'd call right back, if I couldn't go." She took a step forward, then stopped: "I just wish you could go too, Eddie."

"So do I." He smiled at her again, then took a mouthful of brandy and watched her go.

His father looked up.

"Well, young lady…what's on your mind?" Roger Aldworth asked pleasantly. "I can see there's something brooding there."

"Steve just called on the telephone," she told him. "He wants to know if I can go for a ride."

"And I suppose you've already made up your mind about it?" Roger Aldworth laughed lightly. "Sometimes I wonder why daughters even bother to ask their fathers for permission." He turned to the banker. "That's Mr. Delingham's son, you know—Steve. He and my daughter have been close friends since childhood."

Mr. Rydin smiled approvingly. "Fine lad! Going to be just like his father some day."

"Yes, you've got to hand it to Steve," Roger Aldworth said, throwing a critical look at his own son. "He knows where *his* future's at."

Edward caught the meaning of his father's words, but said nothing. The less said now, the better. He drank more of the brandy.

"Well..." Roger Aldworth said, looking at his daughter, "run along, then. But be home early. Steve's a working man now, you know!" And laughed again—telling the banker the mill was back to working half-days on Saturdays.

Edward listened a moment, then threw his head back and emptied the glass: out of the corner of his eye he saw his sister bolting up the stairs. At least she's out of it, he thought. A moment later: "Edward—if you're going to have seconds, at least have the courtesy to refill Mr. Rydin's glass." Edward flushed now—started for the man's glass.

"Oh, don't bother about me," the banker said, holding up his hand. "I've had my fill."

Roger Aldworth cleared his throat now. "Mr. Rydin was just telling me that he's having a collection of fine oil paintings brought down here for the new bank, *Edward.*"

"That's right," the banker said. "By some of the finest young artists in the country. Do you know anything about art, Edward?"

"No, sir," Edward answered, standing there awkwardly with his empty glass.

"Oh—he was pretty good at drawing in grammar school," Roger Aldworth said, giving his son another critical look.

"Well, I always say," Mr. Rydin said, "there's nothing like a few good paintings on the walls, to make people feel at home. And that's what we aim to do. We want the people here to think of the new bank as their second home." Edward nodded now, blinking his eyes slowly—then the doorbell sounded. "Oh, that must be my secretary, Cynthia," the banker said. "I told her to drop off the minutes."

Roger Aldworth stared at his son now: "Well, Edward—don't just stand there! Answer the door for Mr. Rydin!"

Edward put the empty glass down and wobbled over to the door. His legs felt rubbery now. I'm drunk, he told himself, or getting drunk. Whichever. Now all he needed was to have *Cynthia Forst* here. That ought to round out the evening nicely!

Grabbing hold of the doorknob firmly, he pulled the door open wide: a girl stood there—half-hidden in shadows. A dark dress, pointed breasts, and a briefcase. "May I speak to Mr. Rydin a moment?" she asked in a dull, flattened tone of voice.

"Oh, sure," Edward said, backing suddenly into the wall behind him. The girl moved into the light; then turned her face away. From the back Edward could see she was very tall—probably taller than he was, with her shoes on—and very slender; she had a small waist and long thin legs. Her hair was dark and long down her back, and she seemed saturated in heavy perfume. Edward held his nose a second. Well, at least she *looked* like a model, he thought, and shut the door.

"Well, Cynthia..." his father said, rising with a smile. "Sit down!" He pointed to the exact spot Edward had occupied on the sofa. The girl mumbled something, turned again and sat down, crossing her legs. "Well, Edward—a brandy for Cynthia, *please*," his father ordered again.

Edward nodded and returned to the serving cart, picking up his empty glass on the way. He took out another glass and half-filled it, doing likewise with his own, then measuring the glasses side by side, decided to put a little more in his. There was no use trying to get the girl drunk. She was already working at the bank.

Picking up the glasses carefully, trying to steady himself, he walked toward her and saw her face now—slightly blurred but adequate: it was long and slender, like her body, with wide eyes running across it. She had no nose or mouth to speak of.

"Be my guest," he said, bowing before her, as he handed her her glass. She took it—"Thank you," and laid it flat in the palm of her hand. Then, whirling about—noticing that she was sitting in his spot, he reached out for a nearby chair and pulled it over, plunking himself down into it. "Excuse me," he said, grinning now, holding up his glass, "I've been drinking. I'm a little drunk…"

The girl didn't say anything, but there was a glint of amusement in her eyes.

"It's been a long time, hasn't it?" Edward said. "I doubt whether we would have recognized each other on the street. I know I wouldn't have known you—" He waited for her to say something now.

"No, I don't suppose we would have," she said. She didn't move her eyes off him.

"Well—are you surprised?" he asked, laughing suddenly and thinking he was beginning to sound just like his father. "Have I changed much?"

"Not really," she said.

"Well, I must say you have. You're much taller and prettier than I thought you'd be. But then models are supposed to be taller and prettier, aren't they?" He laughed again.

"Are they?" Her voice was dull and flat, as before.

Edward tried something else. "Do you mind," he said, leaning toward her, "if I ask you a very personal question?" She shook her head, watching him carefully now. "Well...I don't know how to say it, but—" He leaned closer. "Could you tell me what happened to those awful black circles you used to have under your eyes?"

"Black circles?" She looked amused again.

"Ah ha..." He pointed to her left eye. "This one used to have the worse one of all, I remember." He studied her face for a moment, knotting his brows deeply. "But they're gone now."

"Makeup can do wonders," the girl said, almost smiling.

"No, I don't think that's it at all," Edward said, suddenly flinging himself straight in the chair, staring out. "*Time.* That's what happens—" He took a hurried swallow of the brandy. "Time passes and erases things..."

"You don't happen to write poetry too, do you?" she asked, sounding as though she were making fun of him.

"No." He turned back to her. "No, I'm a lawyer—that is, I'm *trying* to be one. There's a difference."

"Oh." She drew up her glass now, slowly, dipping her no-mouth into it, and left a delicate purplish smudge on its edge. Edward watched the very long, pointed fingernails encircling the glass. She reminds me of a long thin black cat, he told himself. She could scratch my eyes out without a second thought.

"I guess we don't like each other very much now," he said a moment later, swinging one leg precariously over the arm of the chair. "I mean, because I had to walk you to Sunday School, and you had to go. All that. But I don't blame us." He took another mouthful of brandy, then gazed across the room, at the banker: "And *he*—your boss—doesn't like me either. You see"—he looked back at her intently now—"he just offered me a very good position at the new bank, and I turned it down. Well... I almost turned it down, anyway. He doesn't know it yet, but I did. And..." His expression softened. "And I guess you're part of it too."

"I am?" The girl watched him carefully again.

Edward nodded. "*Circumstances* again!" He looked a trifle sullen now: "You see, I can't work for him because I've already got a job in New York. But he doesn't know it, and neither does my father. Only Steve Delingham knows, and my sister, and they won't tell. Course..." He paused, then went on thoughtfully: "It's just a matter of time when everybody will find out. Actually, it's for the best anyway. It wouldn't have worked out."

"It wouldn't?" the girl said, dipping her blurred face into her glass once more.

"No. You see, I'd only be thinking about that other job, and besides..." He paused a moment again. "It would be too much like taking you to Sunday School again. I'd hate it, and you'd hate it. Wouldn't you?" He waited for her answer.

103

But she didn't give any.

"Well…" he went on, tossing his head back, "I think you would anyway." He emptied his glass and grinned: "I guess I'm *very* drunk, aren't I?" He waited again for a reply but instead saw her set her glass down on the cocktail table, stand up. "I've got to go now," she told him, and he nodded. "I don't blame you. I'd go too."

His father and Mr. Rydin were watching them now, smiling. Roger Aldworth stood up. "Well, Cynthia…I'm glad you stopped by. I suppose you two had a lot to talk about?"

"Not really," Edward said gloomily, slouching down in the armchair.

Roger Aldworth ignored his son now: "I'm sure you were both glad to see each other."

The girl mumbled something again, and the banker got up then. He looked at his host. "I might as well leave too, Roger. I've got these papers to go over," and picked up the briefcase that the girl had brought in.

Roger Aldworth nodded slowly. "I hope the evening wasn't too much of a disappointment," he said a little sadly.

"Of course not!" the banker said in the same jovial voice he had come in with. "I've enjoyed every bit of it. It was a superb meal, Roger! Give my thanks to your wife." He moved toward Edward then: "Well, young man…I suppose we've both got something to think about now, haven't we?" He laughed and put out his hand again. Edward barely managed to get out of the chair, to shake it; then sat down again.

"I'm sorry, Charles," Roger Aldworth said, looking away from his son embarrassingly. "I don't know what's got into him. He's never done this before..." He followed the banker and the girl over to the door, then went to the closet for the man's coat; when he returned, Mr. Rydin already had the door open. Roger Aldworth silently watched the man slip on his coat, then followed the two outside. "I need a breath of fresh air," he said, closing the door lightly behind him.

Edward waited until the door closed, then mumbled something to himself. He looked down at his empty glass. What *he* needed now was another drink! Pushing himself up on his feet, he staggered back to the serving cart, picked up the bottle and was about to pour, when the door swung open suddenly. His father stood there staring at him harshly against the darkness of the night. "I think you've had enough to drink," he said. "You'd better go upstairs to your room before you fall on your face."

Edward nodded and put the bottle down. He thought he'd better go upstairs, too.

7

The next day—Saturday—Edward woke up late again. This time his sister was standing by the bed holding a cup of hot black coffee. She stirred the covers impatiently. "Come on, Eddie! You've got to get up now! Mom and Dad are waiting for you downstairs!"

Moaning softly to himself, Edward rolled over on his back and opened his eyes slowly: just then a terrible pounding began at the top of his head, as though someone were standing there driving in nails. He put his hand over the spot, rubbed it gently, hoping it would go away, and when it didn't realized he just had to live with it. "What time is it?" he asked her hazily.

"Almost eleven again!" She looked a little perturbed now by his slowness. "Dad said if you're not downstairs by eleven-thirty, he's coming up to get you!" She pushed the hot steaming cup close to his face, prompting him to sit up. "Here—you better drink this," she said. "You're going to need it."

He looked at the cup suspiciously. "What is it?"

"Black coffee, of course."

"Oh, no..." Edward turned his face away: a sudden feeling of nausea had come over him.

"Oh, yes," his sister insisted. "I went through a lot of trouble to get it up here. Mom and Dad are watching everything like hawks this morning!" She waited until he had grasped the cup securely, then went on: "They're getting ready for a full-scale war down there, and you're the target. You're going to need all the fortification you can get." She paused to examine his face. "God, you look awful! What did you do last night—run into a truck?"

"Something like that." He tried to smile, but it was still too painful. "I guess I had too much brandy."

"Dad said you practically finished the whole bottle by yourself, and that you almost knocked over the furniture and were very rude to Mr. Rydin, and that you weren't even nice to Cynthia either, when she came over. He said you ruined the whole evening."

"I did all that?" Edward asked meekly.

"Don't you even remember?"

He shook his head slowly.

"Well...it's not your fault anyway," his sister said, folding her arms obstinately in front of her. "Dad had no right to ask Mr. Rydin here without getting your permission first. He got exactly what he deserved, if you ask me!" She tightened her brows into a sulky frown now: "It makes me so mad sometimes, the way people in this house think they can run other people all the time!"

"Oh...Dad didn't mean anything by it, Sis. He was just trying to be helpful."

"No, he wasn't! If he really wanted to help you, he'd leave you alone now. Let you make up your own mind about things. You graduated from Harvard, didn't you? What more does he want?"

Edward didn't say anything. He sipped the hot coffee carefully.

107

"You've got to tell him everything now, Eddie," his sister went on, "before it's too late. Steve said Dad's been telling everybody that you're going to work for Mr. Rydin, at the new bank. That's why Steve was so surprised yesterday, when you told him you weren't, and Mr. Habich too. You can't keep things a secret any more."

"I know," Edward said, thoughtfully now. "I just hope Dad won't be too disappointed though."

"And what if he is?" she said crossly. "He wouldn't care if you were—if you never got to go to New York. All he cares about is that new bank of Mr. Rydin's."

"Well...it's not all Dad's fault, Suzie. I should have told him I had a job right away. I probably would have done the same thing he did."

"No, you wouldn't. You would have *asked* first." She looked impatient. "You've got to stop thinking about other people all the time, or you're never going to get to do the things you want to do."

"I suppose..." He stared off—thoughtful again.

"Dad didn't talk you into anything last night, did he?" his sister asked quickly, watching him.

"Of course not—" He looked back at her with a slow, painful smile now: It was funny how you even got used to pain. "I'm still going to New York—nothing's changed. In fact, I'm doubly sure about it now. Even if I didn't have that other job, I wouldn't want to work for Mr. Rydin. He and I are at opposite ends of the pole, and I think he knows it, too. But—I don't want to hurt Dad. I couldn't go away knowing I'd hurt him, or Mother."

"Well, I could."

"No, you couldn't, Sis." Edward gave her a quiet, tender smile now. "You're just saying that now, but if you were in my shoes, you'd feel the same way."

"No, I wouldn't!" she insisted. "You don't know me any more, Eddie. I've changed. Honest!" She looked at him wide-eyed, hoping to convince him; but he only laughed.

"Well," he told her, "it'll all straighten out now. Once Dad knows I've got a job, he'll back off."

"I wouldn't count on anything too much this morning though," his sister said. "He barely touched his breakfast, and you know how he loves to eat on Saturdays when he's home." She waited for him to drink more of the coffee, then took the cup. "You'd better get dressed. You don't want him barging up here."

"How do I look to you now?" he asked, trying to be cheerful.

"Better. But there's still a lot of room for improvement. Try a cold shower yet."

He nodded and watched her go to the door, thinking how much this morning was like yesterday morning, and yet how different: so many things had happened since then. "Thanks for the coffee anyway," he told her.

"Don't mention it. I just thought somebody ought to try to even out the odds a little."

Downstairs, Edward hesitated by the archway of the kitchen: his heart was pounding rapidly. Well, here it was now, he told himself, the big moment—what he'd been waiting for. Was he going to bungle it too, like he bungled everything else so far?

He could see his father sitting at the kitchen table, reading last night's newspaper through the heavy horn-rimmed glasses; his mother was across from him, brow taut, stirring a spoon in her coffee cup. She's probably wondering what's going to happen between us, Edward told himself. She looked rather pale—almost ashen in her light blue morning-coat, with her hair still rigidly piled high off her face. Even that hairdo complicates things, he thought; it was another thing added to all the other things they had done for him. Well— maybe if he could remain calm through this, they could too.

He pushed himself slowly into the room. His mother was the first to see him.

"Oh…good morning, dear," she said, a tiny nervous smile fluttering across her face momentarily. She leaned toward her husband and touched his arm gently, then got up and went to the stove for Edward's breakfast.

Edward didn't say anything. He just stood there, listening to the newspaper rattling as his father folded it down on the table.

"Oh, you're down finally…" his father remarked, pulling off the glasses and glaring up at him. "Well—what do you have to say for yourself? Did you sleep well?"

"Yes, sir." Edward corrected himself then: "Well, fairly well, sir."

"I'm glad to hear somebody in this house did," Roger Aldworth returned caustically. He waited for his wife to set down another plate.

"Well, sit down—eat your breakfast. What's left of it. Your mother got up bright and early this morning, to make your favorite pancakes."

Edward nodded his thanks and sat down. He began eating.

His father resumed: "I hope you realize the anguish you caused us last night. I don't mind telling you, I was deeply humiliated by the way you carried on. I've been sitting here all morning, trying to think of what reason you might have had for doing it. Whatever it was, you could have at least showed some consideration for your mother and me. After all, Mr. Rydin was our guest. He came here in good faith."

"Roger, please..." interrupted Mrs. Aldworth, nervously. "Wait until he's through eating." She was sitting at the table again.

"*Wait?*" Roger Aldworth shot a disapproving look at his wife now: "That's all I've been doing this morning—waiting!" He shook his head sternly. "No, Adele—some things must be said. If you can't stand hearing them, then you better leave the room."

She nodded and stood up—looked at her son. Then left.

"Your mother's very upset over all this, Edward," his father said. "You can see that."

Edward held his fork still. "I'm sorry about last night, Dad. I didn't mean to upset anybody. I don't know what came over me—"

"Do you do that sort of thing often? Drink that much?"

"No, sir. That was the first time."

"Well, I'm glad to hear that at least," his father said dryly. "I'd hate to think we've spent all that good money to send you to college, just to become an *alcoholic*."

111

Edward didn't say anything now: he could see his father's old prejudices veering up again. Now that the big banker's visit was over, everything had gone back into place.

"I spoke to Mr. Rydin this morning," Roger Aldworth went on, his tone softening a bit, "and in spite of all that has happened, he's still interested. Though I don't know why he should be. He still wants you to think over his offer."

"I can't, Dad."

"You can't, or you won't?" His father looked hostile again.

"I just can't—" Edward laid the fork down now; there was no use trying to eat any more. "It's not that I don't want to, but—I've already got a job."

"You've already got a job?" his father repeated. He looked stunned for a moment—then: "That one in New York?"

"Yes, sir."

There followed now a silence so deep, so eerie—much like the silence before a great avalanche. Neither of the men looked at each other, neither of them spoke. Then:

"So you have committed yourself after all," Roger Aldworth said thinly. "When—last night?" He looked back at his son.

"No, sir. Just before graduation."

"Just like that?..." muttered his father. "You could have at least told your mother and me—"

"I couldn't, Dad. There wasn't enough time. I had to give my answer right away. The people at the Placement Office at school said if I didn't grab it, somebody else would." Edward stopped to catch his breath—watching the grim tenseness straining his father's face. Why did things have to go wrong all the time? He hurried on: "I was going to tell you about it Thursday, on the way home, but Mother seemed so happy about my being home again, and then last night— well—everything started piling up and—"

"I see…" Roger Aldworth gazed off again—then suddenly lifted his shoulders remorsefully. "Well…" he said thoughtfully, laboriously, "it's all settled then. There's nothing more to talk about, is there?" He paused. "So—when are you planning to leave?"

"In two weeks." Edward corrected himself again: "Actually twelve days."

"Not much time either, huh?" His father gave him a wry smile now. "Maybe we shouldn't have even bothered to unpack your things."

Edward didn't know exactly what to say now: but he knew he had to say something.

"I'm sorry, Dad," he said slowly. "I know how much you were counting on my working for Mr. Rydin—at the new bank, but this other job was such a terrific opportunity, I just couldn't let it go. I know that once I tell you all about it, you'll—"

"No!" his father shouted. "Don't tell me about it! I don't want to know about it! You've made up your mind and that's that! There's nothing more to say!"

Edward felt awful now; and he knew deep in the pit of his stomach that his father was feeling awful too. Why did people have to go through things like this? Why couldn't they just know all by

113

themselves, how things had to be, without being told, hurt? He tried again: "I'm really sorry, Dad. I just wish there was something I could say or do—to make you feel better about this."

"There is one thing you can do," Roger Aldworth said, his voice showing some restraint now. "You can make an apology to Mr. Rydin. There's going to be a dance at the church tonight—he'll be there. Unless, of course, you've made other plans again—"

"No, sir. I haven't made any other plans."

"Good. That'll make your mother feel better at least." Roger Aldworth rose quickly from the table now, and scooped up the newspaper. He put the glasses back on his face. "I'm not going to mention any of this to her," he said. "I think it's your place to tell her. It won't sound so bad coming from you. But if I were you, I'd wait until after the dance. There's no point in ruining *two* evenings in a row for her."

Edward nodded. He watched his father leave the room.

8

The band began playing at eight o'clock sharp. Edward and his parents arrived a short while later—Suzanne and Steve were already there, dancing. They had gone ahead in Steve's new red sports car. Suzanne looked especially lovely that evening, in a soft pink, billowy chiffon dress; on her left shoulder was pinned Steve's huge corsage, of pink and white roses. Her dark curly hair shone and her eyes sparkled with excitement. Edward thought, She's her old happy self again. He was glad that things were patched up between her and Steve.

Checking his mother's small black evening wrap in the cloakroom downstairs, he hurried up the wide flight of stairs to the hall, where a group of people had congregated to watch the early dancers pirouetting across the floor. A slow, old-fashioned waltz was playing. The Merry Notes—five overfed and paunchy gentlemen in bright blue tuxedoes—always started off with a few slow pieces for the older crowd which usually dispersed itself rather early anyway, then gradually livened up as the evening progressed, until, when it was almost time to go home, they began to sound pretty good. Edward often wondered what would happen if the procedure was reversed: the sky would probably fall down.

At the top of the stairs, he smiled at all the people he knew—people whose faces had been familiar to him most of his life: there wasn't a single stranger in the crowd. And that was another thing that was wrong with the church dances, the young people said—always the same old faces. Now, of course, if you wanted to see something different, you could go to the Albino's and watch a girl, who carried contraceptives in her purse, smoke men's cigars. The big fat ones.

Edward located his parents now: they were talking to a small, thin woman in a flat-chested purplish dress. Mrs. Habich, the butcher's wife. Mrs. Habich was a staunch member of the Women's Church Auxiliary and one of its directors, and if there was anything you didn't like about the church socials, you could always convey it to her: of course, there was no guarantee that she'd do anything about it. Mrs. Habich had been running the dances for nearly thirty years now, and she was the sort of person who didn't like to change horses midstream. Mr. Habich himself was nowhere to be seen: Edward assumed he was doing his part for the church somewhere, too. Now, Kenny, you didn't even bother to look for. He never came to the dances. He was always too busy. Besides, nobody who ever worked for Marty got a Saturday night off, whether it was for the good of the church or not. Marty was strictly interested in his own business. But if Kenny wanted to know how to run a successful business, it would certainly be from him. Marty had been a successful businessman for as long as Mrs. Habich had been running the church socials.

Edward started toward his parents now, when suddenly a huge man—not so much of size but invulnerability—stepped out of the crowd in front of him: he was of medium height and stocky build, with pitch black hair and heavy jowls. His long, straggly eyebrows stuck out at the sides of his face like threatening, diabolical wings. He was dressed in an old brown suit which had seen its better days a long time ago, and a dull black tie. "Well, Edward," the man said in a coarse, loud voice, pumping Edward's hand a few times, "it's good to see you home again."

Edward smiled. "Thanks, Mr. Delingham."

"I suppose you're getting ready now to conquer the world?" the man asked, loudly again, making a somewhat ridiculous attempt to soften his hard face with a reciprocal smile.

"Well—I don't know about the world, sir," Edward said. "I'm just hoping to become a good lawyer, that's all."

"Well, don't cut yourself too short," the man said again coarsely.

"I won't, sir." Edward smiled now at the woman who was standing between them—she was very tall, very plain-looking, with large bones that of a man. Her hair was of a deep red and there were thick sprays of freckles across her forehead and nose. A dowdy black dress, stiffly collared in white, hung loosely on her long limbed body, and the only jewelry she wore was a thin gold wedding band. It was funny, Edward told himself, how Mrs. Delingham always reminded him of the "stern" matrons at Mapleville High—funny because there was nothing really stern about her. In fact, one immediately detected a certain inbred composure—a quietness about the woman, which came as a relief after the boisterous soundings of her husband. People always felt sorry for Mrs. Delingham, even though she lived in that

117

fine big house on Thorfield Road, and had all that money, and they often asked themselves, how a nice lady like that could stand being married all those years to a man like Morris Delingham. But only Elizabeth herself could have answered that question. The truth was, she couldn't have stood being married to any other kind of man.

Her maiden name was Murphy. Her father, Jacob, had been a quiet, kindly man—a tailor who had succumbed to an early death (he had scarely been forty-five at the time), because of working too hard for too little. Young Elizabeth had actually hated her father's grimy little tailor shop, with its dusty bolts of cloth materials and endless spools of thread, and stacks of used, smelly clothing waiting for repair. Most of all, she had hated the hot greasy smell of her father's sewing machine as it throbbed away to all hours of the day and night, and she had sworn to herself that she would never marry a man like her father. How many times she had wakened at dawn, to find him still stooped over his work—some garment that a thoughtless customer had brought in at the last minute and expected to have ready the next morning. No one ever thought the tailor should have a life of his own. Then, one day, her father just stooped over for the last time, and died. Elizabeth was the one who had found him, of course. She was only seventeen then, and for three long days she had cried hard like a child; then on the fourth, after a brief, stark funeral, she dried up all the tears forever and got ready to open the little shop the following morning, as though nothing had happened. But from that day on, Elizabeth kept an eye out for something better. She started looking for a husband.

Though Elizabeth Murphy knew she was much taller and much stronger than most women—and more capable of taking care of herself—she sought a man who would protect her from the cold indifferences of the outside world. A man who would never succumb to another's selfishness or inconsideration. A man who would be his own boss. And on the day, six months later, when Morris Delingham, a big burly black-haired young man of twenty-seven, who had already acquired a large fortune from the wilds of Canada (nobody knew anything about his past, but it was thought that he had been in the lumber business there), had come into town, she made up her mind he was the one for her. She let it be known that she was considering matrimony.

Morris Delingham was the ideal man for Elizabeth, for he too was looking for a matrimonial arrangement. Although he could have had his pick of the prettiest girls in town, he preferred an uncomely woman, who, because of her lack of beauty, would be willing to occupy herself with things to do, and demand as little of his time as possible. Pretty women sought to be pampered, and he had no time for such frivolity. He had come to this little country town to build a paper mill, and marriage was a secondary thing on his mind. The woman he would marry would have to understand this. He wanted a wife who would be there when he needed her—to cook and sew and keep his house, to see that he was at least decently dressed (he was a very shabby dresser even then), and to provide the few simple comforts he asked for, and the last thing he wanted was one who would clamor all over him, or expect him to clamor all over her. He

119

was not a very passionate man. Had he still been up in Canada, he would have just chosen a woman to live with; but now that he was getting older, now that he was ready to build the paper mill, he wanted respectability. He wanted to live in a fine, large house, with a good woman in it. He had had enough of roughhousing to last him the rest of his life. Also, he wanted a son—he had wanted a son now for a long time. So, on that day when he arrived in Mapleville, he began to look for the plainest and strongest woman he could find, and Elizabeth Murphy, the tailor's daughter, had been his choice. He had met her on a Sunday, had proposed two days later, and had married her on the following Sunday. There had been no romance between them. They had simply began to live as man and wife in the house he had bought for her on Thorfield Road. And on the following workday—Monday—Elizabeth closed her father's tiny tailor shop for good.

She had never regretted it. She had never once felt sorry that she had married this dark, brooding man who knew little about the common, everyday courtesies that women expected from their husbands, but who had never once been unkind to her either. She had never tried to judge Morris Delingham, or to find fault with him, nor had she ever deceived herself with the notion that he might have married her out of love. She knew he had not. She knew that she had merely filled his needs, as he had hers, and she asked nothing more of him than he was willing to give. She was contented to live in his shadow. She ran his house meticulously, kept a stringent budget, and gave him no cause for dissension. She tried to please him in every way she could. Even now, many years later, she still could not say whether he loved her, but she knew she had won his respect, which was far more important to her. Some people thought she was a fool to do all she did for him, that she would have been better off working in the tailor shop, becoming an old maid, but she knew better. She knew that Elizabeth Murphy, the tailor's daughter, had done far better for herself than she had ever hoped. She had married the town's rich man.

There was only one thing that troubled Elizabeth Delingham now—these days, and that was her son, Steve: he was too much like her father. Too good-natured, too easy to manipulate, and she couldn't help worrying about him. Every day she would pray in church that something would happen to change him, to strengthen him. She did not want him to end up like Jacob Murphy, a used-up man before his time. Right now, she knew that Steve wasn't doing too well at the mill, that her husband was pushing him too hard, but she felt he would improve. She was glad though (this was unbeknown to her husband) that he had chosen a strong-spined girl like Suzanne Aldworth to go steady with, and she hoped they would marry soon. Because she was Steve's mother, she sensed things in him that others could not, not even her husband—a striving pride that only needed to be developed; and she believed the right kind of wife would bring it out. The right kind of wife would not mind sacrificing some of her own pride to help her husband. She knew, of course, that being a Delingham was not going to be a bed of roses for any girl; but she felt that if the girl was sensible enough, if she loved Steve enough, she could be happy. Elizabeth wanted both of her men to be strong and successful.

This was the woman Edward was looking at.

"Hello, Edward," she said, wrinkling up the fleshy corners of her eyes in a quiet smile. "How are you?"

"Just fine, Mrs. Delingham." Edward looked back at her husband now and saw that the conversation was closed. Mr. Delingham was already talking to somebody else, about the paper business. He seldom spoke about anything else for too long.

Edward moved on toward the spot where his parents had stood a little while ago, talking to Mrs. Habich; but now all three were gone. Then the music stopped playing, and he saw his sister coming toward him from the dance floor.

"God!" she said, smoothing out the front of her dress, exhaustively, "am I glad that's over. I don't know why Steve has to dance the waltzes. He doesn't even know how to do them."

Edward laughed. "Where is he?"

"Over by the punch bowl." She pointed to the long, rectangular table set back in one of the corners of the hall, covered with a stiff white tablecloth. "He's getting some punch for you too."

Edward nodded and smiled his thanks.

His sister looked around then. "Where did Mom and Dad go?"

"That's what I've been wondering. They were standing here a few minutes ago."

"I know. I saw them." She looked at him. "Did Dad talk to you yet?"

"No. I guess he's still sore."

"Well, just ignore it. The less he says, the less you'll have to fight back at. He's playing stubborn so you feel sorry for him."

"I suppose." Edward looked meditative.

"I hope you're not going to let it spoil the evening for you," his sister said, a trifle short.

"Of course not." He smiled quickly now: he wasn't going to let it spoil the evening for her either.

"You don't want to let him know he's getting to you. That's the worse thing you can do." She paused. "Oh, I almost forgot—I promised Priscilla I'd ask you to dance with her. You don't have to, though, if you don't want to."

"I don't mind." Edward looked around now himself. "Where will I find her?"

"Over by the punch bowl somewhere," his sister said again, "where all the boys go." She looked away and frowned then. "Here comes Steve now. Take a look at that suit he's wearing. Isn't it awful? Mr. Delingham made him go out and buy it this morning. He said Steve can't wear his sport jackets or bow ties any more."

Edward didn't say anything: he just looked out across the dance floor, at the tall, freckled, red-haired young man coming toward them in the dull olive green suit. Steve didn't look like himself at all that evening, but he didn't seem too unhappy about it. He had a big grin on his face as usual.

"I think it's absolutely hideous!" his sister remarked now. "It makes him look *old*."

"Hello," Steve said cheerily, slurping some of the punch from one of the glasses that was nearly brimming over, while holding out the other two. "Nice turn-out for the church, huh, Ed?"

"Seems like everybody and his uncle's here." Edward smiled.

"Not quite. The main attraction hasn't arrived yet," Steve chuckled, his little blue eyes sparkling with mocking delight as he gazed sideways at Suzanne.

"You know who he's referring to," she said sulkily to her brother. "Cynthia Forst."

"It shouldn't be too long though," Steve continued, disregarding her objection. "She's expected shortly. She had to stop off at the Albino's first, for something."

"Oh," Edward said.

"Well, if she's smart she'll stay there," Suzanne snapped, looking as though she were ready to fall back into her bad mood of yesterday. "Serve everybody right, too! All they're waiting for is more to talk about!"

"Oh—I hope she comes," Steve said. "She ought to be really something tonight. She knows everybody's going to be here." He grinned at Edward: "I heard she paid you a visit last night—"

"Well...it wasn't exactly a visit," Edward explained. "She just dropped off some notes from a meeting. Mr. Rydin asked her to." He paused for a while. "What about the Forsts? Are they coming, too?"

"I don't think so. The last thing I heard they were working in the drugstore. They're going to open up Monday."

"Oh," Edward said, "I thought they were open already."

"No, there was some trouble about the stock not getting in on time. And then they had that other property in Worcester to get rid of. Complications." Steve slurped some more punch, then jerked his head up suddenly: the band was getting ready to play again. "Come on, Suzanne," he said, reaching out for her hand, "they're going to play another waltz."

"*Must* we?" she asked irritably. "What about the glasses?"

"I'll take them back," Edward volunteered.

"Thanks a lot!" She made a face at her brother.

Edward laughed and watched them dance off, then started for the punch bowl table. The music seemed slow enough now. Setting the glasses down, he looked around for a young girl who was biting her nails down to the quick; but there was no one like that. Instead, he saw a girl in a very bright green dress sitting motionlessly on one of the wooden chairs by the wall. She had long straight brown hair and her hands were tightly folded in her lap; she stared straight out in front of her, as though she were afraid to turn her head. Edward thought, She's one of us. He walked over.

"May I have this dance, Priscilla?"

"Oh..." the girl said, looking up with enormously frightened eyes, "Suzanne told you. I'm not a very good dancer—"

"Neither am I."

Edward watched the banker dip the huge silver ladle into the crystal punch bowl and set the float of crushed fruit shimmering on its surface, in the pale yellow light. Mr. Rydin was impeccably tailored

125

again in another dark suit whose lapels were right up to fashion. Next to him, Edward thought, Mr. Delingham would look like a pauper.

"Well, Edward..." the banker said, smiling broadly over his shoulder as he steadied the ladle in his hand, "are you enjoying yourself tonight?"

"Yes, sir." Edward smiled back and sipped his drink: he was trying to think of the proper way to start. But maybe there wasn't a proper way—maybe you just started, that's all. "I guess I owe you an apology for last night, sir," he said, finally. "I acted pretty badly."

"Forget it," the man said. "We all have to let go once in a while. I can still remember the time I had when I graduated from college, and it was only beer!" He laughed heartily, and finished filling his glass.

"Well..." Edward went on, "I just want you to know that I appreciate what you're trying to do. If it weren't for the other job—"

"Yes, I know," the man said, trying to make it easier for him. He straightened and looked more directly at Edward: "Your father told me you've decided to go to New York. He seems, though, to be under the impression that you're still not sure what you want."

"Oh, I'm sure, all right," Edward said. He didn't want to leave any doubts behind this time. "It's everything I want."

"Oh, well, then..." the banker said. "That's the breaks, isn't it? We can't win them all." He smiled slowly now. "Who knows— maybe if I were in your place, I'd be tempted to do the very same thing."

126

Edward looked down at his glass now: he felt a little ashamed. This man—*this* Mr. Rydin wasn't so bad, after all. He wanted to be honest with him. "I guess I just can't see myself working in a bank the rest of my life," he added.

"Well, that's an honest answer anyway," the banker said, "and I appreciate your honesty. Now I'm going to be honest with you: I felt the same way, when I was your age. If someone would have told me I'd be in the banking business all these years, I'd have laughed at him. But here I am!" He laughed heartily again.

"Well..." Edward paused a moment. "I know I should have told you all this yesterday, but I couldn't. You see, I hadn't told my dad yet that I had taken the job, and well—he was so set on my working for you, I just didn't know how to break the news."

"You mustn't let yourself feel guilty about it," the banker told him. "It's your life, and you've the right to do what you want with it. Parents can be difficult sometimes, I know. They get too anxious for their children. But all they want is to see that they get started on the right foot. Your father'll come around eventually."

"I know." Edward paused again. "The trouble is, it's not just me—there's another person involved. A friend of mine from college. He's got a job with the firm too. We sort of made a pact that we'd work together after graduation."

"I see," Mr. Rydin said. "Another law school graduate?"

"Yes, sir. Except with him it's a little different—he's black, and well—you know how they feel sometimes. They always think people

127

are against them. He's going to be a great lawyer someday, but right now he needs all the confidence he can get."

"I see," the banker said again, and he seemed as though he really did see. "In other words, you want to back him up."

"Well, I don't know if you'd call it that exactly. He's helped me a lot at Harvard. I just want to be there in case he needs somebody." Another pause. "I know that if I don't go to New York, he won't either."

"That's highly commendable, Edward," Mr. Rydin said. "I almost envy you such a fine friendship. As for your friend, I wouldn't worry too much about him. From what you've told me, I think he'll do just nicely. Life has a way of smoothing out the bumps."

"That's what my father said. Anyway"—Edward took a fast sip of punch—"I probably wouldn't have worked out for you at the new bank. I'm too much like old Mr. Conover."

"Oh, don't say that, for heaven's sakes!" the banker almost shouted. "Not at your age, at least. Never close your mind to progress, Edward, for if you do, you defeat your own self. A closed mind is a *trapped* mind. Remember that."

"I will, sir. It sounds like good advice."

"It is. It's the best I can give you." The banker put out his hand now— "Well, I want to wish you all the luck in the world. And I'm certainly glad we've had this little conversation. I think it's cleared the air for both of us. As for that other—I think you would have worked out splendidly. Even though we must always look to the future, we can never forget the past. For *there* lies all our failures—and the possible solutions to our future successes!"

"Yes, sir." They shook hands now.

"If you should ever change your mind, see me. I'm always interested in a young man who is not afraid to speak his mind."

It was ten o'clock, and the music had livened up. Edward stood by the big dark oak doors and watched the couples swirling by: his sister was dancing with a boy named Rudy Logan—a tall thin young man with long, golden locks. Edward hadn't seen Rudy since he had let his hair grow long and at first didn't recognize him. Suzanne seemed to be enjoying herself now, for she was laughing all the time, just the way she used to in the old days.

Edward smiled at them as they went by; then felt a light tap on his left shoulder. Turning about he saw a pudgy young fellow in a bulky mottled tan suit, grinning happily at him.

"Georgie Mathews! You old sonofagun!"

"Hi, Ed. How're you?"

"Just fine. And you?"

"Okay." Georgie's grin revealed two badly chipped front teeth: as a child, he had had a bad habit of biting the metal edges of pencils.

"You just get here?" Edward asked him. "I've been looking all over for you."

"We were at the Albino's for a while." Georgie pointed toward the stairs— "Tom's downstairs."

"Oh." Edward didn't care about that, though.

129

"'Ever been there?'"

"No. But I've been hearing a lot about it. Must be the place to go now."

"Sure is." Georgie made a clucking sound through his teeth now. "Lots of girls go there. Things have sure changed around here, I can tell you."

"You don't have to," Edward said, laughing. "I can see for myself." Just then a couple tried to pass between them, and they stepped back for a moment. "I hear you're down at the chemical plant now."

"Yeah. Tom got me in. He's in *Sales,* and I'm *Personnel.*"

"D' you like it?"

"Oh, sure," Georgie answered without hesitation. "There's plenty of opportunity there. I should do all right."

Edward didn't bother to pursue that any further, for he could see that Georgie would have been contented going anywhere Tom had directed him. Georgie hadn't changed either.

"Tell me, did Tom ever get that big car he was always bragging about?"

"Hell, no," Georgie said, laughing as though it were a joke, "he'd never spend any of his money on a car. He's been driving the company's now." Georgie looked away. "Here he comes—"

Edward glanced over his shoulder and saw a tall, sleek-haired, sleek-bodied young man, whose face might easily have been called handsome if it were not for its too eager, too hawkish expression, coming up the stairs. Tom Rowley was wearing a tan suit, too, except his was of a darker hue and better cut than Georgie's. Georgie was still trying to copy Tom's style.

"He sure looks mad," Georgie commented. "He's been trying to get something going with Cynthia Forst, but she won't let him. He thinks every guy in town is screwing her except him." He laughed, taking it for granted that Edward knew all there was to know about Cynthia. "See...there she goes, trying to get away from him again."

Edward looked back and now saw a tall, very slender, very attractive girl in a shiny, clinging mauve dress, rushing toward the opposite side of the double oak doors. Her hair was long and dark, thick down her back, as he vaguely remembered it from the other night—but, again, her face seemed blurred, with the distance. She's probably got loads of makeup on, Edward thought, that you can't tell if she is good-looking anyway.

"He's really having a rough time," Georgie went on analyzing. "No girl has ever thrown him like that. She won't fall for any of his lines, but boy, has he got it for her!"

"How did she get here? You had to drive her?" Edward was wondering if Georgie was still playing chauffeur, too. You could never tell what kind of deals Tom had going for himself. Even though Tom had a company car, he could be pocketing the gasoline money and still be using Georgie's. He was shrewd like that.

"Hell, no," Georgie replied. "Cynthia never lets anybody drive her. She's got her own car. She's very independent." He was watching Tom again, who was halfway up the stairs, talking to a cute girl in a short white skirt. She was all goggle-eyed. "He can get any girl he wants. I don't know why he bothers about Cynthia. She wouldn't even give him the time of day."

"Maybe that's what he likes about her," Edward said. "Somebody who can put him down once in a while." He was hoping that Georgie would take the hint, but of course he didn't. Georgie probably never would.

"Yeah," Georgie said. "Maybe that's it. Oh…here he comes. Don't say a word about what I told you, or he'll get sore."

Tom hurried to the top of the stairs now, saw them and put on a quick smile. But you could see he was boiling over from something. "How' you doing, Ed?" he asked, his sharp, beady eyes scanning over the girls who were standing closeby. "Plenty of broads here tonight, huh?" He was still calling the girls "broads," even though everybody had stopped that a long time ago. Tom believed in doing things in his own way. Too bad Georgie hadn't picked that up from him.

"Looks like they're all here," Edward told him.

"Yeah. Sure does…" Tom whirled around then, and saw Cynthia standing on the other side: a group of young men were slowly edging toward her, laughing loudly. "She's nothing but a prick teaser," Tom told Edward bitterly.

Edward didn't say anything: he could see Georgie laughing quietly over Tom's shoulder. The little guy was getting a big bang out of it. Well, that was something anyway.

"The slut!" Tom shoved his hands deep into his pockets and slouched forward, looking somewhat like an old man whose spine had degenerated with age. "So how's tricks?" he asked, looking at

Edward again. "Been getting any here lately?" The same old baloney.

"Sure," Edward said, smiling. "How about you?"

"I do all right." Tom gazed around again. "I hear you're getting ready to work at the new bank," he said.

"No. That's the wrong rumor. I've got a job in New York." Edward thought how good it felt, to be able to tell Tom he was wrong about something.

"Oh, yeah?" But it didn't matter to Tom one way or another. His eyes were still roaming about. "I've been there a few times. Every place is the same, if you ask me."

But nobody's asking you, Edward thought.

"I wish I were going to New York," Georgie said, smiling at Edward.

"What the hell for?" Tom asked roughly, turning all his hostility on his little friend now.

"Oh, you know..." Georgie clucked through his teeth again. "They've got those gorgeous models out there."

"Models?" Tom laughed cruelly. "What the hell would you do with a model? You can't even handle the broads out here." He looked at Edward sharply: "I keep fixing him up with broads for nothing. He needs somebody to hold his hand."

"No, I don't," Georgie said sadly. He looked deeply hurt. Edward thought: Tom didn't spare anybody's feelings, not even that of his best friend. Georgie meant no more to him than those little bugs he used to carry around in his pockets.

"Goddamn slut..." Tom mumbled now, pulling his hands out of his pockets and staring across the hall at Cynthia. The group of young men were talking to her now, and one of them had his arm about her waist. "I've got to go over there and bust that up," Tom said.

Edward watched him walk away. Then: "What's he so peeved at you for?"

"Oh...he's got a double date all set for tomorrow night," Georgie answered, "a screwing party, and I don't want to go."

"What kind of girl is yours?"

"She's okay." But the way Georgie had said it, Edward knew she couldn't be that okay—the kind of girl Georgie would have picked out for himself, if he had the choice. Tom always made sure Georgie got the worst of the lot, to make himself look good. He never did Georgie any favors. Even getting him that job at the chemical plant had to be for a selfish reason. "It's me, I guess," Georgie added. "I just don't care to fool around with any girl that comes along."

"Did you tell Tom that?"

Georgie nodded, his tiny rounded shoulders collapsing a minute. "He said I must be queer or something, that a guy's supposed to get as much experience as he can, before he gets married."

"That depends on the guy, I think," Edward said. "You're not queer. You're just a little more particular than he'd like you to be."

"I guess I'm too old-fashioned," Georgie said with a smile. "I just want to wait for the right girl to come along. You know—the one you bring home to mother." He laughed.

134

"There's nothing wrong with that. A lot of guys feel that way."

"Well"—Georgie glanced down at his brown shoes—"I probably shouldn't complain. I'm lucky even to get a date—a big fat slob like me." He laughed again. "I suppose a good-looking guy like you though—"

"No."

"Not even once? I mean—sex—"

"Not even once. And I don't consider myself queer. I just never met a girl who made me feel that way. I guess I was too busy making it with the books." Edward laughed, too. Somebody had to tell Georgie the true facts of life.

"Weren't we all." Georgie looked away now, to see how his friend was doing: Tom was still battling it out with Cynthia. Even from the distance, the air about them seemed to crackle. "Now you take him," Georgie said, "with all his experience, he still can't make it with her. She hates his guts. Wouldn't it be something, if a guy like you were to go over there and get a dance with her, when he couldn't?"

"Oh, I don't think she'd want to dance with me," Edward said hastily, thinking of the consequences of what Georgie had just said.

"No? Why not?" But Georgie was already hooked on the idea.

"Well…for one thing, I'm not even sure we're on speaking terms." Edward went into some of the details of last night: "I must have said something I shouldn't."

"But you don't know for sure," Georgie said, still holding on.

"No. But my dad said I was rude to her. So I must have been."

135

"Well, you could always apologize, couldn't you?"

"I suppose." Edward hesitated thoughtfully. "I wouldn't want to do it in front of those other guys though—or Tom."

"You wouldn't have to. You could wait until the two of you were dancing." Georgie seemed to have all the answers now.

"That's if she'd dance with me," Edward reminded him.

"Oh, I think she would," Georgie said, with a sudden smile. "She keeps looking over here all the time." Edward glanced back and saw that that was true: Cynthia seemed to be looking in their direction. But then it could be any of the dozen other guys standing there. He didn't want to jump to conclusions. "I bet she'd dance with you, just to spite Tom," Georgie said, laughing now.

"Well..." Edward could see it was no use: Georgie wasn't going to let go. Well, maybe he did owe Cynthia an apology. It wouldn't hurt to try. And maybe if Georgie saw somebody show Tom up for once, he'd start trying to make it on his own. It was for a good cause. "All right," he said, "but don't expect too much."

"I won't." But Georgie was already beaming with excitement.

Edward walked over to the other side of the doors, slowly. There was no use rushing to the slaughter, he told himself. If she was going to cut him down—well, so be it.

The girl's face came closer now—suddenly cleared itself, as though some miracle had happened: wide, darkly fringed eyes (globs of mascara, of course); high cheekbones; immobile, thankless mouth. Edward suddenly felt the urge to turn around and go back, but he knew he couldn't. Georgie was watching. He couldn't let the little guy down.

"Hello," he said to her, very close now, feeling an awkwardness ascending over him. Why did she always have that effect on him? Even after all these years? He hadn't liked her then, and he didn't like her now. Yet— "Would you care to dance?" he asked.

"I don't mind," she told him, surprisingly—in that same flat, toneless voice of last night. She came toward him, and he caught hold of her elbow, guided her to the dance floor: out of the corner of his eye, he could see the astonished expressions of the young men in the group, who had been standing by her. Tom included.

They started dancing. The music was a bit jumpy, but it was still better to follow than those waltzes. Edward felt all feet now: Weren't models supposed to be expert dancers too? Light like a feather, from all that training—parading up and down? Well, he couldn't think about that now. *Some*body had to start the conversation rolling, and it obviously wasn't going to be her.

"Actually," he began slowly, "I wanted this time to apologize for last night. I guess I drank too much. I'm one of those persons who should stop after the first glass..." He laughed lightly. "Anyway, I have a feeling I might have said something to you I shouldn't."

She looked at him for a moment, with those wide, dark eyes; then: "Do you always apologize for the things you do?"

"Well...most of the time I do," Edward answered. "I guess it's one of my shortcomings." He could smell the heady fragrance of her perfume rising from her body, from the soft sheaves of her silkish mauve dress. Too strong again, he remembered. "Anyway, I just want you to know I didn't mean to offend, if I did."

"You didn't. I don't get offended that easily." She seemed to lift the corners of her mouth slightly. "Besides, I like people to drink too much."

"You do?" He hadn't expected that at all. "Well...I don't think you'll ever catch me doing it again," he told her. "It got me into too much hot water with my dad. He doesn't approve of drinking." He realized he had come to the fork in the road, so to speak—it couldn't just stand there. Some explanation was needed. "You see, the brandy was mainly for Mr. Rydin, to impress him. My dad was dead set on my working at the new bank, and well—I've already got a job in New York. 'Course, my dad didn't know that at the time—last night—" He didn't know why he was telling her all this: it sounded almost trivial coming out. "I suppose it all sounds pretty complicated," he finished, laughing again.

"No. You explained it last night."

"I did?" He felt embarrassed now. "Well, it just goes to show you, how much you can forget when you drink too much." He laughed once more, trying to put some humor in it; then felt his face flushing. "I'm talking too much about myself," he said. "I should be asking you how you like being back home. Or have I done that already too?"

"No," she answered. "It's all right."

"I suppose it's not as exciting as Washington was, though—"

"No." She didn't say anything for a while. "But I manage to amuse myself occasionally."

"Well, I guess that's all one can hope for—a little amusement now and then." He didn't try to say anything else. All she was contributing were the answers to his questions.

The music stopped then, and they just stood there looking at each other silently. After a moment: "I suppose you wouldn't care to dance the next one, would you?" he asked her.

"I can't. I've already promised it."

"Oh, well…that's all right." He took her back, then, to where she had been standing. And that was that. For Georgie.

A short time later Edward was standing by the big double doors again: this time he saw his sister dancing with a boy named Robert Healy. It was a little different with Healy though: he was the all-American boy of Mapleville. Healy excelled in all forms of sport—track, swimming, basketball, football. You name it and he excelled in it. But what he really had his mind on was big league baseball, and right now he was trying to negotiate some kind of an arrangement with one of the bigger universities, to play on their team. Besides all that, Healy was a handsome guy—ruggedly built (he had the largest and hardest biceps in the county), with thick chestnut-colored hair and smiling blue eyes. It was the "Irish eyes" that always got you in the end, everybody said. You never quite took him seriously, until he won the game against you. Healy was popular with the girls in the way Tom Rowley was not—he was a thoroughly likeable guy, and if

139

Steve had any competition over Suzanne, it was probably with him. For Healy, too, had been crazy about her since she was fourteen.

Suzanne had never danced with Healy before, probably because she knew it would make Steve jealous. But now she didn't seem to care. She was laughing all the time again, flashing her dark eyes at him recklessly, as they danced.

Edward watched them a minute or two, then looked around for Steve: the tall, red-haired young man in the new drabby olive green suit was sitting all by himself on the other side of the dance floor, on one of the wooden chairs by the wall, near the punch bowl; Priscilla Eckert was just a few seats down from him. Misery must come in pairs, Edward thought. But Steve was still too close for comfort. He looked deeply perturbed. His face was a glowing bright red, his arms tightly folded against his chest, Indian-fashion, as he stared out over the dance floor. It seemed that the longer Suzanne danced with Healy, the redder he got. Well, you couldn't blame Steve for being angry. They were going steady now. Edward thought he'd better go over there and try to ease things up a bit.

He was just about to start when he saw his mother rushing up the stairs toward him: she looked all aflutter in her light beige evening dress. "Oh, Edward..." she said, relieved to have found him so soon, "we've got to go home now. Your father just had a talk with Mr. Delingham, and he's very upset. He said Suzanne's been dancing with all the boys tonight except Steve. He wants us to take her home. He's going to make Steve go home, too."

Edward said nothing. He knew this was not entirely true: Suzanne had danced with Steve—the waltzes, though they never really counted.

He looked across the dance hall again. Steve was standing up now, holding onto the back of his chair as though for support, as he gazed awkwardly at his father who had just walked up to him, waving his arms frantically in the air. Mr. Delingham seemed to be stressing a vital point. The conversation looked one-sided. Well, Edward told himself, Steve had the worst of all of them. He had to prove to his father he was just like him, when he wasn't.

"It's so humiliating..." muttered his mother behind him. She pulled out a lacy white handkerchief from her small black moiré handbag, touching her forehead with it. "I don't know what possesses that girl sometimes. Steve's such a nice boy, too. They're going steady now, and he bought her that lovely corsage of roses..." Adele Aldworth managed to drag her eyes away from the distressful scene and looked toward the stairs. "We'd better go downstairs now," she told her son. "Your father wants us to wait there."

They went downstairs. Edward took out the stub and went to the cloakroom for his mother's coat. While he was helping her put it on, he saw his father coming down the stairway, dragging his sister along with him. Roger Aldworth was grasping his daughter tightly about the arm. Suzanne blurted out, close to tears, "I don't know what everybody's so excited about! I was just having a good time!"

They all went outside then. As they were getting into the car, Edward heard his mother say: "As soon as we get home, you're going to call that boy up and tell him how sorry you are!"

The ride home was a silent one. Suzanne sat crouched in one corner of the back seat, while her mother was in the other; her father drove the old Chrysler solemnly. No one spoke. It was as though a deep heavy black cloak had fallen over the three, smothering out all the words that might have been said, that could have been said, to ease the tremendous tension.

9

Edward sat quietly on the sofa, watching the tenseness play upon his father's face. The living room looked strangely small that night, in the light of the single lamp lit, and warm too, even though a steady breeze came through the parted curtains of the large bay window. Edward felt the perspiration forming on his brow. Things were beginning to close in.

Upstairs, a terrible commotion was going on: doors were being slammed, objects flung to the floor. Cries and accusations tossed back and forth. If, indeed, there was something of an unrest on the first floor of the house, it could hardly be compared to that of the second.

All through it, his father sat quietly too, across from him, in the big brown leather chair; both men stared at each other from time to time, both had their own private thoughts about the matter, about this evening.

Finally, Roger Aldworth spoke: "I suppose your sister has told you she's planning on quitting college." Edward nodded. He dared not say anything. He knew that to say anything at this moment would only be an intrusion. His father's voice sounded crusty, put upon; he was thinking he had had enough trouble already with Mr. Delingham, over the books, yet to have this too. A daughter shaming him at the church social. Only a daughter like his would cause so much trouble for her father. "She says she wants to have fun," he continued. "What kind of reason is that? That's all she's ever had—was fun!" His voice was punctuated now from an inward bitterness. "I've heard of boys saying that, wanting to loaf, but a girl—I suppose I can't make her go if she doesn't want to, but this—this was uncalled for!"

Edward remained silent again. The trial was over, he told himself; the verdict in. Now it was just a matter of having the verdict read to the court, having the punishment decreed.

"The trouble with her is," his father went on, sharply now, "she's had it too good with Steve. Another girl would have appreciated his fine qualities. What is she trying to do, lose him?" He shook his head stiffly. "I don't understand her at all." He paused for a moment then. "Do you know how many boys she's danced with tonight? Twelve! Your mother counted them. I don't know what's the matter with girls today— Your mother would never have done such a thing!"

Roger Aldworth stood up now and began pacing the floor: "I don't blame Mr. Delingham for being upset with her. He's got the right to want a good solid girl for his son. After all, the responsibility of the mill is going to be in Steve's hands someday. He can't be wracking his brain over what *she'll* be doing." His father stopped pacing, then drooped and looked down, "Well... I've done my best with the girl, and so has your mother. We've tried to be patient with all her foolishness. I suppose it had to come to a head sooner or later—"

His father stopped talking now and looked up toward the top of the stairs: a bedroom door had suddenly opened. "I won't, I won't, I won't!" Suzanne shouted in feisty defiance. Then she burst out of the room, ran to the edge of the stairs and gaped down at them. Her face was swollen and red with tears. "I've got an announcement to make!" she said—all nervous and trembly. "Steve and I are officially engaged now! Mr. Delingham is going to take him for the ring Monday! We're going to be married in *four* weeks!" And then, as hastily as she had come out, she ran back to her room, slamming the door behind her.

Below, both men stared at each other again. Then the elder frowned and came back to his leather chair. "Well," he said, half-satisfied, half-relieved. "It's probably the best thing that could happen to her. She'll have to face up to responsibilities now, and the sooner the better. She's just lucky she didn't lose that boy, the way she acted."

Edward got up from the sofa and went to the stairs.

"Going to bed now?" his father asked thickly.

"I'm sort of tired, Dad."

"Well, that's what we all need now—a good night's sleep. We'll all feel better in the morning." Roger Aldworth watched his son climb the stairs. "About that job of yours, Edward—you haven't said anything to your mother yet, have you?"

Edward stopped and looked back. "No, sir."

"That's good. Mr. Rydin told me you apologized tonight, and I appreciate that. I don't want you to feel I'm trying to tell you what to

145

do again, but I think you ought to reconsider things, now that all this has happened. Your mother's going to have enough on her mind with the wedding and all, without having to worry about you going off somewhere too."

Edward nodded, then continued up the stairs slowly.

10

The following week—amidst all the excitement and preparation of the wedding—the old Chrysler decided to break down. It was the most inappropriate time, but there was nothing that anybody could do about it. It just refused to start one morning, while Roger Aldworth was trying to get to work, and Mr. Delingham, again, was forced to pick him up. This didn't make Mr. Delingham too happy, for he had had an important meeting scheduled for that morning with the man, William Triplett, who was putting in the new machines, and it made him somewhat late. Nearly a half hour. Then, too, the tow truck was long in coming. Edward had to call Marty's garage several times before he got any response, and then it was a stranger who had answered, some one by the name of Towers, who had said Marty was tied up with some business, and that Kenny Habich was working under a truck and couldn't come to the phone, but if it was all right, he himself, the stranger, would come to pick it up. Edward told him it was, glad it was finally going to be hauled away. The old car looked rather pathetic though, as it was being dragged down the street by its snoot.

Besides that, the new shipment of bridal gowns, which Emeline had been expecting and had thought would be especially lovely for the Delingham wedding, had arrived just that day, and Suzanne and her mother and the bridesmaids were to go down to the shop to try them on. Since the Chrysler was no longer available, Priscilla Eckert had to drive them there. But, Adele Aldworth said, it was a small favor to ask of the Maid of Honor, and it was an emergency. Everyone knew what a terrible Maid of Honor Priscilla would make: already she was horrified over the thought of having to walk down the aisle. But custom prevailed; the bride-to be had to choose her best friend for that position, and Priscilla it had to be. To make things even worse for the girl, she had gained almost ten pounds in the past few days, over the sudden news of the wedding. It had all gone into her tummy, making her look like a catastrophe in every gown she tried on. But she promised to take the pounds off, and more, if possible, before the wedding, once she had settled down. Too, Suzanne was letting her win more at tennis, which made her feel a little better. Priscilla, however, was not smart enough to notice this; but any one watching the girls play now, could have seen that the old spark just wasn't there any more. But, if Suzanne was missing a little, she had the right to be. She had other more important things on her mind now, besides tennis. Anybody could play a good game of tennis, but everybody couldn't be getting married in four weeks. And to a Delingham to boot!

Though there was no visible friction between mother and daughter now, anybody could have seen that things were not exactly right there, either. Adele Aldworth felt her daughter was being too difficult about many things, and on many occasions. Suzanne seemed to be displeased with every bridal gown that Emeline showed her, finding more trivial faults than should be, whether it was the color or the fabric or the fit, or the fact that it didn't quite match her expectations of what a wedding gown ought to be. And this last shipment of gowns had to do. Adele knew that Emeline was not going to bother too much, after that. After all, she had other customers as well. Other people were getting married too, other people had important occasions in their lives. She couldn't just be wrapped up in one wedding, whether it was a Delingham one or not. And it worried Adele. She felt that her daughter Suzanne was purposely leaving everything up in the air. How could you possibly have a wedding, if the bride refused to be attired for it? Refused to pick out the wedding gown? Worse yet, she was afraid that her daughter would pick out just anything at the very last moment, not care at all how she looked, just to make everybody else miserable. She herself had already chosen a dress: a wispy blue chiffon. It wasn't exactly what she had hoped for, but it would do, and it would go nicely with the gowns of the three bridesmaids, which, in any event, regardless of what style was chosen, were to be pale pink. Very appropriate for a July-August wedding, Emeline had said. The blue chiffon was well-fitted across the shoulders and the breasts, where she had to be careful, and the length was perfect. Little, if any, alteration was needed. At least *she* hadn't tried to make a fuss.

The atmosphere of the family (together) was not particularly good either. None of them really spoke to each other any more. Just Roger and Adele, and then it was mostly about the wedding, how difficult their daughter was becoming. Roger Aldworth was also worried about what his daughter would be wearing for that all-important day; but he didn't let on to his wife. A father shouldn't have to worry about his daughter's bridal gown, if the daughter was at all right with him. He should be able to take it for granted that she would do the correct thing. As for his son—that job in New York—nothing further was said about that either. A father ought to feel that his son would do the right thing also, under the circumstances. Roger Aldworth had simply taken it for granted that his son would be home for the celebrated day. After all, it was a little thing to ask of a son—and a brother. He should want to be home for his sister's wedding. Roger Aldworth had accepted the old adage—that if you didn't talk about something, if you ignored it, it would go away.

So—it can't be said that this important time in the Aldworths' life was an entirely happy one. Though they were glad it was all settled that their daughter would marry Steve, they were still somewhat embarrassed over the way she had acted toward him at the church social. The next social was nearly a year off, and people would remember a good deal about this one. People did not forget so easily, especially in a small town. Because of an unmultitude of things going on each day, everything seemed to be a bit of important news, and lingered about, like old shoes and magazines, photographs of days' gone, faded clothes, lost songs. Memories. Nothing ever seemed to be thrown away. The Aldworths could just imagine what everybody was thinking. But most people, they found out later, were sympathetic toward them: they too felt it was high time for Suzanne to settle down. The girl just had too much energy for her own good.

And then, of course, there was that other segment of population in the town—those with the daughters, who still felt that Steve could have done better with theirs. But, regardless of what anybody thought, they were all looking forward to going to the wedding. They were sure it would be the occasion of the year, and they knew that (regardless of what she wore) Suzanne would make a lovely bride.

Mr. Delingham had his own set of problems. Because the wedding was of such short notice, he was having difficulty fulfilling his promise to his son, about giving the couple a house for a wedding present. None of the houses he had looked at had quite filled the bill—they were either too small or too large, too poorly constructed, or worse yet, too expensive for what they contributed. So he had contacted a builder in the next town, to immediately draw up some plans for a house, and bought a site less than two blocks down on Thorfield Road, where the big Delingham house itself stood. It would be a belated wedding present, but it would still be the house he had promised for his son. Besides all that, he was going to have its interior decorated and purchase all the furniture as well. Nothing would need to be of Suzanne's choosing. The house would be perfectly outfitted, in proper respect, for the Delingham son who would someday have to run the Delingham Paper Mill single-handed. About the only thing Suzanne could have a voice in was the color of the bedspreads in the bedrooms. Of course, anything that was given to her at the bridal shower could be used also. Mr. Delingham realized that he had taken too much upon himself, and though his bark was worse than his bite at times (the housing industry had a certain ego that he could not at all times penetrate), things seemed to move too slowly for his approval. But there was nothing that he could really do about it. No matter how rich you are, no matter how defiant or pushy, you cannot always build a house in four weeks.

The house, he had decided at length, would be a two-storied one—probably of Georgian style, with four bedrooms upstairs (he was hoping Steve would want a large family), two baths, a study, and a large kitchen. It would be fairly modern but not so modern as to leave the housewife too idle. There would be no dishwasher or garbage disposal or built-ins of any kind, except for the porcelain bathtubs. The less work a wife had to do, the more trouble she could cause for her husband. And that girl—Suzanne Aldworth—had to be kept busy at all times.

About the only person who was totally happy during this period of time—this, above all, frustrating but brief time—and who could just sit back and enjoy all of it, was Mrs. Delingham herself. All she had to do was pick out her dress, and she had let Emeline do that for her. It made no difference what color it was, of what style or how much it cost, as long as it was appropriate, and Emeline had a good eye for that. Wasn't that her business? The only important thing to Mrs. Delingham now, was that her son was finally getting married. She expected great things from him from now on. Unlike her husband, Morris, who had "given in" to the marriage, so to speak, she was thrilled over the thought of having Suzanne for her daughter-in-law, in spite of what had happened at the church social that other night. Secretly, in fact, she had always been afraid that something would come between them—that the girl would get away from Steve in the end. Now she was at rest. She knew that her son loved Suzanne deeply (the incident at the dance had proved that), and when a boy loved a girl like that, there was literally nothing that he was not able to do for her. He could climb the highest mountain, if he had to. He could even run his father's paper mill successfully.

As for the other people involved—the wedding couple themselves—nothing had really changed between them. A certain coolness still existed there. In fact, because of the wedding preparations—the wedding preparations taken over by other people— they saw less of each other than before. Each had his own things to do. Oh, occasionally they would talk for a while on the telephone, but there wasn't really that much to say, for both knew pretty well what the other was doing. It was more repetitious than anything else. Steve, of course, was all excited about the house his father was having built, but Suzanne showed no apparent interest in it at all—and again, her parents, the Aldworths, thought it inconsiderate of her. But how can a young girl get all excited about something that was nothing of her own personal wishes or touches—something that was totally planned out for her, right down to the style of the furniture, and the color of the walls and the carpeting? In truth, a deep bitterness was going on inside of Suzanne at this time. Though she seemed much quieter than she had ever been in her whole life (her dark eyes actually looked too big and too sad for her face now), she did everything in her power to hurt her parents—to confuse them, to make them worry. Because she was unhappy herself, she wanted them to be too, and only by some great miracle would she be the pretty, happy bride that everyone expected to see on that important day—the wedding day. To Suzanne, it was not going to be her wedding day but everybody else's.

Toward the end of the week (Friday morning), Edward received a telephone call from the garage. It was Kenny Habich. It was close to ten o'clock and Edward had just finished eating breakfast. He was all alone in the house: his mother had gone to have her hair fixed again, and Suzanne was off somewhere with Priscilla Eckert, probably playing tennis. Edward wondered what had happened. Marty usually made all the calls.

"D' you think you could come down here this morning?" Kenny asked him. "It's about the Chrysler—"

"Sure. Is something wrong?"

"Well...I can't say yet." Kenny sounded rather evasive, and that wasn't like him. "I'd like to talk to you first."

"Sure. Would eleven o'clock be all right?"

"That's okay."

They both hung up then, and Edward hurried upstairs to finish dressing. It wasn't too far to the garage, he could walk over easily, but he didn't want to rush himself. The morning was pleasant, and he wanted some time to think on the way. He kept wondering what it was that Kenny couldn't talk about on the phone.

He got there five minutes to eleven—the office was empty. Edward thought that Marty was probably in the back somewhere. He seldom sat in his office: he was not the telephone-and-paper kind of businessman. Marty was more times than not in the garage, where the action was. He worked right along with his help.

It was a very large long gray brick building, with two dingy windows up front and a pair of enormous overhead doors at the back, for the trucks to pull in and out of. From the outside, the shop might have had a messy, unkept appearance, but everything had been carefully planned—nothing was ever out of place; nothing went amiss. Many years ago, a blacksmith shop had stood on the exact spot, then around 1912 or so, a fire had broken out and burned it to the ground, and then the land lay vacant for nearly thirty years, due to an entanglement of heirs, until one day the next to the last heir died, and, Mr. Carter, the one who was left, sold it outright to Mr. Vossman, of the Mapleville Realty, who in turn sold it to Marty, for the garage. It seemed a befitting ending for the old place, for by then the modern form of transportation—the automobile—had firmly rooted itself across the country, replacing the horse and buggy of old. All the while the big long gray building was going up, people had talked about it—how the new owner must be somebody who knew his business, and could afford it. And Marty did.

Edward walked out to the back slowly: all the lights were turned on, and a foggy, grayish haze seemed to hang over everything. It was rather a dreary place to be, but then most garages are, unless you like working in them. "Anybody home?" he asked, looking about—and a second later, a pair of lean, agile legs wiggled out from under a dark red Pontiac sedan, whose right side was all smashed in, up to the end of the front fender. Edward thought the driver must have gotten a pretty good knock out of that.

All in all, there were three vehicles in the garage that day: the smashed-up Pontiac, a small GMC pickup, and the Chrysler. The old clunker was standing off by itself, in a far corner, looking as though it had gone unattended. A thin layer of dust clung to it, and Edward wondered what his father would say, if he saw it. His father always kept the old car brightly polished.

"Over here," Kenny said, as he smiled and waved Edward on. He was wearing a pair of baggy overalls covered with grease, and he himself looked of grease and sweat. Kenny Habich was a thin, wiry kind of guy, with a narrow pointed face and long dark blond hair that kept poking into the corners of his eyes. Edward always thought he looked like one of the Dead End Kids, in the movies. You never saw Kenny dressed up. He always looked like this, except for the days when he had had to go to school, and then you couldn't exactly call him clean: there was always a smudge of grease somewhere on him. But he looked happy, contented with himself. Kenny lived in a world of his own—a world of carburetors and spark plugs and fan belts, et cetera, and nothing else mattered to him. At the age of eighteen he already had a good head on his shoulders. He knew what he wanted out of life and how to get it. Kenny was probably the luckiest and happiest guy in all Mapleville, when you thought about it.

Edward walked over with his hand out. "How've you been, Ken?"

"Okay." The young mechanic laughed, and drew back. "You better not do that, or you'll get yourself dirty."

156

Edward laughed too, and dropped his hand to his side. "How do you like it here? Working for Marty?"

"It's okay," Kenny replied, unhesitatingly, knowing what Edward was referring to. "He's not so bad. Once he knows you're here to work, he leaves you alone. I've learned a lot since I've been here. He sure knows his stuff." Kenny pulled a grimy rag from out of his back pocket and started to wipe some of the grease off his hands. "'Course my dad doesn't think it's so hot. He keeps harping about college. Now I ask you"—Kenny gave a little pinched smile now— "what would a guy like me do there?"

"I honestly don't know," Edward said, laughing. And he didn't.

"I'd probably have to start taking the place apart the first day." Kenny smiled again. "Now..." he said, looking about him affectionately, "this is all I want. Give me a place like this someday, and I'll be satisfied."

"It's a nice garage," Edward agreed.

"Yeah. It's the best I've seen." Kenny pushed the rag back into the pocket. "Say, you want some lunch? I've got some liverwurst sandwiches, my dad's specialty—"

"No, thanks," Edward answered. "I just had breakfast not long ago." He felt a little funny saying that, for he knew Kenny's day began bright and early in the morning: seven o'clock. He had the right to be hungry now. "But don't let me keep you from eating."

"Okay." The mechanic went over to a long wooden bench where all sorts of motors and apparatus were sprawled out, and opened a drawer; he pulled out a paper bag and set out two bulky sandwiches

157

wrapped in wax paper and a thermos bottle of hot black coffee. Kenny was the only kid Edward had ever known who drank hot black coffee, and he thought it must be because of those blurry hours he kept, and those dreary places he worked in.

"How about some coffee at least?" Kenny tried again. "There's some extra cups in the office—"

"No, thanks," Edward said hastily. He still remembered the bitter taste of that last cup of black coffee he had—the one Suzanne had brought up to his room, the morning after the dinner with Mr. Rydin. It was funny how a bitter taste could linger on. "Don't worry about me."

"Okay." Kenny smiled, then hoisted himself up on the bench. "I hear you're going to New York," he said casually, peeling back the wax paper from one of the sandwiches.

"Well...I've got a pretty good job waiting there," Edward explained. "'Course you can never tell until you try it." He didn't want to sound braggish. "I thought I'd try out corporate law for a while. Seems a good place to start."

"Sounds good to me," Kenny responded. "'Course I don't know much about that stuff."

"Well..." Edward continued, "my dad doesn't think too much of it, though. I guess he'd prefer my staying with the bank. Forever." He laughed.

"Fathers are sure funny," Kenny said, thoughtful for a moment. "They keep telling you about all the mistakes they've made in their lives, then they expect you to follow their advice. The way I see it, it's up to the guy who's got to do the job. I never told my old man to be a butcher."

Edward nodded. He knew Kenny made a lot of sense. There were only two things you could do about fathers—take their advice and make them happy, or follow your own convictions. The latter, of course, meant you had to have the courage to see it through. Kenny had that courage.

"Well, don't let it throw you," the mechanic said. "It'll work out somehow."

"That's what I keep telling myself," Edward laughed again.

Rolling up the wax paper now into a tight ball, tossing it off into the trashcan, Kenny reached for the other sandwich. He still looked hungry. "I hope you didn't mind coming down here this morning," he said.

"No, I was wondering how the Chrysler was doing."

"It's not. That's what I've got to talk to you about. Marty's not going to work on it."

"No?" Edward looked puzzled. "Doesn't he think he can fix it?"

"Oh, sure. He can fix it. He just doesn't want to work on it any more. I guess it's got something to do with the last time your father brought it in. He had to order some special parts for it, and your father said he overcharged him. That all it needed was a good tune-up."

"That sounds like my dad all right," Edward said, smiling slightly. "He gets prices mixed up sometimes." So there had been some words between Marty and his father. That was why Marty hadn't checked the clunker out before the trip to school. He had just said he was too

159

busy. Well...all his father had to hear now, was that Marty was through working on it. That would be the last straw... "What I don't understand though—" Edward added, "if Marty didn't want to work on it, why did he have it brought here?"

"He didn't. He wasn't around when you telephoned. The new guy—Bruce Towers—did it on his own. By the time Marty got back, the Chrysler was already here."

"Oh..." Edward recalled now the strange voice that had answered when he had called up the garage. "Where is this new guy now?"

"He didn't show up for work the last three days. Marty's sore. I guess he's going to get rid of him."

"I hope it's not on account of my dad. I wouldn't want anybody to get fired—"

"Naw. Towers likes to hit the bottle. He's a drifter—from town to town. Marty hired him temporarily, to see how he'd work out. It's too bad though—he sure knows about trucks." Kenny pointed to the GMC. "See that one over there? It was supposed to be ready for this afternoon. I hate to see the guy's face when he comes in. You can't run a business like that."

"No, I guess not." Kenny was already beginning to sound like Marty. But it was true—you couldn't run a business like that. Wait for some guy to do his work. "Well..." Edward said, getting back to the subject, "what does Marty want us to do? Have the Chrysler towed somewhere else?"

"Oh, he'd do that much for you." Kenny tossed the second wax paper ball into the can. "'Course I was thinking—if your dad wouldn't mind too much, I could take a look at it myself. I know how fussy he is about the Chrysler, but me and old cars get along pretty good."

"Would you?" Edward said quickly. "You'd be doing my dad and me a big favor. Mr. Delingham's been driving him to work every morning, and you know how that is. And with my sister's wedding coming up—" They hadn't talked about that, but Edward sensed Kenny knew.

"Sure. I don t mind. I'll look it over this weekend and get back to you Monday—let you know how I made out."

"That'd be great. But I wouldn't want you to get into trouble with Marty over it."

"Oh, he won't care if I do it on my own time. Personally, I think he feels a little guilty about it being here. He'll be glad to see it running again."

"Well…all right. But I'd better tell you now—my dad thinks it only needs a tune-up again."

"Maybe he's right." Kenny laughed and jumped off the bench. "Well, I've got to get back to work."

"Sure. And thanks, Ken."

"It's okay. I know how fathers are."

That evening, Edward told his father that he had gone down to Marty's garage, and that Kenny was going to work on the Chrysler this time.

161

"Well…" Roger Aldworth said, with a short grunt, "I just hope that boy knows what he's doing."

11

A day later Edward had another talk with his father:

"You never told *me* your black friend was involved," Roger Aldworth said indignantly, as he watched his son sit down on the bed and tie his brown shoelaces. He seldom went into Edward's bedroom, but on this particular morning he felt he had to. Standing at the foot of the bed, holding on to the corner post, he eyed his son critically: Edward was wearing a pair of gray trousers and a yellow knit shirt. He looked as though he had just stepped out of the shower, for his hair was still soaken wet. And he didn't look happy this morning. He was thinner, much thinner than he had been when he'd first come home. But his father wasn't seeing any of this: all he could think about was that his son had held something back from him. It hurt him deeply, and this hurt showed in his face. "Don't you think I want to know about your friends too?" he asked.

"Sure, Dad…" Edward finished tying his shoes and gazed across the room: it was nearly nine o'clock, and a bright warm sunlight was streaming through the long, flimsily curtained windows, setting the dull blue of the walls and carpeting and coverlet of the bed all aglow. It was the time of day that Edward always liked the room the best; but this morning he couldn't help feeling unhappy in it. "I just didn't think it would matter so much," he went on. "You were already dead set against my going to New York."

"And do you blame me?" his father flung back. "Do you know what you're throwing away for this friendship? Just the *vice-presidency* of the new bank, that's all! Mr. Rydin told me this morning that Mr. Olson's retiring at the end of the year, and that he wants a much younger man now for the position. That would mean you."

Edward straightened on the bed: "I'm sorry, Dad."

"Is that all you have to say?"

"I wish I could say something more, but I can't."

"You can't! That's all I keep hearing!" Roger Aldworth let loose of the bedpost and took two rigid steps backwards. "I just don't understand it! If somebody would have made me an offer like that, when I was your age, I'd have jump for joy!" He stared at his son angrily for a moment. "Do you know what I got when I came out of college? A crummy job that paid thirty-two fifty a week. And boy, was I glad to get it! And *you* wish there was something more you could say."

"Dad..." Edward pleaded now. "I wish we didn't have to talk like this."

"So do I! Don't you think I wish that too? How do you suppose I feel, when people come up to congratulate me about your graduating, and I've got to tell them you're rushing off to New York? Especially when they know there's a perfectly good job waiting for you at the bank!"

"Then don't tell them, Dad." Edward got up from the bed and went to the dresser, and began brushing his hair.

"All right!" Roger Aldworth said in half desperation. "We won't talk about the bank any more. I know you don't want to talk about it. All I want to know is what's so special about this black guy."

Edward turned back to his father. "He's my best friend, Dad. That's all. We made an agreement that we'd stay together, work together. I can't back out of it now. He's counting on me."

"And what about your mother and me?" Roger Aldworth looked almost beside himself now. "Don't you think we were counting on you too? Your mother knows now, Edward—I had to tell her. How do you think she feels? She's been waiting a long time to have you home. Don't you think it'd make her happy, to see her only son become the vice-president of a new bank?"

"Sure, Dad. I know that…" Edward set the brush down. "I'd like to make her happy. But I'm just not interested in the bank any more." He wondered how many more times he would have to say that, to convince his father.

"You could at least give it a try," his father persisted. "Then, if you didn't like it, I wouldn't say a word. You could do what you wanted, go to New York even."

"But if I did that, I'd lose this other job," Edward said quickly. "Those people out there are expecting me. They're not going to wait forever."

"And neither will Mr. Rydin!" his father said gruffly. "I'm sure he can get *any* number of young men who'd be willing to become a vice-president."

Then let him, Edward felt like saying. Do me that favor, Dad, *let* him. But he said nothing.

His father's voice slackened: "Aren't you happy at home any more, son?"

"Sure, Dad, I'm happy. That has nothing to do with it."

But his father didn't seem to hear him. "If you're not, you could always get your own apartment. There's some nice new ones on the outskirts of town now—"

"Dad, I'm not going to New York just to get my own apartment. I want to work there. I feel that—well, I'll get a much broader experience there than I can get here."

"Now the town's not good enough for you either, huh?" his father said hoarsely. "Nothing seems good enough for you any more." He shook his head severely. "I don't know what's happening to this family... I've got two children, and suddenly I don't know either one of them. First it's your sister—then it's you. But *you* I always thought I knew."

Edward tried again. "Dad, I know how much this job at the bank means to you, and I'm sorry. I really am. I wish I could convince you of that. But this other job in New York isn't just an ordinary one. The firm's one of the biggest in the city. It handles hundreds of clients each year. It's everything I've hoped for—dreamed about in college."

"And I suppose being a vice-president of a bank is nothing at all?" Roger Aldworth snapped back.

"I didn't say that, Dad—"

"Don't you think other people have dreams too? I had mine, like everybody else, but I woke up in time. I realized that the best place for me was in my own hometown."

But I don't want to end up like you, Edward felt like saying now, dissatisfied with my job when I'm fifty. But he knew he could never say that. It would hurt his father too much. Instead: "But I don't want to get tied down in a bank all my life, Dad."

"Nobody's going to tie you down. Mr. Rydin said you could still have your own practice on the side, if you wanted to. As long as you didn't let it interfer with your duties at the bank. Personally"—Roger Aldworth looked critically at his son again—"I think he's being far more generous than he need be."

"Nobody's asking him to," Edward said quietly.

"Is that your attitude now? Toward people who are trying to do you a good turn?"

"I'm sorry, Dad. I didn't mean it that way." Edward moved across the room now, past his father— "It's just that I don't know if I'd make a good vice-president. I don't even know if I'll make a good lawyer yet." He was trying to be completely honest with his father now—if he'd let him.

"What kind of talk is that? Of course you'll make a good lawyer. You graduated from law school, didn't you?"

"Sure. But so did a lot of other guys, and that doesn't mean they'll all be good lawyers."

"I've never heard you talk like this before," Roger Aldworth said, his face hardening. "It's that black guy, isn't it? He's the one who's putting all these ideas in your head. Trying to pull you away—"

"Nobody's trying to pull me away, Dad," Edward said, looking back at his father. "It was more my idea than his, to go to New York. Why—if he thought it was causing all this trouble, he wouldn't even want to go."

But his father didn't seem to hear again. "What's he got on you, son? You can tell me. If there's any reason at all, that you've got to go—I'll understand."

"What do you mean, Dad?" Edward stood still now—his heart pounding.

"Well..." Roger lowered his eyes. "I know how it is, when boys are together too much. Pressures build up. I've seen it happen in the army—during the war—"

"Jesus, Dad!" Edward stared at his father now. "What are you trying to say? That you think we're a couple of homosexuals? That we go to bed with each other?"

"I'm not saying anything of the kind," his father said swiftly. "I was just trying to tell you that—if there was something wrong, I wouldn't hold it against you."

"Oh, God!..." Edward turned away and covered his face with his hands. "God, Dad! you must have really felt rotten thinking that."

"Well…what did you expect me to think? Mr. Rydin told me you felt obligated to this black guy and he *was* your roommate for a long time. You were always writing about him."

"You could have at least trusted me!"

"Of course I trusted you!" Roger Aldworth looked down again. "It has nothing to do with trusting—"

"Oh, yes it has! And he's not *just* a black guy, Dad. He's my best friend. Can't you even accept that?"

"All right!" the father said, almost shouting, throwing his arms up in the air. "He's your best friend! I can understand that you want to help him. But there's a limit even to friendship!"

"*Limit?*" Edward stared at his father again. "Jesus, Dad! I never thought you of all people would turn prejudiced on me."

"It's not a question of being prejudiced. I've never been prejudiced toward anyone or anything in my whole life! But you just don't throw your entire life away—everything you've worked hard for—just because your friend happens to be *black*."

"I'm not throwing anything away, Dad. There's one thing you've got to understand—this firm wants Jonah. They're not doing him any favors by hiring him. If there'd been only one position open, I doubt whether I would have been the one to get it."

"Are you trying to tell me that you think you're second-best to this black guy?" his father asked tightly.

"No, sir." Edward suddenly felt tired. It was like trying to climb an enormous insurmountable mountain: you knew it was impossible, but you still had to keep trying. "I'm just saying he's probably the better man for the job. He'll make a lot better lawyer than I ever will."

"Well…" Roger Aldworth said, making a wry face, heading for the door. "I'm not going to listen to any more of this! If you want to tear yourself down, that's your business. But nobody's going to tell me my son's something he's not, not even you! He was always a good student in school, and he's going to be a good lawyer!"

"I hope so, for your sake, Dad." Edward watched his father wrench open the door. "I'm sorry," he said softly. "I didn't want to hurt anybody. I was hoping you'd see things my way—"

"No! No more words!" Roger Aldworth said harshly. "We've talked enough! You do what you want now. I'm not going to try to stop you any more. You don't even have to stay home for your sister's wedding, if you don't want to," and he shut the door loudly behind him.

12

Monday: Kenny called as he had promised. In the morning—

"I'll have the Chrysler ready for you by tomorrow, okay?" he said.

"That'll be great. What'll we owe you for it?"

"We can talk about that when you get here. Make it in the afternoon, though, around three."

"Okay."

After lunch Edward walked over to the Forst drugstore. He thought it was time he'd call Jonah, for it was already going on the second week, and he knew his friend must be worrying. He also knew he couldn't make the call from home.

He didn't know exactly what he was going to say to Jonah, though: there wasn't much he could say at this time. Everything was so topsy-turvy, more complicated than before. It was funny, he thought, that less than two weeks ago he had been so sure that everything would be all right, settled, by now. And what was really funny about it was, that other things he hadn't even taken into consideration, things about other people, things that had nothing to do with his job in New York, with his leaving home, which had been settled then, were now unsettled too. It was a whole conglomeration of unsettled things, he told himself, like walking through a whirlwind of flying objects coming at you from all sides, sending you off in all kinds of different directions. Each day, he had gone in a different direction.

Well, now at least the Chrysler was going to be taken care of. Thanks to Ken. At least one thing was off his mind.

Mr. Forst's new drugstore on Ames Street was something of a wonder for the little town of Mapleville, and for Edward as well: it was a maze of glittering mirrors and sleek shiny chromium-glass showcases. The walls and floors were a bright, lemon yellow. Everything sparkled shiny-bright. Edward had never seen a drugstore quite like it before, and if Mr. Forst had wanted to surpass all the other stores in Mapleville, he had certainly succeeded with flying colors. Up to now, Ames Street had just been another plain dirt road that eventually led to the main artery of the town, Main Street, a street of nothing more than a handful of old rambling houses and a few plain old-fashioned storefronts (the "freaks" of Time and erosion, Mr. Rydin would have said), but now it seemed to take on a new life. It sparkled with enthusiasm, and with Mr. Forst's new drugstore backing it, it could very well take on a new look of business, also. There was no telling how far this would lead. Edward wondered if the banker hadn't something to do with it. Well, if he had, the Forsts knew what they were doing. They could afford a little splash.

On this day, however, Mr. Forst looked like any other hard-working businessman: he was on his knees unpacking a large cardboard box of fragile-looking perfume bottles, setting up a display on one of the new shiny glass shelves in the Women's Cosmetic Section. The scent of the perfume filled the air aromatically, but gently, and Edward couldn't help remembering the heavy pungency of Cynthia's perfume that night at the house, and at the dance. How much they differed. Cynthia's was probably more expensive too, because models (even ex-models) liked to go to extremes.

"It's nice to see you again," Mr. Forst was saying in a soft, friendly voice, as he held one of the exquisite bottles in the palm of his hand as though it were a live, breathing embryo which might falter, collapse without sufficient, tender care. It was of smooth milky-colored glass shaped into the form of a swan; Edward noted the imitation blue sapphire stones that represented its eyes. "You haven't changed too much," the man added, setting the bottle down carefully, "just grown a bit."

Edward smiled and looked around at all the glittering items. "You've got a nice store here, Mr. Forst."

"Well, we try…" The druggist laughed. He had a somewhat deep, throaty laugh for his size: he was a small, thin man with neatly balding hair. He wore a pair of wobbly wire-framed glasses, and the little shrunken gray eyes behind them shone kindly, intelligently. Mr. Forst's policy was politeness. A sincere service. No matter how hurried he might be, if you happened to run into him on the street, he would always tip his hat for you and smile and say a few words. It might only be about the weather, but the manner in which he spoke would make you feel important. And when you came into his drugstore, whether it was for a costly prescription or a single bar of candy, he would take the time to thank you graciously. Thinking of

173

this, Edward found it hard to associate this sort of person as the father of a girl whose eyes were too wide, too staring, too cold.

"I hear you're all graduated now, Edward, and going to New York."

"Yes, sir." Edward expected some kind of question now, polite as it might be, as to why he had decided not to return to the Mapleville Bank; but there was none. The man went on simply: "Well, that's the place to go, if you can. There's no city like it. I've got a cousin there who's in the confectionery business. Does real well."

Edward nodded: he was glad to hear something positive for a change.

"Well, I thought I'd try it out," he said. "I have a pretty good offer, otherwise I wouldn't chance it."

"You won't be sorry," Mr. Forst said, setting another perfume bottle on the glass shelf. "'Course the bank's really sprouting out too, huh?" Edward nodded again: he realized now that what was on the minds of other people was probably on this man's mind too, but he was too polite to say it. "Heard they're going to put the roof on next week. Those city folks sure move fast, don't they? Before you know it, the new bank'll be all finished. Well…" He laughed and turned one of the bottles slightly, to make the many featherlike crevices shimmer under the spotlight. Edward noticed that the cardboard box was empty now—the proprietor was no doubt yearning to go on with his work.

"Well," he said, "I thought I'd just drop in and say hello. I was out walking when I remembered I had a phone call to make."

174

"Glad you did." Mr. Forst smiled and pointed to the rear of the store: "You'll find the phones back there. We don't have all the directories in as yet though," he said apologetically.

"Oh, that's all right. I have the number right with me—" Edward pulled out a piece of paper from his pocket, with Jonah's telephone number written on it, and then thought what an idiotic thing to do. Why was he carrying the number around with him, if he just happened to remember that he had to make a call? Well, maybe the druggist didn't catch it. He had his own business to take care of.

Edward walked down the aisle now, pass the assortments of hair sprays and talcum powders and after shave lotions; then bubble baths and toilet paper. A sign at the end of the aisle pointed around the corner and said: TELEPHONES. There were two new shiny brown telephone booths. Edward went into the last one, next to the wall, the furthest from where Mr. Forst was working, and took out some change and laid it on the small, narrow metal shelf. Then he slid the door close and lifted the receiver, dialing for the operator.

"I want to place a call to Chicago," he said as softly and plainly as he could.

"One moment *please*," the local girl said. He heard her connecting him, then another voice said: "What number please?"

He gave the new voice the number, and a phone began ringing in the distance.

It rang and rang and rang. Edward let it ring, remembering what Jonah had told him—if his grandmother was coming to the phone, you had to give her plenty of time. He waited patiently.

175

Finally, the receiver on the other end was lifted. A soft, drawling black voice answered, sounding full of pain. Edward pictured a horribly bent figure of an old woman standing there. "Hello," the voice said.

"Hello," Edward said, loudly now, clearly, remembering that he also had to speak up. "I'd like to talk to Jonah Willis, please."

"He ain't home," the voice returned, definitely. "He went downtown. He won't be back till suppertime."

"Oh..." Edward didn't know quite what to say now: he had just taken it for granted that Jonah would be there. Well, what did he expect, that Jonah would be waiting at the phone all this time? The two weeks were almost up.

"You want him to call you back?" the suffering voice inquired. There was something about it now, the uneven tone, the very quiver, that let you know it couldn't hold on for too much longer. Yet it waited patiently too.

"No," Edward hurried now, "I'll call him back. Just tell him Edward Aldworth called—that something came up and I couldn't get to him sooner. And that I'll call again tomorrow afternoon."

"Tomorrow afternoon," the voice repeated. Paused—then: "All right."

"Thanks."

"Your welcome." And the connection was broken.

Edward returned the receiver to its holder, stared at it a moment. Well, at least he had another day. Twenty-four hours more. Maybe something would happen to resolve some of the problems. He slid the door open and stepped out: Mr. Forst was down to the middle of the aisle now, emptying another box—this one smaller than the other. "Get your phone call all right, Edward?" he inquired.

"Just fine."

"That's good. There was some trouble with one of the phones this morning." The proprietor watched him go to the door. "Well, say hello to your folks for me. I suppose everybody's busy getting ready for the wedding?"

"Yes, sir. It's all pretty exciting."

"Well, that's what weddings are for." The druggist smiled. "It's been nice talking to you, Edward."

"Same here, Mr. Forst." And thanks for not asking too many questions.

13

Tuesday turned out to be rainy. The sky was overcast and threatened heavy showers. A fine, steady rain had fallen early in the morning, then cleared, and there were little puddles everywhere, up and down the streets, and the air had a clinging, suffocating moisture to it. You could almost smell the second bout of rain coming.

Now, at twenty to three, the sky hung dark and swollen, ready to break again. Edward snapped the bolt lock of the back door shut, then hurried down the stairs: he didn't want to get caught in a downpour. He wanted to make it to Marty's garage before the rain started up again, but it was no good getting there too early, because Ken had said around three. And there was no telling if he had some last-minute things to do on the Chrysler. Edward didn't want to rush him. He was thankful that Ken had taken the time to help out. Ken was the kind of guy you didn't have to explain things to. He understood beforehand.

Just at three o'clock Edward walked into the back part of the garage; it looked even drearier than it had the other day, with its eerie lights glowing and the prospect of more rain. Marty was in the office this time, sitting at his beat-up desk. His back was turned toward the doorway, and Edward was glad, because he wouldn't have known what to say to him either. Marty was a tall, thickset figure of a man, with matted brown hair and big staring eyes. He always had a sulky expression on his face, as though he were mad or worrying about something. Yet when he talked to you, he was polite enough. Anybody could tell that he was wrapped up only in one thing though: his business. Someday Kenny would be just like him. That was why they were getting along so well.

Kenny was waiting.

"You made it just in time," the young mechanic told him, pointing to one of the murky windows above. A sudden burst of thunder sounded, with little splashes of rain oozing down the glass. "I know," Edward laughed. "Looks like it's going to be a mean one now." Kenny nodded, and then the both of them walked over to the Chrysler. It was standing now away from its corner, and it looked all shined up with a fresh coat of polish. Even under the eerie lights it looked good. Edward thought his father would have been pleased to see it like that.

"You didn't have to bother to polish it," Edward said, running his hand slowly over the smoothness of the hood.

"Oh, I didn't mind. It was getting pretty dirty standing here." Kenny laughed too. "'Course, the rain'll spoil it now."

Edward cast a thoughtful glance toward the office then— "Marty didn't get sore over it, did he?"

"Naw…" Ken's laugh died down into semi-seriousness now, but his face looked at ease. "Naw…" he repeated, "like I told you, he was glad to see it running again." He walked around to the driver's side. "You want to try it? See how it runs now?"

179

"No, you do it—" Edward watched Kenny slip onto the front seat, start the motor running: it purred like a kitten now. "Gee, it sounds great. What did you do to it?"

"Oh, I just changed a few things. Points and stuff." Kenny sounded a little evasive again, as he bowed his head now, to listen carefully: "I think I've got all the kinks out. Your dad shouldn't have any more trouble with it."

"Say, it sounds like new! And that's something. He'll never want to get rid of the old heap now." Edward laughed again.

"Well, I can't blame him," Kenny said, turning off the ignition and agilely making his way out of the Chrysler, "it's a nice old car. If he ever thinks he wants to sell it, let me know. I'll buy it from him anytime."

"I sure will. Now…" Edward dug into his trouser pocket for his wallet, "…for that little matter of what we owe you—"

"Nothing."

"You've got to be kidding."

Kenny shook his head.

"Now, wait a minute—" Edward objected, flicking through the bills he had neatly arranged in the leather billfold, "I can't let you do that. Your time is worth something."

"Naw…" Kenny said stubbornly, stuffing his hands into his pockets. "I did it as a favor." He gave a grin. "Anyway, I always wanted a chance to work on your father's car. If he's satisfied, he can pay me the next time."

"Well..." Edward felt funny about it, but he could see that Kenny's mind was made up. "Well, I certainly appreciate it," he said. "I don't know what my dad would have done, if you hadn't come to the rescue."

"It was no big thing," the mechanic said, tossing it off lightly. "If he ever has trouble again, tell him to see me."

"I will." Edward held out his hand now—and this time Kenny shook it. Then he laughed deliberately. "I told you you'd get dirty. My old man says I'm always contaminating things." Kenny hunched over, shoving his hands back into the pockets. "Well, I better get back to work," he said. "The boss is watching."

Edward nodded. Marty was lingering in the doorway of his tiny office now, waving at him. "Everything O.K., Ed?" he asked, looking a little guilty.

"Just fine," Edward told him, smiling. He got into the Chrysler, started it up, and drove up to one of the big overhead doors. Well, there was no use blaming Marty. It wasn't all his fault.

About an hour after Edward reached home and put the Chrysler away in the garage, the phone rang. It was Kenny Habich again. "'You home alone?" he asked Edward strangely.

Edward replied that he was, hoping that nothing had gone wrong between Marty and him, after he had left. "Is anything wrong?"

"Well, I'm not too sure," Kenny answered, sounding evasive once more. "It's about your sister—I'm just calling to see if she made it home all right."

"She's not here yet," Edward said, beginning to worry. "What happened?"

"Well..." Kenny went on, "she came in here looking for you, right after you left. It was raining hard, and I told her she could wait a while and use the phone, call you at home if she wanted. But she said no, she'd rather walk over to B's and see if she could get a ride from somebody over there. Well, she left—then this Bruce Towers guy I was telling you about—the guy Marty was going to let go—he walked in. Marty had fired him this morning, I didn't know that, and he came to pick up his money. He was plenty sore, had a few drinks under his belt. He screeched out of here, and I saw him turning the corner where your sister was standing and—"

"And?" Edward could tell Kenny was holding back something now— It was the first time for Kenny. "What happened then?"

"Well...I sort of saw her standing there, and then when he turned the corner, she started running toward his truck and then he was gone. She must have got into it. I'm not sure, but it sure looked that way. I thought I better let you know."

"I'm glad you did," Edward said, slowly now. Thoughtfully. "How long ago was it?"

"I'd say about fifteen or twenty minutes ago. She ought to be coming home about now." Kenny sounded apologetic now: "I thought I'd wait and give her a chance to get there."

"Sure..." Edward walked up near the dining room windows and looked out: it was all jumbled up with rain outside. It was hard to pick out a car coming, but he was sure there was none. At least nothing as big as a truck. "You say this Towers guy has a truck?" he asked to make sure.

"Yeah. A dark green Ford pickup. It's pretty well battered up from an accident he had with it." Kenny stopped a minute to meditate. "They were heading toward Reddington Road, that's what worries me. He's staying in one of those motels there. Sunset Lodge, I think Marty said it was. 'Course, he could have just dropped her off somewhere in between—"

"That's probably what happened," Edward said. "But maybe I'll take a ride over in that direction, to make sure."

"I would if I were you," Kenny clarified now. "He's not that bad of a guy when he's sober, but with a few drinks in him, he can be nasty. What I mean is, he's not the sort of person you'd want your sister to be with."

"I know what you mean. And thanks for calling."

"It's okay. I hope she's all right."

"So do I."

They broke off.

Edward grabbed the light weight poplin beige jacket he had worn that afternoon, which lay neatly across the back of one of the yellow kitchen chairs, slipped it on, and rushed out the back door.

The rain was pounding hard now, matching the nervous pounding in his head. Unmindful, he trudged through the widening puddles of the driveway, all around lightning flashing and crackling, but saw nothing. He walked like a blind man, a prisoner of his thoughts. "The thing is," he said to himself, reaching the garage—lifting the heavy, awkward white frame door, "she's never done this before. Why now?"

14

It was one of those low sprawling modern motels—relatively new but already growing shabby. The grass needed cutting, the paint was peeling about the windows and doors. It didn't have an inviting look. There were ten units in all, five on each side of the meager office: a light blue Chevrolet was parked on one side, and the battered dark green Ford pickup on the other. The truck was standing in front of door number 8.

The rain had let up some as Edward parked the old Chrysler, got out and walked over. A soft, diffused yellow light shone through the tightly drawn curtains. Stay calm, he told himself. You don't even know if she's in there.

He stood staring at the door a moment. There was something very positive about it, something very shabby too, that had nothing to do with the unkempt grass or peeling paint. Ordinary, decent people wouldn't want to live like this, Edward thought, not unless they couldn't help it. This man—Bruce Towers—was far from ordinary; he was an outcast. He had no ties, no family—or if he had, he had discarded them somewhere on one of the many roads he had traveled. He was cold, callous, indifferent to the responsibilities of life. His truck was all battered up, he couldn't keep a job even if he wanted to.

The only thing that mattered to him was booze. Hitting the bottle. How could his sister want to get mixed up with someone like that?

It seemed impossible. But then—hadn't so many "impossible" things happened in the past few weeks?

He knocked on the door. A radio was playing—he heard voices suddenly talking above it, then nothing. Silence. He knocked again, this time more forcefully.

The door finally opened, and a huge, brawny man about thirty-five, with a heavy dark unshaven face and ornery eyes, filled the doorway. His hair was rumpled and he stood barefooted. He was naked to the waist, clad only in a pair of grimy brown trousers. "Yeah?" he said, giving Edward the once over.

"Bruce Towers?"

"Yeah," the man said impatiently. "What'd you want?"

"My name is Edward Aldworth. I'm looking for my sister. I was told you gave her a ride this afternoon—about an hour ago."

"Yeah?" The man looked irritable now. "Well, you've got the wrong party. I don't know nothin' about your sister. Try somewhere's else, huh?" He started to shut the door, but Edward stopped it with his foot.

"Somebody saw her get into your truck," Edward added. "That one over there—" and he pointed to the Ford pickup.

"Oh, yeah?" the man said, roughly now. "Well, whoever it was who told you must be blind. I'm telling you I never saw her. Now, just go away, okay?"

"I can't. I've got to take a look inside first."

"Listen, buster—" The man's face came down hard, close to Edward's, as he barred the doorway with his thick, muscular arm. Edward detected the strong odor of whiskey now. "This here's private property, see? Up to now, I've been real nice about it, but you're startin' to get on my nerves. So why don't you run along home, before you cause yourself some trouble?" He gave Edward a little shove.

Edward shoved him back, quickly.

"Why you sonofabitch..." The man stood still for a second, eyeing him—then lunged forward, grabbed Edward by the shirt collar and flung him against the door jamb. "So you want to play games, huh? Maybe a few lumps on the head'll change your mind."

Edward blinked over the hard knot of fists: he felt the man tearing his shirt, but that didn't matter. He could always get another shirt. What he wanted was to see inside that room but the man's massive body was in the way.

If he could only get the door open a little more... He stuck out his foot, gave it a push: it moved an inch or so, then stopped. The man caught on.

"Think you're smart, huh? Well...maybe this'll change your mind—" He pressed his forearm against Edward's windpipe. Edward made a small, gurgling noise.

"Oh, stop it!" a girl shouted from behind the door. "Stop it! Stop it!"

Relaxing his grip, the man looked at her sideways, his jaw dropping in slight amazement. Edward saw his opportune moment now: bending his knee, he kicked as hard as he could, and the door went flying against the wall.

"You dirty bastard!" the man snarled, looking back at him, grappling with the shirt collar once more.

"I said *stop* it!" the girl repeated throatily. There was a certain trembling in her voice, as though she couldn't quite make up her mind whether she wanted to be angry or not.

Edward gawked at the room now, saw its entirety: the new but cheaply made dresser and chest, the chair, the one table and lamp. The bed. One of the pillows had been tossed to the floor, and his eyes fell upon it—followed its almost upright position against the bed rail slowly to the top of the bed, then across the rumpled cover, to where a girl lay crouched with face half-hidden. Dark eyes stared out over the covers: two perfectly round Os.

"Suzie..." he said to her quietly.

"Oh, Eddie!" She turned her head away, burying her face in the soiled pillow. "Why did you have to come here? Nobody asked you to!"

"Suzie...listen to me! We're going home now."

"No!" She shook her head fiercely. "No! No! No!"

The man dropped his arms now, as he listened to the dramatic episode going on between the two.

"Come on, Sis." Edward spoke softly now—carefully, as though to a child. "You don't want to stay here, with him..."

"Didn't you hear what the little lady said?" the man said hotly. "She wants you to buzz off!"

Edward looked at the man squarely: "This is between my sister and me."

"The hell it is!" The man stood ready to pounce at Edward again, fists tight at his sides.

"Oh, leave him alone!" Suzanne told him sharply. "Can't you see he doesn't know how to fight? He's never hurt anybody in his whole life!" She looked at her brother. "Eddie, please go now—before something terrible happens!"

"I'm not leaving here without you," Edward said quietly, firmly.

"I know..." She lowered her eyes suddenly, staring at the rumpled bedcover. Then: "All right...you win. Wait outside for me..." Her voice seemed to trail off somewhere.

Edward nodded. "But remember—I'm not leaving until you come out."

"I'll come out."

"Hey—" the man piped up now, wheeling around to look at her. "I thought you and me were going to Philadelphia."

"I can't—any more."

"It's all his fault!" The man returned a hateful stare in Edward's direction. "I ought to knock his goddamn fucking nose down his throat!"

"Try it," Edward told him. "Anytime."

"Oh, yeah?"

"Oh, leave him alone, you brute!" Suzanne shouted again, her face trembling. "He didn't do you anything." And then she began to cry.

189

15

The rain was pouring down hard, swashing against the driving impact of the windshield wipers, making loud, eerie noises. Edward listened quietly. On the seat beside him, his sister was sobbing. There seemed to be no other sounds in the whole world, just these two—the rain and her crying—as though the Chrysler was standing still in Time. No movement. Just sounds.

At last he had to speak to her.

"Suzie...don't cry any more."

"I can't help it!" She shook her head wretchedly. They were moving now— "Oh, Eddie! Why did you have to go there? Spoil everything. By tomorrow I could have been faraway from here—safe!" She heaved forward with one great sob: "Oh, I wish I were dead now!"

"Suzie... Don't talk like that."

"But it's true!" She jerked her head up to look at him—her face all wet with tears, the small dark curls flattened by rain: there was just the ovalness, the large round eyes staring at him unhappily. "He was going to take me to Philadelphia. I could have done anything I wanted to then. But no, you had to come and ruin things! Now I'll have to do what Mom and Dad want—get married, even if I don't want to!" And she started crying again.

"Suzie... Suzie..."

"Oh, Eddie!" She looked at him imploringly now. "Please don't make me go home! I'll do anything you say, but don't make me go back to that prison!"

"Suzie..." he said slowly. He watched her pull out a handkerchief from her drenched little coat and wipe her eyes, and he thought of all the times he had had to dry her tears away when she was small, when they were both children. Little, inconsequential crises then. A broken toy. A doll's arm out-of-socket; a torn book cover; a missing piece to a puzzle.

His sister could never tolerate anything that wasn't quite right, that wasn't perfect, and that was why things always had been more difficult for her than for him. "Suzie..." he began again, "you know I couldn't leave you back there, with a man like that. It was all wrong. You would have regretted it later. I'd rather be dead first myself."

"You would?" She stared at him thoughtfully—seemed to quiet down a bit. "Yes, I think you would..." She looked down then— "Oh, Eddie, don't you see? It wouldn't have mattered that much. You didn't have to protect my honor, because there wasn't any any more. I tried to tell you once, but you wouldn't believe me—I've changed—"

"Oh, Suzie...don't torment yourself this way—"

"No!" she said, dragging her eyes up to look at him. "You've got to hear it all now. I'm not the kind of girl you think I am any more. I'm not a virgin—it's happened before. I've been with a man already—"

191

He didn't say anything now, for a moment: it wasn't the kind of thing you talked about with your sister, cared to talk about. But something compelled him on. Suddenly he had to know where he was at, where he was going. He couldn't keep blundering on. Too many blunders already... "The spring vacation?" he asked her, softly.

"Yes." She hung her head now, as though she could no longer bear to look at him. "I met a boy at college— He was studying to be a doctor and—"

"Were you in love with him?" He was trying to make it easier for her. He didn't like this tenseness of the confessional—

"No. It wasn't anything like that—a love affair. We were just very very good friends." She raised her chin determinedly. "He was kind, considerate—a lot like you. You would have liked him." She looked back at him. "It wasn't ugly. We had a wonderful friendship, and I'm not ashamed of it. Does that make any sense to you?"

"Yes, it does," he answered slowly. "Nobody knows better than I, how important friendship can be." He gave a short, weak laugh. There was more of course—things he couldn't say to her though. He had made up his mind long before she spoke—told him this—that he would not judge her. That he had no right to judge her. He had had enough time to ask her about the spring vacation (nearly two weeks now), and hadn't—instead he had preferred not to "interfere" (how he hated that word now), so it was perhaps, like everything else, as much his fault as hers. What had happened today. He had put things off, avoided too many things already. Well...at least he was bringing her home now. That was something. Anyway.

He knew that once all this was over, they would never discuss it again. It would be as though it had never happened.

"Is that why you were running away," he asked, giving her a tiny worried smile, "to be with your friend again?"

"No. We're never going to see each other again. It's all over—like passing ships."

"Well…" He was glad about that. He wouldn't have wanted her to run off with somebody he might like, either. "And Steve—what about him? How does he fit in all this? Don't you care for him any more?" It seemed inappropriate now, to even mention the word "love."

"Oh, I guess so…" She flattened the handkerchief against her palm and gazed down at it, gave it a little squeeze. "I don't know any more. Everything's been so rushed—I just don't want to get married to anybody now. I'm not ready for marriage."

That made sense. She was only eighteen. "Well," he said, "I'm sure if you told Mother and Dad how you feel, they wouldn't want you to do something that would make you unhappy."

"Oh, yes they would!" she returned almost wildly. There was a certain bitterness cutting through her face that he had never seen before. "They don't care how I feel! All they care about is themselves, and the things they want!"

"Oh, Suzie…you're so wrong about them. You once said they never gave you any hope—well, I happen to know different. They're always worrying about you. Why—I bet Mother would be all too glad to listen, if you just gave her half a chance."

193

"No, she wouldn't. She's so wrapped up in making the wedding, she wouldn't hear a word I said. She's always been so afraid I'd lose Steve. She can't wait until we're married, so I can live in that big house on Thorfield Road someday and have all that money Mrs. Delingham has, and I hate it! And Dad's no better—he just wants Steve for a son-in-law so he can get even with Mr. Delingham for that raise he never got. Neither of them care if I'm ever happy."

"Oh, Suzie… How can you say that?"

"Because it's the truth!" She brought the handkerchief up to her face and began to cry again: one big tear escaped—rolled down her cheek slowly. "Oh, sometimes I hate them so much! And that house of theirs too!"

"Don't say that. You don't mean that—"

"But I do! I do!" Her eyes clung to him desperately now. "That's why I've got to get away from here, Eddie. If I don't leave now, I'll never get another chance. I'll never have a life of my own!"

"But where would you go?"

"I could take a train somewhere."

"And then what? *Starve?*" He shook his head.

"I could get a job," she said quickly. "Other girls do."

"And other girls get themselves in all kinds of trouble, too," he told her.

"Then let's run away together," she said suddenly. "I could go with you to New York. Oh, Eddie—it's the only way we'll ever be free of them!"

"We just can't run away like that, Sis. That never solves anything. Troubles just follow. Besides, it wouldn't be fair to Mother and Dad."

"That's all you ever do is worry about them," she said to him crossly. "I thought that once you graduated from law school, you'd be different, but you're not. Sometimes I wonder whose side you're on— theirs or ours."

"Ours, of course." He spoke rapidly to her now— "But we've got to try to see their side of it too."

"But when are they going to try to see ours? Dad didn't try to see your side about the job, did he?"

"Well…that was different."

"No, it wasn't. It's all the same thing. Either you do what they want, or they don't like it. Don't you see—this is just another trick of theirs. They're going to make me marry Steve, even though I don't want to, so you have to stay home. They're going to keep on thinking up things like this, until you lose your job."

"Oh, Suzie, that's not true. Mother and Dad love us. You know that."

"Maybe they do, but that doesn't give them the right to own us. Nobody has the right to own *anybody*."

"They don't want to own us," Edward tried to explain. "Oh, sometimes they get carried away with things, I know—but they mean right. They're just trying to make us happy."

"Well, maybe if they didn't try so hard, we would be," she snapped back.

"Sis…" He waited for her to settle down a little. "Believe me—this is the best way. You talk to Mother and Dad. They'll understand. Everything'll be just fine. You'll see."

"No, it won't," she said. "You keep saying that, but things only get worse. We're doomed, Eddie—I know it. We're never going to be happy."

"Sure we will." There wasn't much time left to talk. They were turning down Hobson Road now, and the house loomed ahead—tall and grayish in the foggy rain. The porch light was on. She noticed it too. She stared at it a moment, then shoved the handkerchief back into her coat pocket. She was through crying now—her face looked oddly hardened. "Well," she said, in a tight, small voice, as she glanced down at the clock of the dashboard, "at least they can't say we're late for dinner. It's just six."

Edward watched her get out and run up the broad, glistening stairs; then drove the Chrysler into the garage. He hurried back around to the front of the house: he didn't want her going inside alone, for there was no telling what fireworks would go off, with that mood of hers.

The front door was open, waiting for them. As soon as he stepped into the doorway, he saw his father coming toward them from the dining room. "Well," Roger Aldworth said, appraising his children somberly in their wet clothes, "it's about time you two got home. Your mother was beginning to worry." His eyes settled on his daughter then: "And where were you all day, young lady? Priscilla said she left you at Emeline's at ten-thirty."

"I walked around for a while," Suzanne answered, her back toward her father as she hung up her coat, "and had some lunch at B's. Then it started to rain hard, and I went over to Marty's garage, to see if Eddie could give me a ride home. But he left already."

"Kenny called here, that I should pick her up," Edward put in quickly, not sure how far his sister intended to go with her story. "I thought we might as well take the Chrysler for a little ride, to see how it runs."

"In *all* this rain?" his father asked. But he didn't wait for an answer. "So how does it run?"

"Just fine, Dad. Kenny did a good job on it."

"How much did he charge you?"

"Nothing. He did it as a favor. He said you can pay him the next time."

"Humph." Roger Aldworth looked away briefly. "Well, let's hope we can count on it for the wedding at least," he said, non-committedly.

Later, at the dinner table, Mrs. Aldworth addressed her son:

"Edward—there was a telephone call for you, from Chicago. Just before you came home. Jonah Willis, your friend from college. He wants you to call him back right away. It's urgent. It's about that job in New York—" She stopped to glance at her husband, then continued: "I put his number by your plate."

197

Edward nodded his thanks and reached over for the piece of paper. He folded it quietly and slipped it into his shirt pocket.

Across the table his father made a sudden loud, screeching noise against his plate, as he cut a piece of steak.

16

It was one of those glorious golden summer mornings, filled with warm sunlight and soft breezes, which are so perfect for weddings. A delicate scent of flowers and freshly mown lawns was in the air; and above, fluffy white cloudlets drifted placidly in a deep azure blue sky. It was a memorable day for a memorable occasion. Everyone in the little town of Mapleville was getting ready to turn out in his very best, to see the young couple take their matrimonial vows. After all, it wasn't every day that a Delingham got married.

On the dresser of the blue bedroom of the simple white frame house on Hobson Road, the small ivory-enameled clock showed ten past nine: Edward had already completed dressing and was now appraising his appearance in the mirror. The sunlight was slotting through the many folds of the lace curtains at the windows and, if you stood very still, you could hear the subdued sounds of the day, of the morning—the twittering of a bird on a bough, the breeze rustling the leaves of the old maple down by the driveway, the cawing of a crow flying over a nearby cornfield. Altogether, the moment seemed quite tranquil—peaceful, but it was not; nor was the house; or had it been just a few moments ago. Across the hallway a great deal of bustling had taken place: there was the last-minute problem of the bridesmaids' bouquets arriving late, and amidst all the fretting Mrs.

Aldworth had misplaced one of her long blue gloves which matched so exactly her blue chiffon gown and had to look all over the house before she found it. Now, with both gloves safely on, she was downstairs tending to her husband who was sitting rather soberly in his big brown leather chair, gazing out through the wide bay window of the living room, at the smooth emerald greenness of the lawns that morning, while trying to catch a few minutes' rest before the grand parade began. He was attired in another dark gray, pinstriped suit, much like the one he had worn to Edward's graduation, except this one was more formal, with a softly ruffled-fronted white shirt and a black, gray and white satin tie, and Mrs. Aldworth, with her gloves on, was trying desperately to pierce the tie with the 18 karat gold stickpin. The next moment, upstairs, Edward's eyes wandered off the mirror to the door, his ears alerted for some unsuspecting stirring. But there was none. The house seemed reasonably still now, and so he walked quietly over to the door, opened it, and stepped out into the hallway.

It lay empty now, with its narrow strip of mauve carpeting, like a deserted battlefield, all the soldiers gone, the tanks and artillery moved elsewhere, the blood already spilled. Edward moved cautiously, though, ever mindful of a booby trap.

His sister's bedroom door was ajar, and he stopped and stared at it. No sound came from there either. Then suddenly a flash of whiteness flittered by the opening; and he pushed the door open slowly, walked in.

She was standing before her little dressing table with its flouncy orchid skirt, bent over with the palms of her hands resting flat on its surface, studying her reflection in the oval-framed mirror: she wore a long flowing gown of dazzling white—so dazzling white, that the very sunlight of the room seemed brighter than it really was; and the lace veiling of her tiny beaded cap rippled down softly about her face, blotting out the darkness of her hair, making her eyes look larger than ever, sadder than ever. She looks so very young in all that white, Edward thought, so pale. Where had all the bloom of her cheeks gone to? She caught sight of him and turned.

"I thought I'd just drop in and see how you were doing," he heard himself tell her. "Are you all right?"

"Oh, sure," she said quickly. "I'm just fine." She brushed her hand against her face then, and he realized she'd been crying. "Don't mind me," she said, trying to laugh. "All brides are supposed to cry on their wedding day, you know."

"Yes, I know." He smiled now—just stood there. There wasn't anything else he could do.

"Oh, Eddie!" she cried suddenly, bursting into tears and rushing over to him. "I don't care about myself any more. But they shouldn't have made you stay. Now you're going to lose that job in New York for sure."

"No, I'm not, Sis. Everything's arranged..." He held her in his arms now, and felt the heat of her tears against his shoulder; for an instant she was the little girl again, his little Suzie, running to him with the broken toy. But no one could go back to the past. One had to know that. "Listen…" he said, pushing her away gently, "I don't want you crying over me. There's nothing to cry about. I wanted to stay. Besides—" he lifted the trembling chin carefully, "you didn't really think I'd go away without seeing my little sister walk down the aisle, did you?"

She shook her head and tried to smile.

"Now that's better… No more tears, okay? You don't want to spoil your face."

"It's spoiled already," she said, uncaringly. She looked down at her left hand now—at the small neat diamond engagement ring blinking up at her merrily, near the pointed edge of the white satin cuff, and twisted it on her finger. "It's not your fault, Eddie, I want you to know that. I always knew I'd marry Steve someday—it's just a little sooner than I expected. Anyway—" She looked up at him. "I could have always run away again, if I wanted to."

"Yes, I know. But you didn't."

"No. I guess I knew it wouldn't do any good. Like you said, you can't run away from things." She gazed away thoughtfully. "I guess I'd have come back in the end, anyway."

"Sure you would." He took her hands and squeezed them gently. "Try to be happy—promise?"

"Oh, sure," she said, tossing her head back and looking at him again, with those enormous dark eyes, "I'll be happy. Don't worry about that."

"All right. I won't." He laughed softly. "Now I better get out of here and let you finish—"

She nodded. She watched him back away from her—then: "Eddie…" He looked at her without speaking. "We're never going to talk like this again, are we?" she asked.

"Of course we will, Sis. Many times—"

"No. This is the last time. I know it."

"Well…we'll probably have nothing to talk about then. We'll both be happy and—" He smiled.

"Yes…we'll both be happy." She smiled back but the tears filled her eyes again. Then something happened. Her gaze shot past him to the door—her face froze, the tears stopped as though someone had turned off a faucet. There was a noise outside in the hallway, and the next moment their mother stepped into the room.

"Oh, there you are…" Mrs. Aldworth said, smiling at her son excitedly. She looked very tall, very regal in the long blue gown, her hair coiled high at the top of her head once more. "You look very handsome, Edward," she remarked, and then turning her full attention upon her daughter: "Are you almost ready, dear? We mustn't be late for the church, you know—"

17

The music sounded tremendous.

Edward sat in the pew directly behind his parents', hands folded in his lap, and listened to it. That morning, Mrs. Offerdahl's dexterous, trained fingers glided over the old yellow keys of the church organ with such a powerful intensity, that it seemed she had suddenly been gifted with some unusual "second life" of talent: moving her slight, erect body, which was modestly sheathed in a dark summery frock, with the smoothness of a cobra uncoiling itself from a tiny box that had contained it for too long a time and now ready to slither away into the cool, moist intrigue of jungle foilage, she sent forth such remarkable *crescendos* and *fortissimos* as was never before heard from her. Under ordinary circumstances, Mrs. Offerdahl was a rather shy and conservative person, but today, like everyone else, she was putting out her best. She had become something of an impresario, if anyone cared to notice. But it was doubtful that anyone did.

Now she was playing *Ave Maria*, and Edward felt the song rising and rising, to tremble the very timbers of the old lofty ceiling. The wedding procession itself—the main attraction, of course—was soon to begin: the parents from both sides had already been properly seated, and the three bridesmaids and the maid of honor in their pale pink gowns and floppy wide-brimmed organza picture hats were lining up at the dark archway of the vestibule, while the little flower girl, Germaine, unmindful of it all, was hopping and skipping about much to the dismay of her mother who was pulling the skirt of her lavender dress down about her white-stockinged legs. An effervescence of excitement was building up, as people cranked their necks about to catch the first glimpse of the bride. Edward wondered how long all this would go on, how much more fussing there would be. He was sure God was not fussing. There wasn't anything *artificial* about Him.

Now he unfolded his hands and laid them over his knees, and the music stopped for a few seconds—created such a tension (its non-playing was almost as electrifying as its playing), that he felt a sudden throbbing inside his head; then it lunged out again, grabbed him with one loud plunge, tremolo-ing as though it would break for good. There were gasps of joy, gaping faces all around him and, turning his head, he saw that the bridesmaids were moving forward—their heads lifted high, the small baskets of flowers pressed nervously against their bodies. Poor Priscilla, Edward thought sadly, noting the girl's clumsy trodding. She had taken off the near-ten pounds as she had promised, only to put them back again and more, and now the seams of her gown were bulging from the surplus flesh. Well, what did it matter? What did any of it matter, when there was no heart in it?

Edward diverted his attention now, to the altar—at its simple white beauty: on each end of it stood a tall silvery urn of white roses. A gift from the Mapleville Florist, no doubt. No pretense there. That was just good business.

The little flower girl came along now: soft, blondish curls peeking out from a stiff white bonnet, chin firmly planted onto the lacy pique collar as though her mother had deliberately pinned it there. Children were innocent. No matter what you tried to do with them, they usually turned out to be just themselves.

The music jolted again—struck a familiar chord; and all eyes were swept back to the archway. Edward saw his sister standing there now, in a shimmering cloud of white: the veil was covering her face, as she held her father's arm. How still she looks there, he told himself, how almost lifeless. Oh God, what had happened? What had he done? Had he failed her too? Bungled her life as he had bungled everything else, since he had come home? What good was he, if he couldn't even help those he loved?

That day at the motel, he had held his sister's whole life in his hands. No, he couldn't have left her with that person Bruce Towers; nor, could he have let her runaway by herself. But there had to have been something he could have done, to help her. But instead he had put the blinders on again, let Time take care of things. Time. Was that his real enemy now?

Time was here now, of course—all around him, this day. It moved swiftly, while other things stood still. He had stood still. He had let Time move on, he had let everything slip away, while he had stood still! I am my own enemy, he told himself now, taking a shallow breath as he watched the stilted form of his sister move slowly toward the altar. I am my thoughts, my fears, my hopes and my desires, my failure. I am nobody but myself—and so, as myself, I must be ready to accept my responsibilities, and my guilts.

She was at the altar now; her father had stepped back, to let Steve take his place. Edward could hear the solemn words of the priest's rising above the music: Mrs. Offerdahl was stepping into the background now, too. Well... God was with his sister now. If anybody could help her, it was Him.

He watched the candles flickering quietly on the altar: no sound there. They were like a holy balm, soothing his troubled brow for a few moments. But the pain would return. The pain would return to haunt him again, he knew.

Dropping his arms to his sides, he pushed himself up slightly from the smoothness of the oaken seat, and listened again: the priest's words rang true, of course. Was that to be his destiny now, just to listen? Hadn't he done that all along, listened to what others had to say, while saying very little himself? Nothing, actually—

A sudden hushness prevailed: the Ultimate Moment had finally arrived. The exchange of vows, of rings. He heard his sister speak now, softly—then Steve slipped the wedding ring on her finger, and Mrs. Offerdahl came to the foreground again (you could always count on her), bursting out with *Ode to Joy*. Well, it vas over. Everything. How quickly—it became too late!

A deep feeling of hopelessness came over him. He could stand it no longer! He had to get out of there! Something was crushing his chest; he needed air to breathe. He started to rise, but people all around him were rising too, and, looking back toward the altar, he saw that the bridal couple had turned around and was now facing the smiling, tearful congregation. His sister's face looked drawn without the veil covering it, the huge dark eyes shiny like mirrors. Only I can see into them, Edward thought. Only I...

He moved slowly, steadily toward the queue of people starting back to the vestibule; a wedge had formed at the archway, where Suzanne and Steve waited. His sister was smiling now, holding out her hand to all who came up to her, while Steve, tall and youthful in his white tuxedo, flushed constantly. Well, he wasn't going to partake in that too! Reversing his direction, he headed toward the outer aisle.

The vestibule was also crowded, which was usually the case at all the larger affairs—the bulky overstuffed chairs and two sofas took up too much room; people mulled about seeking a comfortable spot to stand in, to chat in. They were all out there, of course—the parents. Standing to one side was his mother, dabbing excitedly at her eyes as she spoke to a small group of older women in vivid, colorful dresses, while his father, beside her, chuckled from time to time, over something she'd said. Edward had to admit she made the perfect Mother of the Bride. Close to them were the Delinghams and their acquaintances. Mr. Delingham, looking gross and impatient in his dark gray pin-striped suit, was probably thinking of all the business he had had to let go, to get this over with. Mrs. Delingham was the only natural-looking one there: she smiled silently, plainly in her apricot-colored gown. Well, he had enough of that too!

Turning about rather sharply, Edward collided with an elderly man with watery blue eyes, who promptly clamped him on the shoulder and smiled up into his face. "Hello there, Edward," the man said. Edward quickly responded with a smile and a handshake, and the man continued on his way. Thankfully, Edward went on his.

At last he reached the doors. Now there was no one, nothing to stop him. With one hefty shove, he pushed them open and walked out. The bright azure sky greeted him warmly.

Outside, the sunlight was crinkling down through the long branches of the old elms and maples, spilling upon the lawns like bits and pieces of broken golden glass. He wished he could pick up all the pieces and put them back together again.

18

"Now I don't want you to worry about a thing," Roger Aldworth told his son, as he started for the little alcove in the dining room, where the telephone was. They were alone once more, and a steady rain was streaming down the narrow panes of the living room window, making little patches of mist; but Edward only half saw it. He was sitting on the sofa, his head bowed, his gaze fixed to the floor. "I'm going to tell Mr. Rydin this very minute," his father added, "and everything will be all right."

Edward lifted his head. "But Dad—don't you think it's too late? It's almost five months now—"

"What difference does that make?" Roger Aldworth replied impatiently. He had broken his stride and seemed annoyed. "The new bank just opened up last week. He said you could wait until then."

"I know, but—you don't even know if Mr. Rydin still wants me."

"Of course he wants you. Don't talk nonsense. Why just the other day he mentioned how he had thought you would have worked out just fine at the new bank, and that it was too bad you had your heart so set on that other job in New York. That sounds as though he's still interested, doesn't it?" But his father didn't wait for a reply. He continued walking.

"But what about his nephew?" Edward asked. He didn't know how to convince his father, but he had to try. "He's already got him down here from Chicago, for the job."

"Yes, but—" his father said, strikingly irritable now, "he's not satisfied with him. He told me so. He said the boy's more trouble than he's worth, that all he cares about is chasing girls. Personally, I think he's just keeping him here temporarily, until he can find somebody more suitable for the position."

"I don't know, Dad..." Edward cast his eyes down again. "I don't want to put anybody out of a job."

"You won't be putting anybody out of a job. I'm sure Mr. Rydin will find something else for his nephew to do. Anyway—it's not as though he were *hired* for the job, you know."

"I know," Edward said, looking up once again, "but won't it sound as though we're begging now? I don't want to have to beg for a job—"

"Why would we be begging?" His father raised his eyebrows in restraint now, and Edward could see that they were heading down that old familiar road again: *Dissension*. Where very little of what he had to say was heard by his father— "I'll just tell Mr. Rydin that you changed your mind. Anybody can do that. I'm sure he's done that many times himself. Besides, the job was offered to you first. We'll only be asking for what is rightfully yours."

Edward stared at his father a moment. "But I've already turned it down. Mr. Rydin knows I didn't want to work at the bank any more."

"Well, you'll just have to convince him otherwise then," Roger Aldworth said thornily. "I'm sure you'll know what to say. They must have taught you something about *protocol* at Harvard."

"I know what to say," Edward returned slowly, "but it just doesn't seem ethical—"

"Well..." Roger Aldworth looked at his son narrowly. "Sometimes you have to eat humble pie, Edward, when you've made a mistake. You'll learn that, even as a lawyer."

"But I'm not sure it was a mistake, Dad. I still don't know if I want to return to the bank."

"Do you know what you want to do?" his father asked pointedly.

"No..."

"Then it seems to me, if you don't know what you want to do, you probably don't know what you don't want to do, either. Doesn't that make sense?"

"I suppose so." Edward stared at his feet now: it seemed just then that all his hopes and dreams had plummeted there. Lay there in broken pieces, like those bits and pieces of sunlight that had glittered across the lawns that day at the church, that day of his sister's wedding, when he couldn't do a thing about it, when he couldn't put those pieces back together either. "I just don't want anybody going through too much trouble," he said slowly, "in case it doesn't work out. I'd hate to start something I couldn't finish."

"What are you talking about?" his father asked bluntly.

Edward looked straight at his father now— "The relationship between Mr. Rydin and me. We don't seem to see eye to eye on a lot of things. Even he knows that."

"But it doesn't seem to bother him, so why should it bother you?" Edward felt like saying now— "But he's not the one who has to take the job—I am." But he didn't. His father went on curtly: "You need a job now, don't you? You can't sit around the house forever."

"I'd find something."

"But we didn't send you to Harvard just to find *something*." Roger Aldworth studied his son's face now, carefully: "You're not still thinking of going to New York, I hope."

"No." Edward took a long breath. "I'm all through thinking about that."

"Well," his father said, "I'm glad you've finally got that crazy notion out of your head."

"That's just it, Dad. I don't think it was crazy." Edward realized he was risking sounding insolent now—contradicting his father's words, his beliefs, but there came a time in every one's life when one had to be completely honest. Even with one's father.

"Well…you will when you get to be my age," Roger Aldworth returned. "Now, we've wasted enough time. I'm going to call Mr. Rydin up and explain everything. I'm sure he'll understand."

Edward sat silently now. He watched—listened to his father dial the telephone.

"Oh, Dorothy…" Roger Aldworth said, his voice instantly turning syrupy, "would you please connect me with Mr. Rydin? Thank you."

213

He tapped on the edge of the table a few moments, with his fingernail. "Oh, Charles is that you?" Laugh. Laugh. Laugh. "Well…I'm glad I didn't miss you." Another laugh. "I'm calling about that job you offered my son a few months back? Yes…Well, he's finally decided to stay home, and I was wondering if your offer still holds. I know it's a bit late but—better late than never, I always say!" A stronger laugh now. "It *is*? Well, I'm certainly glad to hear that. And Edward will be too. He was worried about your nephew, you know—"

Edward stopped listening. He felt embarrassed now—embarrassed for his father, because he knew his father was incapable of feeling embarrassed for himself. He had never thought his father would stoop this low—

He got up and went over to the window, and watched the rain trickle down the misty panes. At moments, with the wind, it made a swishy sound, almost like a whisper—like the sound of the windshield wipers, that night he had brought his sister home. And he thought of Jonah's telephone call, and the call he should have made back to him.

"Nine o'clock? Fine. I'll see that he's there. And thanks again, Charles. We'll have to have you up to the house for another dinner." The final laugh.

Roger Aldworth set the receiver down now, and eyed his son with a smile: "It's all settled. He wants you to come in Monday at nine o'clock. You're going to have your own office and everything, just like before. Nothing's changed." He waited a while. "Well—what do you say about that?"

Edward didn't say anything. He just kept standing there, watching the rain, his back toward his father.

"Well, it seems to me…" his father said quietly but tightly, "you ought to be grateful about it. You're a very lucky young man, indeed. It isn't everybody who gets a second chance at the vice-presidency of a new bank, let alone a first one."

19

Standing in the somewhat glaring sunlight of that Monday morning in late October, dressed again in his new dark blue suit and light blue tie, Edward took some time out to gaze up at the huge expanse of shiny plate glass which made up a good part of the architectural frontage of the new Mapleville Bank. The house of glass, Edward thought glumly, remembering Mr. Rydin's words—that the new bank was going to be a second home for the townspeople. Well… was this the real bank now, or just an imposter? He would soon find out.

Pushing against one of the tall revolving glass doors, he immediately alighted upon a small rectangular of thick terra cotta-colored carpeting and, standing there for a few moments, took everything in. The lobby of the new bank was large—almost too large for comfort, and yet, surprisingly, at this very early hour of five past nine, it was already bustling with people. They were everywhere—standing in lines before the tellers' cages, writing at the many smooth-topped tables, conversing in the bright orange leather chairs along the rows of spanking new black metal desks, or just walking about looking at the gleaming gilt-framed oil paintings which flowed with almost no interruption down the long stark white walls. Had all these people been waiting for the doors to open this morning? There were pots and pots of tall ferns about too, everywhere you looked. The Mapleville Florist certainly must have had good business here lately. Well, the big banker said he'd do it, and he had. Nothing about this spoke of small-town business. This was business on a large scale. Citywise.

Walking down one of the narrow strips of black rubber matting, which stretched in different directions from the doorways, indicating where one should walk or not walk, Edward made his way now over to the receptionist's desk, where a young girl of about twenty, in a fitted white angora sweater and a long rope of pearls, sat waiting idly for him. "May I help you?" she inquired in a carefully constrained, courteous voice, her eyes going over him as though he were a complete stranger there. Edward had never seen her before either. She must be one of those people Mr. Rydin had brought down from Chicago, he told himself.

"I'm looking for Mr. Rydin's office," he said.

"Oh..." The girl whirled about in her orange chair and pointed a long polished fingernail toward the rear. "You'll have to take the elevator over there. It's on the second floor."

"Thanks." So now there was even an elevator... In the old days, you just hiked up the stairs and liked it.

Following the invisible line the girl had drawn for him, down the middle aisle of the black metal desks, Edward felt a little conspicuous now, walking away. Were the girl's eyes following him? Could she tell that he might be an imposter too? Of course not. She was already directing another person.

Stopping before the elevator door, Edward pushed the UP button and waited a second; then noticed the drinking fountain nearby. Feeling suddenly thirsty, he went over to it, took a few sips and had to stop; the elevator had come down already, and you could never tell about those modern ones, especially in a place so highly precisioned as this. It could very well go up without him—and then what would the girl think?

He got in and listened to the door close smoothly, soundlessly; he barely felt himself lifted. When it opened again, he was facing a long bright hallway of the same stark white walls and thick terra cotta carpeting, except now there were no rubber mattings to guide him. It was just taken for granted that by now his shoes were clean. Here's where all that highly-precisioned thinking goes on, he thought. Everything seemed so still, silenced.

To the left of him were three darkly stained doors, marked LUNCHROOM, WASHROOMS, and CONFERENCE ROOM, and then the hallway turned a right corner. Edward followed it to another reception desk. This time a woman in her late thirties or so sat with short straight black hair and glittery beige eyeglasses. She tilted her head forward slightly, above a thin swanlike neck firmly anchored by a high-necked ivory ruffled blouse, and perceived him an instant above the lenses. "May I help you?" she then said, in the same carefully modulated, courteous tone of the downstairs receptionist. Edward wondered if the two hadn't gone to the same school together.

"My name is Edward Aldworth," he told her. "I have a nine o'clock appointment with Mr. Rydin this morning." He suddenly had to clear his throat. There was something decidedly stifling about this second floor. "I'm a few minutes late, I'm afraid," he added, apologetically.

"Oh, that's all right," she returned matter-of-factly. "Mr. Rydin never comes in before nine-thirty anyway. You can wait in his office, if you like. It's the door on the left—" and another long polished fingernail pointed the way.

The door that had been indicated was closed, as were the other two doors directly across from it, in this part of the hallway. Edward turned the ornate brass knob slowly and entered: the room beyond was very large (by now, Edward was finding it easier to associate "big things" with the banker), soothingly paneled in deep brown walnut. In its center was an enormous walnut kidney-shaped desk matching the walls exactly with a high-backed black tufted leather chair and three smaller black leather chairs fanning out in front of it. On one side of the room was a long row of low, sliding door cabinets, with groupings of what appeared to be family portraits above them; on the other wall, two massive bookcases side by side. A gleaming wooden coat tree stood by the door holding a man's soft-looking camel's hair sports jacket. Behind the desk, a wide picture window stretched out, covered with thick nettish off-white curtains which let in only the barest glimmer of sunlight. The carpet was still terra cotta but seemed thicker here, but Edward thought it must be the dimness and density of the dark paneled walls that made it seem so. He went and sat down in one of the smaller black leather chairs and wondered what had happened to all of Mr. Conover's things—the old oak roll-top desk

219

with its plain wooden swivel chair, the dark green painted bookcase, the rusted metal filing cabinets. Had they all been discarded, swept away into some dark, forlorn basement, as relics of the past, never to be seen or heard of again? Well... things *were* certainly different at the new Mapleville Bank. He hadn't come across one familiar thing yet.

Thinking of this, waiting another ten minutes or so longer, he suddenly heard the office door open and remembered he had shut it behind him.

"Well, well, Edward..." Mr. Rydin said, stepping cheerfully into his office. He switched on the lights. "It's certainly good to see you this morning, but you shouldn't have been sitting in the dark this way." He stopped before Edward and extended a hand.

"I didn't mind, sir. It was sort of restful."

"I know what you mean," the banker said, proceeding toward the desk. "I like to do that occasionally myself, but sometimes we need to throw some light on things, don't we?" He laughed and spun the black tufted chair around, to sit down. Edward thought: He can afford to make a joke now. It's his show. "I was a little afraid that you might change your mind again," the banker went on. "You seemed so positive about going to New York the last time we talked."

"Well," Edward said slowly, "a lot of things happened since then."

"Yes, things do happen." The banker looked thoughtful. He leaned back slowly, regarding Edward more seriously: "I hope you don't mind my curiosity, but I can't help wondering what made you stay after all—"

"Well…" Edward looked down at the terra cotta carpeting. "I guess it wasn't any one thing in particular. Everything just got too complicated in the end. It didn't seem worthwhile any more."

"No?" The banker still waited—patiently, for more. He was the sort of person who enjoyed getting down into the nitty gritty of things; and even though Edward didn't feel like doing that this morning, he knew he had to.

"Well," he explained, "I was only supposed to be home for two weeks. The firm needed someone right away, and they had been nice enough to give me the time off. Then when my sister was getting married, it didn't seem fair to make them wait any longer. So—" He looked down at the floor again. "Besides, my dad was against it a hundred percent. It probably wouldn't have worked out anyway."

"And what about your black friend? Did he take his job?" So the big banker had remembered that. "You seemed pretty worried about him."

"I don't know," Edward answered. "We sort of lost touch. I guess that happens all the time, after graduation." He tried to laugh. "Anyway, I hope he did."

"Well…" Mr. Rydin said, lifting himself forward in the black tufted swivel chair, "that's all water over the dam now. You're here, and we're mighty glad to have you!" He smiled quickly— "I suppose your father has informed you that Mr. Olson, the Vice-President, is retiring at the end of the year?" Edward nodded briefly. "We're going to start training you immediately for his position. We want you all shipshape by the time he leaves. Of course—you'll have to go before the Board of Directors; but that's merely a formality. They're already eager to meet you." The tall leather chair squeaked forward a little. "But for now, I just want you to take it easy for a few days. Just roll along with things. I'm not expecting any miracles the first week!" A hearty laugh now. "Now tell me—what do you think of your old hometown bank now? Isn't it everything I said it would be? That's quite a crowd we've got down there, and it's been like that since we've opened up."

"Well…" Edward hesitated, feeling lost for words. He realized he should have had some kind of speech ready. "I'll just say it's a lot bigger than I expected. I haven't seen one person I know yet."

"Oh, you will!" the banker responded quickly. "Mr. Happle's still with us, and Miss Striver. And of course, you know Mr. Olson—"

Mr. Olson was probably getting the ax *politely*, Edward thought, even though he didn't know it, because he believed in the very same things that Mr. Conover did—that it wasn't how big or new or fancy a bank was, but what it could do for the people, that mattered in the long run. As for Mr. Happle—he was just Loans. He'd always be just that, as long as somebody would let him. Mr. Happle was a small, quiet man, who never mingled too much with anybody because his mind was always on his work. In some ways, he was nearly as eccentric as old Mr. Conover was, except he didn't have as many years on him. Miss Striver, on the other hand, never cared to mingle. She had always carried her head a bit higher than the others, because she was Mr. Conover's private secretary. Miss Striver was the typical spinister—hard working, thoroughly dedicated. Efficiency with a plus! She knew the banking business almost as well as did Mr. Conover, and it was she, not Mr. Olson, who kept ends up when the old man took sick and had to stay at home. Edward wondered if the big banker knew this. He must have. He'd been smart to keep Miss Striver on, if only to show the other gals the ropes.

Well, it was almost too much when you thought about it. Almost too much, for sure, if you wanted to look at things honestly. But he hadn't come here for that, to look at things honestly. He had come to work—at least to try. He wasn't even sure about that yet. If he could.

There were still too many things left dangling. Not his pride—he had taken care of that already. But other things—intangible things that you couldn't put a name to—that stuck down deep inside of you, squirmed about there, every time you knew something was wrong. Things like that.

"Now...I'm going to get you all settled," Mr. Rydin was saying as he leaned toward the intercom. "Miss Forst...would you please come in?" He looked back at Edward. "My secretary will show you around the first few days. She'll be acting as your secretary as well, until we can find one for you."

What else? Edward thought. Now he was going to have Cynthia show him around too.

"Oh, Cynthia..." the banker said, smiling away from Edward quickly. Edward heard a click now, of high heels striking the metal bar of the doorway, and, turning his head slowly, trying to rise at the same time, he saw a tall figure of a girl in a soft gray tweed suit, softly waved dark hair about her face. "Cynthia, would you be good enough to show Edward to his office?" She nodded, and the wide, impeccably black mascara-eyes moved languidly from the banker's face over to Edward's. "Miss Forst is one of our most capable persons, Edward. You won't have any trouble under her guidance, I'm sure."

Edward nodded.

"And now, officially..." The banker stood up stoutly, with a hearty smile, extending his hand again. "I want to welcome you to our little family!"

Later, Edward thought there had been too much pomp over nothing. His office to-be was just across the hall, one of those closed doors opposite Mr. Rydin's. Now, of course, the door of the room he was to occupy was open, and the lights turned on.

Edward saw it was a smaller replica of the big office: it had the same dark walnut walls and off-white net curtains, except the desk was black metal with a bright orange leather chair, like those downstairs. On one side of this room was a short row of low, sliding door cabinets (no family portraits, of course), and on the other, a single, narrow bookcase. No coat tree. Instead, there was a tiny closet in one corner, that was used partially as a storage for office equipment—paper, envelopes, an adding machine. Well, there had to be some difference, hadn't there? But nobody could say the banker tried to cut corners on the second floor either.

Edward stepped aside to let Cynthia enter. She was holding an armful of manila folders and some fresh pens and pencils which she immediately set down on the desk.

"Mr. Rydin wants you to handle the foreclosures for the time being," she informed him, scarely looking his way. She didn't seem particularly friendly toward him, despite the fact they had had that dance together at the church social. But that was some months back, and a lot of things had probably happened to her, too. Besides he hadn't expected *her* to roll out the red carpet for him.

"I've got them all here," she continued, as she rested the tips of her very long, dark red fingernails lightly, in a tapping position, on the pile of folders. Edward had almost forgotten about Cynthia's nails: in comparison to the two receptionists', they had to be the winner. "You can go through them at your convenience," she was saying. "If there are any questions, I'll be glad to answer them or Mr. Rydin."

"Thanks." Edward went to the desk. "There seems to be quite a lot of them. How many are there, do you know?"

"I haven't had a chance to count them," she replied, her cool eyes flicking onto him momentarily, "but I suppose there's at least fifteen."

"*Fifteen?* He really believes in starting off with a bang, doesn't he?" No answer. "*All* foreclosures?"

"No... Most of them are pending as yet except for the one with the red tag sticking out of it. That one's ready for processing. Mr. Rydin wants you to have all the necessary papers ready for the foreclosure by next week Thursday."

225

Edward nodded slowly. He thought a while then. "I suppose most of them are relatively new loans, though—"

"No." She leveled her eyes fully at him now. "They're old ones, from Mr. Conover's time. Mr. Rydin wants to clean out the drawers."

"I see." So the big banker was tidying up. How nice. The new bank had just opened up, and already there were at least fifteen foreclosures. (Fourteen pending, of course!) In all the years—the summers—he had worked for Mr. Conover, he had never heard of even one foreclosure going through. Mr. Conover had seen to that. He had always managed to work something out that was beneficial to both sides. Mr. Conover would always say, the bank was there to help people, not to hurt them. But this man was different. He had known he was different. The big banker's ideas were too big. "Well…" he said slowly, "I'll go through them, like you said. Thanks for answering all the questions."

"It's all right." She walked to the door and stopped. "You'll be taking the same lunch hour as Mr. Rydin and me—one o'clock. Of course you can break any time you want. There's a coffee machine in the lunchroom. It's right down the hall."

"Yes, I know. I saw it when I came in."

"Then you're all set," she concluded.

"Yes, I'm all set." He watched her move again. "There's just one more thing—"

"Yes?" she said, dragging the darkened lashes back to him.

"Well"—he looked about the room— "I was wondering if anyone would mind if I drew the curtains back a little. I prefer working in daylight, if I can."

"Why should anyone mind?" She looked a little amused. "It's your office. You can do what you want with it."

"Well, I just thought I'd better ask first. I don't want to break any rules."

She nodded, and left.

Edward went immediately to the window and pulled the heavy curtains back; then he flicked off the lights. A warm ray of sunlight spilled over the desk now, lighting up one crimped corner of that otherwise dreary-looking pile of manila folders. He sat down and stared at them. Maybe it would help if he pretended he was somewhere else, but that was impossible. He knew too well where he was.

He pulled out the folder with the red tag and shoved it somewhere underneath the others, then flopped open the top folder and began reading rapidly.

At eleven o'clock Edward took a break. He went to the lunchroom, got himself a cup of hot black coffee from the coffee machine (he could scarely believe it himself, since the memory of that last cup of black coffee—the one his sister had brought up to his room the day after the dinner with Mr. Rydin—was still pungently fixed in his mind; but, again, this morning he knew he had to think clearly), and sat down at one of the long narrow white Formica tables by the windows and looked out. While he sipped the bitter, steaming liquid, he thought of those folders waiting for him on his desk. What was he going to do about them? Most of them were pending, sure—just like Cynthia had said, but already they were several months in arrears, and how long they would remain in that state was anybody's guess, except perhaps for Mr. Rydin's. He alone knew the answer to that, how much more time they would be given, before they would be pushed down the drain. Red-tagged, too. So he knew he had to do something fast. He couldn't let them go down the drain without some kind of fight— specially that red-tagged one.

Most of the folders belonged to the small-time farmers from around there—the poorer ones who hadn't even enough money for a telephone, otherwise he might have been able to call them and explain the dilemma they were in. As for the mail itself (there was no evidence, as far as he could see, of any letter sent to them, explaining the situation), they were probably too busy just trying to scrape up enough money for the table, to pay too much attention to that. The last few years hadn't been too good for them, and for some even worse. They were just plugging along now, trying to make ends meet, if they could—thinking that the new bank was going to be as lenient with them as the old one had, that it would give them enough time to make it up in the end. Meanwhile, Mr. Rydin was biding his own time, waiting perhaps for one more missed payment, to clamp the lid down. (Didn't the big banker admit he wasn't particularly concerned about the farmers? What did it matter to him, if they lost their farms?) Well, somebody had to try to help them. Somebody had to warn them, before it was too late, even if it meant going to see them personally at their houses!

Edward stared out of the windows now: beyond the rooftops of the little town, he could see the farming fields rolling far into the distance. How pretty they looked this morning, in their mottled late-autumn jackets. Couldn't the big city banker even see that? Of course not, because he didn't want to! That's why he kept those heavy curtains in his office so tightly closed. Well. He had told himself things wouldn't be the same without Mr. Conover. He had expected as much.

He took a quick gulp of the hot coffee and nearly scalded his mouth. You better be careful, he told himself, or you'll really get burned. Then he put the cup down. A second later the lunchroom door opened, and the girl from downstairs—the receptionist in the fitted white angora sweater and long rope of pearls—came in. She turned her small, lean face toward him and smiled. "Hi," she said, going over to the coffee machine and dropping in her coins. "I just heard you're going to work here. How do you like it so far?" Her voice was no longer constrained—properly polite, but outwardly friendly.

"Well…it's hard to tell the first day," Edward answered with a smile back. "Everything's so new."

"I know." She took her steaming cup toward him. "Somebody said you used to work at the old bank. Is that right?" He nodded. "Oh, then, you don't have to worry. You'll like it here. The old one was supposed to have been just horrible—" She eyed the chair across from him. "I hope you don't mind my joining you," she said, "but I

229

hate to drink coffee alone. It reminds me of the alcoholic, you know—taking a secret sip."

"No, I don't mind." Edward waited for her to settle down. "Do you drink much of it?"

She nodded. "Usually every chance I get. This is my fourth cup already this morning. I have a terrible time keeping awake without it. Anyway…" She lifted her cup. "I'm a Cancerian, and you know how addicted we are to the table."

"No. I didn't know that."

"You mean you're not into astrology?" She looked amazed.

"No, I'm afraid not."

"Oh, well…" She shrugged her shoulders. "Eventually everyone will be. It'll be the only thing that'll keep us alive." She took a mouthful of her coffee. Edward thought it ought to have scalded her mouth; but it didn't seem to. "What sign are you under? I mean—when were you born?"

"October 16."

"Oh, you're Libra. I should have known, you're so quiet. Most Libras are like that. I can usually figure out what a person is, if I study them a few minutes."

"Well…" Edward said, smiling again, "I'll try not to be so quiet."

"Oh, don't do that. We need as many quiet people as we can get, with all the noise going on in the world today." She smiled, then changed the subject. "You're not from Chicago at all, are you?" He shook his head. "I didn't think so. 'Course, it's difficult to tell sometimes, there's so many of us here. It's almost like a club." She laughed.

"Are you all from the same bank in Chicago?" He thought it was time he asked a few questions.

"No. I've never worked in a bank before. I was sent down here by an employment agency. Actually, I'm a stenographer, but there wasn't an opening for one at the time. But the agency said it was still a great opportunity for me—to be starting in a new bank like this."

"Well, I guess they ought to know their business," Edward said. He waited a moment. "How do you like it here?"

"It's nice. I've never lived in a small town before, though, but I'm getting used to it. I'm staying in one of those new apartment buildings, you know—the one next to Cynthia Forst's. Sometimes we come down to work together."

"That's nice."

She nodded again, then rolled her eyes about. "It's such a pretty bank, isn't it?"

"Yes, it's pretty."

"I bet you're all excited about it being here—in your hometown," she said.

"Well, I don't know if I'm all that excited—" Edward started to say.

But she didn't seem to hear him. "You know, you're awfully lucky to be starting up here, on the second floor this way. All the most important people are upstairs. I bet you don't know that all the young men downstairs are jealous of you already."

"No, I didn't know," Edward answered with some caution. He had a strange feeling now, that he was talking to the future "editor" of the Mapleville Bank Gazette. Well—he wasn't alone in this either. Other people were involved again.

"It's not just your job," the girl went on to explain. "They're jealous because your office is next to Cynthia's, and that you two are such good old friends. They're all trying to date her. It's like one big contest, each one trying to win over the other." She lifted her girlish brows. "All the girls are peeved over it, but I'm not. I think it's sort of cute." She leaned toward him— "I'm not one to talk dirty, but I swear they get an erection every time she passes by!" She giggled above her cup.

"Well," Edward said with caution again, "you can tell them for me, there's nothing to worry about. We're not such good friends. I just happened to walk her to Sunday School, when we were kids. Our parents are the good old friends."

"Oh." She looked disappointed. "Well… maybe you'll get to be better friends, now that you'll be working together." She rolled her eyes up to the wall clock now: "I better get back. We're shorthanded today. My regular relief girl had to go home. She got her period. Terrible cramps, you know."

"Oh…I'm sorry," Edward said, and blushed.

"Oh, don't be sorry," she said with a smile. "It beats getting pregnant every time." She rose and pulled the white angora sweater down over her hips. "Well, so long for now."

"So long."

It was incredible, Edward thought. All that, and she didn't even tell him her name.

Later, in the afternoon, Edward went to Cynthia's office. She was sitting at her desk, bowed over a small notebook, flicking the pages back with those long blood-red nails. "Yes?" she asked coolly, looking up. Her eyes were aloof. They seemed to be looking right through him.

"I was wondering where I could find the mortgage papers—the deed, et cetera—on the Benson file. You know—the one with the red tag?" He waited a second. "They don't seem to be in the folder you gave me."

"No," she said, her face unchanging. "We keep all the legal papers in the vault downstairs. But I just happen to have the Benson file up here. Mr. Rydin wanted it brought up, because he'll be referring to it in the next couple of days."

"I see." Edward waited another second. "Well—is it possible for me to see it?"

"Of course." She pulled her long, slender legs out of the cubbyhole of her desk, got up and walked across the floor. Edward noticed now that her office was similar to his—the same black desk and orange chair, the closet, except that she had a filing cabinet instead of the sliding door cabinets—probably for Mr. Rydin's private papers. She reached out for its middle drawer, pulled at it, and handed him the folder over her shoulder. "When you're through with it, I'd appreciate it if you would return it immediately. Mr. Rydin doesn't want the legal files lying about."

"Of course. I understand. And thanks." He started to leave.

"How are you doing with the others?" she asked, returning to her desk.

"I'm almost finished with them."

"Good. When you are, Mr. Rydin will want to talk to you."

"Yes, I know." Then he left.

20

The next day—Tuesday—Edward arrived at the bank early. He was the first one upstairs, and when the receptionist, Mildred Gatt, of the short blunt black hair and glittering eyeglasses, arrived ten minutes later, she was surprised to see him already at work.

"You're early this morning," she remarked pettishly. "Usually, nobody comes up here before nine."

"I thought I'd get a good start today," Edward told her politely.

"It's all right with me. You can come any time you want. Of course, you know, the switchboard doesn't open till nine."

"Yes, I know."

She walked away then, still pouting, to primp herself in the small round mirror hanging on the wall, behind her desk.

Edward went back to what he had been doing; he was glad for the few remaining minutes of complete quietness. He had already figured out all the letters he was going to send out that day, and was now putting the finishing touches to the last one—the Bensons' letter. That one, above all, had to be a perfection of clarity. It had to contain all the right words—the proper punch (*stress* was probably the more suitable word here; but it would not do to go overboard either, in one's own thinking), urgency, to convey the impending danger awaiting them. Though he had never seen the Bensons, he visualized what kind of people they were; he did not want to frighten them. But the letter could hold no false hopes either, for Thursday of next week was not that far off, before the whistle would be blown; if anything was to forestall, prevent the foreclosure, it had to be done now. It could not be dragged out any longer. The Bensons had to know that the boom was about to be lowered.

At nine-thirty he was finished. Pulling the untidy sheaf of papers together, from his desk, he got up quickly from his orange chair and went into the hall. From where he stood in the doorway, he could see Cynthia working at her sleek new typewriter. There was barely a sound from it. It sneaks up on you, he thought. You don't even know it's working. And he thought of all the old Grandfather Royals that Mr. Conover had kept year after year at the bank, their loud clacking sounds filling the corridors. At least they let you know honestly that business was going on, communicating. Well—that wasn't the issue here, he reminded himself. It wasn't the case of old typewriters versus new but human dignity, compassion versus *greed. Greedy* ambition!

He walked into Cynthia's office slowly, waiting for her to look up.

"Good morning," he said pleasantly. "I hate to bother you again, but I was wondering if you could type some letters for me today." She didn't say anything right off. She was wearing a neat caramel-colored suit, and her hair was sort of combed away from her face. She looked very businesslike. At her left elbow stood an open steno book on its edge.

"Do you want me to take dictation?" she asked after a few moments.

"Well...no." Edward smiled. "That won't be necessary. I've got them all written out, in longhand. All you have to do is type them up." He held the papers out for her to see.

"How many are there?"

"At least fifteen." An instant rejection came into her face. "Actually all of them are the same, except for one. It reads a little differently—"

"Oh," she said. "Then I'll make Xerox copies for the others and type the one individually."

"Well...I'd really prefer to have them all typed individually. I don't want them going out looking like form letters."

"Then I'm not sure I can do them all today," she said almost flatly. "I've got a lot of Mr. Rydin's letters to get out."

"Well, that's okay, if you're busy," Edward returned, starting to back away. "I'll find somebody else. Maybe Miss Striver will type them—"

"She can't. She's not allowed to do any work outside the loan department. She's Mr. Happle's secretary now."

"Oh." Edward stood still. "I didn't know Mr. Happle had a secretary now—he never used to."

"No." She looked straight through him again. "Mr. Rydin has expanded the loan department, since he took over. With the new bank, he's expecting a flux of new loans to come in."

"Oh, sure," Edward said quickly. "I should have thought of that." Sure. More loans, more foreclosures. Off with the old, on with the new. How come he didn't think of that himself? "Well, that's okay," he said again. "I'll just peck them out myself then."

"Wait." She reached out for the papers now. "I might be able to do them after lunch. I can't promise anything before four-thirty though—"

"Oh, that'll be fine. I just want to be sure they get out today. They're all pretty short, except for that one—I told you about."

At four-thirty punctually she brought them over. He was sitting at his desk, and she laid them down. They were all neatly typed and stacked together.

"If you want," she said, "you can sign them now, and I'll stamp and mail them for you."

"That won't be necessary. I can do that much myself."

"Very well." She lowered her eyes. "You'll find the stamps in the top right-hand drawer." She waited a minute. "Of course, if you ever want—the mail girl can put your letters through the machine for you."

"Thanks. I'll remember that."

She nodded and left.

Edward signed the letters quickly and slipped them into their envelopes; then set the Benson letter aside, and sealed and stamped the others. Then he tucked the Benson letter safely into his coat pocket. He'd stop there tonight, to see them. It was on his way home.

21

Wednesday, the bank was closed.

On Thursday morning, the first thing Edward did was to go to Cynthia's office, to return the Benson mortgage file. He had examined it carefully, made some notes, and was now through with it; and he remembered her saying it had to be returned as soon as possible. But Cynthia wasn't there. Instead, sitting in her place, in her orange leather chair, was a young man dressed in a bright blue jacket which seemed more appropriate for a sport event than a bank office. He had thin, shiny blond hair and crinkly gray eyes. He sat leisurely, with his feet crossed, and his arms folded over his chest. The moment Edward appeared in the doorway, he leaped up and stuck out his hand.

"Hello," he said most cordially. "I'm Andrew Groves—you know, the nephew?" He laughed. "You must be Edward Aldworth."

Edward nodded and smiled, as they shook hands swiftly.

"It's about time we've met, huh?" the young man laughed, tumbling back into the chair. "Looking for C. F., no doubt. She's been detained for a while. My uncle took her out to breakfast this morning, and you know how those things go." He gave a warm chuckle. "I'm just sitting here, waiting for the both of them."

"Oh…" Edward looked around a moment, confused. "Well… I just came to return this folder." He felt a little awkward holding it now, as though maybe he should file it away himself. He remembered the drawer it had come out of.

He walked toward the filing cabinet.

"How do you like working for my uncle so far?" the young man asked point-blank.

"It's okay," Edward answered, pulling out the middle drawer where the folder had come from. "It's not all that different from the old bank. I used to work there."

"I know. As a teller. You and I probably know a lot about each other." The young man laughed again, leaning sideways in the chair now, as though to hold more of Edward's attention. "I want to take this time to thank you for saving my life."

Edward set the folder down—on top of the others. "You've got to be kidding—"

"No. I'm serious. I couldn't have gone on here too much longer. I'm going back to Chicago now, thanks to you."

"Oh."

"You had me worried, though, for a time there. I really thought you were going to New York."

"So did I." Edward smiled slowly. "That just goes to show you how things turn out."

"Yeah. Here you are, and I'm the one who'll be leaving…" He watched Edward pick up the folder again. "I just want you to know you didn't do me a bad turn, that's all. The whole truth is, my uncle can't stand the sight of me, half the time. Unfortunately, we're related." Andrew Groves gave another laugh. "Actually, I'm a musician—I play the saxophone. But my father felt there was more of a future at the bank, with my uncle."

"Fathers have a unique way of looking at things, I know," Edward said with a nod.

"Well—I'm not kicking though," the young man went on. "I've got it pretty soft. I can practically write my own ticket. And there's always the girls hanging around, trying to get on the good side of me because of my uncle." He laughed again.

"Sounds pretty soft to me," Edward smiled.

Andrew nodded. "I think you'll have it pretty good yourself. My uncle's got big plans for you—that is, as soon as Olson fades out of the picture." He watched Edward fumble through the folders a moment. "God, though—I don't know how you can stand it here. This is really a dead town, and I mean *dead*. I haven't had a good lay since I left Chicago." Another chuckle. "I'm from around Rush Street, and you know how that is on a Saturday might."

"No, I'm afraid not," Edward said, turning to look at him. "I haven't been to too many places, mostly college, and Boston—"

"Boston? Christ, there's no comparison. Chicago's Rush Street, that's where all the action is. *Sex*wise." Andrew leaned far back in the chair and looked at Edward over the tip of his nose: "'Course, I didn't come here expecting to break any records. Anyone can see this is virgin country. God—I bet half the girls here don't even know what FUCK means. A guy could die here just from getting horny."

"Well…" Edward tried to smile now, but didn't say anything more.

"What do you do for excitement?"

"Oh…I haven't had too much of that yet," Edward told him, "but people tell me that the Albino's an exciting place to go to. 'Course I don't know—"

"Oh, hell, I've been there already. There's nothing there. All they do is sit around and talk. I got a date there once, and do you know what the girl talked about all the time we were together? Her daddy's cornfield. Corn, corn, corn. Now that's what I really call a *corny* evening." Andrew made a grimace.

"What are you doing now?—at the bank, I mean," Edward asked him, dropping the arm with the folder now.

"Oh, I'm helping out in Loans until I leave. They're expanding the department."

"Yes, I heard."

"That's a real bitch there though—Striver. I don't know how Happle can stand it. All she does is boss him around. You'd think she was the head of the department."

"Well… I guess he's used to her by now. They've been working together for many years."

"Yeah? Well, I'm glad it's his problem and not mine." Andrew pulled himself up in the chair and crossed his legs again: "I've only one regret about leaving this place, and that's C. F. I'd have liked to screw that; but maybe you'll be luckier. I hear you two are old friends—"

"I wish people would stop saying that," Edward said almost quietly. "We're not even what you'd call friends. We just know each other. I used to walk her to Sunday School, that's all."

"Oh, yeah?" Andrew said, raising his thin blond eyebrows in a wildish way. "Well, she's not Sunday School material now. Did you ever get a good look at one of those blouses of hers?"

"No..." Edward said slowly, "I can't say that I have—"

"Well, try it sometime. That girl's stacked, and I mean *stacked*. I bet she hasn't got much under either. Everything seems to kind of fold right in, if you know what I mean. That's one hot number, I can tell you." Andrew Groves paused, his eyes growing shiny: "Last week we all had to go to a meeting, and she had on this low-cut blouse. Every time she bent over, you expected something to fall out, and she kept bending over. Well, it so happened my uncle forgot his briefcase in his office and sent me out to get it. She was there, waiting for me. I don't know how she got there before me, but she did. She had turned out the lights and I could barely see her, but I heard her breathing hard. So I went over and stuck my hand inside that blouse, and we just sort of stood there like that for a while—"

"Then what happened?" Edward thought he might as well ask—Andrew looked all hot and bothered by now.

"Nothing! I had to stop there. Christ, do you know what my uncle would have done, if he had caught us? Fire the both of us on the spot. Nothing, and I mean *nothing*, interfers with his business. But she was ready for it, she didn't care. I tell you, those nipples of hers were as hard as spikes. What that girl knows about sex she could teach me."

"Well…" Edward said calmly, "maybe you should have made it a twosome for some other time."

"I tried, but she didn't want any part of me after that. It was then or never. She's a strange one, all right." Andrew Groves lifted his eyes away suddenly: "Oh, here they are now. Take a look at that luscious butt, will yah? How'd you like to nibble on that?"

Edward looked down at the open drawer again: the capital letters ran A to G. Holding forward a rather thick folder—"Beacon"—with his left hand, he slipped the Benson one behind it, then turned his head.

Mr. Rydin's office door was open now, and Cynthia was hanging up her boss's coat on the coat tree. She had on high heels, and the way she was standing with her arms outstretched made her skirt ride up her legs. "Wow!" Andrew exclaimed breathlessly. "That's something!" He stood up and buttoned his jacket. "Well, I leave it all to you, with my blessings. It's your territory now."

"What territory?" Edward asked him glumly. But Andrew had already moved out of the room.

Edward pushed the drawer closed.

Later that same morning, Sweater-and-Pearls—the downstairs receptionist—dropped by. She was beaming with joy.

"Hi!" she said, bouncing into Edward's office. "I've got some good news. I've just been appointed your secretary—isn't that something?"

"Yes, that's really something," Edward responded, trying to smile at her. He wondered if it hadn't anything to do with those letters Cynthia had typed for him. Maybe she had spoken to Mr. Rydin about them. Well, they were out—gone anyway. That was the main thing.

"'Course," the girl was saying, her face clouding a bit, "I won't be moving up here right away. I guess they want to see how I'll work out first. But I'm not worried. I can take shorthand at 120 words a minute and type 90."

"You sound like a whiz."

"I know." She beamed again. "Well, I thought I'd let you know. If there's anything you want typed from now on, just call me. Oh—and my name's Angie."

"I'll do that."

"Bye!"

"Bye!"

22

The following week started off hectically. Early Monday morning, as Edward stepped out of the elevator, he was assailed by a nearly hysterical Miss Striver. She was a scrawny, nervous type of woman, sallow-complexioned in a dull plum-colored woolen suit; she had quick, dark, birdlike eyes, and her graying brown hair was rigidly sculptured into waves about her head, in the same fashion of forty-some years ago, when she had first approached Mr. Conover for the job as his secretary. Edward often thought what a terrifyingly energetic woman she must have been then.

Now she was wringing her hands frantically before him, as he stood there wondering what had happened.

"Oh, dear…" she kept saying over and over again. "Edward …the Benson mortgage file is missing from the drawer! Mr. Rydin will want it for the foreclosure Thursday, and he's going to blame me! My name's the last one on the sheet!"

Edward stood still. He hadn't heard as yet about the "sheet" and just assumed it was some form of identification, since those files in Cynthia's office were primarily for Mr. Rydin's use. He suddenly felt guilty. Had he misfiled the folder? He had been sure he'd put it back correctly; but Andrew Groves had been talking so much that first day they'd met.

"Are you sure?" he asked her. "Did you look carefully?"

"Of course!" the woman answered, pulling herself up tightly under Edward's waiting gaze. She looked agitated with him now. "I should think I'd know how to look for a file after all these years! It was there last week. I put it there myself, Monday. Somebody must have taken it out afterwards, without signing the sheet!" She looked away now, toward the receptionist—Mildred—who was sitting there with gaping eyes. "I don't want Mr. Rydin to blame me for it," Miss Striver continued. "There's enough conspiracy going on around here, as it is!"

Mildred said nothing. She lowered her eyes to her work—a stack of small index cards on which she was making notations.

"Well..." Edward said, looking about slowly, "it's got to be here somewhere." He was about ready to say that he had filed the folder away himself, Thursday morning, when the elevator glided open, and Cynthia stepped out.

"What's the matter here?" she asked, her attention focusing on the frustrated woman.

"I was just telling Edward that the Benson mortgage file is missing from your cabinet," Miss Striver repeated diligently. "I put it there Monday, and somebody took it out without bothering to sign the sheet! Now I'm going to get the blame for it!"

"Oh." Cynthia looked away from her now—but not at Edward. "Well—I did it," she said a minute later.

"So it *was* you," the elder woman said, pointing her eyes at Cynthia like fingers. "I thought so. Why didn't you sign the sheet, then?"

"I didn't think I'd need it that long."

"Mr. Rydin explicitly said," Miss Striver raged on, as though she hadn't heard the explanation, "that *any* one taking a file from those drawers had to sign the sheet! *No* one was an exception!"

"Don't worry about it," Cynthia told her. There was a noticeable iciness in her face now. "I'll find it myself."

"Well…" the woman said, her voice subsiding a bit, "you'd better. I don't want to be held responsible for something that's not my fault."

"You won't be." Cynthia turned away abruptly, and went into her office. Going directly to the filing cabinet, she pulled out the top drawer and signed her name to a long yellow sheet, then inserted it back into the drawer again. Not bothering to look at anyone, she took off her coat.

"Well…it's only fair," Miss Striver remarked, drawing back her shoulders haughtily, "if she did it." And with that she stringently walked off to the elevator.

Edward stood there for a while; then walked slowly over to Cynthia's office. She was seated at her desk now.

"You shouldn't have taken the blame," he told her. "It was probably my fault. I put the folder away that morning you came in late with Mr. Rydin."

"It doesn't matter," she said rather indifferently. "The old bitty's been trying to get something on me for a long time, and now she's satisfied. She's jealous she's not Mr. Rydin's secretary."

Edward thought that was very probable; Miss Striver was certainly capable of being jealous over something like that. But he still felt funny about Cynthia taking the blame. However, he said nothing more and walked away.

Later in the morning, Cynthia called him on the intercom.

"I found the Benson mortgage file. I thought you'd want to know," she said.

"Yes," he said quietly, "I'm glad." Then: "Where was it?"

"Stuck inside of another folder. The Beacon file. You must have slipped it in without noticing. It's a very thick file."

"Yes." And he felt guilty again. He should have known.

She clicked off.

Edward leaned back in his orange leather chair, and stared out through the open doorway of his office. Then, a moment later, as though it had been planned that way, he saw Miss Striver rushing by—happily holding the "missing" folder against her scrawny breasts, like a mother hen who has just found one of her long lost chicks!

The next day (Tuesday) Edward waited impatiently for his lunch hour. He kept glancing at his watch for the time. When it was finally five to one, he got up and hurried out. Cynthia was getting ready to leave, pushing some papers aside on her desk.

"I just want you to know I appreciate what you did yesterday," he told her, "and I thought—well, maybe you'd let me buy you lunch today."

"I can't," she said. "I usually lunch with Mr. Rydin." She got up and went to her closet.

"Oh—well, that's okay," Edward said. He watched her pull her coat off the hanger and went over to hold it for her. "I understand."

She almost smiled now. "We could make it for some other time, though, if you want. Dinner, maybe—"

"Oh, sure," Edward said quickly. "That'll be okay too. Anything you say."

"What about Thursday?" She buttoned her coat—with those long pointed blood-red fingernails.

"Sure. Thursday's just fine." Edward thought a moment. "I'll get my dad's car that day."

"Don't bother. We'll use mine."

"Okay." Edward could see something in her face now, that would have resisted an objection. "Thursday it is then," he said, and turned on his heel and walked away.

Down the hallway, standing by the open door of his office, was Angie—his new secretary. She was holding her steno pad and four sharply pointed pencils, waiting for him. Edward suddenly remembered he had asked her to come up to take a short letter.

"I'm sorry I kept you waiting," he told her, hurrying back into his room.

"It's all right," the girl said, giving him a sly twinkle of the eye. "I can see you've got a lot on your mind."

Later that afternoon, while Edward was mulling over some papers at his desk, Andrew Groves poked his head in. His face looked bright and shiny.

"Just got the latest bulletin," he said. "Olson walked out. Took his walking papers. That means you'll be moving up, so you better start polishing the apples. There's going to be a big meeting Monday night. All the bigwigs from Chicago are coming down to meet you."

"Great," Edward said. "Simply great."

23

Thursday: a dreary gray November day. A thin rainy snow was falling in the background of Edward's office, making everything inside look even grayer. As he sat working, the intercom sounded. It was Cynthia Forst again.

"Are the Benson foreclosure papers ready for today?"

"Yes, they're all ready."

"Good. Mr. Rydin wants to see you as soon as he comes in. I'll let you know when he does."

"Thanks."

Edward flicked off the button and gazed down at the desk—at the slightly irregular pile of immaculately white sheets of paper, with their neat, precisely detailed paragraphs. You could almost call them beautiful, he thought. Lifting them carefully between his fingers, he tapped them together against the dark wood-grained top of the desk. Everything had to be neat, of course. Not a single word out of place, not a thought, not an emotion. He set the papers down again, slid them gently inside their folder, and leaned back in his chair, then his eyes went about the room—at the dark paneled wall at the left, with the solitary bookcase (not too many books there. What a waste.), the closet, the door, the other paneled wall with the short row of low built-ins, and then back to the desk and the chair he was sitting in.

We're all like robots, he told himself grimly, sitting in our little orange leather chairs. But what else could he do? The Bensons had said they would call him about their delinquent loan, and they hadn't. There was nothing he could do now.

The intercom sounded again.

"You can go in now," its voice dictated. "Just walk right in. He's waiting."

Edward nodded to it, flicked off the button again, and stood up. Buttoning his suit jacket now, as he had seen Andrew Groves do that other morning, he drew the carefully contained folder to himself. Well, the papers were ready, and the big new bank was ready, but were the Bensons?

He went to the door.

Outside, in the hallway, Mildred Gatt was sorting through the turmoil of the morning mail. She gave him a dismal smile.

"Looks like one of those days."

"Yes," he said. "One of those days."

Edward turned the ornate brass knob slowly. The big banker was sitting behind his big kidney-shaped desk, reading a letter. The curtains were drawn together tightly, the lights turned on.

"Good morning, Edward," he said, putting down the letter and breaking into a smile. "Come in, sit down!" He indicated toward one of the chairs before the desk— "Make yourself comfortable."

Edward sat down, holding the folder carefully in his lap.

"How are things going?"

"All right, sir."

"Splendid." Mr. Rydin's gaze dropped to the folder then: "My secretary said you have the foreclosure papers all ready—"

"Yes, sir." Edward handed over the folder—watched the banker open it, peer through the papers briefly, then set it aside.

"Everything looks fine, Edward," he said. "I only hope you're not taking any of this too personally—"

"I don't think so, sir."

"That's good because"—the tall tufted black leather chair tipped backwards noiselessly— "I'd like to talk to you about it this morning. I had a telephone call from Mr. Benson the other day—Tuesday, just after you left for home—and he said you'd been out to his house. He seemed to be under the impression that the bank was going to extend the waiting period on the loan. Of course, this is not so... We can't."

"Well, sir..." Edward felt himself stirring in his own chair now— "I just thought I'd go out there and talk to them. I couldn't find any copies of letters sent to them, in the files, concerning the delinquencies, and I wanted to make sure they understood the urgency of the situation."

"Mr. Happle holds all the correspondence on loans in his files. You had only to ask him about it. He would have gladly shown them to you." Mr. Rydin's voice sounded calm without anger, but there was a definite message to it. "On the contrary," he went on to say, "there's been a great deal of correspondence on the matter, with no effect."

"I'm sorry," Edward said. "I didn't know that." He stopped— waited a moment; then: "I didn't mean to cause any trouble for the bank, sir. I just thought—well, somebody ought to try to help these people. They've had a lot of bad luck the last few years. Mr. Benson broke his leg a year ago and hasn't been able to work the farm, and with all the medical bills piling up—"

"Yes, I know," returned Mr. Rydin calmly. "We have a complete history data on the family." He almost smiled now. "I'm not trying to reprimand you for your actions, Edward. I fully understand your feelings. These are people from your town—possibly your friends, (No, Edward thought, they're not my friends; I just care about what happens to them. You don't. Neither does the bank now.), so naturally you want to help them. I only wish you had told me about your plans; I could have stopped you. You see, by going out to their house that way, you gave them false hope—hope where there was none. Of course I had to tell them the truth but it was a painful procedure on both sides. You see, Edward," the banker said, looking at Edward steadily from across the wide, polished desk, "the last thing the bank wants to be is cruel. But in this case, nothing can be done. Our hands are tied. The foreclosure must go through—"

Edward said nothing now. He sat still—waiting for the banker to continue; and he did.

"Were you aware of the fact that the Bensons were in arrears *six* times in the past ten years?" Edward shook his head. "That's serious enough," the banker said, "but besides that, Mr. Benson had made a considerable amount of other loans with the bank, for expensive equipment he knew nothing about, nor needed. The man was a poor manager. He knew nothing at all about farming. Of course..." the

255

tufted chair came forward a little, "all of this happened during Mr. Conover's time, when things were quite different. The bank much smaller. Nevertheless, had I been president at the time, this loan would never have gone through. I would have clarified it as a poor risk, and all this pain would have been avoided."

Again, Edward said nothing.

"Now, I know what a great admirer you are of Mr. Conover and his ideals, Edward, and I want you to know I'm not against ideals. Just futile ones. It would be nice, of course, if we could help everyone who came along, but we can't. This is not a charity organization. We have our own responsibilities—to our depositors, our investors, our stockholders. These people look to us for assurance, and we must see to it that they get it. We must travel a straight and narrow path, Edward, if we are to continue to thrive as we are now—to achieve the goals for which we have set ourselves!" The banker paused. Then, slowly: "It is a pity of course, that things like this—foreclosures must happen, but with proper guidance, they can almost be avoided. One never knows the disasters that await—as in the case of poor Mr. Benson; but, with careful planning, one need not always be the complete loser. However—" the banker's voice grew steadfast now, "regardless of which way things go, we must always be prepared to follow through with our commitments. You can see that, can't you, Edward?" The banker waited now for some definite response.

Edward felt his head nodding now.

"Now, up to this point," Mr. Rydin went on more quickly, "we have had no assurance from the doctor, that Mr. Benson will ever be able to work. He may never work the farm again.

Meanwhile, all the burdens are falling on his wife's shoulders." Mr. Rydin paused again. "So you see how futile it would be to go on like this... To extend the waiting period any further would only plunge these people further in debt. No, Edward—the best thing for them to do now is to give up the farm. Then Mrs. Benson can go back to her old job at the paper mill. She's already made application for it; and maybe, in time, Mr. Benson can return there also. They can start afresh."

No! Edward almost shouted within himself, it's never the best thing to give up one's home. How can you say that? It's not so easy to shatter a dream...

"I know all this must sound a bit heartless to you," the banker was saying, slowly again, "but after you think about it for a while, you'll realize I'm right. Some people are doomed for failure, Edward, because they want the things that are not right for them. The Bensons are that kind of people. They should have never left the mill. They belonged there. Had Mr. Conover been more—visionary, shall we say—than sympathetic, he would have seen that. Well—" The banker's eyes fell to the folder. "I've asked the Bensons to come down here this afternoon. I'd like to have you speak to them again. Explain the mistake—"

"Yes, sir." Edward nodded again. "I'll talk to them again."

"Fine." The tall tufted chair sprang erect now. "When today is over, we're going to put it all out of our minds.

Starting next week sometime, I'm going to have you moved down to Investments for a while. I think you'll get a better perspective there, of what we're trying to do." The banker paused now with a careful smile: "I suppose you've already heard about Mr. Olson's leaving us prematurely?" Edward nodded. There was no need to deny it. "Well," the banker went on with a degree of cheerfulness, "we'll just have to get you all shipshape that much faster. There's going to be a big meeting Monday night—at five o'clock, after the bank closes. I want you to be there. A lot of important people are coming down from Chicago, to meet you. I hope you haven't planned anything for that evening—"

"No, sir," Edward answered. "I'll he there."

"Good." The banker stood up now and came around to the front of the desk: "Now, I don't want you to worry about a thing. I've got the utmost confidence in you. You're going to work out just fine! All you have to do is remember that good old golden word: Conformity. It solves a great many problems!" The banker smiled again. "Someday you might be saying the very same things to another young man like yourself, Edward. We all have to go down the same path. There's no shortcuts."

Edward nodded and stood up.

They walked together to the door.

* * *

When Edward returned to his desk, he found Cynthia waiting there for him. She was holding another batch of manila folders, all of which had red tags sticking out of them. She looked strangely aloof.

"Mr. Rydin wants you to finish processing these, before you go down to Investments next week. Of course there won't be any letters to write. That's all been taken care of."

Edward just nodded. He took the folders, sat down, and began working on them.

At ten to three he looked at his watch: it was the fifth time he had done that in the past half-hour, and now it told him it was time to get ready. He stood up and buttoned his suit coat and went out into the hallway. It was quiet there, empty. Mildred Gatt had left her post for a mid-afternoon break.

Edward started toward the door of the Big Office; then the elevator door slid open: it was quiet too, and had there been any other sound about, he might not have heard it. But now, for all its quietness, it had a startling effect. Edward stood still. Then the next moment Mr. Happle stepped around the corner.

He was wearing a dark blue suit and under his arm he carried a shiny new black leather attaché case. Now that's Conformity, Edward thought. Mr. Happle had never worn a suit to the bank before; he had always worked in his shirtsleeves. And as for an attaché case...well, Mr. Happle was coming up in the world now.

The Head of Loans stopped suddenly, startled himself; then continued down the hallway. He gave Edward a small, embarrassed smile. "Hello, Edward. How are you?"

"Just fine, Mr. Happle. And yourself?"

"Just fine." Edward opened the door for him, and the man went in. Edward followed.

They were all there now—the Bensons, Mr. Rydin. Mr. Benson sat brow-beaten in his shabby sheepskin jacket, cane at his side, while his wife, with her little crooked brown felt hat and brown woolen coat, and enormous sunken paled eyes, stared frighteningly at the man who was speaking to them. The big banker stood beside his tall leather chair, with one arm resting along its back, and though his voice had a soft, caressing tone of sympathy, the words seemed to cut through the air with the same sharpness of Mr. Habich's long butcher knife drawing blood. "Of course," he was saying, "we don't like to do this sort of thing, but we have no choice. Too much time has passed already. The foreclosure must go through now—" He paused, waiting for Mr. Happle to seat himself, lay the attaché case carefully on the table, then turned to Edward: "Now, Mr. Aldworth will explain things to you more fully—"

24

At five o'clock the thin rainy snow had stopped and a brisk cold wind had taken its place. Relentlessly, it whipped about the corners of all the old buildings on Main Street, and about the corner of the new Mapleville Bank. Edward pulled up his coat collar and started hurrying for home, when he saw the car waiting. It was parked by the street lamp, its headlights on, the motor running. Cynthia's yellow Mercury. He hadn't expected to find her there, for he hadn't seen her or spoken to her since she had given him those additional manila folders to work on, and he had just taken it for granted that she had called off their dinner date for that evening. He could still remember the strange aloofness of her face, when he had come out of the banker's office. But there she was.

He walked over to the car, and opened the door.

"I didn't think you'd want to go out any more," he told her honestly, getting in and shutting the car door.

"Why not?" She was huddled up in the corner, eyeing him from the thick smooth folds of her black woolen coat. The wide eyes with their heavy dark lashes seemed shiny in the semi-darkness of the streetlight.

"Well…you know, it's been a pretty lousy day all around. For you too, I suppose. With the Bensons coming in about the foreclosure."

"I never let what happens at the bank interfere with my personal life," she said, straightening up and turning off the motor.

"You don't? You're pretty lucky then. Most people can't do that. I guess I'm one of those who brings the troubles home with him, like my father." And he laughed a bit tightly.

She didn't say anything. She looked away and laid her darkly leathered gloved hands on the wheel. Edward could see she was suddenly impatient to go.

"Well—" he said, trying to exude a more cheerful note into the conversation, "where shall we eat? At the Albino's?"

"Is that where you want to go?" she asked, turning to him almost abruptly.

"Oh, no," he replied quickly, sensing her bleak rejection. "We can go anywhere you like. I just mentioned it because everyone seems to be going there. Actually I haven't been there yet myself, so I don't know too much about it—or its food," and he laughed again.

"Well," she said, looking away once more, "I thought we could go to my apartment. I could fix some sandwiches."

"Oh, sure, if that's what you want to do. That'd be fine with me too. I just thought you'd want to eat out somewhere, that's all."

"All right," she said. "We'll go there."

She turned on the ignition, shifted gears and started driving east on Main Street. Edward sat back now and watched how efficient she was at the wheel: she was fast—much faster than his sister was, but there was an undeniable maturity about her fastness. The hands, with their dark leather gloves, with their long pointed blood-red fingernails, were very strong, very precise on the wheel. You can be sure she knows where she's going, Edward thought. There's probably not one thing in the world she's afraid of doing.

The yellow Mercury turned down Baynor Street. It was a short street, not more than three blocks long, and halfway down the second block stood a row of tall, newly constructed apartment buildings: some hadn't their front lawns in yet. They all looked alike—light tan brick faces, wide picture windows with little intricate black wrought iron balconies, deeply recessed double-doored entrances flanked with glistening brass coach lanterns. Very fancy, Edward told himself; just like those robot orange leather chairs at the new bank. They all looked alike too. He noted how the new apartment buildings made all the old frame houses around there look so out-of-date, dreary. That was the trouble with progress that no one ever mentioned: it downgraded the old while embellishing the new. It made people suddenly discontented with the way good things were. What was wrong with an old frame house anyway? He'd lived in one all his life.

Alongside each of the buildings was a long sweeping driveway that led to a parking lot at the rear. The yellow Mercury pulled into the first one and parked in Section 6.

Edward sat still for a moment, watching the deep black darkness gathering from the trees at the edge of the lot. Then he said, "You know, it's funny. My father was talking about these buildings not too long ago."

"Really?" she said. sounding not too interested. Taking the keys from the ignition, she picked up her shoulder bag and got out. And

263

Edward had to hurry back up the driveway, to catch up with her before she reached the front door.

Cynthia's apartment was on the second floor, next to a huge potted fern which looked exactly like those of the lobby of the new Mapleville Bank. Edward thought it must have been a housewarming gift from the big banker. Sometimes Mr. Rydin's generosity simply amazed him.

He watched her unlock the door, turn on the lights.

The living room was dazzling white—so dazzling white that Edward almost had to blink his eyes to look at it. It was every bit as dazzling white as Suzanne's wedding gown that morning in her bedroom, with the bright sunlight shining over it. There was a long white velvet sofa that curved at the end, two white embossed lounge chairs, a pair of large white alabaster lamps on enormous square white plastic-like tables, and a low narrow white marble-topped coffee table that almost ran the full length of the sofa. The walls, the drapes, the carpeting were all of the same stark, penetrating white. No color of any kind. Edward had never before seen so much whiteness in one room. Well, it matched her personality—cold-looking.

He hesitated to step on the white carpet.

"Come in," she said, holding out her hands for his coat. He quickly slipped out of it.

"It's very nice here," he commented. "Very modern."

"Yes. I like things to be very modern." She hung up her coat and his in the closet. She was wearing a soft, clinging beige dress. He wondered why he hadn't noticed it before this. Well…it had been that kind of day. There were probably a lot of things he hadn't noticed.

"You can sit down and make yourself comfortable," she told him, "while I make the sandwiches. There's a bottle of wine on the table"—she pointed to the marble coffee table—"pour yourself a drink."

"Well…if you don't mind," Edward said, smiling, "I think I'll just pass that up this time."

"Suit yourself," and she turned away toward the kitchen.

The next moment Edward heard the refrigerator door bang shut; then she was rumbling loudly amongst the pots and pans. He waited a few moments more, then crossed the white carpet carefully, to one of the white embossed lounge chairs and sat down slowly. Despite its touchy appearance, it was very comfortable—soft, deep, like a cushion. Edward leaned back and scanned the room again. Well, it must have cost a pretty penny. The cleaning bill alone could keep you broke.

His eyes rested then on the bottle: What made her think of that? Did she expect him to make a fool of himself in front of her again?

He hadn't been sitting there for too long a time—possibly ten minutes at the most—when she appeared with a tray of neatly carved sandwiches, of chopped liver, freshly-cut ham, and cheese. This she set down on the coffee table, next to the wine.

"You can start eating, if you like," she said, "while I take a shower. I won't be too long."

"Oh don't hurry on my account," Edward said awkwardly, "I'll be just fine here."

"All right," and she went off in the direction of the bathroom.

Edward listened now to the water running in the bathtub. What a darnest time for a shower, he thought. But it was her right to take one, if she wanted to. She lived here.

He took a sandwich from the tray—chopped liver and began eating absent-mindedly. He had a feeling it was going to be another one of those evenings, with her not talking too much. Well, it wasn't actually a date anyway. Neither one would have broken his neck to be with the other. If he hadn't misfiled that folder, if Miss Striver hadn't made such a stink over it, he wouldn't be here now. Of course, it would have been a lot simpler if they had gone somewhere to eat. To him, it was no big thing being here in Cynthia Forst's apartment, though he knew Andrew Groves would have thought so.

Realizing he had finished the sandwich already, he reached for another chopped liver again. The monotony of himself irritated him now: Why couldn't he have chosen something else—the ham at least? Well, he really wasn't that hungry. It was just something to do.

He heard the water stop running. The bathroom door opened and she came out in a thick fluffy white robe and velvety white slippers (naturally, he thought, why break the pattern of whiteness now?); her hair lay dampish down her back, in ringlets, and her face had a scrubbed-clean look except for the wide eyes which still had the mascara on. Edward wondered if she had taken off the old batch and applied a new one, or just eliminated the eyes altogether when she bathed. It seemed a complicated procedure either way.

She crossed in front of him, sending out a sudden whiff of heavy perfume—that same heavy, nauseating smell he remembered so well from the other evenings. She never wore it at the bank. She must be two people, he told himself—one over there, and one here.

She sat down on the sofa and spread the robe over her knees, then picked up a sandwich. "I didn't know if you liked chopped liver."

"Oh, I like pretty much of everything," Edward declared, flashing a smile. "I'm not too fussy."

She eyed him for a second then. "I hope you don't mind my sitting here like this," she said, fingering the edge of the robe, "but I hate being all dressed up at home. It gives me claustrophobia."

"Oh, say—this is your apartment. You've got the right to do what you want here. Actually, I don't care too much for sitting around all dressed up myself," and he laughed. Then he cleared his throat and threw in the last portion of the second sandwich.

"Would you like another?" she asked promptly.

"Well..." he said, sitting erect, "maybe just one more."

He tried to look over the sandwiches as quickly and carefully as he could. This time he drew a cheese. "I meant to ask you—you haven't had any more trouble with Miss Striver, I hope?"

"No. Everything's back to normal again. We're not talking."

"Oh, I'm glad. I mean I'm glad that that other thing is over. I wouldn't want her to be going at you because of me. She's not really a bad person, once you get to know her. But I suppose she can be

267

rather jealous, if she wants to be," and Edward remembered how Miss Striver had always made sure she was the only one who took Mr. Conover's telephone calls, or gave him his messages, or brought in his mail. No, Miss Striver could be very jealous, if need be. "Well..." he added slowly, "she's another displaced person." He looked down at the sandwich now, waiting in his hand: "I suppose you know your boss is sore at me, for the way I handled the Benson case. That's why he's sending me down to Investments next week." He lifted his eyes.

"Maybe he just wants you to get better acquainted with that part of it," she said, without showing any visible signs of interest in the subject.

"No, he's sore all right. And he wants me to know it. But I don't blame him—I'd probably be, too, if I were him." He smiled suddenly. "I'm just lucky I didn't get the boot, like Mr. Conover and Olson." He listened.

She didn't say anything now, though. And he hadn't expected her to. She picked up the bottle of wine, filled a glass for herself. "Are you sure you don't want any?"

"No, I better not," he answered with a slightly smothered laugh. "I wouldn't want to give you a repeat performance of that other night."

"It's up to you." She leaned back to the concave of the sofa and began sipping slowly, meticulously, the long pointed blood-red fingernails grasping the edge of the glass loosely as though it were made of air. Her eyes were on him.

Edward took a bite from the cheese sandwich. "I suppose you don't remember too much about Mr. Conover, do you?"

"No. I've never met the man."

"Oh, well… you'd have to know him to understand how I feel. He was a nice old guy, always trying to help people out. Some thought he was a little odd at times, but that was just his way. Actually, I think he was afraid of people; but he liked them. I remember…" Edward smiled now: "One time he and I almost got locked in the vault together. It was really funny—he was stammering all over the place. I think he was more afraid of being in there with me than anything else." He laughed a moment, then grew serious: "Anyway, I know he'd never foreclose on the Benson farm. He would have thought of some way out for them. And that makes me feel sort of responsible, you know, as though I've let him down." He paused again not expecting her to reply. "I guess I've just worked too long at the old bank. I was fifteen when I started there. I sort of grew up around Mr. Conover's ideas on things."

"People can change if they want to," she said, still not showing interest.

"I know, and that's what I've been trying to do. But so far I haven't been too successful at it. First, I misfile that folder—then I do all the wrong things, to please the boss." He laughed weakly. "I suppose the whole point of the story is, I should have just gone to New York when I had the chance."

"Maybe you still can go." She was sitting very still watching him, as though she were waiting for something.

269

"No, that's over," he said. "You see"—he smiled slowly—"I've burned all the bridges. There's nowhere to go now, and I'm stuck. Here."

"Well, then, I suppose," she said with almost mocking deliverance, "you'll just have to adjust to the way things are."

"I know," he said, "and that's what worries me. I'm not too sure I can." Why was he telling her all this, opening up this way? She could always carry it back to her boss. But she wouldn't, he knew, because she didn't care. You could talk to people who didn't care, until you were blue in the face, and it wouldn't matter. "Well," he said suddenly, "I guess my trouble is, I get too wrapped up in people. I'll have to stop that." He paused again. "I suppose you never have that problem—letting people complicate you that way? I mean, it probably wouldn't bother you at all, for instance, if your parents didn't approve of your living here...I mean, in your own apartment— like this—"

"No, why should it? It's my life, not theirs." She lifted her head for her drink.

"That's true. Very, very true." Edward nodded. "You're lucky again, that you can be that way. I can't. Well..." he said slowly, "this all must sound pretty boring to you. I'm probably ruining your evening."

"It's all right." She picked up the bottle again, and refilled her glass. "Are you sure you don't want to try just a little?" she asked.

"Well..." Edward watched the red wine sparkle in her glass; it was his intention to say No again, but now his throat felt very dry from all the chopped liver and cheese. Of course, he could always ask her for a glass of water; but how would that look? "Well..." he said almost carefully, "I guess a little wouldn't hurt. We usually have wine at home on holidays. Anyway it's not brandy—" and laughed. He watched her half fill a glass for him, and then reached out for it. He took a few fast swallows and said, "It's very tasty. It must be an expensive brand."

"Yes. Very expensive."

"Well, it'd almost have to be," he said, his eyes fluttering swiftly about the room, "to go with the rest of your things." He leaned back then and tried to be comfortable. "As I said before, my father mentioned these apartments. I guess he thought I'd like to live here, too. We might have been neighbors. But of course, you've already got a neighbor from the bank—Angie, my secretary. She tells me you two go to work together sometimes. That's nice."

"She's lying. We never go to work together. We seldom see each other except at the bank."

"Is that so?" Edward looked somewhat surprised. "Well, I always suspected she likes to exaggerate. Some people do," and he drank some more wine.

They didn't talk after that, for a while; both drank quietly. Then, seeing that Edward's glass was nearly empty, she picked up the bottle again. "Would you like a little more?"

"Well... I guess a little more can't hurt much either." He laughed, leaning forward. This time she filled the glass to the top, but he didn't say anything, Drawing back, he misjudged—the glass tilted a bit, and a small round blood-red blemish appeared on the white marble coffee table. "Oh...I'm sorry," Edward said, flushing— quickly removing it with his coat sleeve.

"It's all right," she said. "It doesn't matter."

"Well, I wouldn't want to damage anything on you," he told her, rubbing again.

"It doesn't matter," she repeated. But now she seemed impatient. She set her glass down and got up, walked over to one of the plastic-looking white tables and pulled out a drawer; then, taking out a small glass ashtray and a package of cigarettes, she lit one and turned to him. "Do you want one?"

"No, thanks. I don't smoke either. I guess there's quite a lot of things I don't do. I'm what you'd call 'very square'." He laughed shortly.

"People do what they want to do," she said flatly, blowing some smoke out the side of her face.

"That's what I always say," Edward said quickly. "Live and let live! That's my motto!" He felt the wine running his words, but now he didn't care. His throat was feeling much better. "Speaking of smoking—I heard you indulge in men's cigars. The big fat ones."

"Who told you that?" she asked instantly. Something lit up in her face.

"Oh...I don't want to mention any names," he told her cautiously, "but someone was supposed to have seen you smoke one at the Albino's. It's probably just a rumor, though."

"No, it's not a rumor." The darkly-framed eyes watched him carefully now. "Would you like me to smoke one for you?"

"Well..." Edward said, "I've never seen a woman smoke one of those before. But I wouldn't want to put you through any trouble. You've already got a cigarette started."

"It's no trouble. I'll be right back," and she set the cigarette in the glass ashtray, got up and went to the bedroom.

"Don't hurry on my account," Edward called after her. He watched her flick on another light; through the opened doorway he could see the stark whiteness of the walls beyond. Another cold-looking room, no doubt, he thought, and went on drinking the wine.

When she came back she was holding a black lacquered wooden box, which she placed on the coffee table, next to the other things. Opening it, she took out a cigar and tore off its wrapper, bit its tip off, lit it, puffing on it deeply for a few minutes. Then she blew out a roll of perfectly shaped smoke-circles into the air.

"Oh, that's very good," Edward said, almost gleefully. "I bet there's not too many women who can do that."

"Thank you," she said, looking at him. She seemed as though she were getting ready to smile now—the corners of her eyes lifted as though she were. Edward waited but no smile came. Then— "I hope you don't mind," she said rather softly, as she stood unbuttoning the robe, "if I take this off. I never smoke a cigar with my clothes on, except in public. It's too confining. I suppose you've already seen a naked woman?"

"Oh...sure," Edward said, stuttering suddenly. "Many times..."

"Good. I wouldn't want to embarrass you." She went on unbuttoning the robe, letting it fall to the floor. Now she stood stark naked. Edward felt himself gawking. She was very slender—very, very slender except for the breasts which hung away from her like softly rounded, inflated pincushions; her legs were long, very slender too, and her hips straight like a boy's. There was something definitely defiant—masculine about her presence. The cigar in her mouth made it more so. Puffing on it again, she blew out now long curdles of smoke; then, tossing a satiny pillow onto the sofa, she lay down and rested her head upon it. "Now, watch," she commanded almost sharply, and took another puff on the cigar. Drawing up her legs slowly, she parted them—Edward saw the hand with the lighted cigar going down…down…down….

He looked away quickly. His brain was whirling now, from the wine, from what she was doing. Why was she doing this? Was she trying to embarrass him again? She had said she didn't want to, but—

"I…think I better go home now," he told her, pushing himself up from the chair. "I…don't feel… so good." Without looking at her, he set his glass down, walked as quickly as he could over to the closet; opening it, he pulled his coat down from the hanger: the metal made a terrible clacking noise. Embarrassed, he groped for the sleeves—

Then he heard it. Her laughter. Softly at first, like a crazy, mixed-up sound coming from somewhere else; then louder and louder, rising, until it became a shrill. It pierced his ears with shame! Groping now for the knob of the front door, he pulled hard, stumbled out into the hallway; but the laughter followed him. It followed him down the long, narrow stairs, and outside, and all the way home. It followed him into his bed, and as he lay there searching for sleep, staring into the turbulent darkness of the night, he asked himself over and over again—why? Why?

The next morning he got up very early. He got down to the bank very early too, but he didn't start working. He just sat at his desk, watching the time, waiting for Cynthia's arrival. When she finally came, he got up and followed her into her office.

She was standing, taking off her coat. She was aware of his presence, but didn't bother to look at him.

"I said something last night that made you angry, didn't I?" he asked her quietly.

She didn't answer. She took off a thick woolen beret and laid it on the shelf. Then— "I hate gossip." Her voice was cold, flat.

"Yes... I don't blame you. So do I." And he turned abruptly, and left.

25

Monday. They started coming in early in the morning—the first, at quarter to nine—the weary, sober, executive-faced lot, some men, some women, in fine dark suits, carrying expensive-looking but slightly battered leather suitcases and attaché cases. Edward watched them disappear one by one behind the darkly-stained door of the Big Office, not to be seen or heard of for the rest of the morning and afternoon. This day, a strange, revered silence had overtaken the second floor of the new Mapleville Bank, not too much different from that other silence Edward had experienced on his first day there, but heavier—more consuming. It seemed to touch the very starkness of the white walls, the resilience of the thick terra cotta carpeting, the shiny, sleek blackness of the metal desks and their orange chairs. And it certainly touched the person of Mildred Gatt, the receptionist, who sat very stiffly, very formally, like a soldier on guard, at her desk the whole day.

By ten-thirty they were all there—the Board of Directors—and Edward saw Cynthia go into the Big Office then. She was appropriately dressed for the "grave" occasion: black suit, white pleated blouse, black suede pumps. I feel as though I'm being buried today, Edward thought; and a moment later, as if triggered off by some secret signal, Mildred popped off her chair and took in a tray of coffee and doughnuts. Edward got up from his desk and went to the lunchroom for a cup of hot black coffee. It was like a morgue in there, too. No one sat about. The room stretched neat and empty. It seemed all socializing was off, taboo. I wonder if anybody's going to the bathroom today, Edward told himself, and he envisioned all the bank workers holding back their bladders just because of the arrival of those few but so cherished persons, up, up, up high on the ladder of success!

When he returned to his desk he tried to work very hard, and though he was able to get most of the things he had to do done, he did not even come close to the quota he had set for that morning. He had filled out some papers, had taken some phone calls, and had made a few of his own, one to Vera Michaelson, who had inquired about a loan for a new car (she was the daughter of a personal friend of his mother's) which had been approved by the Loan Department, but he had promised he would call her back personally, and the other to a Bradley Thomas, regarding a mortgage on a commercial building Bradley was purchasing, and the termination of the old one, on the house in town he had just recently sold. The problem there was Bradley's lawyer, Marcum. Marcum had just had a bad flare-up of ulcers and was recuperating in the hospital. A meeting had been set for next Thursday, but it was not known whether Marcum would be able to attend. Besides, Edward was waiting for Bradley to bring in some necessary papers for the transaction. Edward had lost nearly thirty minutes with that call, and when he was through and had glanced at his watch, it was already twelve-forty-five. Then, Timothy

Hanahan, the bus boy at B's restaurant, brought in a large box of hot beef sandwiches, and the delectable odor filled the corridor, trailing right up to Edward's nose. Seeing it was almost one now, he thought he'd better eat himself. He was not particularly hungry, but he knew if he didn't eat something, he'd eventually come down with some kind of nagging headache, and he didn't want that on top of everything else.

Silently, thoughtfully, he consumed his two peanut butter and jelly sandwiches and drank two more cups of black coffee. He was getting to be a regular coffee drinker, he thought. If that didn't shake up his brain, he didn't know what would. The lunchroom was no longer empty, but those who sat about did not converse. They all seemed deeply immerged in something. Edward was glad. He didn't want idle talk, and certainly not bank talk. He would have plenty of that kind of talk, he was sure, later on.

Though he had twenty minutes left of his lunch, Edward went back to his desk and began working again. He finished looking through some papers, then pushed the intercom button, got Angie on the line. "I'd like you to take some letters this afternoon," he told her. "Sure," she said, "I'll be right up." She sounded as though she were chewing gum, the words minced with saliva. "Well," he said, "you don't have to rush up. Finish whatever you're doing." "It's okay," she said, "I'll come right away." And there was a smacking sound then.

Edward readied himself for the girl. She was up in a few minutes, with her steno book and the usual four sharply-pointed pencils (he often wondered how she had derived at that amount: Apparently, she was more cautious than he figured her to be). That afternoon, however, he dictated very badly—his voice was either too shallow or too quick, and sometimes he would stop for no apparent reason, then slur the words. He could see Angie was rather perturbed about it. But she got it all down, regardless, without having him to repeat anything, not even the spelling of a name or a street, and for that he was grateful. He wanted things to move along quickly. He didn't want to have to repeat anything that day.

When they were all through, Angie closed her steno book abruptly and stood up. "I'll have them ready in a couple of hours," she said, even though they were five rather lengthy and complicated letters.

"Well, you don't have to rush," he said again. "They're really not that urgent. If you have something else to do, they can go out tomorrow just as well." Then why had he bothered her to come up today? He realized he was sounding rather blunderish.

"No," she said stubbornly, probably not catching it, or not wanting to show that she did. Angie enjoyed her new prominent position very much, and did not want to do anything to jeopardize it. Besides, the sooner the letters were done, the better. E. A.'s letters were always so boring. All that legal jumble stuff. She didn't want to carry that heavy stuff home on *her* brain. Why anybody ever wanted to be a lawyer, she couldn't understand. "I'll have them finished by four, no later."

But Angie had them ready by quarter to four, and all five were neatly done, without a single typographical error. Edward wondered how she did it. He couldn't type one sentence without making an erasure. Angie was certainly a whiz of perfection.

"Thank you," he said, "but you didn't have to hurry that much."

"I didn't," and she gave him a somewhat smug little smile and left. Edward read the letters over carefully, not particularly liking some of the phrases he had used, but signed them anyway just to get rid of them. Then he put them in the envelopes, stamped, sealed them, and set them neatly in a pile on the right-hand corner of his desk, for the mail girl to pick up at four-thirty. Then, as though he had at last spent himself, he leaned forward on his elbows and rubbed hard at his eyes for a moment, and stared at the wall ahead. It was then that he saw Andrew Groves watching him in the doorway. He was wearing his gaudy electric-blue suit jacket, and his small, palish lips curled up with the usual friendly, debonair smile. He's suave, Edward thought, recalling all the other vivid jackets Andrew had worn—the vibrant rust, the throbbing apple green, the glowing reddish-burgundy, but today Andrew looked a little frayed around the edges. In the thick, clear yellowish light of Edward's office, his thinning blond hair looked tarnished now—and the skin of his long, angular face stretched tightly over the high cheekbones, as though ready to break. Andrew looked haggard for his twenty-some years; there was already a fixed stoop to his young shoulders. He's going to age fast, Edward told himself, and maybe he knows it. Maybe that's why he's in such a hurry to live it up now.

"Hello," the young man said, stepping in closer. "I thought I'd drop in and see how you're weathering the storm." He laughed but without malice.

"Oh...I'm weathering it all right," Edward said, smiling a bit. "So far anyway." He pushed some papers away, as though he had just finished working on something significant. But there was no need to pretend with Andrew. "Most every one around here seems to have gone into shock though," he added.

"They're a muddy-looking bunch, aren't they?" Andrew went on, not expecting an answer. "I hear this meeting's one of the biggest of the year. They've come to present you with the 'Keys to the Kingdom,' or something like that. 'Course they're going to look you over first, with a fine tooth comb."

"Now I'm really beginning to worry."

"Well, don't panic. You've always got my uncle to back you up. His word is gold. Besides, they haven't drawn blood—yet." Andrew laughed again, "But that's the price you pay, for showing promise. Now, me, I never show promise. They're just happy to have me out of sight." A chuckle now. "Anyway, it'll all pass over soon. They come and they go, thank heavens!" Andrew waited a minute now; then— "What I really came here for, is to say goodbye. I'm leaving for Chicago today. The old stamping grounds. Got the bags packed and everything ready to go."

"Oh..." Edward said, "that's good," sounding a little disappointed though. He realized now he was going to miss having Andrew

281

around. He brought a little sunshine into the place anyway. "I'm happy for you," he added quickly, a minute later.

"Thanks. So am I." Andrew hesitated—then smiled, and shoved out his hand. "Well, keep the chin up, old chum. Look them straight in the eye, don't let them bamboozle you." He laughed once more. "Maybe one of these days my uncle'll send you down to Chicago for a box of pencils, and then I can show you my kind of country. I'll fix us up with a few hot numbers from my little black book, and we'll have a screwin' good time."

"Sure," Edward said, shaking the hand offered to him, "sounds like fun." And he gave Andrew Groves a parting smile.

At 4:27 the mail girl came. Smiling, she took the pile of letters. Then the intercom sounded. It was Cynthia's voice: calm, confident, totally unemotional.

"Mr. Rydin wants you in the Conference Room at five o'clock."

"I'll be there."

Well…he had a half hour left.

At a minute before five Edward stood quietly before the darkly-stained door of the Conference Room. Well, here he was now—there was no use fighting it any more. Hadn't he admitted he had burned all the bridges behind him? There was no other place to go.

He opened the door, held on to it. The Conference Room was twice as large as the Big Office: banquet-sized. It had, of course, the same dark walnut paneling, the same carpeting and drapes, but there was one notable difference: it was empty except for a long, wide, sleek-topped table flanked on all sides by tall, very prestigious-looking brown leather chairs. The chairs appeared to be neither comfortable, nor otherwise, but strictly functional—strongly-built for the pursuit of heavy thinking. If they had a name, Edward thought, they'd probably be called the Profits and Margins Chairs. Above them and the table, a thick blackish cloud of cigar smoke floated about. The air was tight, suffocating, but the people there did not seem to mind at all.

The big banker was seated at the far end of the table, talking; but as soon as he saw Edward, he stood up.

"Ah..." he said, smiling heartily, "here he is now. The young man you've all been waiting to meet: Edward Aldworth—the *new* Vice-president of the *new* Mapleville Bank!" Edward gazed over the smiling faces—the blinking eyes and nodding heads. Then he smiled back and let the door go.

It was very dark outside, raining heavily. Edward felt the rain beating hard against his chest, against the thickness of his overcoat. Under the lamplight, again, the yellow Mercury waited. He walked over to it.

She opened the door for him. "Get in," she said. "You'll get all wet."

He nodded, got in.

Later he told himself it was the easiest thing he had ever had to do.

26

"I'm sorry," he heard himself say.

He was lying quite still on the large rumpled white bed in the white, white bedroom, staring at the stark white ceiling: from out of the corner of his left eye he could see her moving about at the dresser, stirring things—making short, nervous snatching noises, like a tiny mouse hunting for food. She was completely naked again, but now it did not matter, for her body was no longer a stranger to him. Only a few moments ago he had held it close in his arms, felt all the soft ripples of its nakedness, the urgent driving of its passions—the terrible, terrible mountings of its powers, which had, in the end, diminished his totally. "You're not a virgin, are you?" she had asked him, and he had shook his head; but already the little terrors had started to do their mischievousness inside of him, quenching what little power—strength he had left, until finally she had to pull away.

Now, of course, he knew how her face looked. He did not have to see it to know. It looked exactly as it had when she had left him on the bed—cold, pitiless, almost hateful.

"I suppose," he muttered now, "I've ruined another evening for you."

She turned to look at him, "Why don't you drink some more brandy?"

"Yes..." And he reached over for the glass on the bed table, drank from it slowly, steadily. He knew she waited now; but the longer he took the more time he had to prepare himself, to prepare to prove himself to her again, and he knew she knew that, he knew she knew what he was thinking.

At last he finished, and she said, "Why don't you have another for good measure?" and he nodded, filled the glass and drank again. When he emptied it the second time, he returned it to the table and lay back resting on the pillows again.

"Are you ready now?" she asked impatiently.

"Yes," and he watched her come toward him, the long, slender body seeming to cast a long dark shadow across the bed. Then—I'm making too much of this, he told himself.

She switched off the light.

"We'll try it this way, this time," she said, and climbed on top of him.

He lay alone again, on the bed. She had bathed and was now dressing herself in a sheer white lacy nightgown; a narrow, trailing white ribbon held back her dark hair. She was neither beautiful, nor otherwise, just a being standing there. Beads of sweat formed on his brow now—he felt strangely tired.

Suddenly he wondered what time it was. It had to be very late, if she was dressing for bed. He could not remember how long he had been here, in this room—or how many drinks he had had, or how many times she had gone to bed with him, but he sensed there had

285

been quite a few. Everything about this evening—from the moment he had got here—had seemed unfocused, fuzzy. Well, drinking did that.

"I'd better get dressed now," he said, and swung his legs over the edge of the bed, sat up. For a moment the room spun about him, then stopped—settled down. "I must have really drank a lot tonight," he said, rubbing the back of his head and smiling at her.

"You can stay for the night if you want," she offered.

"No, I'd better not. My parents would only think the worst. And they'd be right." He laughed shortly, then made a valiant attempt to stand up: his legs felt a little wobbly. At first he wasn't sure they'd be able to hold him up.

"Do you want me to make some black coffee?" she asked, watching him; but the way she had said it, the way she was looking at him now, told him it would be an imposition to her. She was ready for bed. It would only irritate her again, to make her wait for him. So he replied, "Don't bother. I'll be fine. Once I get outside, the cold air'll shake me up."

"It's up to you," and she started straightening the bed.

Slowly he made his way to the chair, where his clothes lay. He pulled on his underclothes, then his trousers and socks and shoes, then his shirt and suit jacket and coat. He buttoned the coat, and taking the tie shoved it down in its pocket.

When he was all ready to go, he looked back at her: she was already under the covers.

"Well… good night then," he said to her awkwardly.

"Good night," and she rolled over on her side, closed her eyes to sleep.

He let himself out quietly.

27

It was several weeks later—a Sunday. Roger Aldworth, standing half-turned before the wide bay window of the rose-colored living room of the house on Hobson Road, holding the newspaper tightly against his chest, perceived with cold critical eye the sudden sight of his son coming through the front door. Edward was slovenly dressed: his coat, which was improperly buttoned, hung lopsided about his shoulders, the white shirt peeking out from under it badly soiled at the collar, the tie askew. He looked as if he hadn't shaven or bathed for quite some time. The elder man, having never seen his son in so sorry a state, felt acute resentment. He was angry, too, because he had just taken up the newspaper in an attempt to get a few moments of calmness after a rather long, hectic conversation with his worried, near-hysterical wife. Worse yet, the hour was bad. Poor timing. At a quarter to nine the Sunday supper meal had long been over, and the food that lay awaiting Edward's arrival, dead cold.

"So you've finally decided to come home," the father blurted out caustically, turning to face his son fully. "Where've you been all this time, lying in some gutter? You certainly look it!"

Edward said nothing. He just smiled by the doorway.

"Well?" the voice came back sharply. "What have you got to say about it?" The father paused, then continued on hastily: "Have you any idea how worried your mother and I have been? And Mr. Rydin, too? He's been calling here every day, wondering what happened to you. He said you haven't been at the bank at all. You could have been lying dead somewhere, for all we knew."

Again, Edward didn't reply. He was standing a little off balance—suddenly his right shoulder collapsed, and he pulled it up quickly, to straighten it; but to no avail. His father had noticed.

Roger Aldworth sniffed in his son's direction now: "You've been drinking again. Is that how you spent your time—these weeks—drinking?"

Edward gave him a rather idiotic smile now.

"Well...!" the father said curtly. "I can certainly see you've been very busy. One big party after another, huh?" He made a quick wry face. "What are you trying to do, lose your job? Don't you care about your responsibilities at the bank? People are depending on you there!"

Again, no answer. Edward blinked his eyes a moment—then started across the living room slowly.

"Is there something wrong at the bank," the father went on, his eyes following him, "something you don't like? I can talk to Mr. Rydin. Maybe he can fix it."

No answer again.

"Then what is it?" Roger Aldworth said swiftly. A definite hostility was building up in his voice. "Is it that black friend of yours again? Has he contacted you about something? Does he still want you to go to New York with him?"

289

Edward stopped. He gazed back at his father and blinked his eyes again.

Roger Aldworth felt a rejection. "All right," he said more carefully, "if it isn't him, who is it? Me? Are you doing this out of spite, is that it? To get even with me for making you go back to the bank? You can tell me! I can take the blame!"

Nothing. Edward just stood there—blinking his eyes as before.

"All right," Roger Aldworth said tightly. "So you don't want to talk about it, huh? That's all right. I'm used to talking to myself now. I suppose it's your own business, if you want to throw your life out of the window like this!"

Edward looked a bit fidgety now. He began walking about.

"Now what are you doing?" Roger Aldworth asked irritably. He saw his son's eyes alight upon the serving cart in the dining room. Edward staggered toward it. "You needn't bother to look in there," the father said coldly. "It's empty. I took everything out."

Edward looked sad now. He put his finger up to his forehead thoughtfully—then smiling suddenly as though he had remembered something, he dug into one of his coat pockets and drew out a small flask. Unscrewing its top, he drank quickly.

"What's that?" his father demanded harshly. "Whiskey?" He frowned deeply, "So now you carry a bottle around with you, huh? You've stooped to *that!*" He turned away disgustedly.

Mrs. Aldworth came on the scene then.

"Look, Adele!" her husband said shortly. "Your son's back. And he's pie-eyed again!"

"Oh, Edward..." she muttered, half-relieved, half-distressed over her son's disheveled appearance. "Where have you been? We were so worried."

"He can't talk," Roger Aldworth said. "Cat's got his tongue!" He made another wry face. "I've been trying to have a sensible conversation with him since he got here, but so far I haven't succeeded. Either he blinks his eyes—" Roger Aldworth blinked his eyes now, "or smiles like this," then gave an exaggerated replica of Edward's smile.

"Oh..."she said worriedly, scrutinizing her son further. "Maybe he's ill. He looks so drawn."

"Oh, he's fine," her husband said, sarcastically. "He's been partying all this time. We're the ones who's going crazy!"

Edward went on drinking. He seemed unaffected by his father's words.

"See?" Roger Aldworth said, pointing a finger at his son. "He doesn't care about you or me or Mr. Rydin or the bank or anybody. All he cares about is that little bottle!"

She fell into silence then.

Roger Aldworth looked more severely at his son now: "Just how long do you intend to do this? Don't you have any intentions of going back to the bank?"

Edward shrugged.

"You don't know?" his father said, astounded. "What kind of attitude is that?" He paused—waited again for an answer that would not come. Then, "Don't you care about your job at all? Don't you

291

care if people talk? Mr. Rydin, out of the kindness of his heart, has made you the vice-president. Doesn't that mean *any*thing to you?" The tense, dark, questioning eyes behind the bulky horn-rimmed glasses stared out now in near-explosion.

"Roger…please," Mrs. Aldworth said. "Don't argue with him."

"Who's arguing?" he said, throwing a fast look at her over his shoulder. "I'm just talking to him. Can't a father talk to his son any more, or is that supposed to be a crime now, too?"

She fell back into silence.

Roger Aldworth reverted his attention to his son. "Maybe you can tell me one thing at least. If you're not going to work, what are you going to do? Lie around every day and drink?" Nothing. "See?" Roger Aldworth pointed his finger again. "That's what happens, when you give your children a fine education," he said. "In the end, they think they're too smart to even talk to you!" He stared at his son. "In all my born days, I never thought I'd live to see this! A son of mine turn into a *loafer*! A *drunkard!*" The eyes behind the spectacles were bulging out now.

"Roger…remember your high blood pressure," his wife cautioned.

"Tell it to him! He's the one who's giving it to me!"

Through all of this, Edward remained quite tranquil. He took another swallow.

"I don't know," Roger Aldworth said, turning away for a second. "It's like… talking to a dummy!" He shook his head severely. "I just wish somebody would tell me what's so awful about being a vice-president of a nice new bank, in your own hometown. I think that's pretty darn nice, if you ask me!" He looked at his wife again. "The trouble is, it all came too easy. He should have had to sweat his head off for ten or twenty years, as I had to!" He dropped his hands to his sides. "I don't know what's wrong with him," he said loosely then. "I can't talk to him any more. He's not my son any more. He's somebody else."

A long, complete silence followed. Then:

"Just what am I supposed to tell Mr. Rydin, huh?" Roger Aldworth asked, staring back at his son.

Edward gazed at his father quietly—then, in a soft, barely audible voice: "Tell him to go fuck the bank, Dad."

"*What?*" Roger Aldworth shouted now.

"What did he say?" Mrs. Aldworth asked, almost timidly, standing behind her husband and tugging at his shirtsleeve.

Roger Aldworth turned around swiftly. "*Your son said I should tell Mr. Rydin to go fuck the bank, Adele!*"

"Oh…" she said, shrinking back into oblivion again.

"Is that the way you talk in front of your mother now?" Roger Aldworth asked, his face trembling. "Gutter talk? Is that what they've taught you in college?"

"Shhhh!" Edward whispered suddenly, pointing to the flask. "They're listening to you."

"Who? Who's listening?" Roger Aldworth's eyes were rolling about in his face now.

"The little men in there," Edward explained, holding the bottle protectively against himself. "They're listening to everything you say. Levie, Gore, Stan..." His voice mumbled on into nothingness.

"I don't know what's wrong with him," Roger Aldworth said again, shaking his head. "He must have lost all his senses."

Edward screwed the top back on the bottle. Then he went to the stairs.

"Now where are you going?" his father shouted after him. "Up to your room to hide?" Roger Aldworth watched his son climb the stairs: Edward kept going up and up—until the door of his bedroom closed quietly. "Well...I'll tell you one thing," the father said to his wife. "If he thinks he's going to carry on like that under *this* roof, he's badly mistaken. He can just go right back to where he came from!"

28

He lay floating quietly within her, on the huge white bed. It was one of those rare moments of peace that he had had in the past few months—no past, no present, no future, just this floating, this carefree feeling of going nowhere, of belonging nowhere. But he knew it wouldn't last long. Either she would say or do something to spoil it, as she always had. And of course she did.

Stirring, she lifted the long dampened entanglement of dark hair from her face, and the strangely wide eyes with their heavily darkened lashes gazed at him with the same deliberate aloofness of before. And it broke then, in two—the peace inside him—as a twig breaks when someone steps upon it carelessly, severely. A small, thin, fragile twig which has been lying about through all the turmoils of winter, waiting to be broken.

He released her, and she got up quickly. She was always in as much hurry to get out of bed as she was to get into it. He watched the tall, slender, naked body with its long, smooth, model-like strides, cross the room to the bathroom, then the door closed and the tap water ran. It was always like this. First, the passion, then the coldness—the nothingness as though they had never really touched.

He lay still and stared at the sterile whiteness of the wall ahead: how many minutes had passed, he did not know; nor did he care.

Time was of no significance now. A minute here, an hour, a day—weeks, months passed, with no difference. It was always the same; the nothingness never changed, never stopped. Time stood still, uncaring, empty.

Presently the water stopped running and the door opened and she came out. She had on a soft satiny kimono type robe through which the tips of her breasts protruded very erectly, very rigidly. Though in her mind she had spent all her passion, her body had not yet let go of its. It was a hard, driving body, full of endless lust, and it was not unusual for it to demand sex four or five times a day; and on those days when he was so sodden with drink, when he could barely raise an arm let alone make love, it would lie beside him on the bed like a poisonous snake ready to strike. Well, one of these days it would; then he'd be dead. It would be over.

He watched her walk quickly to the dresser; bending over, the shadowy thickness of dark hair tumbling down over her face, she pulled out a drawer and took something out. He couldn't see what it was, but knew it was a cigarette. She always smoked after sex and bathing. A moment later, a thin—as yet indefinable swirl of smoke rose above her shoulders.

"Is that one of the regular ones," he asked, pulling himself up in the bed and settling his head against the pillows, "or those Q.T.'s you buy?" He knew she got all her regular cigarettes from her father's drugstore; the others—the marijuana ones (the Q.Ts. as she called them), from whom and where he did not especially care. When two people were dying together, neither one worried too much what the other was dying from. He only hoped that tonight she wouldn't be smoking the marijuana cigarettes because he wanted to talk to her, and you could never be sure what kind of mood she'd be in, if she did. Luckily, she didn't do it too often. Sometimes she wouldn't smoke one for weeks at a time, then she'd go on a binge like she'd never stop. She did everything that way—on impulse—indulging herself in every whim, to the limit. But in this, she was at least a little careful. He knew that if there was anything in the world that frightened her, it would be to be under the control of something or someone other than herself. She had to be totally free.

Well...he had had his binges too, plenty of them, so many in fact that he couldn't remember when last he had been completely sober. Christmas, yes, probably then—that far back, that long ago. Now it was turning spring, the weather warming and the days growing longer, when there would be more time to drink before the night came with its coal-blackness, its shadows in which one was forced to stare endlessly for hours, thinking of one's endless problems, unless of course one took the necessary precaution of paralyzing one's brain beforehand.

But today he wanted to be sober, to have this talk with her, if she'd let him. He hadn't had a single drink since two that afternoon, and now the clock said six.

Now, however, they were on this thing about the cigarettes, and it was his own fault: he had said something he shouldn't, and she had caught it, and there was no way to retract his words. They were gone, gone like all those days behind him—days of uselessness and moping

297

about, of drinking too much, of just waiting for her to come home so that the nothingness could start again. So he had to let it run its course.

She half-turned, smoking, holding the cigarette up in the air for him to see. But he didn't look at it. "I thought you weren't going to ask that question any more," she said with unmistakable iciness. "I hate people who keep tabs on me."

"You're right," he said. "I don't know what made me ask. I don't really care to know—it's your business." He let his gaze fall to the bed—the rumpled sheet, and with one pale, slightly trembling hand, tried to smooth it out but soon saw his effort was futile, as always, and stopped. "I was thinking today, that maybe we should go out somewhere one of these evenings. It'd do us both some good." He inhaled deeply now—trying to detect a sweet, pungent odor; but it wasn't there. He looked back at her.

"Where? The Albino's again?" She set the cigarette on the edge of a tiny white china ashtray and picked up the hairbrush.

"No, I know you don't want to go there," he answered. For a moment he watched the long, pointed fingernails working swiftly through the tangled ends: soon they'd all be separated, lying smoothly, and then she'd brush and brush and brush, at least a hundred strokes, until all the dark hairs lay gleaming like thick black satin about her face. "No..." he repeated slowly, "I thought maybe we could go somewhere for dinner, or take in a movie. Anything for a change."

"I'm perfectly satisfied to stay here," she said, not looking at him and flicking the brush briskly, "but if you want to go somewhere, you can. No one's holding you here."

"I didn't mean it that way," he said. "I don't want to go by myself. What would be the purpose of that?" He waited but no answer. "But, if you don't want to go, we won't. I just thought you might like the idea yourself. All we do is coop ourselves up here and make love. We never see anybody, or talk to anybody. Half the time we don't even talk to each other." He frowned.

"What do you want to talk about?" she asked, eyeing him in the mirror—the brush idle at her side now. A certain irritance had come into her voice. "Your father, or the bank you hate? Or that job you lost in New York? Or maybe your black friend still waiting to hear from you in Chicago? I've heard all of that a thousand times and it bores me to death!"

"I don't blame you," he said, dropping his gaze again. "It'd bore me too, if I had to listen to it that many times…"

It was true—he had talked and talked about it at least a thousand times, and she had the right to be bored. Anyone would. But it was funny, that the one person in the whole world who could care the least about it, had been the only one he could have told it all to. "No," he said. "I don't want to talk about that any more either. I'm through talking about it." He paused. "It's just that sometimes"—his voice grew slower again— "I can't help wondering where all this is going. When two people are together as much as we are, there ought to be something more than—the bed. Sex."

299

"What? Marriage?" She turned and stared at him with the wide black-mascara eyes: "I told you how I felt about that in the beginning."

"No. Not that," he said. "I don't want marriage any more than you do. God knows we'd never make it in that." He looked at her lingeringly now, as though he half couldn't control his eyes— "But there ought to be something more than this—some sort of decency— commitment."

"I can't live with commitments," she told him flatly. "That's your kind of life, not mine."

"Yes, you're right again." He nodded. "Well...don't mind me. I'm full of old remorses today," and looked away.

"Old remorses?" She put the brush down. "Sometimes I can't understand you at all. You're always talking in riddles. Why do you have to poke into things all the time? Why can't you just leave things alone, as they are?"

"I don't know. I really don't." He smiled a little. "I guess it's another one of my bad faults. I seem to have more than you bargained for."

"Well," she said abruptly, "I can't waste any more time on this." She drew on the cigarette again, then squashed it out. "I've got some work to do for Mr. Rydin tonight."

"Oh, sure," he said. "By all means do it. I don't want to waste any more of your time. I know you can't keep the big boss waiting."

"It pays for your liquor bills." Flatly, again.

"That it does." He turned his head now and smiled at the bottle waiting for him on the bed table: how considerate of her to remind him. It was time for another drink. He picked up the bottle and poured—only a few drops came out. He frowned again.

"There's another bottle in the kitchen," she told him, watching.

"I know. There's always another bottle."

She didn't say anything. She went to the door—then: "Do you want me to get it?"

"No, don't bother. I can still do that much for myself."

"Very well," and she left.

He finished the tiny bit in the glass, then threw his legs over the edge of the bed, and got up. Going to the kitchen, flicking on all the lights, he found the other bottle and brought it back—flung the empty one noisily into the white wastebasket and went into the bathroom, splashed himself with cold water, put on a pair of clean pajamas and climbed back into bed.

Several hours later, she came back to the room. She stood by the bed, naked.

"Are you asleep?" she asked, pulling the covers away from him impatiently, in the semi-darkness.

"No..." He rolled over on his back. "I'm not asleep..." But he had been asleep—partially asleep, a very light sleep—drifting somewhere between unconsciousness and reality. He tried to pry his eyes open.

She switched on the table lamp: it shown with a soft glow over her body: the full, rounded breasts, the strong, firm stomach, the thick black puff of pubic hair, waiting… He moved over on the bed, and she got on. Instantly, she straddled him, her hot breath coming down over his mouth, taking his breath away, while the long pointed fingernails clawed sensuously at his tired, warm flesh. Then they fumbled with the buttons of his fly, and when at last they found what they wanted, made their little insertion.

Gasping now, her mouth still hard upon him, he listened to the quick, steady rasping motions of her body against his. "Come, now," she said, drawing him closer; then, like a slow, lame, half-reluctant horse ready for pasture, he felt himself trotting to her step.

The second time around:

Again she was riding her poor, tired beast, digging the spurs into its aching sides, galloping, galloping wildly—rushing, rushing once more to that inevitable ending, when, at last, thoroughly exhausted, ravaged, its mouth frothed over.

After the love-making:

"Are you still angry with me?"

"I don't want to talk any more. I'm going to sleep now." And she turned off the light.

And he stared and stared into the groping depth of darkness all around him, the darkness that he knew would plague him until morning.

29

About a week later it happened: she came home very late one evening. She had never done that before.

Edward, lying naked under the soft downy white coverlet of the bed, woke suddenly in a state of confusion. What time was it anyway? He could not tell, for the little enameled alarm clock on the dresser, with its luminous hands and numbers, was turned away from him—but the room was in total darkness, as were the other rooms, so he knew it must be late. Where was she?

Reaching out with one groggy arm and turning on the light, angling his head severely to one side, chin tucked determinedly into the folds of the cover, eyes blinking profoundly, he finally saw what the clock said: 11:30. That *was* late. Where could she be at that hour? She certainly wasn't working at the bank.

Straightening now against the enormous white pillow that guardedly raised his head, Edward tried to remember—rather, to distinguish—what day this was. But all the days seemed to mingle together now, tightly, and at times it was difficult to tell which was which. So he tried the logical approach of dividing them into categories, which might help. For instance, he knew it couldn't be Sunday, for if it were she'd be home now; and it probably wasn't Monday, because he might remember that yesterday had been Sunday. Wednesdays the bank was closed, and Saturdays were half-days, and she'd have been home too. So that left Tuesday, Thursday, and Friday. On Fridays, the bank was open until eight and she was usually back no later than nine, unless something held her up. What could have held her up this long? This was no hour to be held up.

He kept trying to think. He could call the switchboard and find out what had happened; but that didn't make any sense. The bank was closed at this hour, and the switchboard wouldn't answer.

While all these things were jabbering and bouncing about in his tired, yet sleepy brain, calling for some kind of conclusion, Edward became aware that his mouth felt very dry. In fact, it was getting drier by the minute. His stomach felt empty too, but he gave that no consideration. If someone were to ask him at that moment, when he had last eaten, he would not have been able to say. The truth is, when a man reaches a state such as this—of mental stupor, oblivion— neither sober, nor drunk—the latter course seems the simplest to take. Decline is always so much easier than the climb back up to where one has lost footing in the first place.

So, now, Edward's mind was solely on having a drink. Pulling himself up from the cover, he gazed down at his naked navel but for a second: where his pajamas were, had gone to, did not interest him at all. For already the Pearly Gates of Decline had opened, beckoned him, and he was descending; and in a short time (Time moved quickly at this point), he would be feeling no pain, no stress, no bewilderment, of mind or body.

With head turned sharply sideways, eyes set in full admiration of a tall, dark, vaguely labeled (labels meant nothing either) bottle on the night table, he reached out and drank rapidly from its uncorked, heavenly aromatic mouth. As he was doing this, a key turned in the front door and she stepped, with her high, clicking heels, into the gray shadowy foyer. Edward saw her lay her coat on the chair there; then, seeing the light in the bedroom, she came directly toward it.

He quickly picked up the glass next to the bottle, filled it, and put the bottle down.

"Oh, you're up," she said with disappointment, noting his upright position in the bed. "I thought you'd be asleep by now."

"I was. I just woke up a little while ago." Thoughtfully he watched her move to the dresser—look at herself in the mirror. "What kept you so long? It's nearly midnight."

"There was a last-minute meeting," she answered matter-of-factly. She took some pins from her hair and fluffed it out. She seemed a-ware that his eyes were watching her constantly, but avoided looking at him. "Then we all went out to eat," she added.

"Oh, that explains it," he said. He rested back against the pillow: So it had to be Friday. That was the day the big banker held most of the meetings, last-minute or otherwise. "Gives everyone something to think about over the weekend," he'd say with one of his hearty laughs. Well, he wasn't going to make the mistake now of asking what day it was, for he had done that once, and she had only given him an odd look. Instead: "Who's 'we all'?"

"Mr. Rydin and I, and the new vice-president, Mr. Markin."

"It must have been a full course meal," Edward remarked now, "to last this long."

305

"No…" she said, turning toward him. Then she began unbuttoning her blouse. "Larry didn't bring his car along, and Mr. Rydin asked if I could drive him home, which I did. He wanted to drop off some papers at Mr. Happle's house."

"Oh, so it's *Larry* now?" No answer, Edward diverted his thoughts then to the Head of the Loan Department—poor, meek Mr. Happle, of the dark blue suit and shiny new black leather attaché case. He wondered if the suit and briefcase weren't beginning to show some wear by now. "I suppose it was some more of those 'surprise' foreclosures," he said somewhat broadly. "They must be pretty busy at the bank these days, to work this late."

"I didn't ask." Coolly.

Edward watched her slip off the skirt now—carry it to the closet: "This Larry—is he married? With wife?" His voice sounded a trifle sarcastic.

"No."

"How convenient." He gazed deeply into the glass he was holding and took a mouthful. "I suppose he's good-looking, too?"

She turned around abruptly now, stared at him a minute, the wide, black mascara eyes bolting straight through him. "I won't be cross-examined this way," she told him, "by you or anyone else. This isn't a courtroom. If you're that interested, why don't you go down to the bank and find out?"

"I would, if I thought it would do any good." But he wouldn't, and he knew he wouldn't, and so did she. It was just another excuse.

"I can't talk to you any more," she said irritably. "You're always going off in different directions."

"Don't let that bother you." He smiled above the glass: "I can't talk to myself so good any more, either," and took another swallow.

"I suppose you were doing *that* all day?" she questioned, watching him drink.

"Nearly. The other times I slept."

She turned away in disgust.

A relatively long silence prevailed then between them, and Edward thought it the perfect time—interlude—for another drink. He finished the one he was holding, poured another and finished that, then, pouring the third, leaned back again and rested the glass precariously on his bare chest. It felt pleasant, soothing there. Closing his eyes, he suddenly realized he was feeling quite warm—very warm in fact: the cold-looking white bedroom seemed to generate a sudden impossible heat. He kicked off the cover a little, stuck one naked leg out to cool.

She stopped what she was doing, gazed down at it dangling there, then went on undressing. Soon she was standing before the dresser completely naked.

"Well," she said impatiently, "are we going to fuck or not?"

"Must you use that kind of language?" he said with a frown.

"What difference does it make?" She looked annoyed again. "You make too much out of everything." But he knew if she wanted to, she would have said it again, just to displease him.

He set the glass back on the table and kicked off the cover all the way, lying there waiting for her to come to him: the high, perfectly rounded full breasts swayed gently with her every movement, like two platters suspended in air. She could be beautiful, he told himself, she could be, if she wasn't so hard, so cold. But she wants to be this way. And no one as hard and cold as she can ever be beautiful.

She paused at the bed, the wide, thickly-fringed eyes staring down at him in chilling scrutiny; then the cold, white face softened somewhat, and she swooped down over him, like a deep, dark enveloping shadow. Like those deep, dark, enveloping shadows of the nights he dreaded so much. She's part of them, he thought. She's part of them.

Instantly, the fingers began their probing—manipulation. The black mascara eyes were very close now, blurring like lobes of sunflower centers into the cold-whiteness of the face. He touched one breast, thinking. She has no feeling for anyone or anything, except this. Only her body is warm. The face, always cold; the eyes, even colder.

She pressed her lips to his chest now, and the long tapered fingernails made soft, dragging sounds through the tufts of hair; then laid herself on top of him, her favorite position. The firm, young ridges of her body sank heavily, mercilessly into his tired, aching, half-drunken flesh. Then her mouth clamped down over his, tightly, like a vise, and she bit him, parted his lips, the scorching heat of her throbbing breath cutting painfully into the wound, filling him, engulfing his soul. The thick dark puff of pubic hair thrust itself now against him—eagerly, lustfully. This is Whoredom, he told himself; my own particular hell. Each day I'm raped of my thoughts and feelings, my own desires, until one day there will be nothing left of me but a dried-up shell. And she won't like that either.

The thick dark puff thrust again—alerting, impatiently. She's an unending element, Edward went on thinking, constantly working on my mind and body, breaking down my defenses. The more I give to her the more she wants, and the more she wants, the less I have to give. I'm like a light bulb she turns on and off whenever she chooses. What will happen when I finally burn out? Will she toss me away and get a new one? Again—the dark puff thrust. The whole strength of human dignity, Edward theorized now, is totally shattered in this one act, this one gesture, which necessitates that one humble oneself completely; yet it is man's whole existence, his common function and his plight, and when it is over, he is expected to go on with some sort of dignity again. Well, why should he feel so ashamed? It wasn't he who had made love to her all those times, but the bottles—the many, many, many bottles... The dark puff pushed hard now, grinding all its anger into his genitals. He seemed to ache all over. God! how he wished he could have another drink.

He tried to make love now, he tried so hard, but the more he tried the more difficult it became, and the less there was to try with. "I can't," he finally said silently. "Can't she see that—that I'm dying inside? Passion is only for the living, the very alive—" But he remained silent. He knew how much she hated his weaknesses.

So he kept on trying, and her hands, her body, kept making their vigorous, sensuous demands; but nothing. The minutes seemed to spin off into hours, long, hard, cruel hours (he felt so tired now), then at last something happened, something he had almost not been aware of: he felt a slight urging. A tiny fire had lit itself inside him, so small though, and she knew it, and she kept pumping, pumping, trying to give it more life, trying to make sure it would not go out. And still that feeling of hopelessness, of failure, kept clinging to him. All around him he could feel the cold-whiteness of the room, watching. So much like her face, he thought. The trouble is, he explained now to himself, there has never been anything between us—she and I—but this—this eternal whiteness, this eternal coldness, this eternal defeat. I am of defeat. I *am* defeat.

He went on trying; but as before, the more he tried the more wrongly it went. Despite all his efforts, his body persistently went its own way—slowing down, retracting itself, growing limp again. Finally, it was gone, all gone; it had all slipped away. The tiny fire, which had burned for so short a time, had died out, deserted him. He made yet another effort; then stopped. Lay still.

She lay still now, too, for a second, waiting—waiting for that which was not coming; then she raised herself and looked down: the horrible deflated thing lay smugly now, on its side.

He expected her to get up now, leave him, but instead she lay back on him, and slowly the fingers began moving again—subtly now, though, making soft, tranquil ripples across his flesh. Her mouth rested on his in almost comforting warmness. She won't let me go, he thought. Placing both hands on her breasts this time, he could feel the hardened nipples pulsating in his palms. She's ready again, Edward thought glumly; she's always ready. If only she could be someone else—someone kind and gentle, someone capable of loving and being loved...She was fondling now that which she desired, and he listened to the passionate, stealthy motions of her body; she was being very cautious this time, lest she move too quickly, too vigorously and all too consumingly, all might be lost again. Well, he wouldn't look at her. He didn't have to look at her. He knew that cold white face by heart.

Now she lay tightly over him, they were almost like one and the smoldering flames of her body were penetrating his, warming all its cold parts. Oh God, he thought, help me to complete it this time. Help me to feel like a man. He listened again—to their muffled stirrings on the bed. The eyes, with their thick black sockets, seemed to be floating up to him now ...I must not think any more, he told himself. I MUST NOT THINK! Then a moment later, it all gave way inside him, bittersweet joy filled him. Suddenly all his thoughts seemed too burdensome, and he closed his eyes, moved slowly with the quiet, regular beat of her body. The fire lit again, and this time he caught it, ran with it. He ran and ran, and ran, until he was nearly out of breath, his heart pounding frantically. I'm alive, he thought; I'm still alive!. Then, as though in retaliation, he turned her over, lay upon her instead, pounding his weight against her body. He heard her take a deep, agonizing breath—then the moisture of her body flowed over him like warm milk.

When it was over, when he had finished as best as any man could in his predicament, he rolled off her onto his back and stared up at the ceiling. She lay there motionlessly for a few seconds beside him— then her body stiffened, molded itself back into the aloofness. Brushing the long muddled strands of dark hair from her forehead, she sat up without looking at him, and moved away. The falseness of it all, Edward thought; sex. We each put on our little masks, pretend to be something we're not, and when it's over, we're but ourselves again. It's a farce—this masquerade of sex.

He watched the strong, unblemished back move further away. Well, she was angry—angrier than before; angrier than she'd ever been. Their love-making had been too long, too laborious for her to enjoy it completely. She hated things dragged out. She liked them to be over with quickly, so she could start anew. He would have to apologize.

"I'm sorry it took so long," he said as she headed toward the bathroom. "I guess I must have drank and slept too much today."

She spun around suddenly—the cold white face with its black mascara eyes glaring at him now. "You're always drinking and sleeping too much!" she said sharply. "That's all you ever do is drink and sleep too much!"

"I'm sorry," he said again. "I always thought that was the one thing you approved of—my drinking."

"That was before it made you into a bore!"

"Is that what I am to you now—a bore?" He smiled at her sadly.

The glaring face went on, pitilessly: "I can't stand people who feel sorry for themselves all the time! All you do is lie in that bed all day and drink. If you're not drinking, then you're thinking your morbid thoughts!"

"When I stop thinking," he told her, "I'll be dead. That's all I've got left to do, think and die."

"Die?" she said. "Is that what you want? Why don't you drink yourself to death, then?"

"I'm trying to."

She turned away disgustedly. "You don't even take baths any more. You smell bad!"

"I'll take one tomorrow," he said.

"Tomorrow, I don't care what you do!"

She went into the bathroom and slammed the door.

Edward picked up the glass again, and finished the drink, then poured another. A few minutes later, she came out. She was still naked.

She went over to the closet again. He thought she was going to put on her nightgown now, get ready for bed, but instead she took out a pair of black slacks and a red sweater. She began dressing—put her bra back on, and panties.

"Where are you going now?" he asked her.

"I've got an appointment to meet someone," she answered without looking at him once.

"At this hour?" Edward glanced at the dresser-clock once again: "It's almost one."

She didn't say anything. She kept on dressing.

"Who is it? You can tell me."

No reply.

"It's not business this time, is it?"

"No."

She put on the slacks and sweater, and took a leather belt from the rack on the back of the door, encircled her waist with it, tightly. Then she sat down to put on her shoes. Edward watched her silently for a moment—then, slowly: "It's all over for us, isn't it? There's somebody else now? We're never going to make love again—" Why should that bother him now, though—making love? Wasn't that the most degrading, demoralizing part of it all? He ought to be glad to be free of it. "Tell me who it is. I want to know."

"What difference does it make?" she said, looking at him wearily. She stood up and straightened the slacks about her hips.

"It makes all the difference in the world to me," he said. "I think I've got the right to know." No answer. "Is it that new vice-president, Larry? Are you going to bed with him now?" Again, no answer. "Or maybe it's the big banker himself. His wife is still in Chicago—" Still, no answer. "All right," he said, "if it's not one of those two, then it's got to be the old man with the Cadillac. From Philadelphia. Maybe he's here for another visit. Maybe he's the one who supplies you with those other cigarettes—the Q Ts."

'Who told you about him?" she asked immediately.

"Everybody knows about him. The whole town knows." Of course there might be a few who didn't—his parents, for instance, or hers. But there was no need to go into details. She was sufficiently infuriated.

"I should never have come back here!" she told him.

"No, you shouldn't have. And neither should I—but we're here just the same."

She began to move about swiftly now—she went to the dresser, ran the brush through her hair a few times rearranging it a little about her face, then pulled a tissue from the white cardboard box and blotted her lips. She's in a hurry, Edward thought; there was a certain carelessness about her he had never seen before. He watched her draw a scarlet line with the lipstick. Then she began working on the eyes, putting on another thick coat of mascara. When she was done they looked like two black slits in the cold, white face.

"I know I'm not a very good lover," Edward told her slowly, "that I've spoiled a lot of your times, and I'm sorry. Most of all, I'm sorry about being sorry all the time, because I know you hated that, too."

"Talk, talk, talk!" she said. "That's all you want to do! I don't want to talk about it any more!"

"Then we won't."

She came back to the bed and pulled out a faded blue over-night bag from underneath it, and set it down near Edward's feet; then she began taking things from the drawers—stockings, bits of lingerie, a fresh nightgown. Well, at least she wasn't taking too much. She wasn't planning on staying away too long.

"Maybe we could try a little harder," he began again. He couldn't help it.

"For what?" she said, glancing at him coldly. "Nothing? There's nothing to try for."

"You're right. Absolutely right." So she knew about the nothingness too. That made it unanimous. "Then it's finished—just like that?" he asked her in a soft voice.

She looked at him again. "You're not the first, and you won't be the last. I told you in the beginning, my life is my own. I made no promises. No one forced you here."

That was true: no one had forced him. He had come at his own free will. On that cold, rainy night of the board meeting, she had waited for him in her car, had opened the door and said, "Get in. You'll get all wet," but it was he who had gotten in. No one had pushed him. So, why had he come then? He hadn't wanted to, he hadn't even wanted to stay. He had come here because it didn't matter any more. He had done so many things he hadn't wanted to do, that this one more thing didn't matter any more either.

Well, now that he was down, really low, she was through with him. Well, what else had he expected? When you start with nothing, you end up with nothing. You can't get something from nothing.

She had said he had bored her; how many people had he bored in his life? His parents, his sister? Jonah, too? Had he bored them all with the promises he knew he could never keep? Well, it was over now, all the useless efforts, the hopes, all gone, done with, finished! And whose fault was it again? *His.* He had gone along blindly in everything, waiting too long, waiting until it was too late, hoping that something would come along to change things, when it never had, when he even knew it never would. It was the pattern of his life. Everything had a pattern.

He took another mouthful. He was getting very drunk now, he supposed; he could go on no further. The whiskey was churning up inside him, climbing the sides of his face, and soon it would reach the top, his head, blow it off. That was good. Without a head he couldn't think any more. Hadn't she said she hated his thinking all the time too?— He raised the glass to his mouth again, then stared off across the room into the dresser-mirror: a stranger's face gaped back at him—bearded, gaunt, disheveled. I don't know you, he thought. Where am I? I'm lost. I'll never find myself again…

"But where will I go?" he heard himself ask her, despairingly. Why was he holding on, still to nothing? Didn't he hate begging? Hadn't he hated it when his father had begged for that job with Mr. Rydin? So why was he doing it now, himself?

"You can always go back to your parents," she told him. "I'm sure they'll take you back."

"Like this?" He pointed to the distorted image in the mirror: "I can't go back looking like this!"

"That's your problem, then," she said coldly. "We all have our own problems."

Well, there it was again! His old contender come back to haunt him— "Conformity," he mumbled, half to himself, half to her.

"*What*?" she asked irritably. The black slits suddenly widened in the cold, white face—

317

"I was just thinking about the Great American Trap," he told her, "how once it gets you, it never lets go. You start out being yourself, and then it keeps taking pieces out of you until one day you don't even know what you are any more. But you don't have to worry, it'll never get you. You're immune."

"I don't know what you're talking about," she said. "I never know what you're talking about." The black slits widened once more.

"Well…it doesn't matter now." He threw his head back, finished drinking, and returned the glass to the table. When he looked back at her, the eyes had changed again: now they were running—running across her face. Soon they'd fall off! He put his hands up, to catch them.

"What's the matter with you now?" she asked with cold sharpness, the eyes becoming intact again.

"I just thought I saw something falling in the air," he told her quietly.

"I think you're sick." But she kept standing there, as though she expected something more to happen, and when it didn't, "You'd better see a doctor."

"Probably." He resettled himself against the bed pillow and watched her go back to the dresser. She took a bracelet from the jewelry box and snapped it closed quickly over her wrist, then reached for one of the perfume bottles, and sprayed herself lavishly. Instantly the room reeked with heavy scent. "I thought you were through using that horrible stuff," he told her gloomily.

"I've decided to go back to it." She picked up the hairbrush now, and the make-up, and tossed them into the bag with the other things.

"You know..." he said softly, "you're just one step up from a whore."

"Yes, I know." She stood still for a moment, then smiled—the first smile she had ever given him, and the black slits lifted themselves pointedly, standing almost on end; the nostrils flared; the scarlet mouth dipped uncouthly into its corners. Don't smile, Edward thought, don't ever smile. It only makes you ugly.

She moved again, and suddenly he felt a chill come over him: the room seemed so cold now, like a sheet of ice holding him. Maybe I'm dying, he thought. Well, when one procrastinated enough to oneself, and to others as well, a part of one had to die. She'd die someday too, when all the passion of hers ran out. The room was dead already, though. A white sheeted death...

She finally zipped up the bag. "I'm going now."

Go, he thought, I don't care any more. But deep inside him, he could hear the boys at Sunday School laughing again. They were always laughing.

She picked up the overnight bag and slung it over one shoulder, and went to the door. "I won't be back until late Sunday night. If you want, you can stay here till then." Her face, her voice were impeccably cold. "Just drop the key into the mailbox downstairs."

"Thanks." He looked away. "It's funny...isn't it?" he said slowly, hollowly. "We never even got to the part of liking each other." But she didn't answer. And when he looked back she was already gone.

He lay very still then, listened—waited for the sound of her closing the front door; when she did, he rolled over on his side. Shutting his eyes tightly, he wished he would die soon.

30

Suzanne Aldworth Delingham closed the bedroom door softly behind her, shutting out the accentuated shouts of her parents that were coming from downstairs. Here, though, all was quiet. Too quiet. She looked about the room, at the blue walls and blue carpeting and still bluer sky at the window, which was slowly deepening into shadows, morose clouds, waiting to put on its early evening wrapper. She never liked this room, never would, for it was always too sad, too dreary. And now the quietness in it frightened her. The evening coming also frightened her.

She walked up to the bed and looked at the motionless, sleeping form lying there. Her brother looked so quiet, too. Not a quiver, not a sound. He slept so deeply.

She gazed down at the tousled head resting against the pillows: how pale the face looked, how drawn and tired. Oh, God, don't let her brother be sick. She cupped her hands to her breasts, sat down on the little maple chair next to the bed and began to weep.

"Oh, Eddie! Eddie!" she gasped suddenly, the tears flowing down her cheeks unchecked. "Why couldn't you fight them? Why did you have to let them win again?" She laid one hand softly on the sheet; for an instant she thought he stirred, took a deep breath, but she could not be sure. His sleep was so deep, so deep.

He's dreaming. He's dreaming of something pleasant, she thought, seeing the calmness on his face. Her poor, misguided brother…Oh, God, help him!

She began to cry heavily now: she had promised herself she wouldn't. She mustn't wake him. Better he sleep, grow stronger. He was home now, at least he was home—where he could be looked after.

She looked about her again, and saw the half-empty bottle of whiskey on the bed table. She picked it up and put its top back, held it as she sat there. The more she looked at her brother, the tighter she held the bottle. It was as though that was all that was left of him, this bottle—where had his smiling, hopeful, dear face gone to? Surely, this object before her, looking more dead than alive, could not be him. Oh, God! God! Frightened tears came into her eyes now.

What could she do? What could anyone do? He lay there, so still. He was like a veil of blue darkness, himself. Gaunt. So gaunt. He had always been thin, but not so thin as this. Hadn't he eaten at all those months he'd been away?

Suddenly, they seemed to be all alone in the world—she and him. All alone.

She sat there, and the room grew darker. Her eyes held the sleeping form of the man as though they were afraid to let go. She heard the minutes ticking off the little maple wall-clock. Minutes! What were minutes? A whole lifetime could go by now, for all she cared! Something had to be done for her brother. He couldn't go on sleeping this way.

How long she sat there, she did not quite know. The room was getting very dark now. She could see the stars twinkling in the sky, beyond the window. Her brother was a dark blob on the bed, and soon his face would be lost to her, as though forever. "I must put the light on," she told herself. "I must not leave him in the dark this way."

She knew she had to go now. She started to cry again, but stopped—that, nothing like that could help. Still holding the bottle, she stood up and switched on the lamp on the table, and tried to smile down at her brother. Maybe if he could see her smiling at him, he would be better. Oh God, please make him better.

She touched his hand, his face, the cover near his chin. One soft little dark curl against the pillow. "I'll be back," she told him. "Don't worry. I'll be back."

She tiptoed away then—tears spilling from her eyes again. He must not see her cry. No good. She must be brave. She must be brave for him, as he would be for her. "Sleep good," she said, turning back to the quiet form. "Tomorrow we'll think of something."

She opened the door. The hallway was quiet now, thank God. She tiptoed out, closed the door softly—holding the bottle tightly against her.

31

"Yes! Yes! Yes!" Roger Aldworth shouted into the phone. "I told you before! I want an ambulance immediately! It's my son—Edward Aldworth. He's locked himself in his room, and he won't come out." Roger Aldworth's voice grew stouter by the minute, "Yes! Yes! That's the correct address." A brief pause. "Is Dr. Schuyler there? He can't come to the phone right now? Well I spoke to him earlier. He knows all about this." Another pause. "Yes, yes. All right! Of course we'll wait."

Roger Aldworth set the receiver down now and frowned. "What else do they expect us to do?" He looked over at his wife then, who was hunched in her chair, sobbing. "Oh, for heaven's sake, Adele! You've got to get yourself together."

She nodded and fumbled with her handkerchief. "It just seems so heartless..."

"Well..." her husband said, "we can't let him stay up there like that! You don't want him to come out dead, do you?"

"No..." She calmed herself a bit and wiped her eyes.

"It's the only thing we can do," Roger Aldworth went on, less provocatively. "It's our duty—our responsibility as parents." He frowned again. "They'll know how to handle him. They won't take any of his nonsense."

"But he's our son, Roger..." she protested again.

"No! That's not our son up there, Adele," her husband counteracted almost hostilely, pointing up toward the stairs. "Our son wouldn't do such a thing! What we've got on our hands, now, is a *Mr. Hyde*. And we've got to act accordingly!"

His wife looked dismal.

"Dr. Schuyler's handled hundreds of cases like this. He told me so. He'll know what to do."

"But I read somewhere..." she said, looking teary-eyed again, "that they put alcoholics through so many things—"

"Edward's not an alcoholic," her husband corrected her. "There's never been an alcoholic in my family, nor yours. He's just been lying around too much, that's all, with nothing to do. They'll straighten him out, you'll see."

"I hope so." She looked thoughtful then.

The doorbell rang now.

Roger Aldworth went to the door and opened it: three men stood there in long white coats, one carrying a small black bag. "It's upstairs—first door to the right. You'll have to push it in. He's got it bolted from the inside."

Two of the men—younger, thinner and more animated than the one with the bag—climbed the stairs immediately. Roger Aldworth watched them dully.

"How long has he locked himself up there?" the remaining man asked, setting the bag down and bringing forth a clipboard he had hidden under his arm, on which he jotted down something. "Four days," Roger Aldworth told him, looking away.

"Why didn't you call sooner?" The white-coated man looked slightly upset, raising one impertinent eyebrow.

"Why?" Roger Aldworth assailed him indignantly. "Because we thought he would eventually come out, that's why!"

The man calmed himself instantly and made a notation. "Has he eaten anything in all that time?"

"How would we know? He won't even talk to us. We've been putting food by the door, but he hasn't touched any of it."

The man picked up the black bag now, and climbed the stairs too.

"Questions!" Roger Aldworth muttered to himself grimly. "That's all they do, is ask questions! If we knew the answers, we wouldn't need them!"

"They won't put Edward in a strait jacket, will they?" his wife asked worriedly, from across the room.

"Of course not! He's not *insane*. There's nothing wrong with his mind."

A loud, thudding sound was heard now—then some muffled skirmishes. Roger Aldworth watched the stairs attentively now: a minute later, the two men who had gone up first, came down running.

"What's the matter?" he asked them, his face looking suddenly strained.

"We're going to have to use the stretcher," one of them answered excitedly, gulping.

"Oh…" Adele Aldworth moaned in the background.

"It doesn't mean a thing," her husband told her, trying to console her in his gruffy way. "They always carry them out that way, when they're boozed up."

The two men came back into the house, bounded up the stairs again.

"We mustn't let ourselves start worrying for nothing," Roger Aldworth added. "There's nothing to worry about. He's in capable hands." He stood still though and listened carefully: there were more noises, but softer, more subtler ones. He sighed thankfully. "He's probably just asleep," he remarked then. "That's all he's been doing here lately—sleeping. I can't understand how a person can get so tired from doing nothing. He hasn't worked a day in almost a whole year!"

There was another rumble, then the three men came down with the stretcher, the man with the bag in front of the other two. He stepped toward the Aldworths again.

"How is he?" Roger Aldworth asked instantly, dragging his eyes away from the still, white sheeted form on the stretcher—which now was supposed to represent the son he had raised, the son he had been so proud of, for graduating from Harvard Law School, the son he had had such high hopes for.

"He seems okay," the man answered. "He might be a little dehydrated, though."

"*Dehydrated?*" Roger Aldworth gave a quick, caustic laugh. "With all that liquor in him? I think that's hardly possible!"

"It happens occasionally," the man said, calming once more, "when there's not a proper balance of food and other liquids for a long period of time." He pushed the clipboard under his arm then: Roger Aldworth could see there were many, many notations on it now and wondered what all he could have written in so short a time.

"You won't do anything to hurt him, will you?" Adele Aldworth put in. "He was always such a good boy."

"No ma'am." The man looked into the fretful face—the swollen, red eyes. "We won't hurt him any more than he's been hurting himself already."

"That's fair enough, isn't it, Adele?" her husband asked her, looking swiftly at his son. "What more could you ask for? You want him well again, don't you?"

She didn't say anything more.

The other two men were grappling now with the stretcher, trying to pull it through the doorway, and the third one went over and held the door open for them.

"I suppose you'll want us to follow you?" Roger Aldworth asked, watching dully again.

"I don't think that'll be necessary," the man with the bag answered, looking back into the face full of distraught—the swollen, red eyes. "Dr. Schuyler'll call you later. You can make arrangements then." To the wife, he said: "All we'll be doing today, ma'am, is making tests. We won't know anything concrete until tomorrow at least."

"Very well," Roger Aldworth said, looking relieved. The very thought of having to drive down to the hospital, following the screeching sound of the ambulance, with his wife sobbing on the front seat beside him, did not especially appeal to him just then. He needed some time to get himself together too. He'd sooner wait for the doctor to call first.

Finally the door closed. He was alone with his wife again. "Well...that's done," he mumbled, sighing heavily. He stood quietly and listened to the sound of the ambulance starting up, then looked toward the stairs: "I suppose we ought to go up now, and see how bad the damage is."

"Do you think we have the right?" his wife asked hesitantly. She rose from her chair and stared about her: This was the house she had known all her life, the house she had been born in—and her children too, but now there was a strange kind of stillness in it, that almost frightened her. "It's his room—" she added.

"Of course we have the right," her husband said, looking at her almost angrily. "It's *our* house, isn't it?"

She nodded.

They went up the stairs together, slowly.

The door to their son's bedroom was partially open, its fine old varnished mahogany splintered and spoiled in spots; from its jagged side a crude block of wood protruded out like an odious wart—whose sole purpose had been to shut out the rest of the world. "I don't know why he had to do that," Roger Aldworth said, his eyes resting upon it. "All he had to do was tell us he wanted to be left alone." He touched the door almost devotedly: "Well...I suppose we'll have to get a new one. They don't make them like the old ones any more," he commented.

329

He pushed the injured door open all the way now, and a yet greater disorder revealed itself: the room beyond seemed torn apart— emotionally as well as physically. The lace curtains at the windows, normally crisp and sparkling white, were cut in places, held back shabbily with pieces of dirty string; the bedclothes, soiled and dismembered also, lay in a careless heap on the floor; and there were endless empty bottles of liquor about, broken glasses strewn across the carpet. A heavy, stale odor covered everything.

Roger Aldworth stared into the room, unbelievingly. "What a mess," he muttered. "You'd think he was brought up in a pig pen." He stepped inside and walked about for a moment, then stopped short— "My God..." he said in a deeply vibrating voice, covering his nose instantly with his hand. "He could have at least had the decency to use the *bathroom!*"

32

Doctor Schuyler's office was large enough to be comfortable and yet, with its explicit frankness, small enough to be otherwise. In almost its entirety, it was "hospital white," the walls and doors, the sleek polished tiled floor, the laminated broadness of the impeccably uncluttered desk, and the vagueness of the sheer curtains, which, somewhat hopelessly, made a futile attempt to shut out the visible signs of the outside world. In this hospital, within the four gigantic, squared-off walls, was a world of its own—a private kind of prison full of pain and suffering, of life dissipated, of shattered hopes and dreams, lonely hearts, broken hearts, mending hearts, retreat, screaming childlike innocence and sadistic calmness, of roguish restraint and medicinal expectorants, enema bags, stomach pumps, tourniquets, of glazed derelict eyes staring out of deadlike, masked faces. In this world, its world, were all the quiet and stormy rages of tormented souls.

Beyond all this whiteness, however, of physician-and-nurse-and-patient, was one breakthrough of color—vivid, surging life: an enormous fish tank stood the length of the wall behind the doctor's desk, groping out through the soberness of the format with glowing, almost hellish carnival colors. Roger Aldworth, sitting quietly, perceptively, watched the tiny fish fluttering and skeltering about, through the illuminated bubbly waters, like children at play. How simple it was to be a fish, he thought; to be put on this earth to do just one thing—swim, an inborn talent and capability. If man could only have it as simple. His wife, too, beside him, gazed quietly at the colorful tank, hands folded motionlessly in the lap of her gray flannel skirt. Beside her, to the left, on a chrome-and-wooden chair was a staggering heap of coats, her thick mauve woolen and her husband's black one, which altogether made something of a barrier between her and the huge white door which was soon to open. She spoke suddenly: "Do you think they'll let us see Edward today?"

"I don't know," her husband answered, taking his eyes off the fish tank a moment. "We'll ask."

Then a minute later, the door swung open and a man entered with quick, springy, agitated steps. He was lean—very sparse-looking in a starkly white frock coat. He had olive skin, black hair and black little eyes, a tightly clenched mouth, and small, impatient hands which promptly shook Roger Aldworth's extended hand, then pulled the chair out from the desk. Though he could be no more than thirty-four or so, he was already balding severely, as if the heavy prostrating burdens of the profession had vindictively robbed him of the vigors of his youth. His face showed the worn map of life. Just moments before, he had disassociated himself from a young girl, scarcely seventeen, with both wrists slashed. A flower not yet fully bloomed but already plucked and ravished. Pregnancy. Drugs. Betrayal, regret, guilt, loathsomeness for life. Parents, wide-eyed, unforgiving: love, hurt, bewilderment, fear, anger. Well, here now was another such near-casualty, another case of such faces. What could he tell them, he wondered, that would make them stop looking like that? He had seen too much, he was so full of the miseries and failings of the world that sometimes nothing would come out. He could say nothing. He did not even know what to call it. He knew what it was, saw it immediately, yet it had no name. It had too many names, perhaps, all turned and twisted together, like a labyrinth with seemingly no end. The holocaust of mind and body. The computerized age of modern parenthood: planned babies, planned childhoods, planned adulthoods. It wasn't "parents" or "children," though at times he had to admit parents had the upperhand. They fed upon their children's minds like little worms. Some loved their children to death. They cuddled, pampered, protected, suffocated them. Soft beds, soft lives, soft bodies. They raised soft, bloodless children. They did everything for them, their thinking, their worrying, gave them all there was to give except two sturdy legs to stand on. Then, when they thrust them into the "great pressure pot" of society, saw them fall on their faces, blamed society for it. Well, it was no easy task to be parents. Perhaps parents ought to be given some sort of gauge when their children were born, to guide them over the bumps and tribulations, to warn them how much affection, attention, caring and support, should be given. Well, maybe there was no right answer. He'd never find it. He had been put here just to pick up the pieces, from each side, and try to put them back together again. Now, he had these people to deal with. If there had been a better time for it, he would have arranged it, but there was never a better time. There was never enough time.

333

What would they like him to say? That their son was fine and ready to go home, of course. They had come almost every day of the past four weeks to ask the same old question.

He reached over and closed the door. Then he sat down and, looking at them thoughtfully, folded his hands tightly together on the desk. "I'm sorry I had to keep you waiting so long," he told them in a stiffly, apologetic tone, "but we had an emergency—"

"Yes, we know," Roger Aldworth said. "We heard the sirens." And he remembered how they had reminded him of the screeching, frightening noises of that day his son had been brought there. The father fixed himself more comfortably in the chair. "How is Edward doing now?"

"Quite well."

"I'm glad to hear that. We'd like to see him today, if possible."

"Yes, I know." The doctor made an invisible frown now—deep inside him. "I spoke to Edward this morning, told him you were coming. But he still refuses to see anyone."

"But you can override that," the father said swiftly. "It's been nearly two months now. Surely we have the right to see our son."

"Yes, you have." The doctor spoke slowly, carefully now— "But I must caution you—that any pressure put upon him at this time could cause a serious setback." He waited a moment. "It might be like opening Pandora's box."

"Well...I don't know too much about Pandora's box," Roger Aldworth returned rather brashly, "but I think I know *some*thing about my son. He wouldn't be acting this way, if he hadn't started drinking."

"No. Probably not."

"And you *did* say he was doing quite well now," the father reminded the doctor, trying to pin him down somewhat.

"Yes. Physically." The doctor went on to explain: "He's eating regularly now, sleeping adequately with the minimum amount of sedatives. He's even put on some weight. From all outer appearances, he looks completely recovered. But if you were to take him home today, he'd just slip back to drinking."

"Then he is an alcoholic, after all," the father said bleakly.

"'No, not in the strictest sense. He doesn't need to drink in order to function. He doesn't even like to drink. He could have stopped drinking any time he wanted, but he didn't want to."

"Then, what you're trying to say is—our son had some kind of nervous breakdown," Roger Aldworth said a little impatiently.

"No, again. His thinking—reasoning powers—are all quite excellent. However, he is going through a mental anguish—a deep mental anguish. The problem is, he doesn't care to talk about it. But we managed to get some things out of him." The doctor re-adjusted the fold of his hands and continued: "He mentioned the position he had been offered in New York, with the law firm, Pratt, McPherson & Rettig. This position seemed very important to him, possibly the root of his anguish." The doctor stopped for a second. "He also spoke of a mountain he was supposed to climb—"

335

"A mountain?" Roger Aldworth gave a short strained grunt. "Well, I can assure you of one thing, Doctor. My son is not a mountain climber. He doesn't care about mountains."

"Well," explained the doctor slowly, "that might merely be a symbol of something else. Many people feel at some time in their lives that they have a mountain to climb. It can be career related, marriage, health—" The doctor slackened the fold of his hands now, let them cling to each other loosely. "Then there was the unfortunate love affair with a girl named Cynthia Forst. Did you know about that?"

"No..." Roger Aldworth looked at his wife. "We didn't even know he was seeing her, except at the bank. They've known each other since childhood. Cynthia was always a nice-looking girl, on the quiet side. Edward used to walk her to Sunday School." Roger Aldworth stopped—then went on, "The Forsts were close friends of ours, until they moved away to Worcester. Then, when they came back and opened up their drugstore, we never really got back together again. I suppose business people don't have too much time for social activities." He gave a coarse laugh.

"Then you were never aware that your son was living with a woman—this woman?" the doctor asked, returning to the subject—trying to establish a fact as he watched the father closely.

"No. He'd go off from time to time, but we never knew where he went."

"As I understand it, they lived together for approximately three months," the doctor added, establishing another fact.

"Well..." Roger Aldworth said slowly now, himself, "we never kept track of the time. As I said before, he'd just come and go. The last time he was gone—which was the longest—we thought he might have left for New York, after all."

The doctor went on. "He also mentioned his friend Jonah Willis, who lives in Chicago. He seems to feel you resent their friendship because the young man is black—"

"That's not true!" Roger Aldworth returned quickly. "I've never resented anybody because of their color in my whole life! But I *did* resent this young man's interference in my son's life. He was poking his nose into a family matter of which he had no business! He was trying to pull Edward away from us. My wife and I wanted Edward home. We had waited a long time to have him home. I would have felt the same way if his friend were white."

"Then you knew about the pact they made—about working together after graduation?"

"Yes, I knew about it," Roger Aldworth admitted freely, shamelessly. "But I didn't take it seriously. After all, everyone makes promises at college that can't always be kept."

"Then, I take it, you were a college man yourself, Mr. Aldworth?"

Roger Aldworth nodded—lifted his shoulders slightly. "'Course my school wasn't on the same level as Harvard," he said, "but it's held me in good stead through the years."

"I see," the doctor said, looking thoughtful again. "Then I need not tell you what an ecstatic event graduation from college can be, for a young man such as your son—and parents too. All the hopes and dreams involved—the fears too—" The doctor stopped a moment again. "Did you ever discuss the New York job with your son? Find out what it all involved?"

"No." The shoulders dropped back into place. "I didn't feel there was any reason to. He already had a fine position waiting for him at the bank. There was no need for his flitting off to New York."

Flitting? thought the doctor. *Is that what you called it?* "Then"— very carefully—"it never occurred to you that it too might have some merit?"

"Oh—I supposed it did. Otherwise he wouldn't have taken it."

"You didn't feel he could be successful in New York?"

"My son would have been successful anywhere," Roger Aldworth said proudly. "He's not a shirker. He always worked hard at everything he did."

"You seem to have a very high opinion of your son, Mr. Aldworth," the doctor let out now—softly, smoothly, "except when it comes to choosing his own job." He moved on quickly then: "Did you ever ask him later—if he was happy working at the bank?"

"No." Roger Aldworth made a sudden stir in his chair. "I knew he didn't want to go back there. But then he seemed to settle down to it. I thought he saw the light, after all."

"The 'light' being"—the doctor treaded most cautiously now— "that the Mapleville Bank was the best place for him?"

"Yes." Roger Aldworth stopped now, himself, to study the man's dark, inquisitive face. He didn't like him too much; nor the questions he was asking. There was a caustic quality about their intimacy, as if they were trying to imply something. "I didn't see anything wrong with that," he went on. "My son was going to be the vice-president of a brand-new bank in his hometown. Eventually, the president. How many young men fresh from college can say that, *I* ask you?"

"Not too many, I'm afraid," the doctor replied calmly, seeing he was getting the father's dander up. He transferred his cool, penetrating gaze over to the wife then, who was still sitting in the chair with her hands folded in her lap, exactly the way she had been when he had come into the room. How quiet she was. She might not have been there at all. The uterus that had given birth. What could she be thinking through all of this? Did she completely agree with her husband? Well, Doctor Schuyler thought, another still, small voice. Sometimes those voices were enduringly still—hidden for what seemed forever beneath the debris of hopelessness and despair. Well, at least now he knew where the son's submissiveness had come from. The mother.

He remembered now the gaunt and senseless form of the young man who had been brought into the hospital nearly two months ago, sunken-eyed, half-starved. How still that face was. Then the Rush—the cleansing and building up of the body, the mind too. Hopefully, a whole new outlook on life. Well, he had learned too quickly, too sadly too, that all was not always possible. Some you had to lose. And there were always the walls to knock down, tall ones, short ones, thick, thin, down they had to come, while Time itself, the belligerent crusader, marched along in perfect unison with the damages. Well. He could do just so much. He wasn't God. Nobody had asked him to be God, either. Today, he had to try to make these people see—understand—especially the obstinate father—what had happened to them, and to their son. Of course, half the battle lay with the father. He loved his son but loved his convictions even more.

"I suppose you think it was my fault that Edward started drinking?" Roger Aldworth asked in a hoarsely tight voice.

The dark little eyes snapped back reviewing the indefatigable tenacity of the father's. Sometimes the stronger the parent, the weaker the child. But that wasn't always true either. "I'm not here to judge anyone, Mr. Aldworth, just to help your son. I'm sure, like most parents, you've done your very best for him. However"—again the highly-professional voice moved cautiously—"I don't think you fully realize what a seriously unhappy young man your son is."

"Of course he's unhappy, with all that drinking. He's made a mess out of his life now. He's even lost his job at the bank."

"When one flounders, one usually makes messes." The doctor paused—then pressed on: "Edward has placed a terrible burden upon himself. He blames himself for every one's unhappiness, including his own. He hates his weaknesses. He feels he's failed as a man—"

"Failed? How could he have failed? He graduated from one of the top schools in the country." Roger Aldworth stared almost angrily at the doctor now. How could this man, who had known his son for so short a time, feel he knew him better than he himself, the father, who had known him all his life? "Do you think he failed?"

"No. But what I think doesn't matter. Every man has his own particular measure of himself."

The wife—the mother—intervened then: "Edward was always a very good boy, doctor. He never gave us any trouble before. Do you think all this could have been brought on from all that studying at school—for the final exams? He looked so thin when he came home—"

"I wish it were that simple, Mrs. Aldworth," a gentleness seeping through the cool granite-like face, "but it's not."

"Well," Roger Aldworth said succinctly, "I'm sure you've got some kind of medicine here, that can fix him up."

"We have all kinds of medicines here, Mr. Aldworth," returned the doctor evenly, "but none are for what ails your son. We can take the bottle away, but we can't dig out the thoughts from the mind. They have to be replaced—pushed out by other thoughts, and that takes time." The doctor paused again, looking directly at the father. His voice remained calm. "The job in New York meant a great deal to your son. It was a chance to work with his friend—a friend who had stood by him all through college, a friend who had helped him achieve all the honors you are so proud of today. When Edward realized he couldn't go to New York, he felt he had let his friend down. His whole world began to crumble around him." Another pause. "You see, Mr. Aldworth—your son had only two choices: he could either hurt you, or hurt himself. Since he couldn't hurt you, he had to hurt himself. The drinking was part of that hurt. Possibly the affair with the girl also."

"Are you saying that Edward tried to destroy himself by drinking?" Roger Aldworth asked.

"I hope not."

"Well!" Roger Aldworth said, shaking his head. "I just don't understand any of this."

"Sometimes the truth is difficult to see, when one stands very close to it."

"But Edward will get well, won't he?" asked the mother hurriedly.

"Yes. But it's all up to him. He has to start believing in himself again." The doctor stood up behind the desk. He had said all he had come here to say, all there was to say. Time was running out. He had to move elsewhere.

"Well," Roger Aldworth said, standing himself—taking his wife's coat from the heap on the chair, "we won't keep you any longer. We know how busy you are."

The doctor nodded appreciatively. He watched the couple dress. "There's one thing more," he said. "Edward told me to tell you he loves you both very much, and that he's sorry he has caused you all this worry."

"Well..." the father said, softening a bit. "Tell him we love him very much too, and that from now on"—his voice dropped an instant— "whatever he wants to do, will be all right with us."

"I will." The doctor almost smiled.

The next day—in the same office:

"I'd like to talk about the girl again, if you don't mind—"

No answer.

"Did you enjoy having sex with her?"

"No."

"Why not?"

"I—just didn't."

"Was it because of the drugs she took occasionally?"

No answer.

"Did she make you feel inadequate—as a man?"

Again—no answer.

"Were you in love with her?"

"I could never have loved her."

A pause.

"Your parents were here yesterday, as I told you they would be. They were very disappointed that they couldn't see you again. Do you suppose the next time they come, you will want to see them?"

No answer.

"Would you like to go home soon?"

No answer.

Part Two

Jonah

33

It was one of those old rehabilitated buildings just off Halsted Street, whose jagged brick front had been painted bright engine red. It had a white cupola at the top. The whole first floor had been gutted out and made into one long room which sparsely housed two rather badly marred second-hand oak desks, a pair of triple-drawer filing cabinets, and a crudely carved bookcase containing a row of worn law books, an encyclopedia and Unabridged Webster's Dictionary, Thesaurus, and a street guide of Chicago. Between the filing cabinets, by the wall, stood a large circular floor fan which on unbearably hot humid summer days would be dragged to the center of the room, to circulate the air on both sides.

Upstairs, on the second floor, was a small, untidy furnished apartment where a widow lived with her three mongrel dogs. On a clear, windless day, when all seemed right with the world, all the dogs could be heard yelping.

Outside, the wide plate glass window lettered in gold read:

RAVIN B. MONTEZUMA
Attorney at Law

Criminal	Divorce
Traffic	Real Estate
Personal Injury	Foreclosure
Collections	Bankruptcy

This day, in April, a huge bulky-framed black man sat at the front desk in a dark brown suit, a white shirt, a shiny yellow tie and yellow socks. His face was round and fat, smoothly cut with prominent features; the long curly graying hair that reached his shoulders stood out like a halo about his face. He was sitting leisurely, while his thick, bulbous fingers worked through a pile of unopened letters. Each of his fingers except for the thumbs, had a flashing gold ring on it. At the other desk, a young slender black man with closely cropped hair, dressed in a dark blue suit and white shirt and pale blue tie, sat pondering over his one and only letter. He held his chin up with one hand, in solemn thoughtfulness. The first older black man gazed at him a second, then went back to his pile of letters.

"What's the matter, kid? Got a problem there?"

"I don't know. Maybe..."

"Maybe I can help. I've got good broad shoulders." Ravin Montezuma looked strangely friendly when he spoke: his large shiny dark eyes rolled with perceptive ease in the smooth, round face.

The younger black man let go of his chin. "Rav—what would you do if you were waiting to hear from a friend a long time, then you got a letter from him dated back almost two years ago—July?"

"Your college friend in Massachusetts?" The front swivel chair turned around.

The younger man nodded.

"Well," Ravin said, "it'd all depend on how I felt at the time. Two years' a long wait. If I was pretty sore by then, I might just toss the damned thing into the wastebasket there and say to hell with it. Then, again, I might not. If he was a real good friend, like your friend is, I might think he was in some kind of trouble and wonder about it."

"You would?" The younger man's face took on a glint of hopefulness.

"Sure. What does he say?"

"Well...he says he's been having a lot of family problems and that his sister's getting married soon—"

"Family problems, huh? I get the picture: whitey boy mustn't go with black boy to New York."

"I don't think it was that, exactly. From what he told me they didn't seem prejudiced. I just think they didn't want him to go, period. They're a tight-knit family."

"There's always the first time, kid. Parents can be surprising. Now take my mother—I never knew she didn't want me to be a lawyer, until one day she told me. She said I should have been a basketball player instead, make a lot of money. Me, a nice fat boy—" Ravin laughed.

The younger man laughed for a second, too, then pondered again. "Well...maybe it had something to do with the sister. She was pretty young—eighteen. He was always worrying about her." A pause. "The thing that gets me is, he didn't finish the letter— He just stopped writing in the middle of a sentence, as if he changed his mind. But if that was true, why did he bother to send it at all, then?"

"Hm...now that's intriguing. I'd be real curious about that. In fact, I might even be curious enough to want to go down there and find out what it was all about."

"Oh, I couldn't do that, Rav."

"Why not?"

"Well...for one thing, you've got all those new cases coming up. I couldn't stick you like that. It wouldn't be fair."

"Listen, kid, I did it all before you came, didn't I? I haven't grown soft yet. Besides, how much good do you think you'll be, sitting here and worrying about that letter all the time?"

"Not very much, I'm afraid," the young man answered, smiling rather shyly and watching the gold-laden fingers flashing up. He knew those hands well by now: he had seen them in action in the courtroom. At any given moment, they would thrust into the air, with swift, striking movements—maneuvering, manipulating, flashing, like constant searchlights probing muddy waters, paralyzing the victim's face, for truths, justice. Some called Ravin Montezuma the "Magician"; others, the "Performer." But whatever he was, he bore it proudly; he was a constant, diligent campaigner for the good of mankind. You'll never grow soft, Rav, the younger man thought. I admire you. If I'm half as good as you are someday, I'll he satisfied.

"In fact..." Ravin Montezuma added, "maybe you ought to start right now."

"Right now?"

"Sure. The sooner you get there, the sooner you'll get back. Believe me, kid, it's the best thing to do. Clean out all those cobwebs once and for all."

"Well..." the other said, still a bit hesitant, "I did promise to go down there."

"So now's your chance. And that letter's your invitation."

"Do you suppose he intended it to get me down there?"

"Who knows? But one thing's for sure—you ain't going to find out sitting here."

"No."

Later that same day, a weary, painful-faced elderly black woman in a faded blue and yellow apron-dress climbed the stairs to the second floor of her old frame house, then stood quietly tottering on her cane. Through the open door of her grandson's bedroom, she saw him standing at the bed preparing to pack a battered brown suitcase. A certain sadness came over her; but she didn't allow it to show in her face.

She moved into the room. "You going someplace, Jonah?"

"Yes, Granny. I've got to take a little trip down to Massachusetts, to see my friend Edward Aldworth. I think he's in some kind of trouble."

"Bad trouble?"

"I don't know. I hope not."

"Well..." She patted his arm slowly. "You do what you've got to do."

He nodded and watched the frail, twisted body pull itself over to the dresser. Every step, he knew, was a torment for her. But she never complained. She never spoke of her illness, as though it were not there. She's a real soldier, he thought. Loving respect filled his eyes.

"You don't have to do that, Granny," he said, as the bony, gnarled hands scooped up a handful of clothes, then slowly turned, leaned on the cane again, "I can manage."

"I've done it all these years, Jonah," she said, "and I can do it now." She pressed the clothes down into the suitcase. Then, without looking at him, said, "You don't worry none, Jonah. You hear? The Lord's got a way of taking care of troubles long before you do."

"I hope so, Granny. I truly hope so."

34

Jonah gazed out through the cold, cutting rain, at the house: it was tall and white—almost grayish in the mid-morning's misty pallor. He got out of the car, walked down the path and up the front stairs, pushed on the doorbell, then pulled down the collar of his drenched raincoat.

He stood there for a few minutes before the door opened. A short, stocky, bloaty-faced woman in a dreary dark green dress faced him. "Is this the Aldworth residence?"

She nodded dully.

"Well... my name is Jonah Willis. I'm a close friend of Edward Aldworth. We went to college together."

"Oh—" she said, interrupting coldly, "you must be part of the mourning party. They all left already, for the cemetery."

"Cemetery?" Jonah shied. "I didn't—know anyone died—"

"Oh," the woman said, looking at him suspiciously now, guarding the doorway a little with her stocky body. He was the tallest black man she had ever seen—at least six-five—and very slender, but neatly dressed. The collar of his dress shirt peeking out from the drenched raincoat was snowy white. She had never seen better. "You're not from these parts?"

"No, ma'am. I've come all the way from Chicago."

"Chicago?" she said, looking now as if she had already spent all her patience on it. "Well—" she said rather stiffly, "I suppose you ought to know, if you've come that far. Edward Aldworth's dead. He died in the hospital three days ago. They're burying him today."

Jonah stood still for a minute or two. Something inside of him wouldn't let him speak. Then his hand slowly moved to his coat pocket; he drew out the letter. "I don't understand..." he managed to say. "I just received this letter from him last week—"

"I don't know anything about that," the woman said, dismissing it with a brief gesture of hand. "I was just hired to stay here today. Mr. Delingham sent me down from the mill to keep an eye on things. Answer the phone and such. The only person who might be able to tell you something about it is the sister, and she's locked up upstairs. She's been there all morning and won't come out."

"Suzanne?" Jonah asked quickly.

The woman nodded briefly, shifting the weight of her body to one side, in the doorway.

"Well...maybe you could ask her if I could please speak to her for a few minutes?"

"I can ask her," the woman said, with some outward resentfulness now, "but I'm not promising anything. She won't even talk to me." She watched the wind whipping about Jonah's coat collar and stepped aside. "You might as well come in out of the rain, while I find out."

"Thank you," Jonah said, stepping into the warm dryness of the house.

"What did you say your name was?"

"Jonah Willis."

"All right. You wait here."

Jonah watched the woman start up the stairs, then turned away and looked about. The long, wide living room, with its bay window and rose-colored walls and flowery slipcovers, stretched out drearily in the gray light; through the archway he saw that the dining room table was set with candles, china, carefully folded napkins. All waiting. He shivered suddenly, as though the cold clamminess of the rain had just entered. He looked back at the stairway. The woman was coming down already.

"You can go up," she said brusquely. "It's the first door to the right." She looked at his wet raincoat again. "You better hang that up first," she said, "in the closet there," pointing to the nearby door. "You'll get everything wet."

Jonah took the coat off and hung it up on one of the metal hangers and went up the stairs. At the top, the door at the right was waiting partially open. He knocked lightly. "Come in," a young girl's voice sounded from inside, and he opened the door all the way.

A girl with bouncy dark curls sat cross-legged on the bed, clad in a pink fuzzy night robe; her face looked red and swollen from tears.

"Hello," she said.

"Hello."

"I knew you would come when you got the letter."

"Then it was you who sent it?" Jonah asked her.

She nodded. "I found it amongst Eddie's things. I thought you should have it now—"

355

"Yes."

She looked toward the door. "Would you please close the door?" she almost whispered. "She *listens.* She's been standing behind it all morning, trying to hear what's going on in here. I'll be so glad when she's gone." Jonah obliged. Then: "Please sit down." She pointed to a chair by a small maple desk and waited for him to be seated. "Did she tell you?—Eddie's *dead!*"

"Yes," Jonah said quietly. "She told me he died in the hospital."

She shook her head suddenly. "He killed himself! He committed suicide!" She hung her head and began to sob, tears streaming down her face. "It's so awful—so awful! I've been sitting here all morning, thinking about it, how awful it is. Sometimes I wish I were dead too!"

"You mustn't do that," Jonah said. "That won't help anything."

"I know. But I can't help it!" She looked up at him with wet, shiny cheeks—wet, shiny enormous dark eyes! "They tried to tell me how it happened, but I wouldn't let them. I don't want to know. I never want to know! Never!" She sucked in her breath—tried to hold back the tears now. "They wanted me to go to the funeral this morning, but I wouldn't go. I locked myself in here instead. I'll never go there—to the cemetery. They can bury him, if they want to, but I never will!"

Jonah said nothing now. He watched the anguished, tear-stained eyes stare into space—

"The doctors at the hospital said Eddie was very depressed, that he lost his will to live. But they—my parents (she finally gave 'they' a name, but with some vindictiveness)—don't believe that. They blame his drinking. But I know the truth. Eddie was so unhappy. He wanted so much to go to New York with you, but they wouldn't let him. He had to go back to the bank and work there instead. He never cared about being a vice-president of a bank or anything like that. That's why he started drinking—" She began to cry again.

Jonah remained silent. There was nothing he could say, should say. If she had to cry, it was better that she let it out.

She took a deep, hurried breath and went on. "He was supposed to come home today. Instead he's..." She stopped and gazed at him forlornly again. "I thought if you came here—if he saw you again, everything would be all right. He'd be happy again. Maybe you still could go to New York together. That's why I sent the letter."

"I'm glad you did."

She wiped her eyes quickly now, with the backs of her hands: "Do you think people really die? I mean, *really, really* die?"

"No. Not if they're loved."

"Neither do I. I never want Eddie ever to die—" She stared away again. "My father said it's a mortal sin to kill yourself, but I think God'll understand. I think He'll know how good Eddie was—won't He?"

"Yes. I think He knows a lot more than we'll ever give Him credit for."

"Oh, I hope so! I wouldn't want Eddie to suffer that way too." She wiped her eyes again. "This was his room, you know—"

"Yes, I know. He told me all about it in school."

"Even the *yucky* blue walls?" she asked, wrinkling her nose suddenly.

"Yes, I'm afraid so," Jonah said, having to laugh now. But it was a soft, polite laugh that even Remorse itself could not have taken offense to.

"I've always hated this room," she said. "It was always blue. I don't think Eddie liked it too much either, but he never said anything. He never complained about anything." She rolled her eyes about. "He locked himself in here, too, for four days. He didn't eat anything, just drank brandy. That's why my parents had to put him in the hospital."

"I hope you're not planning on doing the same thing," Jonah said cautiously.

"No. I wouldn't do that to them again. I'll come out as soon as they get home."

"Good."

"That's his last bottle of brandy over there," she said, pointing to a half-emptied bottle on the night table. "I confiscated it. Otherwise my father would have thrown it out with all the others. There were twenty-six bottles in all. I'm going to finish drinking this one and keep it as a remembrance."

"Do you think that's wise?" Jonah asked, carefully again. "I don't think your brother would have wanted to be remembered that way."

"No, you're right. He wouldn't have. He was always putting other people on pedestals—" Her voice became soft, thoughtful again. "Do you think people can love too much? I mean they can hurt other people with their love without even knowing it?"

"Yes. I think anything is possible."

"So do I." She spoke slowly now: "I thought I would hate my parents now that this has happened, but I don't. Instead, I pity them. I guess you can never really hate the people you love, just because they made mistakes."

"No."

"Oh—I know they loved Eddie," she went on. "That's why they were always trying to run his life. But they never understood him, or tried to." She sighed a terrible heavy sigh. "We all loved each other, but Eddie loved the most. His love was unselfish. So it's all our fault he's dead now."

"No..."

"Yes, it is!" She looked at him with almost calm determination now. "He was always worrying about us, whether we were happy or not. He never worried about himself, until it was too late—" Her eyes began to fill with tears again; but she held herself in check. "I want to show you something," she said, and turned and groped under one of the pillows. She took out a thin, badly mangled book. "I found this this morning—Eddie's book of Quotations. He must have been reading it a lot before he went into the hospital..." She opened the book to a marked off page and handed it to him. "Especially that page," she pointed, "it's so full of smudges and things." Jonah slowly gazed down at the book, at one of the quotations which had been circled many times with a blue pencil, and read:

> "When we have lost everything,
> including hope, life becomes a disgrace
> and death a duty."
>
> Voltaire, *Merope*

When he had finished, he closed the book and gave it back to her; she slipped it back under the pillow. "I think he knew how it was going to end all along," she said, looking at him. Jonah looked back at her silently. The face that was watching him was so full of misery, so full of its own hopelessness, what could he say? Even the rain seemed to make soft, mournful sounds against the windows...

"Well," she was saying almost quickly now, "I guess he wouldn't have made a very good lawyer anyway. He couldn't even defend himself." She gave an agonized laugh.

"I don't believe that," Jonah said, "and neither do you. He would have made a fine lawyer."

"Yes. Oh, yes!" She tried to smile—then uncrossed her legs, stretched them out in front of her, leaning on her hands. Pink furry booties peeked out from satiny pajama-legs. "Are you happy?" she asked. "I mean, did you find a job you like?"

"Yes, I'm happy," Jonah told her. "I'm working for a great guy— a great lawyer. I'm learning a lot of things from him."

"I'm glad. Eddie would have been, too. He was always afraid you would never get your chance." Another try for a smile. "He was so proud to be your friend. He said you were the smartest person he ever knew."

"Well," Jonah said, trying to smile too, "I think he exaggerated quite a bit there."

"No. He could tell. So can I. You look smart. In fact, you look exactly as I imagined you would. Just like Sidney Poitier. You even got his smile. He's one of my favorite movie actors. Did you see 'To Sir With Love'?"

"No, I'm afraid not. But I'll consider it a compliment."

"Please do."

"Thank you," he told her. "And now, what about yourself? The letter said you were getting married— Did you?"

"Oh, sure, Steve and I got married. We had a big, fancy wedding, and now we're getting divorced."

"Oh," he said, "I'm sorry to hear that."

"Don't be. We're not sorry. It's the best thing for both of us. It could never have worked out. Oh—maybe it would have, if there hadn't been so much family pressure. I guess I never cared for Steve enough—I liked him a lot, but I didn't love him. But we're still friends, which is good. And he'll be happy now. He's already got a girlfriend—she's a waitress at B's Restaurant. She's always fussing over him, and that's all he ever wanted. I could never do that. And she likes the mill, which I've always hated. Her father put in some new machines for Mr. Delingham. It'll be one big happy family now."

"Well," Jonah said, "it sounds as though everything has been worked out."

"Oh, sure. I haven't told my parents yet, though. I mean about the divorce. They think Steve and I just had a big fight. I'm waiting until the funeral is over."

He nodded understandingly. "Then what? What will you do—about yourself, I mean?"

"Oh…I'll probably just go back to school, finish college. That'll make them happy a little at least. Then someday I'll get married again. But the next time it'll be somebody I pick out and when I want to."

"Sounds fair to me."

She nodded. "It's almost funny though—" she said, looking sad again. "All of this was for nothing. Eddie's going to Harvard—my marrying Steve." She paused a moment. "Well… I'm all they've got left now. I'll never be as good as Eddie, though."

"You sound good enough to me," Jonah said.

"No. You don't know. I can be very bad when I want to. I'm what you call 'the black sheep' of the family."

"Well, you certainly had me fooled," Jonah said, laughing now. "I would never have thought that."

"Well, I am," she said, almost stubbornly. She looked at him differently then. "You know, you talk just like Eddie. You say all the things he would have said, if he could be here. Now I know why you were such good friends."

"Well," he said, looking serious again, "we were together a long time. I guess a little of each one rubbed off on the other."

"And you shared things. Hopes and dreams."

"Yes."

She smiled now—a tiny, tired, childlike smile; but it was good enough. A good beginning. "I'm so glad you could come. I feel so much better now. In fact—I think I'll try to take a little nap—"

"Good idea." Jonah rose quietly now, watched her stretch out on the bed.

"Would you please cover me with the blanket, before you go? It's kind of chilly in here."

He unfolded the blue woolen blanket at the foot of the bed and pulled it over her, gently.

"Thank you." She closed her eyes. "You're going to the cemetery now, aren't you?"

"Yes. I—"

"I know..." She turned her face away. "Maybe... someday I'll..."

"Yes."

"Goodbye..."

"Goodbye."

He walked to the door quietly and opened it. When he looked back she seemed already asleep.

35

The cold dreary rain followed Jonah all the way to the cemetery. He parked the car and got out and walked through the iron gates. At the rear of the sodden grounds, through a misty maze of tombstones, he saw a small group of people dispersing, solemnly—bent, etching dark umbrellas across the swollen sky. Two women cradled the shoulders of another, who was tall and slender, dressed in mourning black, sobbing in a handkerchief as they walked along. A middle-aged man, graying profusely at the temples, remained alone at the grave site. Umbrellaless, the rain splattering on his face and clothes, he gazed down, pressing his hat tautly against his side.

Jonah pulled up his coat collar and walked over. He watched the man reach out and touch one of the flowers on top of the bronze coffin, then the hand fell away, slowly. Jonah took another step: the soggy earth made an eerie squishy noise against his wet shoes. The man seemed to hear. He turned about and stared at him.

For a moment he did not speak. "You're Jonah Willis, aren't you? Edward's friend from college?"

"Yes, sir." Jonah waited—then: "I happened to be passing through on business and thought I'd stop at the house for a while. Your daughter told me what happened."

"So she finally decided to unlock herself, did she?" the father said, almost irately. "Well...I always knew you would come here someday. But it doesn't matter now, does it?" He looked back at the coffin. "I don't understand this...I never will," he said slowly. "Do you know what my son did? He hanged himself—with a *bedsheet*. A Harvard Law School graduate!..." The elder man paused—then went on, his voice growing ponderous: "He was our only son. We gave him everything we could. He had a fine education. Everything to live for. He could have been the vice-president of a new bank, but he didn't want that—that wasn't good enough for him. Instead, he wanted this...Why? Why?" The father looked at Jonah with a sudden aggrieved expression.

Jonah stood quietly, silently. Again he listened to the sounds of the rain all around him, just as he had in that bedroom, with the sister—except now, it wasn't pattering against glass, windows, but soft petals of flowers, the smooth surfaces of granite, marble—the soppy circles of grassy, drowning earth...

"Maybe you know," the father was saying now, his face straining against the rain. "Maybe you can tell me. You probably knew him better than anyone else did, those last years at school. Maybe you can tell me why something like this has to happen." The father waited now for a reply.

"I'm sorry, sir—I don't know."

"You don't? Well..." The bereaving, tenseful face turned away. "Maybe fathers aren't supposed to understand these things, I don't know..." The elder man gazed off to the distance. "I better go now," he said, bringing the crushed hat to the front of him. "My wife's waiting…" He stared back at Jonah again: "Maybe you'd like to come back to the house with us. We're having a few friends in for dinner. I know she'll want to meet you. There's so many things she'll want to know now, about Edward, about those years you spent together at college."

"Well, I'd like to, sir," Jonah told him, "but I'll have to call the office first. They're expecting me to start back this afternoon."

"Of course," the father nodded. "Well… try to make it if you can." He walked off then.

Jonah watched him make his way toward the gates, then looked back at the bronze coffin: how still it looked there, how cold. The final process of Life. A terrible chill came over him. The cemetery had suddenly become unbearably cold. Nestling his chin deeply into the warmth of his coat collar, he hurried to the car.

The first thing Jonah did when he got to his hotel room was to call Ravin Montezuma, in Chicago. "Hello. Ravin?"

"Sure, kid, it's me," the low, gravelly voice responded. "Where are you?"

"I'm here—in Mapleville. I arrived this morning."

"Made good time, huh?" A pause. "How're things going?"

"Well…I'll have to explain all that to you later. I just thought I'd let you know I'm leaving here this afternoon."

"So soon? You just got there. Listen, kid, you take your time, huh? Make it like a little vacation. There's no hurry."

"I know." Jonah smiled into the receiver now, to give his voice a lift: "How's the Robinson case coming along?" It was one in particular that he and Ravin had been working on together: a lot of money was involved, graft, and some slimy characters, and Ravin couldn't wait to get his teeth sunk into it.

"O.K. We've got a court date three weeks from this Thursday, which gives us plenty of time. We should have it wrapped up around the middle of next month. The bastard on the other end is itching for a deal, but he's still afraid to scratch."

"That's good to hear," Jonah said, smiling again. "Well... I've got to go now, Ravin."

"Sure, kid. Have a nice trip home. And don t rush yourself. Take some pretty pictures to show me, huh?"

"Sure. I will. And thanks. Thanks for everything, Ravin."

"Hey, now," the gravelly voice said swiftly, "don't be running up the toll for that kind of stuff." A soft chuckle sounded from the other side.

"I won't. So long."

"So long, kid."

Jonah put the receiver back on its cradle, thoughtfully, then went over to the small table by the windows and sat down. Taking a sheet of the plain white stationery paper and a ball point pen provided by the hotel management—The Mapleville Arms—he began writing:

Dear Mr. &. Mrs. Roger Aldworth:

I am sorry that I will not be able to join you for dinner, but urgent business requires that I return to Chicago as soon as possible.

With deepest regret—and sympathy,

Sincerely,

Jonah L. Willis

Then he put the pen down, folded the letter carefully, slipped it into an envelope and addressed it, and went back to the phone and rang the desk clerk downstairs.

"Would you please come up to room 201?"

"Yes, sir."

He sealed the letter then and waited for the desk clerk's arrival. A few minutes later a knock came to the door. He opened it.

A youth about seventeen or eighteen, with thin curly hair and a sweaty white shirt and crooked red tie, gazed up at him slowly and said, "Yes, sir?"

"I was wondering if it's possible to have this letter delivered within an hour? It's very important."

"Oh, yes, sir," the youth replied quickly, taking the letter, "we take care of things like that." His eyes moved about the room, quickly too, then rested on the bed, where an open, empty suitcase lay. "Will there be anything else, sir?"

"Yes. One more thing—" Jonah told him. "I'm leaving this afternoon. I won't be staying the three days as planned."

"How come, sir?" the youth asked, losing some of his civil pomposity. "Is there something wrong with the room or the service?"

"No, everything's fine. There's just been a change of plans."

"Oh," the youth said, looking relieved, "I'm glad to hear that, sir. We aim to please, you know, sir."

"Yes, I know." Jonah dug into his pocket and took out a five dollar bill and gave it to him. "This is for your trouble."

"Oh, thank you, sir!" the youth said, tucking the money into the pocket of his shirt. Then he looked up at the long length of the black man standing before him. "I hope you don't mind my asking, sir— but are you one of those Chicago basketball players?"

"No. I'm a lawyer."

"Oh—I'm sorry, sir. I didn't mean to—"

"It's all right." Jonah smiled. "It's a natural mistake."

"Yes, sir! I'll see to the letter personally, sir!"

"Thank you."

"Thank *you* sir!"

The youth left and Jonah began packing.

36

An hour later Jonah stood before the train station. It was still raining. He hurried up the three uneven wooden steps and pushed the door open.

It was a small, square, frame building with a large window on two sides; the ticket man sat crouched behind a caged-window, in a circle of yellow light, wearing a green plastic visor over his eyes. He had a thin, pinched face that fell into deep folds about his mouth, like parentheses, whenever he looked down.

Jonah went up to him. "I'd like to know when you're expecting the train to New York City."

"Ten to fifteen minutes," the ticket man replied, adjusting the visor with one hand as he gazed up at the huge wall clock, "if there's no delay."

"I'll take two tickets."

"Round trip?"

"No—one way." The ticket man stretched his neck a bit now, to see if he had missed something. "They're for a friend and me," Jonah told him. "He'll be coming along soon."

"That's your business," the man returned grumpily. Jonah felt that the dreariness of the day had gotten to him. "Your friend better

370

hurry though," the ticket man added. "The train doesn't stop for more than ten minutes, usually."

"He'll be here in time."

The ticket man shoved the tickets uncaringly through the opening, and Jonah paid him. Then Jonah pushed the other door open and stepped out onto the platform: a narrow hip roof jutted out over it for shelter, but the rain had managed to soak through its old weathered boards, giving it a ruffled-looking edge. The platform was empty except for a husky little man in a dark tan raincoat and floppy hat. He wore a bright green striped tie, and his stomach protruded down over his narrow brown leather belt. He wobbled over. Jonah noticed how clumsily he walked on the outsides of his shoes; then he smelled his breath. It was heavy from whiskey. "Going to New York City?" the little man questioned, resting against the one lonely pillar there. Jonah nodded. "Glad to have the company. Hate this run alone. I come a couple times a year, to see my sister and her kids. She had a belated birthday party for one of them."

"I've never been to one of those," Jonah said, smiling. "Are they any fun?" He thought it was best to humor the little man.

"Nope! Too many damn relatives around. You can't have fun with relatives." The little man jostled himself against the pillar now, looking ready to fall. Jonah stood by to catch him, but he steadied himself. "Ever been to New York City before?"

"No. This is the first time."

"Aw—it's a great city. You haven't been anyplace, until you've been there. I'm going to a convention there now. Sales. Ladies' lingerie. Now that's going to be fun." The little man's face lit up. "You know all those jokes they tell about salesmen?—they're mostly true." He laughed, then looked steadily into Jonah's face. "Say— you're not a bad-looking black guy. Why don't you come along? I'll fix you up with a girl, and we'll have a ball."

"Well...I'd like to," Jonah answered carefully, not wanting to hurt his feelings, "but I'm going along with a friend. He's supposed to meet me here."

"Is he black or white?"

"White."

"That's great. I'll fix him up, too. Three's the merrier."

"Well... we've got some important business to take care of out there. We'll be too busy—"

"Busy!" The little man sulked now. "That's all I hear nowadays. Everybody's too busy! What the hell are they so busy about? Screwing up the world?"

"That might be it," Jonah said.

"Too much screwing up already." The little man swayed—free-standing. "Ought to stop screwing up already, or there won't be any world left to screw up." His voice was getting loud, boisterous, and the ticket man inside the building stretched his neck out again, trying to determine what the problem was.

"I guess the whole world's pretty busy nowadays," Jonah commented, cordially.

"You're telling me. Nobody takes the time to have real fun any more—" The little man looked as though he were about to cry. Then: "What kind of line are you in?"

"Law."

"Law. You a cop?"

"No. A lawyer."

"Well..." the little man said in a slurpy voice now, "you can't say I didn't ask you in a gentlemanly way." He studied Jonah's face again. "You don't look much like a lawyer."

"I know. That's what everybody says. I guess those who do, aren't, and those who are, don't." Jonah laughed.

But the man kept looking serious. "I know a few who look like damn lawyers, all right."

"Well, I guess it's something you have to work into, like everything else," Jonah said.

A soft tooting sound came then.

"Looks like the train's coming now," Jonah added.

"That's no news." The little man looked away—at the dark form emerging in the near distance. "Your friend better hurry now."

"I know. The ticket man said the train only stops for about ten minutes."

"It all depends on how long the guy takes to piss or drink."

The tooting sounds got closer and closer. The little man leaned silently for a moment, against the pillar again. "Screwing big world, that's what it is," he muttered. "Too screwing big for fun any more." He looked miserable.

"Well, you'll have fun at the convention," Jonah told him, trying to cheer him up, "when you get there."

"Oh, yeah. We always have fun at them. The trouble is, they don't last too long. Then the fun's gone again."

"That's life, I suppose."

"Yeah. Nothing lasts forever any more. If they could come out with fun that'd last forever, I'd buy some myself."

The train was close now.

"Your friend better hurry," the little man said, "or he's going to miss the train."

"He'll be here."

"How come you're so sure? I can't see him anyplace at all." The little man looked about.

"He told me he would."

"I think he lied to you."

"No. He's not that kind of person."

"You've got too much faith in human nature," the little man said coldly. "When you get as old as me, you'll find out. Everybody lies sometimes."

The train arrived then—came to a slow, screeching, brake-grinding stop. Then the motorman stepped out.

"We better get on," the little man said, straightening, steadying his step the best he could. The rain and the air seemed to sober him up some. "We'll get in the first car. Your friend ought to see you in there. I just hope the motorman has to piss or drink a long time, for your sake—" Jonah laughed and took hold of his arm lightly, helping him up the steps. The first coach car was nearly empty except for a young couple in the back, who looked like students. They had a stack of books on their laps. They were talking, jabberishly, between kisses. "Young people got it too easy today," the little man commented, almost bitterly. "All they do is play," and he set his husky form down next to the window. "I like to look out. Hope you don't mind."

"No, that's all right," Jonah said, sitting down beside him, on the warm dark blue leatherlike seat. He thought it would be impolite—downright rude—if he didn't. The little guy was expecting company.

"It's about three minutes gone now," the little man said worriedly. "Your friend better really hurry now."

"He'll be here."

"You keep saying that," the little man said almost angrily, "but I still don't see him coming."

The conductor came along then, to collect the tickets. Jonah held out his two— "One's for a friend. He'll be here in a second"; then the little man, his. He gave a crackly smile to the conductor, who was black and poker-faced. "Now, I'd never ask *him* to the convention," he said, when the black man moved away. "He'd never know how to have fun."

Jonah moved to the edge of the seat. The motorman was coming out of the building.

"Looks like it was a short piss or drink," the little man said. "Your friend won't make it now."

Jonah stood up. "I'd better get off."

"What for?" The little man grabbed hold of his coat sleeve for a second. "You're going to miss the train yourself, if you get off. The hell with your friend."

"No—I've got to find him."

"You're crazy. He ain't going to wait for you," the little man said, pointing at the motorman who was about to climb aboard.

"I'll be back," Jonah told him. He stepped out and the motorman got aboard. The little man was watching him nervously through the window.

Jonah went inside the building again; he looked at his watch, then at the clock on the wall. The ticket man gawked at him from behind the cage but said nothing. Jonah picked up one of the newspapers from the cardboard box on the floor and began reading.

The train tooted again. The little man was standing up now, hat off, his face pressed against the window, waving Jonah on. Jonah smiled and waved back. Then the train made a sudden lurch forward, and the little man kneeled on the seat, mouthed something through the opening of the window; but the loud hissing, grinding noises of the wheels dulled it away. Jonah waved again, and the train started up. The little man kept waving, frantically, his nose pressed hard against the glass.

Jonah finally put the newspaper down: the train was gone. The ticket man was still gawking. "It probably won't rain all day," Jonah told him.

Then he went outside, down the three uneven wooden steps. The rain seemed to have let up some now. He looked up at the sky and saw the sun trying to peek through the grayness.

He began whistling, softly.